"BEING A PROTECTEE TAKES SOME GETTING USED TO.

"If you want to go out in public, you have to follow a few rules," Hawkins said. "I have limits, Ms. Kavanaugh."

"Really? And what exactly are those limits?"

An unexpected hint of amusement warmed his eyes. "I'd tell you, but you're having such a good time trying to figure them out yourself that I'd hate to ruin your fun."

Surprised—and a little chagrined—that he'd seen right through her, Lili regarded him narrowly. He had great shoulders, beautiful eyes, and a sexy voice. It wasn't fair that he was intelligent, too. That had to be breaking some law of biology.

"Where did you learn to read people so well?"

Hawkins smiled, making him look almost boyishly handsome. . .and downright approachable. How had she ever considered this man ordinary-looking?

"In bodyguard school."

"Of course," she said dryly. "And did they also teach you how to dress like a million bucks there?"

"Yes, ma'am, and which fork to use for each course, so my table manners are decent, too." This time, beneath the wry humor lurked a faint warning.

ATTENTION: ORGANIZATIONS AND CORPORATIONS
Most Avon Books paperbacks are available at special quantity discounts for bulk purchases for sales promotions, premiums, or fund-raising. For information, please call or write:

Special Markets Department, HarperCollins Publishers, Inc., 10 East 53rd Street, New York, N.Y. 10022–5299.
Telephone: (212) 207–7528. Fax: (212) 207-7222.

Michelle Jerott

Her Bodyguard

AVON BOOKS
An Imprint of HarperCollinsPublishers

This is a work of fiction. Names, characters, places, and incidents are products of the author's imagination or are used fictitiously and are not to be construed as real. Any resemblance to actual events, locales, organizations, or persons, living or dead, is entirely coincidental.

AVON BOOKS
An Imprint of HarperCollins*Publishers*
10 East 53rd Street
New York, New York 10022-5299

Copyright © 2001 by Michele Albert
ISBN: 0-380-81317-3
www.avonromance.com

First Avon Books paperback printing: October 2001

Avon Trademark Reg. U.S. Pat. Off. and in Other Countries, Marca Registrada, Hecho en U.S.A.
HarperCollins ® is a trademark of HarperCollins Publishers Inc.

Printed in the U.S.A.

10 9 8 7 6 5 4 3 2 1

For Mom and Dad . . .
thanks for always being there

PROLOGUE

Big Moccasin Lake Lodge, Wisconsin
August 22, 1933

"Why can't I come with you, Joey?"

Joey Mancuso raised his head from Rose's perspiration-moistened neck, and kissed her breast as he breathed in her warm fragrance—attar of roses, mingled with the musky scent of sex. As he traced the curve of her breast with the tip of his tongue, she shifted restlessly.

"Don't," she whispered. "Answer my question. You know how I hate it when we can't be together."

He raised himself on his elbows, and looked down into the face of the woman he loved more than life itself, the only person on this lousy earth he'd ever trusted. She was so pretty, his million-dollar-baby—her short red hair worn in marcelled waves, and wide brown eyes topped by pencil-thin brows like Myrna Loy, her favorite picture show star—but tonight, the sadness in Rose's eyes nearly tore him apart.

"They'll be looking for us back in Chicago, so I want you to lay low at your cousin's place in Racine. When

I'm not so hot no more, I'll come for you and we'll go to Canada, like we planned." For her sake, he smiled. "And maybe I can finally make an honest woman outta you."

Rose sighed, and ran her foot along the back of his thigh. "This trouble is about that last job you pulled, isn't it?"

He kissed her lips as he eased out from her, catching her soft gasp, then kissed the tip of her nose, her forehead. "You know the rules, baby. Don't ask me no questions, then I don't gotta tell you no lies."

"Joey, I hope you're not thinking of going to Kansas City. You know the laws there are still looking for you over those killings at the train station."

Mood plunging to black, he swung out of bed. "I didn't have nothing to do with killing them cops."

"You used to muscle for Johnny Lazia, and that's all Mr. Hoover's boys care about," she said in a warning tone. "The laws want you real bad, sugar, and they'll do whatever they can to take you down."

Joey rubbed his thumb over her warm, soft cheek, then reached for his undershirt and began dressing. "Just remember what I told you—and keep your dancing shoes close by, because when I see you again, baby, I'm taking you out on the town in high style. Promise me that when I come for you, you'll be wearing a big smile for your fella, and your favorite dancing shoes."

Her gaze met his, but he shook his head in a warning before she even asked the question he saw brimming in her eyes. Not telling her the truth was the only way to protect her from the laws.

Turning slightly away from her, because sometimes Rose was too smart for her own good, he rubbed away a spot of dried mud from his trousers that he'd somehow missed earlier.

"I promise, on both accounts." Rose smiled brightly—

too brightly—and swung out of bed, small breasts bouncing in the lamplight. She picked up her flowered blue dress from the floor, where he'd thrown it a half hour ago. "And maybe I'll buy me a new dress, too. A red one. Would you like that?"

"I sure would." He pulled a roll of bills from his trouser pocket and pressed half of it into her hand. Nobody could say he didn't know how to take care of what was his. "I figure this'll keep you in style until I see you again."

Rose sat on the bed, putting aside the money, and began rolling her silk chiffon stockings up her legs. He never tired of looking at her pretty legs.

"I don't understand how anybody knew where to find you," she grumbled, clipping her stockings to her garter belt. "We're way out in the wilderness. Hell, *I* don't even know where we are."

"Willis ratted on me, that's how," Joey said tightly. With angry, jerking motions, he strapped on his shoulder holster over his shirt and vest, then pulled on his suit coat.

And his buddy Willis Conroy, partner and onetime cellmate, knew all the truths that his girl didn't.

Trusting Willis had been a mistake.

"Willis would never rat on you, sugar," Rose said, frowning. She slipped on her dress, and began buttoning it. "He's your friend."

"People like me don't have friends."

Outside, the pine tree branches scratched across the window and the wooden siding of the lodge, like something trying to claw its way inside.

Rose looked at him, her red mouth a pretty pout. "What about me?"

"No, baby, you ain't no friend, you're my life."

She smiled, love shining in her eyes. Nobody but Rose had ever looked at him like that. She'd always made him feel like he was worth a damn, even on the bad days when his past rolled over him like a drowning wave. To keep that light shining in her eyes, he'd do anything for her.

"Besides," Joey added, "Willis would spill his guts to the laws if it meant getting out of the chair."

Earlier, he'd received a cryptic call warning him that his partner had been arrested in Minneapolis the day before, and was singing away. By now, the laws in Chicago would know where to find him and Rose. Life being what it was, any number of those cops were sure to be tight with Mike Riley, the meanest Irish gangster in Chicago's North Side, and ol' Mike would be keen to get to Joey before the laws or the G-men.

No doubt about it, Joey the Joker was a popular fella lately.

He had pals who could hide him, even hot as he was, but he had to get Rose away. If the laws or bureau agents found her, it would go hard on her. They'd slap her around, call her whore, and play games with her mind. So long as they got their man, they didn't care how they did it. And all those lawmen, alone with a girl they considered a floozy, wouldn't think twice about using her in other ways. He couldn't let that happen.

He pulled out a leather bag and shoved his clothing inside. Rose was already packed and ready to ride. They should've left hours ago, but he'd had to repair the car engine, and then Rose had start kissing him and fiddling with his shirt buttons, and one thing had pretty much led to another.

Joey fastened his coat to hide his gun from their hosts, but he didn't think the old man and his wife were awake. He suspected they'd guessed the identity of their only guests, but they'd treated Rose right so far, and he had no cause to be suspicious. Leastwise, no more than usual.

He'd be sure to leave enough money behind to pay for the nights they'd stayed.

Nobody would ever say Joey the Joker would stiff an old man. He wasn't as heartless or without morals as the newspapers claimed.

"I'm taking the bag down to the sedan. You sit tight. I'll be back for you."

Rose nodded, suddenly going long-faced and moist-eyed.

"Aw, Rosie, baby, don't," he muttered, tensing. "I hate it when you cry."

She sniffed. "I'm feeling blue just thinking about not seeing you. I get so lonesome when you're gone. And I'm worried. This one don't feel right, Joey."

A chill shot through him at her words.

Rose was still watching him, and the light wasn't kind to her tonight. She wore more lines than a twenty-two-year-old woman should, and her eyes were weary. The same weariness touched him now, the same bleakness that forced him to admit he'd never live to see twenty-six. Rose knew it, too, but they never talked about his dying. It only made her cry.

"I don't know where all the good times went," Joey whispered. "It started out as a game . . . I never wanted it to be like this."

For a long moment, she said nothing—all the memories of their five years together hanging thick between them—then smiled. "You better quit jawin', boy, and pack those bags. I want us out of here before the laws jump you."

Or Mike Riley's triggermen. Mike wasn't about to forgive Joey for double-crossing him. All this, because Riley's slut had bad-mouthed Rose. Jesus, skirts could be death on a fella.

He almost smiled. Even at times like these, he could still find a joke.

Grabbing the bag, he headed to the door. Nobody was in the lodge's common room. He didn't turn on the lights, suspicion second nature. He slipped out back and headed to the black Ford V8 sedan. He'd stolen it outside of Chicago, but had switched license plates. Times were hard lately, and few folks had the money to travel much. Out-of-state plates would tip off the local laws right quick.

And Henry Ford's big V8s were roomy enough for living in, for sleeping—even for lovemaking. Those big backseats of the cars he'd stolen had sure seen a lot of action. The best times of his life.

Joey looked away from the backseat, his gaze falling on the back floor where blankets hid boxes of shells, his two Browning automatic rifles, a Thompson submachine gun—his best chopper—and a half-dozen other rifles and handguns.

All at once, that ball of dread in his belly burst, overwhelming him with a powerful sense of helplessness. Two years of gun battles, police chases, roadblocks, and living on the lam . . . it was no kind of life, with nothing to look forward to but being shot down one day like a dog on the highway.

He'd been born to nothing, and if he died tonight, what would he have?

Nothing.

Except for Rose, and for a while, it had seemed he might make something of himself.

Joey sagged against the sedan and lowered his forehead against the cool, black metal roof and breathed in deeply, smelling the tang of pine needles and the nearby lake, the loamy scent of ground dampened by a recent rain.

He swallowed back the tears. Crying was weak, and he'd always known it would end like this . . . he'd just hoped to string his days out a little longer.

A sudden sound cut across the silence of the heavily wooded northern wilderness and Joey looked up, listening, his heart pounding.

Tires on gravel—and too late at night to be anything but trouble.

"Fuck," he snarled, and grabbed the chopper. He was silently slipping toward the front of the lodge when lights snapped on in the common room.

Rose . . .

She must think it was him, bringing the Ford out front.

"Rose, shut off the lights! Shut them off . . . get down, get down!"

His frantic warning was lost in an explosion of gunfire and shattering glass. A short scream cut across the thundering noise—an animal sound that raised the hair on his arms and the back of his neck.

"No!"

As the guns fell silent, Joey's bellow of rage echoed through the darkness, long and drawn out like the howl of a wolf. Heedless, knowing it was too late, he ran toward the front porch, chopper blazing whitely as he sprayed a wide arc of bullets.

From the darkness, the flash of returning fire erupted from the trees, the rat-a-tat-tat of machine guns.

The first bullet slammed into his chest. He staggered back as another two bullets hit his shoulder and arm, and by the time the last bullets took him, he'd fallen to the soft, spongy ground, still clutching his smoking chopper in his hand.

"Rose," he gasped over the white-hot pain, each breath a struggle to pull more air into his lungs.

Sorry, baby . . . so sorry . . .

As blackness washed over him, he heard the sound of running footsteps, and a voice, muffled as if coming through a thick blanket, "He's dead! Goddammit, I told you I needed him alive!"

"He was shootin' to beat the band, Lou. It's not like we had a choice."

"I needed that bag, you idiots. Where's the shoes? Get me the shoes!"

"Lou!" A new voice shouting, so tinny and far away. "Lou, the laws are coming . . . three cars, down the road. They must've been right behind us."

"Aw, Christ! Get to the cars. We'll have to shoot our way outta here."

"What about the money, Lou?"

"We got no choice but to come back for that later . . ."

As blackness swallowed Joey Mancuso, his last thought was of Rose, laughing and twirling in a shiny red dress, kicking up her heels in her dancing shoes.

1

Chicago
Some seventy years later . . .

"**D**amn good thing I wore my best silk undies today, because if I had to go and faint in front of three hundred people, at least I did it with style." Lili Kavanaugh stopped her barefoot pacing on the carpet of her posh suite at the Drake Hotel and briefly closed her eyes. "Three *hundred* people . . . my God, I could just die of embarrassment."

"You nearly died for real," said a male voice from behind her, the tone sharp. "Embarrassment is the least of your worries right now, Lil. Are you sure you didn't hit your head when that cop knocked you down?"

Resuming her restless pacing, Lili glanced over her shoulder at her business manager, who was also her sister's boyfriend. Jared Sayers reclined on the pastel striped love seat: brown-haired, lean, and wholesomely handsome, but the lines of stress etching his face betrayed his casual sprawl.

Of course he was right, but he'd missed the point. Embarrassment she could handle and deal with; what she couldn't handle was that only a few hours ago a man had rammed a gun against her neck and almost dragged her out of the Morton Auditorium at the Art Institute of Chicago, where she'd been lecturing.

"Well, it's my guilty secret that I'm totally spineless." She smoothed the skirt of her red shantung silk dress. Damn, her hands were shaking again. "Fainting certainly doesn't do much for my suave and sophisticated image, does it?"

Jared didn't answer, and with a sigh, she gazed out her window at the grand view of Lake Michigan and the Oak Street beach. The sky was a cheery turquoise blue, sunlight streaming down and sparkling off the water. Although it was early October, the beach still swarmed with sun-worshippers, joggers, children, and people walking their dogs. She watched with a frustrated longing.

"Jared, do we really have to do this bodyguard thing?"

"Yes," he said with flat finality. "In case you've forgotten, somebody tried to kidnap you today."

As if she could forget. Lili rubbed her arms, wincing as her fingers reached the painful spots where her assailant had grabbed her with such vicious force. By tomorrow, she'd have a lovely collection of bruises.

And here she was, without anything in her suitcases to accessorize purple or yellow.

She continued to stare outside at all the people and activity, at the bright colors and endless blur of motion, and the suite she'd found so charming and spacious that morning closed around her, growing smaller and duller and ever more suffocating.

Lili glanced at the small knot of suit-clad detectives and uniformed officers talking by her door, including the off-duty cop who'd been in the auditorium and chased off her assailant. Outside her suite, hotel security stood guard. She wanted nothing more than five measly minutes to herself so she could wallow in a good bawl, but the police insisted on hanging around until this bodyguard person arrived.

Bodyguard. Images of a grim-jawed G-man in black popped to mind, and she gave a shiver of dread.

In all her thirty-one years, she'd encountered nothing more troublesome than the occasional jerk. Ever since the attack, she'd asked why anybody would want to harm her. No one had an answer, but at the moment it didn't appear that it was a onetime, random event.

A knock on the door cut across her thoughts, and Lili turned as the serious-faced young man in charge of hotel security poked his head into her suite. "Professor Kavanaugh? The gentleman from the security agency is here."

Lili stiffened, her breath catching, but when the tall, dark-haired "gentleman" walked into the suite, her apprehension eased into surprise.

The man coming her way with an easy, self-assured grace had a strong, angular face with the faintest hint of a cleft in his chin. He wore his hair cut short, and was one of those men who, no matter how often they shaved, always had a shadow of a beard. While not particularly handsome, he had pleasant, attractive features.

He was no thick-necked brute, anyway, and while Lili wasn't sure what a bodyguard *should* look like, she hadn't expected someone resembling an executive.

"Matt Hawkins," the man said, walking forward, hand extended. "You must be Professor Kavanaugh."

"Mr. Hawkins," she said as he took her hand in a firm, warm grip.

Standing so close, Lili couldn't help notice the color of

his eyes—light gray, almost silver in the strong afternoon light—and that an incredible pair of broad shoulders filled out his suit.

The man discreetly cleared his throat, and Lili realized she still held his hand. She released it with a rueful smile, and quickly sized up the rest of him. Hawkins wore an expensive, conservative suit—the steel-gray color did wonders to enhance his silvery eyes, and she had a feeling he was well aware of that. Armani, most likely, with a Breuer tie and a fine cotton shirt.

Gaze moving lower, she eyed his shoes. She didn't recognize the designer, but these were definitely pricey and Italian.

Obviously, guarding bodies paid rather well. And with an outward package like this, she'd bet the Kit Kat in her purse that he wore silk boxers, too.

A sudden heat stung her cheeks, and Lili looked back up, meeting the bodyguard's unwavering gaze.

Wonderful. She'd been threatened with a gun, manhandled, dragged across a floor, and had keeled over in front of a packed auditorium—yet she was speculating about the underwear of a man she'd met fifteen seconds ago.

Well, really . . . in a day rife with aberrations, what was one more?

Jared stepped up beside her and took Hawkins's hand in a quick shake. After introducing himself, he said, "Thank you for coming. Dan told me you initially declined the assignment, but I'm pleased you reconsidered. Trust me—you won't regret it." Jared shot Lili a quick look. "Dan Armistead is part owner of the security agency, and an old friend of mine. I asked Dan for the best, and that would be Mr. Hawkins here. He's a certified personal security specialist. Top of the line."

It sounded as if Jared were describing a luxury Lamborghini or a state-of-the-art stereo system, not a man.

Frowning, Lili tipped her head as she sized up Mr. Hawkins's shoulders again. "So . . . you're the crème de la crème of bodyguards?"

"The best." His eyes locked onto her, seeming to pin her to the spot where she stood. "And technically, I'm a personal security specialist, ma'am, not a bodyguard."

The sound of his voice washed over her: a deep, rich voice, like that of a nighttime deejay on the radio, the kind you could listen to for miles and miles as you drove that white line into the darkness. A sexy voice that invited trust—maybe even a fantasy or two.

But before her fancy could take that thought and run with it, two other men wearing suits entered her suite, and Hawkins turned, breaking eye contact.

Immediately, her tense muscles relaxed.

"My team," Hawkins explained. "That's Manuel Mendoza standing by the flowers, and to his right is Dallas Farrell, my driver."

Lili summoned a smile for both men. Mendoza was a lanky Latino of middling height, sporting a sleek black goatee. Farrell looked surprisingly young and slender for a bodyguard. He had reddish-brown hair and brown eyes framed by long, thick lashes, and Lili's first thought was: *Does your mother know what you do for a living?*

With some surprise, she noted the baby-faced bodyguard wore a wedding band. Before she could check herself, she glanced quickly at the left hands of the other two men. Neither Mendoza nor Hawkins wore rings.

"I need to talk with the police for a moment," Hawkins said, reclaiming her attention. "Then I'll have questions for you. Sit tight. I'll be right back."

Lili knew an order when she heard one, no matter how politely stated. She glanced at Jared, who shrugged and dropped back down on the love seat. She resumed pacing, casting occasional curious looks at her bodyguard.

Odd, how a man who wasn't particularly out of the ordinary—and who wore an unobtrusive gray suit, albeit expensive—stood out among all these cops. His voice wasn't overly loud, his movements weren't overly aggressive, and yet he drew her attention again and again.

In a room where testosterone all but crackled in the air, that was no small accomplishment. In his own quiet way, his entire bearing seemed to proclaim: *Watch out. The big dog has arrived.*

Within minutes, Hawkins had gathered his information, and the police and detectives filed out of her suite. Mendoza and Farrell followed them, which left her alone with Jared and a complete stranger who was now in charge of every hour of her life for the rest of the week.

Hawkins headed back her way, and with a renewed sense of unease, Lili noticed his frown.

"Is something wrong?" Realizing how ridiculous that sounded, she quickly added, "Beyond the obvious, I mean."

He regarded her just long enough for something uncomfortable to flutter in her chest. "Sit down. Please."

It wasn't a request, and she sank down onto a wing chair. He took the opposite chair, perched on the edge of the seat, hands loosely clasped between his knees, looking dark and ominous against the sherbet hues of her suite.

"I need to ask you a few questions about what happened."

At his words, the panic she'd been holding off for the last couple hours came rushing back, filling her with a cold, dark dread. "You just talked with the police. What more can I add?"

"I know you'd prefer not to talk about it," Hawkins said. "But it's important, Professor Kavanaugh."

Professor.

Lili managed a small smile. "Please. Just Lili."

He didn't smile back. "Tell me what happened. I need to hear it from you."

"Is this really necessary?" Jared demanded as he sat forward. "Can't you wait an hour or two? She's been through a lot this afternoon. Give her time to rest up and—"

"It's okay," Lili interrupted. Jared, like everyone in her family, tended to be overprotective of her.

Letting out her breath in a long sigh, she focused on the vase on the end table, filled to bursting with a lavish arrangement of calla lilies, irises, and asters in hues of yellow, lavender, and white. "I'm a fashion shoe designer, Mr. Hawkins, but I'm also an expert on shoe history. I own an extensive collection of shoes that belonged to famous American women, which is what I was lecturing about earlier."

"The attack came toward the end of your talk, correct?" Hawkins asked. He pulled a small notebook from his inside jacket pocket—and Lili glimpsed a shoulder holster and the dark gleam of a gun.

Fear gathered in her chest, tight as a fist. Her heart pounded.

Of course he'd have a gun. Somebody had threatened her earlier with one, so why wouldn't he? Still, having an armed man sitting mere inches from her wasn't as comforting as she'd expected.

"Yes," she answered. "I'd thanked everybody for coming, took Rose's shoes from where I'd stashed them in the podium, and made my way to the edge of the stage."

"Rose?" Hawkins repeated, looking up from his notepad. "Who's Rose?"

"Are you from Chicago, Mr. Hawkins?"

Hawkins hesitated, then answered, "I was born in Pittsburgh, but I've lived in Chicago for years."

"Then you should've heard of Joey and Rose. You know, the star-crossed gangster lovers." At his blank expression, she added, "She was the moll of Joey 'the Joker' Mancuso, and was gunned down with him back in the thirties. My collection includes shoes from bad girls and floozies, too."

Recognition dawned in Hawkins's eyes, and he nodded once. "Okay. Why did you take the shoes with you?"

"Rose was one of Chicago's most notorious personalities, so I figured a chance to see the shoes would bring in more people to my lecture. The more the merrier, that's my motto."

Briefly, Hawkins's gaze slid over her, taking in her fitted red dress designed to play up her modest curves and show a generous length of leg—and now her skinned knees, unfortunately.

His gaze moved upward to her hair, which she deliberately wore in a classic bun—her own little joke, playing off the stereotype of a professor. This month her hair was inky black. The last few months it had been red; a deep, unabashedly fake shade of red.

"Are the shoes worth a lot of money?" Hawkins asked, his gaze locked onto her face once again.

"It cost me nearly twenty-five grand to get my hands on them. Gangster paraphernalia commands a high price these days. A few years back, Clyde Barrow's bloody shirt sold at auction for eighty-five thousand bucks." Suddenly registering the meaning behind his question, Lili hastened to add, "But he wasn't after the shoes. I had the shoebox with me, so if that was what he'd wanted, he could've easily just yanked them away from me."

"You held on to the box the entire time your assailant had you?"

Lili shrugged, and glanced toward the mangled box, its musty-smelling pink cardboard faded with age. "I guess I was too petrified to let go. Smashed the hell out of it, too, which makes me mad. That was the original shoebox. Very rare, you know."

Hawkins didn't look impressed. "Tell me exactly what happened after you walked to the edge of the stage."

Lili took a deep breath, seeing again in her mind's eye the dark blur rushing toward her. "I'd just sat down, and I was watching people walk down the aisles toward me. Out of the corner of my eye, this big dark shape caught my attention, mainly because it was moving so fast. I looked over and saw it was a man dressed all in black. For a second or so, I didn't think much of it, because artsy people often wear a lot of black. But when—"

She broke off, shivering at the memory, and how terror had hit her with such paralyzing intensity. Jared came to stand behind her, rubbing her shoulders soothingly. She smiled, patted his hand, then looked back at Hawkins. The bodyguard watched her and Jared with interest.

Lili knew what he was thinking, but didn't feel like correcting his assumption just yet.

"When I saw his face was covered by a black ski mask, I knew I was in trouble," she continued. "I tried to run, but he was too fast. He grabbed me and yanked me against him." Again, she ran her hands over her tender arms, a sense of violation and revulsion filling her. "Something cold touched my neck, and I knew it was a gun. That's when I sort of froze."

"Most people do. It's okay," Hawkins said—and only then did she realize her tone had been apologetic. "Go on. What happened next?"

"He told everybody to stay away or else he'd kill me." Angrily, she blinked away a fresh burn of tears. "He dragged me toward the emergency exit, the gun still shoved under my ear. I knew that if he took me through that door I was as good as dead . . . and I decided if he was going to kill me, he'd have to do it right there in front of all those people—"

Once again, she broke off, struggling to regain her composure as Jared continued to rub her shoulders. Hawkins waited with quiet patience.

"There was an off-duty cop in the auditorium . . . he'd brought his wife down for the lecture and, luckily for me, decided to stick around. He yelled an order to stop, that he was the police. I remember trying to turn and break free, but the man jabbed the gun into my neck really hard."

Hawkins glanced at her, taking in the angry red mark just under her jaw that would ripen into a nasty bruise by the next day. Self-conscious, she touched it, then clasped her hands together in her lap to keep her fists from clenching.

"All I remember next was feeling this burst of rage, and I started kicking and screaming and biting. I was *not* going through that exit, no matter what." She met Hawkins's expressionless gaze, but couldn't hold it. "At that point, he shoved me away and ran for the door. All these people were around, screaming and trying to get out of the way, and Officer Wheeler tackled him, knocking me down in the process. They fought . . . for a few seconds, maybe, then he kicked Officer Wheeler in the face and escaped."

She stopped. Silence filled the elegant suite, the moment stretching on.

"Then what?" Hawkins prompted.

With another glance at him, she murmured, "I don't know. I . . . fainted."

"You fainted?"

"Yes." She narrowed her eyes and squared her shoulders. "It was an unnerving experience, Mr. Hawkins, and I—"

He held up his hand in a calming gesture. "I'm only verifying you weren't knocked unconscious."

A blush heated her cheeks. "No, I just fainted. And when I came around again, all the excitement was over."

Until now, anyway. She eyed his suit coat, detecting the bulge of his holster now that she knew to look for it.

A sudden vision flashed to mind: the roar of guns, the stink of gunpowder. Bodies lying on the ground, leaking blood.

"Have you ever shot anyone?"

If her abrupt question surprised him, it didn't show. "If I have to discharge my firearm, then I've failed to do my job. I don't fail."

Not quite a yes or no answer—but probably the company-approved one. She supposed he thought it a comforting answer, anyway.

"Did you get a look at your assailant, Ms. Kavanaugh?"

"Not really. His face was covered. He even wore black leather gloves."

"Was he white or Latino? Black?"

"White," she said. "I could see a little skin around the eyeholes of the mask, and his eyes were blue."

"Size? Age?"

She'd already told all this to the police, but she reined in her impatience. "About five-nine or five-ten, maybe. I'm not sure about his age. Obviously not too old, the way he was hauling me around."

She was five-seven, and one hundred thirty-five pounds on a good day—not exactly petite or dainty.

"Did you notice an accent? Speech impediment? Any other means of identification?"

"No accent. Nothing else. He was just a scary man in black with a gun."

"Did he seem nervous to you? In control? Angry?"

Lili worried her lip, thinking. The police hadn't asked her this. "No, he didn't seem nervous, just very . . . matter-of-fact. Like dragging off women was something he did every day."

Hawkins nodded, making another note. "A couple more questions," he said. "Background information, mostly."

Lili stood and resumed her pacing as she spent the next ten minutes detailing the wildly exciting life and times of Lilianne Kavanaugh: yes, her father was a surgeon and her mother an English professor. Yes, they were on good terms with her, and yes, she was the youngest of three sisters. No, she wasn't worth *that* much money, and even if her parents were well off—and could afford his undoubtedly exorbitant fees—they weren't billionaires. No, she hadn't any disgruntled employees or students, and as far as she knew, no business rivals who hated her designs enough to want to snuff her. No, she had no ex-husbands or disgruntled boyfriends, either.

At that, Hawkins glanced at Jared, once again sprawled on the love seat.

"Jared's not my squeeze," Lili said, smiling. "He's my sister's. Sometimes."

Jared shot her a reproachful look—whether for the "squeeze" or the "sometimes" crack, she didn't know. Probably both.

Again, if she'd surprised Hawkins, he didn't let it show. She wondered what it would take to get at least one eyebrow to arch, or one side of his mouth to curl. He had a nicely shaped mouth, and would have a lovely smile.

Hawkins turned to Jared. "What's your relationship to my client?"

Client. Such a cold, generic little word—and hearing it made her go hot with a sudden anger. How *dare* he reduce her terror to nothing more than a business transaction?

"I'm a family friend, and I've known Lili since she was ten," Jared replied in a clipped, professional tone. "I'm a financial analyst for a Boston firm, and in my spare time I keep Lil in the black, oversee advertising and sales, payroll employees, and contract with factories and distributors. I'm here to discuss a catalog layout for the summer collection, and I'm leaving tomorrow. Lili is staying in Chicago for the rest of the week."

"How long have you been working with her?"

Jared glanced at Lili. "About a year. She's only recently gotten things up and running to the point where she needs someone like me."

"Does she pay you a salary?"

"Not really," Jared said, impatiently drumming his fingers on the love seat's arm. "As I just mentioned, I help her out because she's a friend."

"And to impress upon my sister that he's a nice guy," Lili added, catching Hawkins's gaze. "And he really is a nice guy. Jared, better than anybody else, knows I'm not worth killing or kidnapping."

"That's right," Jared muttered. "You're a pain in the ass, is what you are."

Hawkins watched the two of them for a moment longer, plainly assessing. "This shoe collection you mentioned. Is it worth a lot of money?"

"Yes, but we're talking about old *shoes*, Mr. Hawkins," Lili said. "Not jewelry or other assets easily fenced or liquidated."

"I'll need to know your schedule. Where, when, contact personnel, and other details so I can begin securing all routes and buildings." Hawkins glanced at Jared. "Do you keep her schedule?"

"*Excuse* me, but I keep my own schedule. I may be the victim here, but I'm not helpless." Lili retrieved her leather briefcase, pulled out a bulging file folder, and handed it to him. "Everything you need is here. I'm sorry I don't have a neat itinerary typed out, but that's not how I operate."

After another quick, cursory glance, he nodded. She'd translated that curt nod to mean: *Yes, I can see you're not the most detail-oriented woman on the planet.*

"So what's next?" Lili asked as Hawkins stood with a self-assured grace she couldn't help but admire.

"I meet with my team. I usually have more time for advance planning, but this shouldn't take long."

"Do you need anything more from me, or can I grab a glass of wine and unwind in a long, hot bath?"

"I'm done with questions for now." Again, he spoke in that cool, polite tone so at odds with his sharp, ever-watchful eyes, powerful shoulders, and faintly menacing aura.

What an unexpectedly intriguing man.

Still watching him thoughtfully, Lili fished her shoes out from under the love seat, where she'd kicked them earlier. Nothing like a killer pair of shoes to chase away a girl's blues—and these were hot red pumps, topped with an extravagant white organza bow. It was one of her own designs, and as she slipped them on, the four-inch heels raised her nearly eye to eye with Hawkins.

Almost imperceptibly, he arched a brow.

That she'd finally managed to get a reaction out of him made her feel marginally better, more in control—even if she didn't have a gun or shoulders thick with muscles that would scare away would-be attackers. Yet as she passed the window overlooking the beach and paused to watch all those people—so unrestricted, so trouble free—a sudden resolve hardened within her.

Lili turned to her bodyguard and said with a calmness she didn't feel at all, "I want to go swimming."

2

The professor was going to be trouble. Matt knew it the minute he'd walked through the door and got his first look at the hot number in the red dress.

It looked like she wouldn't disappoint him.

"Lili," said the sister's sometimes squeeze. "There's no pool at the Drake. And it's too cold for the beach."

"This is Chicago," she said with a shrug, and the glint in her eyes told Matt none of that mattered to her. "I'm sure we can find a YMCA."

Now that was something his usual CEO clientele didn't bother with. The occasional hooker, yes, but never the YMCA.

"Isn't that right, Mr. Hawkins?" She turned on him a look that was a dicey mix of challenge, anger, and shrewdness.

Matt shifted on his feet, suddenly wary. His client dressed with a classy sexiness and wore her hair in a pseudo-secretary bun intended to look demure, but a don't-jerk-me-around intelligence sparked in her sharp blue eyes.

"Assuming you're a YMCA member, then yes, we can find a facility," he said in a carefully neutral tone.

She didn't look like the YMCA type, and something of his skepticism must've shown on his face, because she arched one dark brow and said, "I hate snobs, and I always preferred the Y to those pricey fitness joints. Besides, the Y offers belly dancing classes."

Turning, she headed toward the bedroom area of the suite, hips swinging, the high heels rounding and defining the muscles of her calves.

"I don't think going for a swim in a public pool is a good idea, all things considered," Sayers called after her in annoyance, bringing Matt's gaze back up from his client's legs. "I'm sure Mr. Hawkins will agree."

But Matt said, "If she wants to go swimming, she can go swimming."

Sayers stared. "Are you sure? What about—"

"I'd prefer she stay in the suite for now, but if she doesn't let off a little nervous steam, she's going to make herself sick. I've seen it before. You people are paying me to keep her safe, so you might as well get your money's worth."

"Mr. Hawkins."

Matt turned. His client stood by the wooden room divider separating the bedroom from the parlor, one hand on the divider, the other on her hip—a pose that pulled her red dress tightly across a very nice pair of breasts.

"If you don't talk about me as if I'm not here, I can assure you this next week will pass by in a much more pleasant manner. And by the way, I didn't bring a suit, so we'll have to go shopping first." She smiled. "Bloomie's is just a block away."

He opened his mouth to answer, but she turned away before he had a chance. After a moment's silence, he turned back to Sayers.

"You don't have to take her anywhere," Sayers said quietly. "Go do your plan of attack or whatever, and let me handle Lili."

"Don't bother. She doesn't strike me as the type to be handled."

More like the type who'd grab life by the ears and kiss it full on the mouth.

Sayers shrugged, but his stiff muscles broadcast his feelings of angry helplessness and resentment of Matt's authority. A typical Type A personality response.

"So she's really a professor?" Matt asked, partly to ease the tension, partly to satisfy his own curiosity. From behind the screen came a flurry of slamming suitcase lids and snapping fasteners.

Sayers shot him an insulted look. "Lili has an MFA from SUNY at Stonybrook. That's the State University of New York, in case you didn't know."

Matt nodded, impressed. He might've stayed in high school—and paid attention—if his teachers had looked like Lili Kavanaugh. "That means she's pretty smart, huh?"

As soon as the question was out of his mouth, Matt regretted asking it.

Sayers frowned, hesitating, then said, "Most of the time."

The comment struck Matt as important in understanding his client, but before he could pursue it, a brisk knock sounded and Manny Mendoza called through the door, voice muffled, "Gotta talk to you."

With a last glance at Sayers, Matt walked to the door and opened it to admit Manny and Dal. "What's up?"

"We have a problem," Manny said. "There's no open rooms on this floor until Monday. There's a wedding and some sort of convention going on."

From behind Matt, Sayers said, "I wasn't sure if I'd have to stay an extra day or not, so I booked my room through Monday. I haven't canceled it yet. Your men can stay there. It's a couple doors down, by the elevator. But you'll be sleeping in here, Hawkins."

Matt turned, meeting the challenge in Sayers's gaze.

"Like you said," Sayers continued. "We're paying you a small fortune, and may as well get our money's worth. So you'll stay right in this suite with Lil, and that way, she gets more bang for her buck."

Damn poor choice of words. The image of how she'd looked standing by the room divider flashed to mind: all long legs, high heels, red dress, black hair, and full breasts.

"With my team lodging on the same floor, that won't be necessary," Matt said, his tone cool. "Staying with a client in their room isn't usual policy."

"I don't give a damn about policy, Hawkins. Lili's safety is not negotiable," Sayers snapped. Lowering his voice, he added, "She won't admit it, but she's nervous about staying alone in the room, and I insist you stay here with her."

At that moment, his client emerged from the bedroom area, a thick terry robe draped over her arm, and walked past them to the far side of the room, where the bathroom was located.

"Do you want me to stay in the room with you?" Matt asked, because it was what she wanted—not Sayers—that mattered.

She stopped outside the bathroom door and turned. "I suppose I'd feel safer if you did."

With a quick glance around the suite, Matt added, "You won't have much privacy."

"Somebody shoved a gun against my neck. Privacy isn't a priority right now." She smiled faintly. "And in case you haven't figured it out by now, I'm not exactly the shy sort."

She opened the door and shut it behind her, lock clicking. He heard the sound of running water soon followed by soft singing: a song about sweet, sweet surrender.

Matt glanced at Manny and Dal, who stared back blankly. Smart boys. Frowning, Matt surveyed the parlor again. The sleeper love seat looked comfortable, and the suite was big enough that he and his client could move around without tripping over each other. The room divider provided a little privacy, and since the client's needs were paramount, and the request wasn't unreasonable—only unnecessary—he decided against further argument.

"All right, I'll stay here. What time on Sunday is Ms. Kavanaugh leaving?"

"She has a three o'clock flight back to New York," Sayers answered.

Turning to Dal, Matt ordered, "Book his room through next Sunday, and tell the front desk I'll need an extra blanket and pillows up here. Get a pass for the cars from George in security. Have them bring up our bags—and put my bags in your room." He glanced briefly at Sayers. "I'll be showering and dressing in that room, not this one."

An hour later, after going over his client's schedule and making phone calls over the whine of a hair dryer—apparently she had to look nice to go shopping—it was time to head to Bloomingdale's, then off to the closest YMCA with a pool.

As Dal waited in the company's armored four-door

sedan, with its bullet-resistant glass, Manny stood at the main entrance to the Drake's ornate lobby—all dark wood, gilt bronze detailing, walls and draperies in tones of maroon and gold, its ceiling dominated by a massive crystal chandelier—and signaled that the location was secure.

"Let's go, Ms. Kavanaugh," Matt said quietly, taking her elbow. "Stay close to me."

"I still can't believe you won't let me walk a block . . . I feel like an idiot with you hovering over me like this," she muttered. "And I told you to call me Lili."

Matt merely guided her through the lobby, past a towering floral arrangement in an Oriental vase. His quick survey took in the registration desk to his left, and the Palm Court Lounge to his right, where water trickled out of the dolphin fountain as piano music played. He nodded as he passed the watchful concierge.

He was alert to every detail of his surroundings and the ever-present threat of danger—or trying to be, anyway. He kept getting distracted by his client's electric-blue knit dress, which looked as if it had been painted on. Its high neck, long sleeves, and short skirt drew attention to how she dipped in and curved out in all the right places.

Her hair briefly brushed against his face, and her shampoo smelled citruslike, and fresh. Under the dim, moody lights of the lobby, her hair gleamed pitch black. Matt figured her true color couldn't really be this dark—not with such fair skin and blue eyes—but it sure was eye-catching. She'd gathered her hair back in a ponytail secured with a large barrette, and the only jewelry she wore was a silver watch and big, square silver earrings.

As she moved ahead of him, Matt trailed his gaze downward, from her swinging ponytail past her curving bottom to her feet. She wore black open-back shoes with thin ankle straps crossing in an X in back, and a big rhinestone secured the straps where they crossed. The flashing rhinestone, and that bit of sexy bare heel, caught his attention.

Irritated at this slip in professionalism—he'd never ogled the asses or feet of any of those middle-aged CEO clients—he looked back up and surveyed the lobby again.

Manny, as the point man, went through the door first, and Matt followed Lili, sandwiching her safely between them. Exactly on cue, Dal pulled the car up to the curb as they walked out, and the doormen and valets stepped back. While Matt kept her between his body and the car, Manny opened the back door. With a quick efficiency, Matt helped the professor into the backseat, then climbed in beside her. As she slid across the seat, her skirt inched upward, providing him a great view of her thighs—and the angry red scrapes on her knees.

Radiating barely concealed anger, his client sat as far from him as she could—and in a Lincoln Town Car that left a pretty wide space.

Matt didn't take it personally. It was a typical victim's reaction. She couldn't get angry with the man who'd attacked her and turned her life upside down, but Matt was a convenient outlet, especially since he was now calling the shots and invading her space.

He even understood her demand to go swimming as a knee-jerk attempt to exert some measure of control. He let her think she'd succeeded, because right now she needed to believe that. In a day or so, she'd calm down and be less confrontational.

If going to either the store or the YMCA were dangerous, Matt would've refused to take her. But both were easily secured areas and, whenever possible, he encouraged his clients to go about their normal daily and business routines. They were under enough stress, and didn't need him to go commando on them, too.

Manny climbed into the front passenger seat as Dal, his eyes shaded by dark Ray·Bans, glanced over his shoulder and asked, "Ready?"

"Yeah." Matt suppressed a sigh. "Let's go shopping at Bloomies."

After spending forty minutes shopping for a bikini—and an emergency trip to the sixth floor for a box of Godiva chocolates—Lili now sat staring out the tinted car window as the buildings along Clybourn Avenue whizzed past. She was more than a little dismayed to be in this monstrous black car, surrounded by pistol-packing he-man types, and on her way to a place where she really didn't want to go anymore.

At some point, getting out of her room and going for a swim had made sense. She'd needed it. Or, at least, wanted it.

Now she wanted nothing more than to go back to her suite, but couldn't figure out how to wiggle out of events she'd put into motion. It was as if she were standing outside her own body, watching in fascinated horror as she plunged toward a certain crash-and-burn.

All she had to do was casually inform her G-Man in Black that she'd changed her mind. But she couldn't bring herself to do so.

Lili sent a sideways look at Hawkins, who stared straight ahead, face expressionless. For all she knew, behind those dark sunglasses he was taking a snooze—eyes open, like some cold-blooded lizard—while she sat beside him all but crawling out of her skin.

A guy like this would never understand her misgivings, and she hated the idea of showing any fear in front of Matt Hawkins. Somehow, acting like a spoiled brat didn't seem nearly as bad.

Silence reigned in the big sedan, except for the CD playing a retro big band song, with a whiskey-voiced woman jazzing about some man who done her wrong.

Didn't they always?

With a sigh, Lili rested her head against the seat and turned to the window. Most of the time, stubbornness had its advantages. Pride and determination had given her purpose when her family had dismissed her dream of becoming a designer as frivolous and "just a phase she was going through." It also kept her sane and grounded in the cutthroat fashion world, and helped her to stay focused on the positives when she wearied of the traveling, long hours, and intense pressure to outperform herself again and again.

But at moments like this, her stubborn streak was a pain in the butt.

She glanced again at her bodyguard and, after a hesitation, cleared her throat to get his attention. Hawkins turned, and she stared at the tiny double image of her face mirrored in his sunglasses.

"There won't be any problems, will there?" she asked. "With me getting into the Y, I mean?"

"I called ahead. The management is expecting us."

"Oh." Lili looked away. Great. Being trailed by men in suits should cause a nice little spectacle—something else she'd failed to consider earlier.

"Here we are," Mendoza said from the front seat as Farrell pulled up to the New City YMCA at North Halstead. Not exactly a great part of town, but there'd been nothing with a pool closer to the Drake.

Maybe she should've gone to a nearby Hyatt or Sheraton. Lili sighed. Well, she'd have to make the best of a bad situation, and maybe she'd find a swim therapeutic. It might help her forget, for a little while, that somewhere in this city one man patiently waited for another chance to hurt her.

"The manager said to park wherever you want," Hawkins told his driver as he opened the door. "I'll call when we're ready."

Farrell only nodded, his gaze on his mirrors, watching the flow of traffic and pedestrians around the car. Mendoza walked to the Y's front door, scanning the area as if he expected an assault team with missile launchers to pop out of the pavement. After a moment, he gave the all-clear signal.

Lili thought the cloak-and-dagger stuff was a bit of overkill, but all the same, her gaze darted along the busy street scene, seeking out potential terrorists, killers, and kidnappers.

Though she doubted they'd walk around carrying a sign that said: *Hi, my name's Bill, and I'll be your deranged stalker during your stay in Chicago* . . .

Lili jumped as Hawkins touched her back and nudged her forward at a brisk pace toward the door. Flustered, she found herself inside the building before she could protest. Glancing back over her shoulder, she glimpsed Farrell still curbside. He waited until they were inside before pulling away.

"I wish you wouldn't do that," she grumbled, but without much heat, staring at Manny Mendoza's black suited back as he walked ahead of her.

"Being a protectee takes some getting used to at first."

"*Protectee?*" she repeated, offended, her body stiffening. "I don't think I like being labeled as a *protectee*."

Hawkins released her, but stayed at her side—not crowding her, yet still playing merry hell with her nerves. "It's what you are, and if you want to go out in public, you have to follow a few rules. I have limits, Ms. Kavanaugh."

"Really? And what exactly are those limits?"

His gaze met hers, and a sudden, unexpected hint of amusement warmed his eyes. "I'd tell you, but you're having such a good time trying to figure them out for yourself that I'd hate to ruin all your fun."

Surprised—and a little chagrined—that he'd seen right through her, Lili regarded him narrowly. He was very attractive, with great shoulders, beautiful eyes, and a sexy voice. It was hardly fair to other mere mortals that he was intelligent, too. That had to be breaking some law of biology.

"You think you're pretty smart," she said dryly.

Hawkins smiled, and she nearly gawked at how it transformed his even, regular features, making him look almost boyishly handsome . . . and downright approachable.

How had she ever considered this man ordinary-looking?

"Smart has nothing to do with it. I read people. It's part of the job."

"And where did you learn to read people?"

His gaze closed, and while his smile remained, it had lost some of its warmth. For a moment, she focused on his chin, its faint cleft—and squelched an irrational urge to rub the back of her hand over his cheeks and chin, and feel the roughness of his dark beard stubble.

"In bodyguard school," he answered at length.

"Bodyguard school," she repeated, looking up again. "Of course. And did they also teach you how to dress like a million bucks in bodyguard school?"

"Yes, ma'am, and which fork to use for each course, so my table manners are decent, too." This time, beneath the wry humor lurked a faint warning.

She reached the pool entrance, and would've walked

in if not for Hawkins's hand on her shoulder, holding her back. Startled by the heavy, almost intimate warmth of his hand through her dress, Lili glanced at him.

"Hold on. Manny has to clear the women's locker room first."

She nodded, very aware of him: the scent of his cologne, the brush of his body against hers when he moved, and his almost possessive stance that marked her as off-limits.

A young man walked quickly toward where she stood by the door, and Matt immediately stepped in front of her, forcing the man to take a hasty step back.

"Next door, please," Matt said, his pleasant voice a contrast to his aggressive stance.

"Sorry," the man said, looking startled, and cast a curious glance back at them as he walked through the farthest door leading to the pool.

Though Lili was embarrassed at such aggressive protectiveness, a small part of her found it comforting to know all this muscle and attitude was at her disposal.

Once Mendoza had determined the women's locker room wasn't bursting with wild-eyed maniacs brandishing guns or dynamite, Lili went to change, ignoring the stares of the college coeds, young families, and seniors in the pool.

When she emerged from the locker room and Hawkins and Mendoza turned to her, she wished she'd bought a suit that didn't bare quite so much skin. Not because of modesty—she'd been competing for attention from the moment she'd learned to crawl—but because this one time she wanted out of the limelight.

No chance of that, though. Gathering her composure, Lili stood on the edge of the pool and dived into the water. She concentrated on swimming laps, stealing peeks at her bodyguard. Hawkins was back in bloodless-reptile mode, standing still, constantly on the lookout. The other swimmers watched him and Mendoza with unease—even a kid could tell they were hired guns—and the looks they turned on her were plainly curious, speculative.

She surfaced, treading water, and glanced at Hawkins again, where he stood a short distance away. He must be hot, yet showed no discomfort. He should look ridiculous, wearing a suit while everyone else ran about half-naked, but the presence that set him apart from everyone else was working full force here.

He just looked dangerous.

Before long, his relentless calm and control began to irritate her, largely because she was anything but calm. In an effort to redirect her irritation and restlessness, Lili joined in a game of pool volleyball. Even that failed to distract her. Twice, she deliberately hit the ball hard enough and close enough to Hawkins to splash him with water—but he didn't so much as flinch, and merely looked at her as if she were a bug.

Finally, caught in this strange, silent battle for something she didn't quite understand, Lili hoisted herself out of the pool. She walked toward Hawkins, water sluicing down her body. As she squeezed the water out of her hair, his gaze darted toward the small lips-and-tongue tattoo peeking from her cleavage. She caught a flash of emotion in his eyes, but he lowered his lids before she could read it.

Probably she'd just made him mad.

"Why not come in for a swim?" she asked. "You must be getting hot."

It was more a challenge than an actual suggestion, of course, and Lili could tell by the look in his eyes that he didn't take it seriously. He didn't even bother to answer—but she was an old hand at dealing with people who ignored her or didn't take her seriously.

Knowing she at least had his attention, Lili slowly surveyed his body, from his fascinating dimpled chin and powerful shoulders right down to his fine Italian shoes, the leather slightly darkened with water.

"Oh, I know," she murmured, looking back up. "You can't go swimming because there'd be no place to hide your gun."

He frowned, his gaze sharpening, and there—barely visible; she'd almost missed it—a small twitch of his jaw muscle.

Brazenly, she dropped her gaze to his groin. "Of course, you could just put it where everybody expects to find a big bulge. And all that extra firepower would really, *really* impress the girls."

He caught her gaze and held it. After a moment, he said, "Don't."

Although unnerved—she didn't doubt for a minute he'd shoot a man without blinking—Lili didn't back down.

"What does it take to get a rise out of you, Mr. Hawkins?"

"I don't think you want me to answer that, ma'am."

"Don't be so sure of that."

Stepping closer, Lili pressed her body against him, her hands resting lightly on his shoulders as she stared directly into his gray eyes, so close she could see the rim of black around his iris. His heat radiated toward her, the texture of his suit rough against her skin, and the woodsy scent of his cologne chased away the heavy smell of chlorine.

He wasn't as cool as he acted. He eased back, his lids lowered, and tiny beads of perspiration dotted his upper lip and forehead. Again, he glanced at the tattoo on her breast, and when his muscles beneath her hands went taut, she knew she had him.

Ah, sweet success. She wasn't a faceless, generic "protectee" to him now. She was a human being. A bothersome, pain-in-the-ass human being he'd be forced to deal with on a personal, face-to-face level.

"I keep thinking I can find something that will liven you up," she said, with an exaggerated tone of thoughtfulness. "Like maybe an 'on' switch."

She slid a hand downward from his chest—and within a split second, anticipating her intent, he'd grabbed her wrist before she'd reached her target.

A bluff, really. She'd have never reached for *that* if she hadn't been damn sure he'd stop her.

Again, their gazes locked. Anger flared in his eyes, and Lili smiled. "Gotcha, G-man."

Satisfied that she'd made her point, Lili moved to pull away, but he didn't let go of her wrist. He tightened his fingers—ever so slightly, but enough to warn her.

"If you wanted my attention, you got it. And now that I have yours, I'm going to repeat that I have boundaries you will not be allowed to cross."

Her little rush of triumph rapidly faded. His grip wasn't gentle, but she'd rather have her circulation cut off than ask him to let her go.

"You're scared and feeling out of control, and you don't like it. I understand that." Hawkins released her. He hesitated, then gripped her shoulders with the tip of his fingers, as if he couldn't bear to touch her, and moved her away from him. "You came here to prove you're still calling the shots. I understand why you want that, too, and because I judged the risk to be low, I allowed it. I may work for you, but you have to let me do my job and follow my rules. I won't be responsible for your safety otherwise. If this is too much trouble, you can hire yourself another bodyguard, Ms. Kavanaugh."

Hot with humiliation, Lili stared at the damp stain

she'd left on the front of his Armani suit. "Why won't you call me Lili?"

"Familiarity with a client is not proper protocol," he answered, his expression closed.

"I've never been much for protocol."

Lili backed away, her gaze touching on dozens of bemused and fascinated stares. Only Mendoza wasn't watching her and Hawkins, instead staring stonily in the opposite direction.

Great. She'd provoked Hawkins, but made a spectacle of herself in the process. Lili sighed. One of these days, she'd learn to look before leaping. Really.

Without giving Hawkins a chance to further chastise her, Lili turned, angled over the side of the pool, and dived again. The cool water muffled sound and distorted her view of everything above her. Hawkins was now only a wavering, gray smear.

The chlorine stung her eyes, and when she surfaced, she wiped away the mingled water and tears. Not the place she'd have picked to have a good, purging cry, but at least she could pretend it was the chemicals making her eyes red and teary.

She swam hard, often kicking deeper below the water, so no one could tell something was wrong. Between the physical exertion and the release of her pent-up tears, her fears faded, replaced by anger and frustration over this unknown, faceless threat. Hawkins was right. She needed his help, and had no choice but to abdicate control over her life and accept that for the rest of this week, she was, first and foremost, a "client" and a "victim."

Gee, just what she'd always wanted to be—a victim.

Lili surfaced, and through the blur of water watched as Hawkins hunkered down beside her. His face was emotionless, but there was something in his manner that didn't seem as cold, or detached. "You ready to go back?"

But he was really asking: *Will you behave?*

When she nodded, he extended his hand—tanned, strong, and large. She stared at it for a long moment before he said quietly, "Lili, please. Let me help."

Maybe it was only a lingering film of tears, or her sudden weariness, but she thought she glimpsed a hint of sympathy in his eyes that, oddly enough, left her feeling safe and on solid ground for the first time since the attack.

It was all she'd wanted, to know that he cared in some small but personal way.

Lili took his hand, and let him pull her from the pool. They stood close for a moment, an awkward silence between them, before she pulled away and walked, with as much dignity as she could muster, to the locker room to change.

3

Matt had turned off the lights in the suite's parlor except for one lamp. He sat on the love seat—coat tossed aside, shirt sleeves rolled up over his forearms, tie loosened—and hunched over a coffee table scattered with paper, filling out reports he hadn't had time to finish earlier.

Hollywood never showed the unglamorous side of being a bodyguard, or the paperwork and long hours of mind-numbing boredom.

Rolling his shoulders to ease a slight, tired ache, Matt looked over his notes. He'd be up half the night doing risk analyses, routing reports, and gathering advance information on all the restaurants, museums, schools, and shindigs Lili would attend throughout the week. A class at the Art Institute, lunch at Spiaggia, dinner at the swanky Savarin, and a meeting with somebody named Pippa at the Redhead Piano Bar. He'd also found a scrawled note that said: *Go see Sue*. He'd have to ask what that meant.

On Thursday, she had a second lecture at the Chicago Historical Society—another auditorium, hundreds of people, and plenty of opportunities for the situation to go south real fast. On Saturday night, the day before he'd take her to the airport, she was attending a private fundraiser, also at the historical society. Private was good, and easier for him to control.

But it would be a long week, and it couldn't pass fast enough. Grimacing, he stood and stretched, then glanced toward the room divider and the bed he could just glimpse. Silence, and no lights. She was sleeping, finally.

Hopefully she didn't sleep in the nude—though he wouldn't be surprised, seeing as how the woman had a tongue tattooed on her breast.

With that unsettling thought came the memory of the stunt she'd pulled at the pool, surging through him on a heated rush: how her damp hair had smelled of chlorine, and how her wet, half-naked body had felt pressed against him. Luckily, his suit jacket had hidden his reaction. God knows what he'd have done had she grabbed his hard-on.

His exasperation had lasted only until he'd realized she was crying as she was swimming, and doing her best to hide it. He'd had a crazy urge to take her face in his hands, look into her eyes, and tell her everything would be okay. He'd sensed Lili Kavanaugh was proud, that any show of weakness would humiliate her, and because pride like that was something he could understand, he hadn't said a word, feeling alarmingly helpless.

Helpless. Christ!

With a low curse, Matt scrubbed a hand over his face. A client had never rattled him before, not like this.

He wanted to blame his impaired focus on the fact that she was his last detail, and he was already thinking like an ex-bodyguard, letting unprofessional thoughts and responses slip more easily past his defenses. But he knew better. He was trained to identify and isolate the source of danger, and this particular danger wore tight dresses and high heels, and looked sexier fully dressed than many woman did showing as much bare skin as legally possible.

She might not be the sort of pretty most guys went for; not pretty in a sweet, cute, or model-perfect way. She had a strong, striking face that reminded him of a young Katharine Hepburn, and her body was nicely rounded, not too thin or overtoned. His kind of female body.

Matt briefly closed his eyes in frustration.

No, not his kind—she was his *client*, and despite the tattoo and the attitude, this woman was classy, rich, and smart. Way out of his league.

He walked around the room, working out the kinks in his shoulders, and tried blocking out thoughts of the woman sleeping just behind him. He stopped at the window, leaning against it as he looked out through the darkness at the cars on the streets below, and the dense blackness of the lake beyond.

As he turned away, still lost in thought, a sparkle caught his eye, and he glanced at the open, beat-up shoebox Lili had clutched to her during the attack.

Maybe he shouldn't be so quick to dismiss this as the cause for the attack. It seemed far-fetched—nobody in their right mind would go to such extremes for a pair of old shoes—but his years of working security had taught him people could be counted on to do the unexpected, if not the downright stupid.

Curious, he picked up one of the shoes, and turned it carefully in his hand. Except for the toe area, most of it was embroidered with black and silver crystal beads. A fringe of beads, in a curving line from one side of the ankle to the other, spilled low over the toe. Matt could almost imagine this fringe shimmying and swaying with its wearer's every Charleston, cha-cha, and kick.

Rhinestones outlined the gracefully flared heel, their facets sparkling. Large circular ornaments, reminding him of the brooches his grandmother used to wear, were fixed to the shoe at either side of the ankle. Each ornament was made up of concentric circles of small rhinestones surrounding a single large rhinestone in the middle.

He weighed the shoe in his hands, surprised by its heaviness. The leather was slightly scuffed, and the soles showed wear marks. Here and there, a bead was missing, and a few rhinestones jiggled loosely in their fittings, but other than that, it was in pretty good shape. Eye-catching, flashy . . . very much a part of the era that had produced it.

"Beautiful, isn't it?"

Startled, Matt turned to see Lili standing by the divider, wearing a thick, white terry robe and her long, black hair loose over her shoulders.

Not happy at being caught off-guard by his own client, Matt looked down at the shoe to hide his frown. "It's nice."

"Rose had lousy taste in men, but she had great taste in shoes." She walked to him, and as she took the shoe from his hand, he caught a wisp of a spicy scent that reminded him of incense. "Joey Mancuso had these specially made for Rose in 1929. Her initials are on the inside of the heel . . . right here. That's how I verified their authenticity."

She ran a finger through the fringe, and the tiny beads made a whispery, clicking sound.

Matt moved back to a safer distance. "Having trouble sleeping?"

"A little." She also moved away, walking toward the love seat and coffee table strewn with his work papers. She picked up a sheet, and looked back at him, eyes wide with a sudden alarm. "This is a list of hospitals and ambulance response times."

"Routine paperwork," he said quickly, to head off any brewing panic. "I don't anticipate trouble, but I need to be prepared for the possibility. Half the work of being a bodyguard is being prepared."

"You make it sound like being a Boy Scout." She sent him a quick look from beneath her lashes, her gaze touching on his mouth before shifting to his shoulder holster and gun. She returned the shoe to its box, gave it a fond pat, then replaced the lid. "Aren't you tired?"

"I don't need much sleep." He started to sit down, expecting her to do the same, but when she began pacing, he straightened again, not sure what to do.

The silence stretched on, the air in the room practically vibrating with her nervous tension. Finally, she stopped at the window and looked outside, her back to him, spine straight, shoulders squared.

"I'm sorry for how I behaved earlier."

"It's okay," Matt said, careful of her pride. "You've had a rough day."

She bowed her head, hair spilling forward, and tightened her fingers on the windowsill. "That's still no excuse. I shouldn't have tried to make you angry, or touched you like I did."

"Don't worry about it." He returned to the love seat, sat down, and picked up his pen. "People respond in different ways to danger. I've been in this business a long time, and there isn't much I haven't seen."

"Thanks. That's very gallant of you." She still hadn't turned, but the line of her back relaxed. "My two older sisters are the ultimate in practical and proper, but I've been charging off without thinking ever since I was a little kid. My parents still wonder where they went wrong with me."

Matt stared down at his pen, rolling it between his fingers. "There's nothing wrong with you."

She turned from the window and leaned against it, smiling faintly. "In my family, you act with decorum and grow up to be a doctor, lawyer, professor, or MBA. Or, at the very least, you marry one. My sisters went right from high school to Harvard and Cornell, but I wandered around Europe for a year, living in hostels, doing the starving artist thing, and suffering for my art."

Matt held back a smile as he glanced around the suite. The Drake had hosted presidents, even visiting royalty. "Doesn't look like you're suffering too much now."

"Suffering is highly overrated." She pushed away from the window and began pacing again. "Jared said you didn't want to take this job. Why?"

Surprised by the question, Matt leaned back. "It's personal."

"I see." Her mouth flattened slightly. "So my father must've made you an offer you couldn't refuse."

He returned her challenging gaze. Against his better judgment, he said, "Just because I'm being paid to protect you doesn't mean I see you as a walking dollar sign."

Lili studied him for a moment, as if trying to read his sincerity, then said, "I wish I understood why that man attacked me."

Another abrupt change of subject, and he quickly adapted to the thread of worry in her voice. "The police are doing everything possible to find him."

"I know they are." She passed by him on a wisp of smoky, exotic scent. "Do you have any ideas about the attack? Who it might be, or what he wants?"

Matt looked down at his pen. "I'm not paid to investigate or solve crimes."

"Then take a wild guess."

At her arch tone, he looked up again, and rubbed the back of his neck. "From what you told me earlier, I can't see much of a motive, so I'm treating it like a stalking detail for now."

"That's what I was afraid of." She briefly closed her eyes. "But why *me*? I'm not famous or rich, and it's not like I have my face plastered in *Harper's Bazaar* or *Vogue* every month."

"You have a presence." Her pacing put him on edge, and he wanted to take her by the shoulders and sit her down in a chair. Instead, he leaned forward, hands clasped together. "Lots of energy. Colorful. You're noticeable."

She stopped and turned, eyes widening in surprise. "What you're saying, in your polite and professional way, is that I'm a showboat."

Matt smiled. "Yes, ma'am."

She laughed, and resumed her pacing. "According to my mother, I was born with a flair for the dramatic."

"Lili, maybe you should sit down and try to relax."

"Oh." Again, she stopped. "Sorry. I'm distracting you from your work, aren't I?"

"Don't worry about it."

"You say that a lot."

"It comes with the job."

"You say that a lot, too. I need a drink." She veered toward the tall, narrow slatted door that hid the mini bar. "You want something?"

Another abrupt change in subject, and he briefly wondered if she was still nervous or trying to keep him off balance on purpose. "No, thanks."

Lili bent to look through the fridge, and again he

watched the fall of her hair, mesmerized by the slow, rippling tumble of silky blackness. After pulling out a small bottle of wine, she shut the door with a smooth swing of her hip.

She walked toward him and, suddenly aware that he was watching her hips, Matt looked back down at his notes and paperwork. "Who's Pippa?"

"A friend. She owns a gallery downtown . . . specializes in fiber sculpture and wearable art." She stopped at the coffee table, and leaned over to examine his still incomplete advance form. Her hair swung downward, wafting a citrusy scent toward him. "You're not going to hassle Pippa, are you?"

"No, but I need to keep informed about who you're meeting with."

Matt looked up, and nearly swore. Her breasts were eye-level, inches away—and her robe gaped enough for him to glimpse her tattoo.

The sound of Lili clearing her throat snapped his attention back up to her face. Amusement glinted in her eyes. "Noticed my tattoo, huh?"

The heat of embarrassment spread through him. Great. What the hell was he supposed to say to that? "Professionally, I'm not supposed to notice."

"Nice save." Lili grinned, not appearing at all offended, then peered down at her chest and sighed. "It was one of those charge-ahead-without-thinking moments. I was twenty-two, and doing the Paris café scene with some Dutch girls I'd met. Too much wine, I guess."

"It often happens that way. I was dead drunk when I got mine."

"You have a tattoo?" Her gaze held his for a moment longer than was comfortable. "Where?"

Matt tapped his left biceps.

"I want to see." As he opened his mouth to flatly refuse, she said, "Oh, come on. Why not? You've seen mine. I want to see yours."

Christ, was she coming on to him? Their eyes met, stirring a familiar heat of arousal. He couldn't seem to move.

"I'm not asking you to strip, Hawkins. Just roll up your sleeve." She arched a brow. "And I'm not making a pass at you, so don't get all excited."

He rubbed the back of his neck, her poise and cool amusement making him feel foolish and clumsy, and said, "All right."

While she watched, he rolled his sleeve up his forearm and over his biceps until he'd bared his eagle-and-flag tattoo.

"Impressive," she said, and the next thing he knew, she'd touched his arm with a long, ruby-red nail, rubbing the pad of her finger over his skin.

"It's a standard tattoo, no big deal."

"I was talking about the muscles," Lili said, smiling, and as he went still in surprise, she added, "You were in the army."

"Yeah." He swallowed. "I was an MP."

The words came out sounding forced, and her eyes turned wary. "I shouldn't be touching you, should I?"

"Probably not a good idea."

Matt held her gaze a moment longer, then she dropped her hand to her side. He looked away and focused on rolling down his sleeve.

"Right," she said, taking a step back. "I was going to play solitaire. I won't bother you, will I?"

Hell, yes.

Matt shook his head, and picked up where he'd left off on his paperwork while she retrieved her little bottle of wine and sat to his left. He listened to the soft *fr-r-r-i-i-i-p* of the deck as she shuffled, and finally he stopped to watch her slender fingers and long red nails expertly fan the cards.

A woman of many talents, his client.

"You're still okay with my staying in your suite?" he asked.

She looked up, and nodded. "Like I said, choosing between privacy and staying alive isn't difficult. Are you okay with it?"

"It doesn't matter what I think. You're paying me. I do as you ask, providing it doesn't compromise your safety or break any laws."

Her brows shot up. "You have clients ask you for things that are illegal?"

Matt shrugged. "I won't procure drugs or prostitutes. Most of my regular clients respect that."

"Well, don't worry. I haven't any urge to hire a gigolo, or shoot up."

"Good. I can sleep easy tonight."

Lili didn't respond to his wry comment, and Matt directed his attention back to his paperwork. He worked in silence through the preliminary reports, and when he'd finished with that he pulled out his notes. "Who's Sue, and where are you meeting her?"

Lili glanced up from her half-dealt game of solitaire. A smile crossed her face, crinkling her eyes in a way that made him want to smile in return. "Don't you read the hometown papers, Matt? Sue's a *Tyrannosaurus rex*."

Surprised yet again, he stared at her. "You want to go look at dinosaurs?"

She looked faintly amused. "If it isn't too much trouble."

"It won't be a problem." At least not one he and his team couldn't handle.

Silence blanketed the room, except for the sound of his pen on the paper, the shuffle of her cards, or a soft muttering when a deal didn't go her way.

Looking up at a quiet "Damn," Matt watched as Lili took a swig of wine, mesmerized by the smooth, sliding movement of her throat as she swallowed. Slowly, he lowered his gaze, stirred beyond good sense by her nearness—and that way she had about her, that confusing mix of cues and signals that made him want to handle her as if she were fragile as glass, and at the same time, fuck her mindless.

She sat with her legs crossed, ladylike and proper, but with a length of smooth thigh bared. She held the bottle between her fingers, and as she stared down at her cards, absently stroked her thumb along the neck up to the ridge of the lip, her finger leaving a path in the wetness caused by condensation.

He shifted on the seat cushion, his mouth tightening as he forced himself to ignore the need pulling at him. Animal instinct was all this was, and he knew all about controlling the animal inside.

"So what's up for tomorrow?"

Her question cut across his randy thoughts, and he glanced at the clock—a lot safer than looking at her—and noted it was after midnight. "I start out with a team briefing every morning. Looks like your schedule is light. You're meeting most of the day with Sayers, with dinner here at the hotel before he heads to the airport." He shuffled through a few papers. "On Monday you go to the Art Institute for a nine o'clock class, followed by two meetings at the institute, then a late lunch meeting at Spiaggia. After that, you're clear for the rest of the day."

When he looked back up, she was staring at him.

"Have I made a mistake?"

"No. Not at all." She shook her head, idly twirling a jack of hearts between her fingers. "You *are* good."

"I'd better be," he said quietly, holding her gaze. "Your safety and your life are my responsibility. And they're not responsibilities I take lightly."

Her face paled, and she flinched, dropping the jack. After a moment, she asked, "Are you almost done with your paperwork?"

"For now. Why? Do you need something? I can send my driver out if—"

"No, it's not that. I thought I'd ask you to play a game of cards with me."

What he'd like was for her to either go back to bed, or get dressed. The shapely length of her exposed leg begged to be touched, and he thought what it'd be like to run his hand upward along her smooth, warm skin.

Ah, hell. It'd make no difference if she was dressed or not; this woman would look sexy in a flannel nightgown that covered her from neck to toes.

Matt shrugged. "Sure. I can play a game or two."

"No poker, though." She scooted her wing chair closer. "I'm not playing a bluffing game with a guy who learned to read people in bodyguard school."

He'd mostly learned it on the streets and in the dump he'd grown up in, but all he said was, "What do you want to play?"

"How about war? Easy rules, and it's boring enough that it might make me sleepy." She shuffled and dealt out the deck. "Not to mean *you're* dull company. Spending the night playing cards with an armed stranger isn't something I do on a regular basis."

Matt scooped up his cards, watching her. Her tone was light, almost flip, but he knew the bravado was for his benefit.

"Being a bodyguard must be an exciting job."

"Most of the time it's boring, just standing around and waiting. But boring means we're doing our job, so that's okay."

"Has it ever been not boring?"

Keeping his gaze focused on his cards, he said, "A few times."

"You're not a very talkative guy, are you?" But before he could answer she added, "Never mind, it doesn't matter. I'll talk enough for the both of us."

Matt smiled, fairly certain she was also trying to charm him and make up for her earlier bad mood. He almost wished she was still angry and confrontational; she'd be easier to resist.

They played cards, Lili making small talk about the weather, the hotel, and Chicago, while her gaze strayed repeatedly to his shoulder holster and the grip of the Glock 23 jutting outward.

"The gun bothers you," he said, and put down his cards to unbuckle the holster. "I'll take it off."

She didn't argue, but watched his every movement. He removed the holster, and when he bent to put it aside, out of sight by the love seat but still close at hand, she said, "Can I see it?"

Matt hesitated, then pulled the gun from the holster, removed the clip, checked the safety, and handed it to her grip first. "There's still a round in the chamber, so be careful." He paused, then added, "And it would be best if you didn't mention to anyone that I'm armed."

"Why?"

He met her gaze squarely, thinking she asked too damn many questions. "Because guns make people nervous. It's best if nobody knows."

Especially since it was illegal for him to carry concealed, but her father was paying a hefty under-the-table incentive to make sure his little girl was protected—*completely* protected.

Matt's willingness to take risks was the reason Dan Armistead had called him in on the detail; he and Dan had an understanding about jobs like this.

"It's heavier than I expected." She examined the gun, holding it with the tips of her fingers, as if it might bite, then handed it back, her gaze solemn. "Are the others armed?"

When he gave a noncommittal shrug, she added, "Your driver, Farrell . . . he's married?"

Matt returned the Glock to the holster and put it aside, wondering what Dal's marital status had to do with anything. "He married a few months ago."

"And his wife doesn't mind what he does for a living?" she asked, picking up her cards again.

"Not that I know of, but I've never asked, either." Matt also retrieved his cards, aware that the tension in the room had returned.

"Are you married?"

As she took his jack of spades with her king of diamonds, Matt looked up, suddenly uneasy. "No." He paused. "I'm uninvolved at the moment."

Like that mattered to her. Jesus, what was he thinking?

"I know it's none of my business. I'm just curious if your kind of job makes it difficult to have a steady relationship."

"Sometimes," Matt said, surprised by a sudden twinge of disappointment over her obvious disapproval of his work.

But most people didn't understand. And why should he care, anyway? He made good money, traveled often, stayed in the best hotels, and ate in the finest restaurants. His clients appreciated his work, and he was good at it.

"I think it would take a special woman to put up with a

man in your line of work." Lili didn't look away from him, and the pupils of her blue eyes were wide and dark—and sharply observant. "But I know I could never do it."

4

"Mr. Conroy, how are you today?"

Willis Conroy turned from his half-packed suitcase to see one of the beefy male attendants—Bart? Bill?—standing in his doorway, a short old broad at his side.

"Still breathing," he said. "Betcha you're sorry to hear that."

Silence. Then Bill-or-Bart gave a too-hearty laugh. "Mr. Conroy is quite the joker some days."

Willis wanted to grab his cane and crack it over the fool's head. Dammit, he was old, not stupid, and he could still read fake in a man's eyes.

"Mr. Conroy, this is Mrs. Etta Schulmann. She's just moved in with us, and I'm taking her around to meet all our residents."

Residents, his ass. Prisoners was more like it. And he ought to know.

"Mrs. Schulmann, this is Willis Conroy. He's been with us for four years."

The old dame's eyes popped wide behind her thick glasses. "Oh," she gasped. "He's that ex-con all the girls in the dining room were talking about!"

"That's right, sister," Willis said, his voice a cheerful growl. "I've got myself a rep. You like us fast types? You're lookin' pretty good. Maybe you and me could have a good time. What do you say?"

The dame squawked like a goose and shuffled off. Bill-or-Bart glared. "That wasn't necessary, Mr. Conroy."

"Bite me."

He'd heard the phrase from somebody or other's grandkid, and liked it. Short, sharp. Got the point across.

Bill-or-Bart shot him another glare, then went after the old broad. Willis grunted, and returned to his suitcase. A couple pairs of pants, some shirts, socks, and his favorite red suspenders. He wouldn't need much. He didn't expect to be gone long.

He paused, his gaze falling on the newspaper on the faded polyester bedspread, and the short news story at the bottom of page six: DESIGNER ATTACKED DURING LECTURE.

Unwillingly, his gaze settled on a single name in the story, surprised all over again to find the pain as strong as ever, even after nearly seventy years.

"Ah, Rosie, Rosie," he whispered.

This little designer gal down in Chicago had no idea what kind of trouble she'd let loose. How could she? Few people were still alive who knew the truth. He was one of them. Lou Graziano's boy was another, and Crazy Tony never gave up when he'd set his mind to something.

Now Willis had no choice but to go back to Moccasin Lake where all the trouble had started—or ended, depending how you looked at it—and wait. Sooner or later, someone would come nosing around, and then he'd have to decide what to do about it.

With another grunt, he reached under his narrow mattress and pulled out his Colt .45, wrapped carefully in an old handkerchief, its yellowed linen embroidered with tiny rosebuds and a decorative "R" in one corner. He hid the gun at the bottom of the suitcase.

Better safe than sorry.

A knock sounded at the door, and he looked up to see the smiling face of the little redheaded nurse he liked. Patti, her name was.

"Willis, your niece Susie is here to pick you up for your visit to the resort. Are you ready, or should I ask her to park and come in and wait?"

"I'm ready." He tossed a checkers set, pill bottles, and the newspaper into the suitcase, clicked its fasteners closed, and then grabbed his cane.

"I'll take the suitcase for you," Patti said.

Willis didn't protest, biting back his pride. At ninety-three, he was sound of mind and body, but not so strong anymore, and he didn't move too fast. Once, he'd moved fast. He'd had to; it was all that had kept him alive. Not that keeping himself alive was anything to be proud of— and he sure as hell never thought he'd live long enough to see this day.

"Let's go," he snapped. "It ain't like I got a lot of time to waste."

Patti grinned. "We'll miss you, too, Willis. You old charmer, you."

After a moment, Willis grinned back. He never could resist a pretty smile or a pretty girl—especially a pretty, redheaded girl.

5

Lili was in the bathroom, clipping her hair back in a barrette, when the phone rang. She reached for the doorknob, but stopped at the sound of Matt's low, even voice from the other room.

"Yes, ma'am, this is the bodyguard."

She smiled at his wooden tone. It must be her mother. Again.

"Would you like me to get her for you? No problem. Hold on."

A firm knock sounded on the door and she swung it open. Matt stood an unnerving few inches away, dressed to kill—literally, she supposed, but hopefully not today—in a charcoal-gray suit with a steel-blue shirt and a gray tie in a chevron pattern. His dark hair was still damp from a recent shower, and he'd shaved, for what little good it did him. He wore a faintly harassed expression, and when he glanced down, his brows drew together in a frown.

Belatedly, Lili remembered she was wearing only a

black full slip. Too late to do anything about that—and he'd seen her in far less over the weekend.

"Your mother is on the phone," he said, mouth tight, then spun around and walked away. As her gaze followed him, she noticed Dal Farrell staring at her, a donut halfway to his mouth, a bit of powdered sugar on his black suit coat.

Lili walked quickly to the nightstand by her bed, aiming for a little privacy, and picked up the phone. "Hi, Mom."

"Lili!" Her mother's voice sounded high with worry. "What's going on? Are you all right? I expected you to call us by now!"

"Mom, it's seven-thirty. I just got out of the shower, and the only crisis so far this morning is that I can't find my black stockings."

Silence, then, "What's that bodyguard doing?"

"At the moment, they're all eating donuts and drinking coffee."

"How can they protect you if they're all eating donuts?"

"Because they're no more than ten feet away from me." Lili sighed. "Both hotel security and the men from the agency are doing their jobs. The only way I could be safer is if one of them crawled into bed with me at night."

An image of Matt Hawkins with his sleeve rolled up around his arm, showing his eagle tattoo and nicely defined muscles, flashed to mind.

Then again, maybe not so safe.

"Don't get flip with me. You may be an adult, but I'm still your mother, and I have a right to be worried. You don't sound very upset about all this."

While she'd never admit it to her mother, she was beginning to consider "all this" something of an adventure. The crazy stalker part still made her light-headed with fear, but being the focal point of a small army of males who radiated power and aggression brought her a little thrill. The feeling wasn't enlightened or modern, true, but if she would be tripping over hunky men all week, why not go with the flow?

"I'm fine. Really. And Mom, the man who answered the phone is the team leader. His name is Matt Hawkins, and he prefers to be called a personal security specialist, not a bodyguard. You might keep that in mind."

"I'll call him whatever he wants, so long as he keeps you safe!"

Lili spent another ten minutes reassuring her mother she wasn't in imminent danger of violent death, then talked with her father, answered a barrage of questions, argued—to no avail—about paying the bodyguard fee herself, and then hung up, repressing an urge to scream.

She adored her parents, but when the hell would they stop trying to micromanage "their baby's" life?

For that matter, when was she going to stop letting them?

Her mind blanked. One too many complications to deal with right now. Her immediate problem was what to wear that would impress a classroom of twenty-somethings with make-me-care stares.

She pondered the clothes in the closet. Definitely something black and sophisticated, with killer heels. No power bitch suits, though, and nothing too severe; she didn't want to look like a vampire, either. Good thing she always overpacked when she traveled.

After a few more minutes, while listening to the sound of low male laughter from the parlor, she selected a black gabardine wool suit with a short skirt and fitted jacket. A more thorough search turned up her black hose, and she dressed.

The opaque pantyhose disguised her scraped knees,

but weren't much help for the ugly bruise under her jaw. She frowned. Not even makeup could disguise it, and she hunted through another suitcase, pulled out a black-and-gold leopard print scarf, and tied it around her neck.

Another quick look in the mirror convinced her she'd pass muster, and she went to find shoes—always the most difficult part of getting dressed. She narrowed her choice down to three pairs, and finally settled on matte black pumps with gold metallic heels. A little something to catch attention.

When she walked out into the parlor, silence fell over the room. All the men turned, and their appreciative gazes—and one in particular—made her go hot with a fluttery, unfamiliar awkwardness.

"Good morning," Manny said, in his quiet, sexy Latino lilt. She smiled a greeting in return.

"Are you ready to go?" Matt asked, putting down his coffee cup.

"Once I make sure everything I need is in my briefcase," she answered.

Matt turned to Dal. "Get the car."

Dal nodded, and as he walked past her, he smiled shyly. He was so fresh-faced and cute that Lili wanted to chuck him under the chin. Except that if she did so, he'd probably flip her over his shoulder or throw her against the wall.

Cuddly, but deadly.

Lili retrieved her briefcase and clicked it open, checking for her slide carousel and notes. She glanced up, and couldn't help smiling at the sight of Matt and Manny standing like the Wall of Jericho in front of her, arms folded across their chests. Manny was wearing a dark brown suit, with a black shirt and a skinny gold tie. Very trendy—and a good choice for his black hair, chocolate-brown eyes, and olive-tinted skin.

"Nice suit," she said. "Ungaro? Ferragamo?"

Manny grinned. "Ferragamo."

"You guys make pretty good money at this job."

"When I was a cop, I couldn't afford Ferragamo," Manny admitted.

"We dress according to the detail," Matt said.

He was all businesslike again this morning, as he'd been all day Sunday. Lili missed the warmth she'd glimpsed the night they'd sat across from each other, comparing tattoos and playing war.

"When we work the Drake," he added, "we wear our expensive suits."

"Ah. I see." Everything she needed was already in her briefcase—surprise, surprise—and she clicked it shut. "So if I were staying at the Sheraton, what would you wear?"

"Good department store suits," Matt said, and a hint of amusement glinted in his eyes at last. "Lord and Taylor. Bloomingdale's."

"And if I were staying at the Motel 6?"

"If you were staying at the Motel 6, you couldn't afford me," Matt said.

"And I probably wouldn't need you in the first place."

"Good point." He slid his hands into his trouser pockets, and rocked back on the balls of his feet. "All set?"

"Except for the shoes." At Matt's blank look, she explained, "I'm bringing four pairs of shoes from my bridal line to the class, and afterward I'm donating them to the school. Can you grab that big bag over there, by the window? I'll be right back."

Lili gathered four white boxes—the cardboard printed in a pale brocade design—and returned to the parlor, where Matt waited with the large canvas bag. She placed the boxes in the bag.

"Okay. Now I'm ready."

Her words set in motion a now-familiar routine. Manny left the suite first, then she and Matt followed. They greeted the hotel security guard sitting by the elevator, and waited a few moments as Matt talked with Dal briefly on the two-way radio. The elevator doors opened with a *ping*, and Manny entered first. She followed, Matt close behind her.

It was a small elevator, but elegant, and graced with a tapestry-upholstered bench against the back. Two middle-aged couples were already in the elevator, forcing everybody to stand close together. Lili pressed back against Matt's body, and his chest rose as he took a long, slow breath. Enveloped in his warmth and the scent of his cologne, she felt pleasantly safe and secure.

No doubt about it. Go with the flow, that's what she'd do.

Shortly before nine A.M., Matt found himself slouched in a chair at the back of a classroom. In a way he couldn't identify, the place even smelled like a school—a smell that always brought back painful memories.

You're stupid . . . just a dumb-ass punk kid! Go on and quit, it don't matter to me. You're flunkin' anyway, and it ain't like you're ever gonna be somebody . . .

Just words, in the usual drunken bellow, and words he'd heard often enough. But on that day, his sixteenth birthday, and for whatever reason, those words had hurt like never before, and were burned into his memory. It had taken him a couple more years to figure out his best revenge was to be everything his father wasn't, rather than be just like him, only meaner. Too bad the bastard was dead now, and couldn't see what his dumb-ass punk kid had made of himself.

Matt took a deep breath, then glanced around the classroom packed full with some forty students, most of them women. Bright-eyed, fresh-faced, and so young. Beside them, he felt old and jaded. He'd never been as innocent or eager as this—or as lucky—and he bet most of these students took their good fortune completely for granted.

Pushing that thought aside, he focused on Lili, who stood at the front of the classroom fiddling with a slide carousel while the room buzzed with voices full of anticipation. The instructor, an older woman in a dark pantsuit, spoke to Lili, and then signaled for silence.

A hush fell over the room, and the woman said, "Today we have with us a very special guest. Lili Kavanaugh is an instructor at New York's Fashion Institute of Technology, and the owner and designer of LiliPads, an exclusive line of bridal footwear. Professor Kavanaugh is here to talk about her experiences in designing specialty footwear, so let's all give her a warm welcome."

Applause sounded in the room, and as Lili flashed her wide, friendly smile, Matt glanced at the four pairs of wedding shoes she'd arranged on a separate display table.

One pair was made of a white brocade, very Victorian-looking, and sported a pouf of netting at the toe held in place by a rhinestone buckle. The pair next to it looked plain, made of satiny ivory fabric with a flat ribbon bow, but he bet it boasted a price tag in the triple digits. The third pair was made of a heavy-looking ivory lace dotted with beads, so delicate and airy that it didn't seem possible to walk in them. The last pair was more showy: white and pale pink sequins in a tiger stripe pattern, and decorated with some sort of white feather plume thing—just the ticket for the well-dressed jungle bride.

Lili's shoes were like Lili herself: pretty, feminine, and impractical. A touch of humor and fun. Nice to look at, but soft and frivolous didn't have much of a place in his life.

He looked up again as the instructor added, "As you also know, Professor Kavanaugh was the victim of an attempted assault on Saturday. Because of this, she has with her several security agents, one of whom is sitting at the back of the room, and the other is outside by the stairs. We ask that you do not distract either of these men. Thank you. My class is all yours, Lili."

Despite their instructor's warning, several girls continued to sneak peeks at him, their gazes a mix of curiosity and frank sexual interest. One in particular, a small-boned, pretty Asian woman with short, dark hair and purple lipstick, caught his gaze and winked.

Kids. Matt glanced away, holding back a grin.

"All right," said Lili, "it's time to get started. You girls in the back stop ogling my bodyguard. The show's up front."

The sound of shifting bodies, creaking chairs, and whispers followed. With one last cheeky grin, the young woman turned away from Matt. He looked to the front of the classroom where Lili perched on the edge of the table, looking sexy as hell in her form-fitting black suit. She'd slipped on rectangular half-glasses with thick black frames that made her look both bookish and elegant—and pure New York style.

"Earlier this semester you studied shoe construction, covered the basics of shoe design and history, and learned how shoes evolved from mere protection against the elements to symbols of status and wealth."

As Lili launched into her lecture, Matt settled back in the chair, folding his arms over his chest. The students in front of him were nodding their heads.

"So what I'm discussing over the next hour is the more

ephemeral—and emotional—elements of our culture's enduring passion for shoes."

She pushed herself away from the table and surveyed the class, a small smile on her face, hands on her hips—a stance that pulled her jacket tight over her breasts.

"It's my philosophy as a designer that shoes are female in spirit, and little else in our culture speaks to a woman like the luscious line of an arch and the sensual curve of a heel." Lili moved her hands sinuously through the air in an hourglass shape, her voice low and throaty. "Or the flirtatious allure of bows and baubles, buckles and beads. Shoes evoke fantasies, embody romance and desire. They can symbolize a cherished memory, and allow us to change personalities and moods in an instant."

Lili's smile widened a fraction and her gaze locked on his, as if she were speaking only to him.

"When a woman slips on a shoe, she's sending a signal, not just about who she is, but who she wants to be. Whether it's a pair of professional flats, or sinfully decadent heels, it's all about making a statement. About expectations. About sex."

An expectant silence filled the classroom, and the word lingered in the air, rich in its complexities and possibilities.

Sex . . .

Short, sweet. Certain to grab attention—and this woman, in her tight suit and high heels, looked as if she knew plenty about it.

At the inconvenient tightness in his groin, Matt shifted on his chair, trying to head off any further thoughts of sex and his client.

"No matter what our personal views on sexuality, we understand the basic biological drive behind it. How we present ourselves is part of the eternal mating courtship— a desire to be noticed, adored. To feel attractive." She pulled a chair toward her, positioned it next to the table, then looked at Matt. "Mr. Hawkins, can you come up here, please?"

As heads swiveled around to stare at him, a flush crept upward to his face. Ignoring it, he stood and made his way to her side.

She was grinning, enjoying herself, knowing he was uncomfortable. What the hell was she up to?

"I want to stand on the table, and my skirt's tight. Can you lift me up to the chair? From there, I can make it the rest of the way to the table without too much trouble."

Several students laughed. Others exchanged startled looks, obviously not sure what to make of professors who stood on tables any more than he did.

Matt took her by the waist and hoisted her up onto the table, bypassing the chair completely. She gave a yelp of surprise, bending her knees to clear the table, scrambled to secure her footing, and then stared down at him.

"Going straight to the table works, too." She smiled. "Thanks."

He returned to the back of the room to the sound of more low laughter and leaned back against the wall, arms folded over his chest, trying not to smile. Christ, she was something else.

"I know you're wondering what I'm doing, and I'll get to that in a minute. But now that I have your attention, I want to make one point very clear. Your creations are a reflection of your personality and how you view the world around you. This quality is unique to you and will define your work, so don't be afraid to use it. And never, ever let it go."

She paused a moment to let her words sink in. "I have a romantic streak a mile wide, and I enjoy all aspects of being a woman. This is why I design very romantic and sexy shoes, and so it's no surprise my designs are often described as 'sweet confections' and 'dreamy fantasies.' You may have a philosophy completely different from mine, but I'm sure you get my point. We must remain true to our uniqueness, our vision."

Matt didn't know about points or visions, but she sure had his attention, and the vibrant emotion in her voice, her passionate conviction, touched a familiar chord deep within him.

"Sexuality pervades every aspect of our culture, especially in the fashion world. Over the decades, fashions have evolved to reveal more of the body, but I believe there's nothing sexier than a woman's bare foot or, better yet, a partially revealed foot. Never underestimate the power of imagination."

Slowly, Matt ran an appreciative gaze over her. She knew exactly what to reveal, what to hide, what to hint at—and she'd used it on him with the skill of a master. No wonder he couldn't think straight around her.

"Quite often, our instincts acknowledge that something is feminine or sexually tantalizing, but we don't know exactly why," she said, bringing his attention back to her face. "To help you get a better feel for what I'm talking about, let's discuss high-heeled shoes. Many women like how stiletto heels make them feel and look. Men seem to fixate on them. But why?"

She walked the length of the table, and every gaze in the room—including Matt's—locked on to her gold heels, the arch of her feet in the black shoes, the rounded muscles of her calves, and long, long line of her legs.

"Does anybody want to take a guess?"

Hands shot into the air, and Matt listened to a series of answers: heels made women taller. Made them feel more powerful, more dominant. Kept the leg muscles toned. Made a good weapon.

Laughter followed the last suggestion.

Grinning, Lili nodded. "Good points. That's all part of it, except maybe the weapon bit, but what's really behind the allure of high heels is a sexual signal. You've all heard stiletto heels referred to as 'fuck me shoes,' right?"

Another round of nods. Fascinated—and surprised by her casual use of "fuck"—Matt stared at her, aware that he was finding all this talk of shoes uncomfortably arousing.

No doubt exactly what she intended.

"Now, there's a reason for this besides crudeness. Sex researcher Alfred Kinsey points out that when a woman wears high heels, her foot arches and stretches into the same vertical position that signals sexual arousal, or to be more specific, the moment of climax."

"Cool," said a young male student in front. "I didn't know that."

Looking down at the floor, Matt took in a long, slow breath as an image of Lili, naked in a bed, flashed to mind. He imagined himself on top of her, inside her, and her feet in the air, arching and stretching as she cried out—

Whoa. Brakes on, buddy. Full reverse.

"Look at the posture of a woman wearing high heels."

Matt looked up—and immediately regretted it.

"A woman stands straight, lower back arched, chest thrust outward." As she spoke, Lili turned sideways to the class. "What does this posture do, if not proclaim a woman's femininity? It's a signal to a male that she's feeling self-assured about herself and her sexuality. Somebody once called high heels the shoes of goddesses, and I think that's dead on."

The energy in the room was near palpable. Every gaze was locked on Lili, every student sat with spine straight, leaning slightly forward.

Man, she was good. Really good.

Lili turned to face her class again, her movements

graceful, her expression serious, as if standing on a table was an everyday occurrence—and for all he knew, she taught all her classes from tabletops. "This is what you can't forget when you sit down to design your first pair of high-heeled shoes. Sure, you can tone down those shoes by making them virginal white and adding a girlish bow on the vamp. And as we'll see in a few minutes when we look at the slides, you can make your shoes elegant and sophisticated, playful or clever—but the essence of the design is still sexual, and always will be."

Trying to gather his composure, Matt glanced at his watch—and almost swore. He was late for check-in. He leaned over, and spoke quietly into his hidden radio piece, "Status report."

Manny's voice sounded in his earpiece, "All secure. Nothing much happening with me, over."

Matt wished he could say the same. "Farrell?"

"In position."

"Roger. Next check-in at oh-nine-thirty."

"Mr. Hawkins?" At Lili's call, he looked up. "Can I bother you to come sweep me off my feet and back onto the floor?"

Every inner warning told him not to touch her. Especially now, when his awareness of her as a woman pulsed dangerously strong and undeniable.

But refusing wasn't an option, so he walked to the front of the room, reached up, and grasped her waist. He brought her down to the floor, holding her against him, her hands resting lightly on his shoulders, and he had an instant impression of soft warmth, narrow waist, and full, firm breasts.

Her eyes met his, and she asked, "Enjoying the lecture?"

"You could say that."

A low titter of laughter spread through the room, and then a student asked, "But isn't everything you said sexist, Professor Kavanaugh? And objectifying women?"

Matt released Lili, but as he stepped back to make his escape, she snagged his jacket sleeve.

Now what?

"There are some who'll say it is, but dressing up to look nice is biologically instinctive. Men and women want to feel good about themselves, as well as look attractive to the opposite sex. And all fashion objectifies gender to some extent. For instance, let's look at Mr. Hawkins here."

No, let's not look at Mr. Hawkins.

Hot with discomfort, Matt faced forty-odd pairs of eyes—and the possibility Lili might start discussing his biological urges in front of a room full of kids.

At the moment, his biological urges didn't need any further urging.

"The suit he's wearing plays up male sexual attractiveness in much the same way high-heeled shoes do for a woman," Lili said, resting her hand on his shoulder. "The ideal male beauty is broad shoulders and narrow hips. The cut of this suit accentuates broad shoulders and chest, and its lines narrow down toward the hips, in an inverted triangle shape."

As she talked, her fingers quickly, lightly, traced a triangle, starting at his left shoulder and moving to his right, then down his belly and back up to his shoulder. When her fingers touched his belly—a little too low for comfort—he flinched.

"A suit like this broadcasts power, authority, and virility," she continued, as if she hadn't noticed his reaction—except she'd been standing against him, and there was no way she could've missed it. "All considered typically desirable male traits. You could say the suit is our society's version of male plumage."

She made him sound like some damn cockatoo.

Matt didn't look away from the staring students, who were blatantly checking him out. In a neutral tone, he asked, "Are you done with me?"

"For now." Lili smiled, a hint of mischief glinting in her eyes. "You and your plumage can go sit back down. You've been very helpful."

With a deliberate nonchalance, Matt returned to his seat at the back of the room. Lili talked on, flashing slides on the screen, and fielding questions from inquisitive students.

Every time he came close to getting a handle on this woman, she said or did something that knocked him off balance. Half the time, he swore she did it on purpose.

From the start Matt had pegged Lili as impulsive and spontaneous, a doted-upon baby of the family who sometimes let her domineering parents control her life.

He'd known that impulsiveness could get her into a tight spot, but he hadn't considered how it might make trouble for him as well. He'd best be on guard, or he'd make a fool of himself—not to mention he couldn't keep an eye out for danger if his dick was doing his thinking for him.

After the lecture, Lili spent an hour mingling with faculty and students, then met with one of the institute's head honchos to discuss the possibility of lending her historical footwear collection to the museum as a temporary exhibit.

Through it all Matt remained in the background, repositioning Manny as needed, and checking in with Dal at the car. He made a special effort to ensure his rookie agent was alert. By now, Dal was probably sick and tired of hanging out in garages and parking lots, and day-dreaming of going back home to his waiting wife . . . who'd probably meet him at door wearing nothing but a smile and four-inch, red, fuck-me shoes.

Lucky little bastard.

Taking a long, slow breath, Matt once again forced his thoughts back where they belonged—on his work, and not on what Lili would look like wearing nothing but stiletto heels.

After she'd finished, Lili asked to return to the Drake to change before heading to her lunch meeting. Matt hailed Dal on the two-way, and when the car pulled up to the side entrance, he and Manny escorted her outside.

"I really do appreciate how you helped out at the lecture today," Lili said, a little breathlessly, as Matt hustled her toward the car. "It's hard sometimes to get young people to pay attention, and they tend to respond better if you play them a bit. I find that drama works wonders."

"Looks that way."

At the car, she twisted, looking at him, her face a touch anxious. "So you're not mad? That I brought you up front like I did?"

"I'm not mad," he said, and pushed her head down through the open door before she could ask more questions. "Please get in the car, goddess."

A soft laugh sounded from inside, and a murmured, "So you *were* paying attention. I wasn't sure. You looked bored."

Damn good thing she hadn't been able to read his mind.

Manny leaned over. "Goddess?"

"I'll explain. Later."

"Man, I can't wait to hear this," Manny said, stroking his goatee.

When they arrived back at the hotel, Matt stepped out of the elevator to find several uniformed police officers and hotel security gathered in the hall outside Lili's suite.

"What happened?" he demanded, fixing his gaze on the officer who appeared to be in charge.

"An attempted entry to Ms. Kavanaugh's suite," the cop said, his gaze shifting behind Matt's shoulder.

Matt turned in time to see the color drain from Lili's face. He told Manny, "Get her in the room now."

With Dal following close behind, Manny led Lili away, a supporting hand at her back. She cast a last glance over her shoulder at Matt before she went inside.

"Tell me exactly what happened," Matt ordered once the door had closed, holding back the hot rush of anger that, if he gave it free rein, would only cloud his judgment.

The hotel security guard answered. "A guy in a maintenance uniform came off the elevator, and said he'd got a call that the thermostat in Ms. Kavanaugh's room needed to be fixed. You didn't say anything to me about it when you left this morning, so I thought it was suspicious. When I questioned him, he took off."

"You didn't catch him?"

The security guard shook his head. "I tried, but lost him in the stairwell. We searched the building, but didn't find him."

"How did he know which room she was in? I ordered that no one was to give out Ms. Kavanaugh's room number."

The guard shrugged. "I don't know. The front desk people swear nobody took any calls or answered any questions about Ms. Kavanaugh."

"Shit." Matt rubbed the back of his neck. She'd had her name and appearances plastered in the local papers and campus bulletins for weeks; he'd checked. Plenty of time for someone to make plans. "It's possible he found out what room she was in before she arrived this weekend."

"Probably," the cop agreed.

He didn't like it, and gut instinct warned him this was no ordinary stalker. Matt turned to the security guard. "You got a good look at him, right?"

It was the cop, one hand on his gun belt, who answered. "We've got a description. White male, early to mid thirties, brown hair and blue eyes. About five-ten, one-eighty pounds. A small scar on his chin. We'll have a composite drawn up as soon as possible. We have a call in to Mike Payton."

Payton was the detective handling Lili's assault case. From his brief talk with the man the other day, Matt had judged him competent and smart.

"When did it happen?"

"About thirty minutes ago."

"Shit," Matt said again. He glanced at the security guard, who was looking uneasy. "You didn't do anything wrong, and you kept him from getting into the room. That's all that matters now. I doubt he'll try again, but I want the watch at the elevator doubled, just to be safe."

A few minutes later, after asking more questions and answering several for the officers, Matt returned to Lili's suite. She was pacing by the window and Manny and Dal stood close by, waiting in silence.

The instant he walked into the room, Lili spun to face him. "Somebody tried to break into my room?"

"It looks that way, but the guard did his job. He was suspicious, and his questions scared the guy off."

"Oh, my God," she whispered. "This is for real . . . the bastard isn't going to give up, is he?"

"I think you should sit down, Lili," Matt said, briefly glancing at both Manny and Dal. When she did as suggested, he added, "We have a description, and the police are preparing a composite drawing. They'll run it on the news, in the papers. Maybe it'll scare the guy off for good, or turn up a lead that will let the cops bring him in. You're okay. You've got nothing to worry about. The security I've put in place is working."

Eyes closed, Lili rested her head back against the love seat. "I'm going to cancel my afternoon meeting."

Matt hunkered down in front of her. "Don't let him get you running scared. That gives him exactly what he wants—power over you."

"But I *am* scared," she murmured, opening her eyes, and he saw the tears brimming—but this time, she looked more angry and frustrated than terrified.

Right then, he knew she'd be all right. She had more guts than she gave herself credit for, probably because for the first time in her life, she was forced to stand on her own. Mom and Dad and their deep pockets couldn't make her trouble go away. Some people shone under adversity, and it looked like Lili was one of them.

"I know you're scared," he said, "but you let me and my team worry about him. You get on with your life. Go to the lunch meeting. Don't let the fear control you."

"Will you make me go?"

He shook his head. "I can only advise. I know your first instinct is to hide, but it doesn't have to be that way. I can keep you safe."

She didn't look away from him, and after a long moment, she asked quietly, "Promise?"

For her sake, Matt smiled. "I promise. I won't even let you so much as chip a fingernail."

She smiled back and then, before he realized what she intended, leaned over and kissed him on the cheek, filling his senses with her dusky perfume, the soft tickle of her hair, and the warmth of her lips. "Thank you."

6

Lili stared at the black-and-white photograph of Humphrey Bogart, who stared back at her from the wall, wearing his signature fedora and slant-browed expression of worldly ennui. "I don't know," she said with a sigh. "The one with Godiva chocolate liqueur sounds very tempting."

"Oh, come on, Lil, be adventurous." Pippa Dowling rolled her eyes. "Try the Chopin martini. Look at that . . . one hundred percent potato vodka, chilled, and served straight up."

"Potato vodka, ugh . . . that sounds disgusting."

She and Pippa were sitting in the Redhead Piano Bar, working their way through an impressive list of martinis, and soaking up the atmosphere. The bordello-burgundy walls looked dark in the dim, smoke-hazed light, and dozens of framed photographs of sloe-eyed screen sirens, suave movie idols, and smiling lounge singers looked down on the crowded room. In the background, the

Wednesday night piano man was crooning Frank Sinatra's "Fly Me to the Moon," accompanied by what looked like half the bar patrons, who'd gathered around the piano.

Pippa suddenly giggled. "Hey, look! Here's a James Bond martini. Maybe we should order a couple for those two guys from Thugs-R-Us."

"They're not thugs, they're my bodyguards," Lili said, trying to look severe. "And they can't drink on duty, anyway."

She glanced at Matt and Manny, sitting several tables away and nursing along something dark and nonalcoholic. Probably root beer. For once, they didn't look out of place, since the Redhead mandated a dress code, and most of the other patrons, both male and female, were urban types in suits.

"The Latino guy's not too bad. I always liked them dark and debonair," Pippa said, giving both men an assessing look. "But that other guy, he gives me the creeps."

Surprised, Lili turned back to her friend. "Matt? Why?"

"I don't know. Maybe it's his eyes. He just looks dangerous to me."

"He's supposed to look dangerous. That's how he scares off the bad guy who's after me."

"So what's going on? Do you want to talk about it?"

Leaning closer, Lili filled Pippa in on the latest report from the police, which was basically zilch. "Matt thinks it's a stalker. A persistent one, since he tried to get into my room at the Drake. Hotel security ran him off."

Pippa rested a hand against her throat. "Oh, my God. You must be terrified!"

"Sometimes," Lili admitted. "Other times, it almost feels like something out of a TV movie."

"What happens after you go back to New York?"

"Matt says I should probably increase security once I'm home. He knows a couple of security professionals in New York who can help me out."

"You think that's necessary?"

"I don't know . . . I never had trouble like this until I came to Chicago. No weird phone calls, nobody follow-ing me around, so it's hard for me to think I'll have trou-ble once I'm home. I keep hoping it'll turn out to be a local nutcase."

"Does anybody know why this guy is after you?"

"No." Lili frowned at her drink. "Matt suggested it might be because of what I am."

"Oh?" Pippa's expression grew ominous. "And what the hell is that supposed to mean?"

Lili shrugged. "Basically, he's saying I'm loud and at-tract attention. Which of course I am, and that's the point. I just never encountered the negative side of it before."

Pippa reached across the table and squeezed Lili's hand. "I don't think we should talk about this anymore. We're here to have fun, to relax, catch up on old times. Let's order a couple more drinks. I'm going for the one with gin, Grand Marnier, and cranberry juice. It sounds kinda . . . pretty."

Pippa was right; they hadn't seen each other in almost a year, so why waste time talking about this bastard? Matt was right, too—she couldn't let the fear control her life.

"I'm sticking with the Godiva," Lili said. "I feel deca-dent."

It was hard not to feel a little decadent in the Redhead, with its dark glamour reminiscent of days gone by. Plus, she was wearing a body-skimming dress of glittery gold nylon spandex, with a scoop neck and fringed hem. The fabric ended at mid-thigh, but the long fringe brushed her knees. She wore a pair of gold leather pumps with chunky heels and no jewelry, except for a thin gold ankle bracelet.

She was in a minimalist monochrome kind of mood tonight, and her boys complemented her quite nicely, since they were both in basic black.

The thought made her smile, and after Pippa ordered their drinks, Lili said, "I better slow down on the martinis. You know I can't hold my liquor."

Pippa grinned. "I figure each martini knocks off about five years in age, and this will be our second, so that makes us mentally on par with a twenty-one-year-old, and means we're technically allowed to act twenty-one."

Vintage Pippa logic.

"I did a lot of dumb things when I was twenty-one. Remember Bjorn?"

"How could I forget?" Pippa laughed, tucking a strand of long blond hair behind her ear.

When they had their new drinks, Lili asked, "How's business at the gallery?"

"Not bad, but it's never going to make me a rich woman, and that lawyer I'm dating is looking more and more like prime provider material every day."

"Like you'd ever need a man to support you." Lili smiled. "The place looks great, and I love what you've done with that fabric sculpture display."

"Thanks." Pippa stirred her martini. "It keeps me busy, that's for sure. I don't know how you manage everything you do . . . the teaching, the traveling, the shoe line. You're amazing."

"Truth is, I'm getting a little overextended." Lili stabbed her stir stick into her drink. "Something has to give, and soon. Probably the teaching, as much as I love it. My designs are finally beginning to attract some serious attention but it's been a lot more work than I expected, and Jared keeps harping on me to diversify."

"I hear you on the hard work part," Pippa said with feeling. "And how are Jared and Olivia doing these days?"

"The usual. Every time he makes matrimonial noises, she bolts. She's currently in bolt phase, and he's cranky as hell."

Pippa smiled. "Your sister is nuts."

"I know."

"Jared's still helping you out, then?"

"Sort of. It's getting harder for him, on top of his regular job. Besides, he's an investment guru, not a real business manager. I'll probably have to hire somebody else to run things pretty soon."

"Why not do it yourself? If you quit teaching, wouldn't you have time?"

Lili sipped her martini. The vodka and chocolate liqueur mix was different, and not too bad. "Detail work isn't one of my strong points. I'm better off sticking to the creative stuff."

For as long as she could remember, her parents, sisters, or friends had said things like: "Lili has a wonderful imagination and dreams big, but she's not very good at following through." Whenever she'd planned adventures, grand schemes, or practical jokes, somebody else always insisted on taking care of the details for her—and she'd always let them do so without protesting.

She frowned at her drink. "I don't know . . . maybe I could oversee most of the business stuff. Just because I never have before, doesn't mean I can't."

"It wouldn't hurt to try," Pippa agreed. "You'll still have to hire on help, but I think it would be good for you to be more involved on the business end. If nothing else, you need to keep informed so people can't take advantage of you. You've always been too trusting, Lil."

Lili glanced over at the next table. Matt was watching her, an unreadable expression on his face, while Manny scrutinized a loud group of middle-aged businessmen who'd imbibed a few too many martinis. She smiled, and he nodded in acknowledgment.

Lili looked down at her hands, nail tips drumming on the table surface. She stopped it as soon as she realized what she was doing. "I keep thinking about what he said, that I'm 'colorful.' I'm thirty-one. Is it time to start wearing longer skirts and shorter heels? Think about settling down?"

"I'm the wrong person to ask. I believe that if you want to wear hot-pink miniskirts when you're ninety, you should do it. Your family and friends know you're a hopeless romantic with a big heart, Lil, and we love you just the way you are." Pippa glanced toward Matt's table. "Is there a reason you're feeling this sudden need to change?"

"Maybe," Lili admitted, going warm.

"You don't have to change yourself for anybody."

Lili nodded in agreement, but a vague sense of dissatisfaction still nagged at her. "Colorful isn't really how I want people to see me, though."

Especially Matt.

"Who cares what people think? You're just getting sappy. You always get like this when you drink."

"No, it's not that. Seriously." Lili sighed. "I think I'm developing a sort of . . . thing for him. I get all jumpy and nervous around him, and he has the sexiest voice. God, I get the shivers every time I hear him talk."

Pippa looked startled by Lili's sudden admission. "You've got to be kidding."

"Why? He's the kind of man that reminds me I'm a woman, and that I want the things a lot of women want . . . and I'm not just talking hot sex here."

"It seems to me you'd be better off lusting after a guy who doesn't make a living by banging heads together and shooting people."

"I'm sure he's banged a few heads together, but I don't know that he's ever shot anyone." Lili glanced again at Matt. He was surveying the room, keeping a lookout for trouble. "I asked him if he had."

"What did he say?"

"He said that if he had to, that meant he wasn't doing his job."

Pippa sat back, and took a long sip of her drink. "What kind of wussy answer is that? It's either yes or no, right?"

"I don't think he wanted to tell me."

"Which means he's probably whacked a whole bunch of people."

"Or not," Lili retorted.

"Give me a break. I mean, he looks like he should be extorting money for some crime boss, and answering to the name Guido or Luigi."

"And people tell me *I* have an overactive imagination. I think he's good-looking, in a sort of quiet, intense way."

Lili plucked the cherry from her drink and popped it in her mouth, sucking off the tang of liquor before chewing it as she considered Matt. She recalled the little shiver of desire that had swept over her when he'd lifted her off the table during class. And sometimes when he looked at her, she swore she saw the heat of attraction in his eyes. There was something between them; exactly what, she didn't know—but something that shouldn't be there, that was certain.

Twirling the cherry stem between her thumb and index finger, she said, "I wonder what he'd be like in bed."

Pippa's pale brows shot upward. "Excuse me?"

"You heard me." Lili continued to watch Matt, assessing him from beneath half-lowered lids as he leaned over to say something to Manny. "I go back to New York on Sunday, so if I make a complete idiot of myself, it's not like I'd ever have to see him again."

"You're not joking, are you?"

"There's definitely an attraction. And he's different from most of the men I've known."

Pippa made a rude noise. "Just how many of your ex-boyfriends wore guns?"

"None of them, and you know it."

"Exactly. I don't think there's much long-term potential here. And if I'm hearing you right, that's what you're after." Pippa peeled the orange rind away from the slice in her drink, and ate the fruit. "Look, I understand. For whatever reason, some women have a thing for tough guys. But this Matt isn't playing the part of a bad boy—he's the genuine article. He may be exciting and different, but he's way out of your league."

"A few minutes ago you told me I should be more adventurous. Maybe you're right. Maybe I could use a little excitement in my life."

"Not *his* kind of excitement." Pippa sat forward, scrutinizing Matt, and when he noticed both of them staring at him, his brows drew together. "But I have to say, he looks like he'd have plenty of stamina. I bet he has a great ass, and if he has a dick to match the rest of him, I wouldn't blame you for wanting to take him for a test drive.'

Lili giggled, and tossed back the rest of her martini. A light-headed, cozy warmth slowly spread through her. Two drinks, and she already had a buzz.

My oh my, she was getting old, all right.

"Now, the other guy . . . he's definitely more my type," Pippa said. "I think it must be that hot Latin lover thing. Cha-cha, baby!"

"Isn't that a bit of a stereotype?"

Pippa winked. "Honey, some stereotypes aren't so bad."

Lili giggled again, because by now both Manny and Matt were exchanging glances, looking wary and baffled. "They know we're talking about them."

"And it's driving them nuts," Pippa said, sounding way too satisfied with herself. "Shit. My drink's gone. We need another."

The suggestion sounded good, if problematic. "That'll knock us back another five years. I'm not sure I feel up to being sixteen tonight."

"Oh, God, I can't even remember what sixteen was like. Probably subhuman, though." Pippa laughed. "We'll stop at three. I swear it."

Manny leaned toward Matt and asked, "Why are they staring at us?"

"Beats me." Matt tipped back in his chair and eyed his zipper as discreetly as possible, just in case. It'd be pretty hard to look menacing with his pants unzipped and his package wagging free. "Probably too many martinis."

He was glad to see Lili laughing and enjoying herself, but he didn't want her relaxing too much. Lili unnerved him under ordinary circumstances, and the thought of dealing with her when her inhibitions were lowered made him sweat—from apprehension or anticipation, he wasn't quite sure.

Just three more days, that was all. Then he'd put her on a plane and she'd be somebody else's problem.

While he watched, Lili stirred her new drink with her pinky finger, and then licked it. His dick shot to hard in an instant.

Okay. Three very, very long days.

"What's going on between you two?"

At Manny's question, Matt looked away from Lili. "What?"

"We've known each other a long time, and I can tell when something's wrong."

"It's nothing you have to worry about."

"You're still spending the nights on the love seat, right?" Manny asked, gaze unblinking—but he was stroking his goatee, a dead giveaway that he was bothered.

"Do you think I'd sleep with a client?"

"No, but if there was ever a client to mess you up, it would be this one."

Matt turned his attention back at Lili, her dark head bent close to her friend's blond one, then surveyed the room. "I'm not going to lose it over her."

"Maybe not, but she's under your skin. I can tell."

No point in denying it. "Manny, the only way Lili Kavanaugh wouldn't get under my skin is if I were dead."

The piano player launched into Billy Joel's "Piano Man," with the warning that this was the last time he'd play it for the night, or else the bartenders would shoot him.

Matt continued watching the crowd. Men far outnumbered the women, and most of them were white urban professionals in their thirties and forties. While he didn't see anyone who matched the police sketch, he knew that in a crowded bar, with all the noise and the motion, it would be easy for a single individual to stay out of sight and wait for the right moment to strike.

He checked in with Dal, who was exactly where he should be—sitting in the car. His rookie agent was doing all right, and well on his way to earning himself a top-notch recommendation for his file.

"So this is your last assignment, huh?" Manny asked, sitting back, but still alert. "You're gonna move your sorry ass on out of here?"

"Guess so."

Manny shook his head. "I wish you the best, man, but I'm gonna miss working with you. We were a good team."

Matt smiled. "When I get my agency up and running, you can always come work for me."

"I might do that. Decided where you want to go yet?"

"I've narrowed it down," Matt said with a shrug. "The security business is booming right now. I could go anywhere."

The generous fee Lili's father had offered, plus the fact he owed Dan Armistead a favor, had been the deciding factors in taking this final, high-profile detail. The plans he'd put into place over a year ago were finally coming together, and after this week he'd have the rest of the startup cash he'd need to get out of the front line and open his own security business.

"How about Miami? Nice weather, and lots of pretty girls in little clothes."

Matt watched Lili and her friend. Pippa was a classic wet dream—tall, slender yet busty, with a wholesome, blond beauty. Yet she did nothing for him. She paled beside Lili, who was all color and energy and vitality.

He looked back at Manny. "Pretty girls are nice, but I've always wanted a house on the ocean. Seattle would work just as well as Miami for that."

"I hear the sun never shines in Seattle."

"Nothing in life is perfect." Matt sat forward, focusing on a man—mid-thirties and of average build—sitting at the bar. Earlier, he'd noticed the man staring at Lili. In a see-and-be-seen bar like this, with men and women checking one another out, his behavior wasn't unusual, but now the man was pulling at his trousers, compulsively smoothing the fabric over his thighs—obviously agitated, and looking at Lili with increasing frequency.

"Manny, check out the guy at the bar, in the tan suit."

"He's eyeing our lady, and it looks like he's working himself into making some kind of move."

Matt nodded. "Stay here. I want to get close to him."

He stood, his movements casual, unhurried, then made his way to the bar. The bartenders were busy mixing drinks and working the tap with quick efficiency, and managing to hold conversations at the same time. Matt positioned himself as close as possible to the man he was watching, although it took a few piercing stares to convince people to move out of his way.

Lili and Pippa were oblivious to the possible threat, just laughing and smiling and talking. Her laughter didn't do much to keep her profile low—although a low profile was near impossible to begin with, considering that gold dress she'd painted on.

His fingers itched to peel it off, sliding it upward, one slow inch at a time, freeing the spicy scent of her, letting it rise from her soft, warm skin.

Oh, yeah . . . Manny was dead-on; if ever there was a client to mess him up, it would be Lili.

Jaw set, refocused, Matt moved closer to his target, pretended to trip, and bumped into him.

"Hey, watch it," the man snapped, shoving Matt back.

"Sorry. My fault."

During the bump frisk, Matt detected no concealed weapons. The guy was probably just a drunk businessman hoping to score, but Matt took no chances. As with any bodyguard, distrust was second nature.

The hot-to-trot businessman leaned forward, balanced on the edge of the bar stool, his gaze locked on Lili—and his position warned Matt, as clearly as words, that the guy was ready to make his move.

By the time the businessman was off the stool, Matt already stood between him and Lili, senses on hyper-alert.

"You again. What's your problem?" The business-man's eyes narrowed with annoyance, his words a little slurred. "Get lost."

"The lady in the gold dress is not to be disturbed," Matt said, his voice calm and nonconfrontational. "You should sit back down, sir."

"Who the fuck are you, her daddy?"

"No, I'm her bodyguard." Matt moved closer, invading the man's space, forcing him back a step, and smelled the alcohol on his breath. "And I asked you nicely to sit back down."

The guy was drunk. Either he'd back down or become aggressive, and Matt waited, watching for a signal as to which way this one would go. The businessman's eyes flared with fury a split second before he lunged at Matt.

Anticipating it, Matt grabbed the man's arm, twisting it until he heard a startled grunt of pain. "I don't want any trouble, but I'll protect my client's privacy with force if necessary," he said quietly. "Don't make me have to do that. My advice to you is to forget the lady, and move on. This is a nice place. You don't want to cause a scene. You're just here to have a drink, have a good time."

"That's right," the man panted, face pinched in dis-comfort. "A good time. Just a drink or two. Let me go!"

"When I release your arm, sir, you'll move on to the other side of the bar and make no further attempt to en-gage my client."

"Yes, yes!"

Matt released him, ignoring the startled stares of those around him, the wary glances of the bartenders. He'd worked the Redhead before and knew the staff wouldn't interfere, but he didn't want to jeopardize his professional standing here. Force was a last resort. Always.

The businessman hastily retreated, straightening his

tie and smoothing back his hair as if nothing had happened. Matt turned. Lili was staring at him with a blank look, and her cat-eyed friend pressed back against her chair, as if to get as far away from him as possible.

For a brief instant, intense regret hit him. Regret that Lili had to see that bit of ugliness . . . regret that she had to see him in action at all.

A quick glance showed Manny standing with a deceptive casualness, but at Matt's curt nod, he sat back down.

Matt made his way to Lili's table and leaned down. "It's okay. Nothing to worry about."

"Did you hurt him?"

Again, that hollow, sinking feeling of regret in his chest. "Just his pride."

She nodded, blinking rapidly for a moment. "I have to go to the bathroom."

"If Conan here will guard our table and fend off any more would-be invaders, I'll go with you," said Pippa in a biting tone. She stood, tall and willowy in her black dress, radiating disapproval as she moved in front of Lili.

A sharp irritation lanced through him at the woman's protectiveness. Why did everybody think Lili needed to be coddled?

"I'll escort my client to the restroom," Matt said, with an iciness that had more to do with his own irritation rather than mother-hen Pippa's disapproval.

Pippa took a quick, sharp breath and sat down. "Okay. You do that. I'll wait here." As Lili stood, the woman added, "Remember what I said, Lil. This is the genuine article."

As he led Lili away from the table, Matt tried to shake off his anger. He was what he was, and not ashamed of it, and it didn't matter that Pippa Dowling looked at him like he was some low-life street thug. Not that a woman like Pippa would know the first thing about street thugs.

He did, though, and it was the reason he was so good at his job.

The piano player launched into Jerry Lee Lewis's "Great Balls of Fire," and despite his grim mood, Matt couldn't help smiling as he watched Lili be-bop through the bathroom door.

Lili called it quits a little after midnight, and after Pippa departed in a taxi, Dal pulled up in the sleek black Town Car to whisk everybody back to the Drake. The effects of her three martinis were wearing off, although she still had a good buzz going. Sounds were muffled, colors appeared oddly bright—and Matt looked even more tasty than usual.

She was sober enough not to giggle at the thought, if still fuzzy enough to wish she could purr and rub up against him in the backseat. She smiled, imagining the look on his face—and Dal and Manny's—if she did so.

"Hey, Dal," she said over a crooning Sheryl Crow. "I understand you just got married."

Dal met her eyes in the rearview mirror, and grinned. "Three months ago."

"Congratulations." After a moment, she added, "You know, I feel a little guilty for taking you away from your new wife like this."

"No problem. It's not like you planned to get into trouble," he said. "My wife, she's used to it. And I call when I'm off duty."

"How about you, Manny? Is there a special lady in your life?"

Lili ignored Matt's stare. She was being nosy, but she wanted to understand how a bodyguard's wife or girlfriend dealt with the absences and uncertainty of her man's profession. Tonight, it somehow seemed important to understand.

Manny glanced back at her, and his teeth flashed whitely in the darkness. "A steady girlfriend, but nothing too serious. I'm not ready to settle down yet."

She smiled, and silence settled over the car. She was very aware of Matt beside her, although he'd hardly exchanged a handful of words with her since they'd left the bar. She couldn't forget Pippa's warning—and it didn't help that she'd witnessed how quickly and effortlessly Matt had fended off that drunken businessman. She wasn't sure yet how she felt about it; part of her was grateful for his protection, but his controlled capacity for violence troubled her.

She wondered if Dal's wife ever looked at him and thought: *He could go out and kill someone today . . . or get killed himself.*

As if aware of her scrutiny, Matt turned toward her. For a moment their gazes met and held. This time, she looked away first.

The alcohol had to be responsible for all these gloomy thoughts. And what did it matter, anyway? Matt Hawkins, and his equally capable team, hardly needed her to fuss or worry over them. It wasn't as if anybody had forced them into this line of business. They'd made a choice.

Nor did it matter to her, because she certainly wasn't going to ask any of them out on a date.

All right, so she was contemplating a little hanky-panky with Matt. A perfectly normal reaction. All those years of teaching and working, delaying starting a family, and now this tension, this brush with death and danger—how could she not physically respond to a good-looking man who was keeping her constant company, not to mention keeping her alive?

Basic biological drives; that's all this was.

Back at the Drake, she smiled at the guard by the elevator, bid goodnight to Manny, and walked into her suite. Foremost in her mind was ridding her hair of the bar's smoky smell. Matt already had his briefcase out, settling in for the night's usual routine of work, so without a word she went into the bathroom and took a long, hot shower.

She didn't bother drying her hair, letting it hang loose and damp. Barefoot, she padded out to the parlor, wearing the white terry robe over her blue satin and lace night-shirt. As she'd expected, Matt was bent over paperwork, his jacket tossed aside and tie loosened. He still wore the gun, but she was getting used to the sight of it. He looked up briefly, and nodded an acknowledgment.

In silence, she wandered around the room, stopping to smell the fresh flowers, a hundred thoughts tumbling through her mind: the talk with Pippa, her lecture the next day, the frightened and angry look in the businessman's eyes when Matt twisted his arm behind his back.

All his calm, cool professionalism hid something darker, volatile. She sensed it, glimpsed it in his eyes when he didn't know she was watching him, and it intrigued her. She couldn't stop imagining what it would be like to be with him, to break through that cool, careful reserve and find his hidden heat and passion.

"You okay?"

At Matt's question, Lili stopped and turned. "Sure. Why?"

"You're orbiting the room again."

"Oh." So she was; a bad habit, that pacing. "I have a lot on my mind. Am I bothering you?"

He smiled, and it caused a little catch in her chest. "No more than usual."

After a moment, she asked, "The man at the bar . . . why did you do that?"

"It's what you're paying me for," he said mildly, his expression closed. "I'm sorry if I frightened you."

"I'm not used to violence like that. I didn't see why it was necessary. He wasn't dangerous, just drunk."

"He might have been dangerous. To me, everybody is a potential threat."

"That sounds paranoid, Matt."

"It is." His tone was terse. "But that's part of being a bodyguard."

What kind of life was that where paranoia was expected? She wanted to ask him why he did it, but asked instead, "The man who tried to break into my room . . . do you think he'll try to get to me again?"

For a long moment, he held her gaze, as if deciding whether to answer or not. Finally, he said, "It's likely."

A chill stole over her, even as she was grateful for his honesty. "Do you have any ideas where? Or how?"

"I assume every opportunity provided is one he'll take, and my job is to eliminate those opportunities as best I can. Or, when I can't eliminate them, to control the parameters."

She sensed resistance, as if he wasn't telling her everything, but dropped the subject, uncertain she wanted to know, anyway. She wandered the room for a few minutes longer, watching him work, then stopped.

"I should probably go over my notes again for tomorrow's lecture. To make sure everything's there."

"What will you be talking about?" Matt looked up. "You're not going to stand on any more tables, are you?"

He'd mentioned this a couple of times. For some reason, it had made quite an impression on him.

"No, no standing on tables. I'm talking about my historical collection, with a special emphasis on Rose McIntyre's shoes."

She pulled her briefcase from under the love seat, and sat next to Matt. "Do you mind sharing the table with me?"

"It's your suite, not mine." He slid as far from her as possible, taking his piles of paper with him. She didn't miss the faint flush on his high cheekbones.

A twinge of guilt pricked her for what she was doing. She could've easily sat elsewhere, but couldn't help pushing him a little. Feeling him out, seeing if she could rouse that spark of awareness between them—seeing if it was real, not just wishful thinking.

For a few minutes she worked in silence beside him, trying to concentrate on her notes even as she soaked in the heat of his body, watching the play of his muscles beneath the shirt as he moved, and how the white cotton pulled against its seams. His scent surrounded her: the smoky scent from the bar clung to him faintly, and beneath it, his woodsy cologne and a hint of male sweat.

A heady combination. She wanted to lean closer, and sniff at the skin of his throat, exposed where he'd unfastened the top button and loosened his tie.

She swallowed, and peered down at her notes. Eventually, the words focused. "Did you know she was only seventeen when they met?"

Matt looked up, puzzled. "What?"

"Rose was only seventeen when she met Joey Mancuso." When he said nothing, she added, "I suppose a young girl like her would've been impressed by Joey. He was good-looking, in that smoldering Italian way, and he'd already been in prison twice, even though he was just twenty-one."

"Too bad her mother wasn't smart enough to lock her away," Matt said.

He returned his attention to the expense report he was filling out, but not before Lili noticed how his gaze snagged on her robe, which had fallen open to reveal the length of her leg and a glimpse of her blue satin nightshirt.

As casually as possible, she pulled the ends of her robe

back together. "Mama McIntyre ran a brothel for Mike Riley, Joey's onetime boss, so I don't think she cared one way or another about what happened to her daughter," she said, surprising herself with the calmness of her voice.

At that, Matt looked up, his pupils dark and wide in the low light. For a moment his face softened, and then he dropped his gaze again.

Intrigued by what she could've sworn was a flash of compassion, Lili added, "Poor Rose was probably looking for a way out. Joey must've seemed like the answer to her prayers."

"Some answer. He got her killed."

"I think he loved her." Lili sat back, glancing down at her scrawled notes. "He had a few redeeming qualities."

"Joey Mancuso killed people. It wasn't like they were a couple of nice kids who got a little confused about the difference between right and wrong."

The vehement tone of his voice surprised her—and also a bitterness she didn't understand. And while Lili recognized the truth in his words, she couldn't help feeling protective of Rose.

"She was just a kid, so maybe you can understand the excitement part. At some point in our lives, we all look for a little excitement."

"Not from guys like Joey. Not if you're smart."

Lili sat back, brows drawn together in a thoughtful frown. "Maybe even killers and losers can fall in love."

Matt grunted, and turned back to his paperwork.

She tried another tack to get his attention. "Al Capone's vault and John Dillinger's missing millions are urban legends, but Joey really did make off with a small fortune in bootlegger profits. He was gunned down before he could tell anybody where he'd hidden that bag full of money, and nobody's ever found it."

"Sounds like you've been studying up," he said, but his tone was flat, neutral—uninterested. And he'd eased another few inches away, slowly, as if to prevent her from noticing.

That, combined with the suspicion he was only humoring her, kept her from pursuing the subject. She wanted to, though. Joey and Rose's story fascinated her.

She'd read what books she could find on her gangster lovers, although Joey and Rose weren't as famous as other Depression-era desperadoes. Joey hadn't achieved the notoriety of John Dillinger or Clyde Barrow, and he'd died a year before J. Edgar Hoover declared war on gangsters and bank robbers. Had Joey the Joker gone down at the hands of lawmen and, more specifically, Mr. Hoover's bureau agents, he'd probably have earned a little more fame.

Still, she'd found enough information for her needs, and a helpful woman at the Chicago Historical Society had filled her in on a few colorful anecdotes and facts that she'd use to spice up the lecture. Some of those anecdotes and facts were downright ironic.

"What are you smiling about?"

Matt's question cut across her thoughts, and Lili looked at him. God, he was sitting so close. She really should get up and move to a safer distance—but doing so would only draw attention to this tension between them. Better to stay put and pretend nothing was wrong.

"I wouldn't want to bore you to death or anything," she said.

One corner of his mouth tipped up in a smile. His gaze flicked down toward her robe, which had fallen open again, then back up to her face. This time, she didn't pull the robe closed.

Let him look. It's what she wanted, really.

"Okay," he said at length. "I'll bite. What's so funny?"

"Not funny," she corrected with annoyance, thinking he was altogether too sure of himself. "Only kind of strange."

He arched a brow, waiting.

"Did you know Joey's partner is still alive?"

"I didn't even know he had one."

He was humoring her, but trying to be polite about it—and Lili found herself wondering if Matt Hawkins ever let go of that deliberate wariness.

"Well, he did have one, so now you know. Willis Conroy is his name, and he must be nearly a hundred or something by now. He lives in a nursing home in northern Wisconsin."

Matt's smile widened. "Even bad-ass gangsters gotta get old someday."

She frowned at him, then continued, "Conroy's father and uncle spent a few years making a quick buck off tourists by showing off the murder site. People still drop by to check out the bullet holes in the walls. Anyway, some Conroy girl fell in love with a local boy and they built a resort next door to where Uncle Willis's pals went out in a blaze of glory. You have to wonder what Conroy thought about that."

"Probably sorry he was in prison and not getting a cut from a bunch of gullible tourists. How many of those bullet holes were faked?"

Lili crossed her legs and started jiggling her foot, which immediately drew his attention to her partially revealed legs.

Yesiree, never underestimate the power of imagination.

"A lot, I'm sure," Lili admitted when he looked back up. She smiled at the faint frown on his face. He wasn't so cool after all. "But stop ruining my fun. You know, you're much too serious."

His frown dissolved into an almost comical expression of surprise.

"Oh, don't give me that look. I'm sure you kick back and relax sometimes, so tell me, when Matt Hawkins goes out for a good time, what does he do?"

Matt tossed his pen on the table and sat back, turned slightly toward her, one arm resting along the love seat's back. His leg brushed hers and she went still, heat flooding her.

All right. So she wasn't as cool as she pretended, either.

"He grabs a beer from the fridge, sits in a chair, and turns on the TV."

"Doesn't the poor man ever get *out* to have a little fun?"

"He sometimes goes to the bar with friends, sails on the lake in his sailboat, plays softball, or takes in a movie. Basically, Matt Hawkins lives a pretty dull life when he's not out playing secret agent man."

"I like a guy with a sense of humor, especially the self-deprecating variety."

A smile tugged at his lips. "And I like a lady who can throw around big words."

Lili grinned. Was he flirting back? Even a little? "I bet you're a lot of fun when you're not working."

The half-formed smile froze. "I work most of the time. There's always enough business around to keep me busy."

Then again, maybe it wasn't flirtation. Maybe he was just trying to be nice. Disappointment washed over her.

He hadn't looked away, and in the low light of the room, his face seemed darker, harsher—and Pippa's warning suddenly came to mind, which in turn reminded her of something else.

"The fund-raiser I'm going to Saturday night is a costume party."

"I know." He looked a little startled by the change of subject. After a moment, he prompted, "And?"

"And if you're going to be there with me, I want you to dress up."

"All right."

"I don't want you acting like a bodyguard. There'll be lots of important people there, people I want to impress. Could you just pretend to be my date?"

He regarded her for a moment. "If that's what you want. You're the boss."

Lili nearly rolled her eyes. Yeah, right.

"That way I won't have to answer a bunch of awkward questions." When he nodded, she added, "I'll take care of getting you a costume. It shouldn't be a problem; I know exactly what I want."

"I'm almost afraid to ask."

She laughed at the sudden wariness in his eyes. "I'm wearing a twenties flapper dress, and Rose's shoes—"

"Why?" he interrupted.

She blinked. "Because wearing the shoes of a notorious gun moll will get me a lot of attention, and in my line of work, attention is very important."

Not to mention they were gorgeous, and she was dying to wear them—even if they didn't fit very well and her feet would hurt by the end of the night.

"Anyway, I think it would be funny if you go as yourself . . . as hired muscle, sweetheart," she said, in her best Humphrey Bogart voice, pronouncing every "S" as *sh.* "Pin-striped gangster suit, fedora, wing tip shoes . . . a carnation in your pocket. Whaddya say, pal?"

Matt's smile faded, and he went very still. Dismayed, Lili realized she'd angered him, but didn't know why. The silence stretched on as she waited, certain he would refuse, but then he shrugged.

"Whatever you want goes. It doesn't matter to me."

Still uncertain of his mood, and hoping to recapture their previous warmth, she smiled and said, "And you know how to dance, right?"

"I can waltz and foxtrot, and I know a few other ballroom dance steps." He leaned over the coffee table again, and picked up his pen. A dismissive gesture, a cue telling her he needed to get back to work. "In bodyguard school, ballroom dancing is an elective."

Lili eyed him suspiciously, but his expression was impossible to read. "I don't believe you."

"It's true." His lips twitched, as if he wanted to smile, but wouldn't let himself. "As a matter of fact, I'm pretty good at dancing."

"So prove it."

"Lili—"

"Keep your client happy," she chanted. "The customer is always right. A satisfied customer is a—"

"All right, all right," he interrupted in exasperation, and pushed to his feet. "I get the message."

Matt moved to the middle of the room, his eyes dark, jaw shadowed by beard stubble, and his shirt unbuttoned to reveal curling black hair at the opening. He was still wearing the shoulder holster, gun in place.

He crooked a finger at her. "Come here."

At his quiet order, a little shiver overtook her—along with a sense of recklessness. Lili stood, meeting the challenge in his eyes, even as an inner voice warned: *Be careful . . . think, think!*

"Okay," she said, chin raised, as she moved to within inches of him. "Impress me."

"Closed position, or promenade?"

Lili slowly smiled. "I've been had."

"Never bluff with a bodyguard—you'll lose every time."

She made a disagreeable noise, then said, "Closed position. Despite the way I carry on at times, I do appreciate the traditional."

As he drew her close, he laughed, a low, easy sound that sent goose bumps rippling over her. He slid his right arm around her left arm, fingers resting just under her shoulder blade, and elbow at a crisp ninety-degree angle.

Lili laid her arm against his, her hand holding on to the firm muscles of his shoulder. His warmth enveloped her, and when he took her right hand in his left, her breath caught briefly.

His form was absolutely perfect. Of course, *he* was absolutely perfect.

No more than six inches separated them, and Lili raised her lashes and met his gaze . . . watchful, intent. Unnerving.

"We don't have any music," she said, a wistful note in her voice.

"Who needs it?" Matt leaned forward slightly, and as she instinctively took a step back he murmured, "Boom-tick-tick . . . boom-tick-tick-and-lean."

Lili laughed, moving gracefully with him through the basic box step, following the subtle, guiding pressure of his fingers against her back. "Boom-tick-tick?"

"Hey, it's easy to remember."

As he spoke, his breath stirred the hair over her ear, and it was all she could do not to shiver again. Against the soft satin of her nightshirt, her nipples tightened with an almost painful ache of need. She was suddenly very aware she wore next to nothing beneath her robe—the only thing keeping her decent was the knot in the belt—and that he was fully dressed.

And packing. The shoulder holster—or "rig," as she'd heard him refer to it—bumped against her, and she was on eye-level with the strap. Well worn and dark brown, it smelled of oiled leather, and there was something decidedly unnerving about waltzing with a man wearing a gun.

Under her fingers, she could feel the play of his muscles as he moved, and his hand was warm, strong. She loved the scent of him tonight, the lingering cologne, the faint tang of perspiration, even the smoky tobacco scent she'd hated on herself. It smelled so male and earthy, arousing, and she took a deep breath, closing her eyes briefly as she fought back an urge to press closer against him, run her fingers down his back, then up into his short dark hair, and drag his head down for a long, hot kiss.

Oh, boy. Too bad she was sober now; she couldn't blame these crazy thoughts on martinis. Maybe Pippa was right, and this attraction was nothing more than the fact he was off-limits to her and she damn well knew it.

Yet she didn't put a stop to it. Instead, she joined her voice with his in a singsong "boom-tick-tick" rhythm that carried them around the parlor, until she could no longer resist temptation and tightened her fingers over his arms. At once his muscles tensed, and his smooth steps faltered. She shifted, meeting his eyes.

Hardly aware of what she was doing, Lili slowed, not looking away. Her mouth was a few inches from his, and a single thought pounded away inside her: *Kiss me. Kiss me, kiss me . . .*

"Matt," she said softly.

He stopped, but didn't release her. "What?" he asked, his voice low, a shade cautious.

Her heart pounded, blood roaring in her ears. She opened her mouth, to ask him for what she wanted, but a sudden flatness closed his face to her, bringing her quickly back to her senses.

"Nothing," she said, sighing. "I'm just having another one of those leap-before-thinking moments."

As if nothing had happened, she moved toward him—intending to pick up on their dancing—only to run against his hand.

Slowly, gently, with just enough force to make his point, he pushed her away.

"I think you'd better go to bed, Lili." As he spoke, he turned from her and walked stiffly to the nearest wing chair. He sat and leaned over, hands held loosely between his knees, still looking over at her.

His face was unreadable, yet she sensed a sudden hostility, and tension . . . a tension shot through with desire, all achy and hot and demanding.

She nodded, looking away, feeling a blush creep along her cheeks. As she walked toward the bedroom area, she realized her hands were shaking.

At the divider, she hesitated, then turned, observing the rigid line of his back, the pull of his shirt against his shoulders, and how the fabric bunched beneath the X-shaped back piece of the holster.

She read the anger in the deliberate posture of avoidance, but realized the anger wasn't directed at her as much as at himself.

On a rush of guilt, understanding dawned: He was furious with himself because she'd broken through that oh-so-important professionalism of his. She hadn't thought what her flirting might mean to him, not this way.

"Matt, I—"

"Just go to bed," he interrupted, roughly.

She let out her breath in a soft sigh. "I was only going to say good night."

At that, he turned. Their eyes met—and that angry, edgy hunger stretched between them, taut and vibrating. His gaze moved lower, before locking on her face again.

Beneath his piercing stare, physical as a touch, she fought the urge to pull together the lapels of her robe.

"Good night, Lili," he said at length, his voice low. "Sweet dreams."

7

Another long, lousy night on the love seat, catching a total of maybe three hours of sleep. Another night of tossing and turning, thinking about the woman only a few feet away, sleeping alone, her sheets whispering and bed groaning as she shifted restlessly. And him thinking of all the ways he could help tire her out enough to sleep.

Matt stood at the suite window, staring out at the lake, jingling the change in his pockets—and stopped abruptly, cursing under his breath, once he realized what he was doing.

He was in no mood to spend another day fighting this damned urge to lay her down on the bed, explore her soft warmth, and discover just how sweet her mouth tasted.

Not to mention finding out if she was really a little bit wild, or if it was all a front. He couldn't be certain—and it was driving him crazy, distracting him when he shouldn't be distracted, as well as keeping him awake at night.

Getting personally involved with a client sometimes

happened, even with the best training to avoid it, and he'd be a fool to think Lili was interested in Matt Hawkins— the guy who collected the paycheck for the work he did— rather than the image and mystique of a bodyguard.

Danger and hormones were a dicey mix. He *knew* that, dammit, and taking advantage of her vulnerability wasn't an option, even if he couldn't help thinking about her. He was only human, after all, but he was also a trained professional. He was—

"Good morning," Lili called, and Matt turned to look at her.

He was in deep shit, that's what.

"Morning," he answered.

He kept his voice deliberately cool with an effort. She wore a fitted dress with a matching jacket that had a pleat and a big bow sitting at the small of her back, reminding him of those old-fashioned bustle dresses. The suit was red—a color she looked damn good in. She'd pulled her hair back in her quasi-secretary bun, tendrils framing her chin, not too sexy, not too severe. Almost without thinking, he glanced at her feet—and saw she was wearing only pantyhose, her toenails painted pink.

What the hell kind of signal was she sending him with that? In self-disgust, Matt pushed away from the window. Maybe she wasn't *signaling* anything at all. Maybe she just didn't want to put on her shoes yet.

She smiled at his approach, but her eyes were wary. "Where's Manny and Dal?"

"Outside talking to one of the security guards," Matt answered, his voice sharper than he meant.

"Oh." Her gaze darted away, then returned. "You're done already with the morning briefing?"

Matt nodded, and after glancing again at her feet, forced himself to meet her eyes, and remind himself to act as if nothing had happened the night before.

And nothing had—despite how close he'd come to kissing her, he hadn't.

"We've gone over the details at the historical society, and they're providing additional security in the auditorium," he said. "Do you still want to go out to the museum afterward to check out the dinosaurs?"

She nodded. "But I'll want to come back first and change."

Lili crossed the room, keeping a distance between them. Not that it did much good. She could be clear on the other side of the room, and a wisp of her perfume would tell him exactly how close or how far, and he'd track her every movement from the corner of his eye, hear her every breath.

"Could you guys dress casually for the museum trip? I'd really like to blend in a little more with the local tourists."

"I'd advise against it."

Disappointment flashed across her face. "Why? Matt, I am tired of getting stared at, and—"

"Would you prefer to get killed?" he interrupted, and when her eyes went dark with hurt, he wanted to kick himself.

He had no reason to act like this to her. His physical discomfort was *his* problem to deal with, not hers—even if she'd caused it.

"Look, I'm sorry . . . I didn't get a lot of sleep last night, and I'm tired. I didn't mean to snap at you like that."

Lili hesitated, then nodded, accepting his apology. "Can I ask why you advise against not looking like the Goon Patrol?"

She had every right to know what he was doing, yet he held back—until he realized he was coddling her, as everybody else seemed to do "Because the image I project when I'm in the dark suit with the radio earpiece is psychological. It's a warning to anybody who's considering harmful action against you that I will protect you with any and all necessary force. In security lingo, it's called 'hardening the target.' "

"With me in the starring role of target," she said.

"Yes."

Instead of turning pale or getting upset, as he'd half expected, she nodded. "I see. That makes sense. Thank you for explaining it to me."

Because he wanted her to fully understand—and to compensate for his earlier bad temper—he added, "Every detail is different. Usually all I need to do is stand around and keep an eye on things, blend in with the family or guests. But in a situation like yours, where a high risk for danger has been verified, a show of strength works best. My team and I will make every effort possible to maintain a nonconfrontational situation, but there are never absolutes."

Again, Lili nodded. She was back to orbiting the room; a bright slash of color on the move. Just being in the room with her acted on him like a jolt of caffeine.

"We should probably get going," he said, reaching for his suit coat. "Traffic at this time of day is pretty bad."

"We can go as soon as I decide what shoes to wear."

Her comment struck him as funny, and despite his lingering tension and unease, his mouth curved in a reluctant smile.

Her eyes narrowed. "Are you laughing at me?"

"No. It's the whole shoe thing. To me, a shoe's just a shoe. But to you, it's like this . . . religion or something."

"Hmph." She turned on her stockinged heel and marched back toward the bed. "Philistine."

Thinking maybe he'd pissed her off—he wasn't doing so hot in the tact and sensitivity department today—he went after her with the intent to smooth any ruffled feathers. He stopped short when he saw the black suitcase, containing a jumble of shoes, lying open on her bed.

Staring, he asked, "How many shoes did you pack?"

She turned, and blushed slightly. "Fifteen pairs."

"*Fifteen?* You're only here for a week! God, Lili, you're—" He clamped his mouth shut before he said something stupid—again—and shook his head instead.

"I'm what?" she demanded, folding her arms over her chest, chin rising.

"Nothing."

"Come on, Matt. What were you going to say? Spit it out."

After a moment, he scratched his nose, and grinned. "You're such a girl."

A look of surprise crossed her face, and then she laughed and gave a philosophical shrug. "A girl's gotta do what a girl's gotta do. We have a saying in this business: If the shoe fits, buy it in every color."

"Looks like you already did."

"Oh, ha-ha. Very funny."

Matt came up behind her, curiosity getting the better part of his good sense. He eyed all those shoes. "No wonder you have a hard time making up your mind. Just how many black shoes do you need?"

She sent him an arch look as she pulled out a shoe— one with a narrow, wickedly spiked heel—and he raised his hands in a mock gesture of defense.

"Hey, I'm just asking."

Lili turned to face him, and as a wisp of her incense-like perfume hit him, Matt's inner warning alarm went off. He stood too close, and the bed behind her, still rumpled and unmade, seemed to beckon.

Like a sleek cat that had been hiding in the grass, waiting for a chance to strike, that sharp, taut hunger rose to taunt him.

"And you're such a boy." Smiling, completely oblivious to the fact he was contemplating ripping off her clothes and tossing her down on the bed, Lili reached up to straighten his tie. "A good-looking one, at that."

Her touch and words took him completely by surprise—although, by now, he should've expected the unexpected from Lili.

Two days. Just two more days, and if he could get through them without further bungling anything or making an idiot of himself, he'd be in the clear.

He rubbed the back of his neck, and stepped to a safer distance. "Lili, there's something I need to talk to you about."

She tipped her head, studying him, still smiling. "I know. I shouldn't flirt with you. It's against all the rules. Right?"

Matt clamped his mouth shut, all the precise psychological explanations suddenly sounding too cold, too clinical. Too lame. "That about covers it."

"Hmm." She moved away, and sat on the bed. Lifting one foot, she slipped on a black pair of heels with a red toe. "You have a lot of rules."

"Rules are necessary," he said, squelching a sudden spurt of irritation. "Believe me, I wouldn't be where I am today without them."

Not to mention he'd probably be dead, or worse.

"Maybe." A long silence followed, and she watched him with interest as she slipped on her other shoe. "Mostly, I'm just trying to be friendly."

"There's no need to be friendly," he said carefully. "You leave on Sunday. There'd be no point in a relationship beyond the professional."

His own answer startled him; he'd meant to say "an interaction," not "a relationship." Relationship sounded way too . . . intimate. But it was too late now to call back that telling word.

Lili's gaze suddenly sharpened. "I won't think less of you because you show me a human side. Emotions like kindness and friendliness aren't criminal. There *is* a point to them."

"But they're a distraction," Matt said quietly. "When I'm responsible for somebody's life and their safety, I can't afford distractions."

"The less you care for me, the better you can protect me? What kind of logic is that?" She made a sound of disgust. "In my mind, you're responsible for me regardless of whether or not you like me, so it seems we may just as well be nice to each other."

"I *am* being nice." Hands on his hips, jacket pushed back, he stared at her, working at not letting his irritation show.

"Really? All I see is a guy who gets human for a moment or two, and then freezes me out again. I'm getting whiplash from all this hot-cold-hot-cold."

"Lili—"

"Oh, be quiet and humor me a moment."

Her eyes remained watchful, studying him, measuring and weighing. Sexual awareness still swirled around them, and beneath her even tone of voice, he sensed she was angry.

"Tell me a little about yourself, Matt."

And stubborn. If nothing else, he had to admire her persistence.

"Like what?" he asked.

"Something simple and basic. Like . . . where do you live?"

Caught between the desire to appease her and the distrust instilled in him over the years, he didn't answer.

After a moment, she said dryly, "You do live somewhere, right?"

"I don't give out my home address or phone number to anybody except team members and my employer."

"Did I ask for an address or a phone number?" Her tone was cool. "I only asked where you live. A house? An apartment? In the city, in the suburbs? Do you have a yard? A garden? A dog?"

"I have a townhouse in the Lincoln Park area. I have a yard, but no pets or garden. I'm not home enough."

"You live in a *very* nice part of town." She stood almost eye-level now that she wore heels, and for some reason it put him on edge. "Am I allowed to ask why you don't you give out your address?"

"Sometimes I protect people whose lifestyles, politics, or professions are controversial . . . like abortion doctors, or lawyers defending child killers. It doesn't matter what I think about a client's beliefs or actions, I just do my job." He paused. "There are people who don't see the difference, and who'd take out their hatred of a client on an agent or an agent's family. Early on, we learn not to give out personal information."

For a long moment, she stared at him, then shook her head. "What kind of a life is that for you, Matt?"

"I make six figures a year, Lili. That's what kind of life it is."

She didn't understand; he could see it in her eyes. Disappointment—irrational, pointless—nipped at him. Just like last night, when she'd said it would be a good joke for him to go to a costume party as what he was: hired muscle.

Lili hadn't meant it to hurt—and that she saw him this

way *shouldn't* have hurt. Yet for some reason he didn't care to look at too closely, he wanted her to see him as something more.

"Some things are more important than money," she said at length.

Easy for her to go all preachy; with her family's old money, her surgeon father, and her professor mother. Heated anger, tinged with something too like shame, rushed through him, but he tamped it down. "It's time to go. I'm sending Dal off for the car."

Without another word, Matt turned and walked away.

8

Matt watched night fall over the city. In the gathering dusk, cars and taxicabs moved as ribbons of light, streaming through the streets. The sidewalks below teemed with shoppers, workers, and tourists headed toward their destinations, be it home for the night or a Saturday night out on the town, as he and Lili had planned.

She was in the bathroom, humming to herself as she dressed for the fund-raiser, and a strange, sharp pang tugged at him as he realized this was his last night with her.

He'd miss her energy and quick smile, those expressive eyes, and her blunt honesty. He'd even miss playing cards with her in the dead of night—not to mention those tantalizing glimpses of her tattoo and those great legs.

It still surprised him how easy and comfortable she made him feel after such a short time of knowing her—so easy and comfortable that he had to remain constantly on guard against letting slip a word or action that would let her know his interest in her had moved way, way beyond the professional.

Lili made him think, and for a guy like him—a doer, not a thinker—that wasn't always good.

Right now, he was thinking about his pricey townhouse in its upscale neighborhood. Yellow brick, built in 1898, with hardwood floors. A four-year-old BMW 323 sat in the garage. The house had three bedrooms, two of them empty, and a family room—but he had no family to put in it. The place echoed when he walked the floors during the rare days when he was home.

All show, he had to admit—and for whom? Those he'd wanted to prove himself to were either dead or gone away. All he'd done was buy an expensive stage, on which he could play at being a regular guy with a regular life.

And then along came Lili Kavanaugh, making him think it was time to quit playing. His restlessness and dissatisfaction hadn't suddenly started the day he'd met Lili—it had been there long before—but being with her made it clearer, stronger.

He was thirty-five, not getting any younger—a job like his wasn't forgiving to aging bodies and reflexes, and life wouldn't stop just because he wasn't ready to hit forty.

Ah, hell. Even if he wanted to give his chances with Lili a shot, he couldn't have picked a worse time. Once he quit Armistead and Flannery, his future would be less stable. He shouldn't start something with a woman like Lili unless he had something to offer, and right now he only had a lot of maybes.

Still, the temptation to start something stayed with him, every moment of the day. The temptation that, even if it was against all good sense, just one night would be enough. Especially tempting because he sensed her attraction ran as deeply as his—and resisting temptation was a lot more difficult than he remembered.

Taking in a deep breath to clear his head, Matt turned from the window, his hands in the pockets of his trousers, and looked down. He wore a gray pin-striped suit with a solid gray vest, a white shirt, and a wide tie in burgundy and black stripes. The pants were baggy, as had been the style of the day, and Lili had scrounged up a pair of wing tip shoes, as well as a red carnation from the Drake's floral shop, which she'd tucked into the breast pocket. He'd already shrugged into his shoulder holster, and as he glanced at the vintage gunmetal-gray fedora resting on the coffee table, he smiled.

He looked like a gangster right out of Al Capone's Chicago, and had to resist the urge to talk out of the side of his mouth and call Lili "doll" or "sister."

When Manny had seen him in full gangster regalia, he'd laughed so hard his eyes watered. Matt had playfully punched him in the shoulder—well, mostly playfully— and told his friend that being a team leader meant sometimes you had to do weird shit that made you feel like an idiot.

Now, as Manny and Dal stood outside in the hall in their tuxedoes, laughing over some joke and waiting for a word from Matt, Matt waited for Lili to finish whatever the hell it was that took women hours to do in the bathroom.

As if on cue, the door to the bathroom cracked open. "Matt?"

He turned. "Yeah?"

"Turn off all the lights except for the one in the closet."

He raised a brow. "Why?"

"Just do it, please . . . you have to see this dress the way it was meant to be seen. I am totally in love with it! I don't want to give it back."

Right, the dress. She hadn't let him see it earlier in the day when it had arrived and, curiosity getting the better of him, he did as she asked. The suite went dark one lamp at a time, until only the dim closet light cast a soft glow over the room.

"Okay. Show time," he said, and stood back, arms folded over his chest.

She killed the light in the bathroom, then walked out. Speechless, Matt watched her slow approach as he took in the dress. It was sleeveless, with a waistline around her hips, the skirt brushing just below her knees, longer in back than in front. Made of a soft, pale gray fabric— chiffon, he guessed—the entire dress was embroidered with silver and pearllike beads in a Deco-style floral pattern.

Lili stopped before him, smiling with delight, and spun. The beaded fringe of the skirt flared outward, the reflection from thousands of beads sparkling against the walls and ceiling. As she moved, the heavy skirt swung from side to side around her hips, and she twinkled with every step.

"What do you think? Isn't it beautiful?"

"I've never seen anything like it," Matt said with complete honesty, although the woman wearing the dress was by far more beautiful. She'd arranged her hair in a tight chignon, and wore Rose McIntyre's gaudy shoes on her feet. On any other woman, it would've been too much— on Lili, it was just right. "It looks great on you."

She twirled again, shooting more sparkles around the room. "It's a little tighter than it should be. Whoever wore this was a good ten pounds lighter than I am. Lucky for me the styles were so boxy. My boobs are too big, though." She peered down at her chest. "And that's a first for me . . . but the idea of binding them makes my teeth hurt."

The rueful comment brought Matt's attention to her

breasts, which pushed against the low neckline. He eyed the softly rounded swell with appreciation, thinking it'd be a shame to flatten a great pair of breasts like hers. He cleared his throat, and mumbled, "Looks okay to me."

"Really?" She sounded worried.

"Really." Beads of perspiration dotted his upper lip, and his fingers tightened into fists in his pockets. He risked another glance at the plunging neckline, smooth column of her neck, and bare skin of her arms, and took in a long, slow breath. "It's warm for October, but won't you be cold dressed like that?"

"Oh, I have a black silk satin wrap to wear. It's a reproduction, but just gorgeous. It'll keep me warm." She smiled, and held out her arms. "Let's do a dry run of a waltz. I want you to take me and my dress for a practice spin." She laughed suddenly, a low, husky sound. "A test drive."

Seeing her wicked grin, he raised a brow. "What's so funny?"

"A private joke. C'mon, Matt." She smiled, her tone entreating. "I'm counting on you tonight. Don't disappoint me."

Matt hesitated—sensing something else shading her words, the playful gleam in her eyes—then took her outstretched hand.

What harm could there be in enjoying the feel of her? Holding her in his arms this last night, before he put her on that airplane back to New York, wouldn't break any rules.

Pulling her closer, Matt rested his hand on her back, rather than below her shoulder. A look of surprise flashed across her face before she smiled and began humming a waltz melody.

For several minutes, Matt close-danced her around the parlor. "You ready to dip?"

Their eyes met a split second before he smoothly spun her under his arm. He tipped her back, his other arm supporting her, and bending so close that he was a fraction of an inch from her mouth.

In that moment, his need overwhelmed him in a hot rush that burned away every last shred of his hard-held resolve.

To hell with the rules and all his reasons to keep his distance. This was his last detail, and his last chance with Lili. He wanted her, if only for the one night. If he offered her the chance, and if she accepted, he'd take her in a heartbeat.

"Is that what you wanted?" he asked, his voice low.

A slow smile curved her mouth. "You're getting there."

Stealing a quick peek at Matt as she sat beside him in the car, Lili admired how he filled out his broad-shouldered, boxy suit. Not every man could look that damn sexy in a fedora. On him, it oozed mystery and danger.

The car was quiet except for Dal's latest CD playing softly on the speakers, and Lili felt a change in Matt's manner toward her. Something had altered between them earlier, and her woman's senses whispered that, at long last, she'd snared the attention of the man, not just the bodyguard.

One-night stands didn't appeal to her, yet men like Matt Hawkins didn't happen along in her life every day—and she was powerfully attracted to him. Not only to his good looks, but to everything about him: his quiet strength, his unobtrusive intelligence, his dry sense of humor, and the way he made her aware of herself as a woman—and, especially, his protectiveness, even though he was only doing his job.

If she passed up the opportunity to seek a deeper, more

intimate connection she knew she'd regret it, and while she could accept her mistakes and failures, she absolutely loathed regrets.

Shifting, Lili forced her thoughts away from Matt and eased her feet out of Rose's shoes. She'd have aching toes by the end of the night, but hopefully they'd earn her a mention in the style section of the local paper, as well as a few business contacts.

This was, after all, why she was in Chicago in the first place—to sell her shoes, not to get laid.

Also, three different museums in the Chicago area alone wanted Rose's shoes for display, and although she'd become very attached to them, she was feeling expansive, magnanimous. Tonight she'd be willing to bargain, and maybe work a deal that would make everybody happy.

Tonight was a night of possibilities. Who knew what might happen?

"We're coming up on the building now," Dal said, switching off the CD player. "What do you want me to do?"

"Drive around the perimeter," Matt ordered, leaning forward.

With a nod, Dal continued along North Clark, driving by the red brick mass of Moody Church. After he passed the historical society—which suffered from an architectural schizophrenic personality; the back Greek Revival, the front a boxy, sterile postwar addition—he swung the big car onto LaSalle.

Lili glanced at Matt, then Manny. Both men were looking intently out the windows as they drove down the busy streets. Dal made a circuit of the area and came up again toward the rear of the building, which faced Lincoln Park.

"What's going on?" she asked, puzzled.

"A drive-by check," Matt said, still looking out the window. "Slow down."

"There's no good spot," Manny muttered as Dal slowed the car to a near crawl. "The semicircle drive is the best for drop-off. Better than the front, since they've locked the main doors."

"Matt," Lili said quietly. "What's the problem?"

"I don't like the setup." He glanced away from the window. "Entrance is through the rear of the building, and it's easy for someone to hide in a park."

"But the front of the building isn't any better," Manny added. "There's heavy pedestrian and vehicle traffic on a Saturday night. Anybody walking around out there could be our guy, and the cars and buildings along the street make it hard to secure the area."

"In other words, you feel I'm vulnerable entering and exiting the building."

"Yes," Matt said.

"So where do you want me to drop you off?" Dal sounded calm.

"The circle drive, as we planned. We'll have a five-minute walk to the back steps. Lili, you do exactly as I tell you."

"Do you think something is going to happen?"

He met her gaze briefly. "There are extra guards patrolling the grounds, so there shouldn't be any problems. But I'm taking no chances."

Dal turned into the semicircular drive off North Boulevard. As he brought the car to a rolling stop, Matt reached inside his jacket and unsnapped his holster.

On a flutter of fear, Lili considered telling Dal to turn around and go back to the hotel, but she remembered Matt telling her not to let fear run her life. Refusing to give this man who terrorized her power over her, she forced back her apprehension.

"I'll check in every half-hour on the hour," Matt said as Manny stepped out of the car.

"Okay." Dal smiled. "Have fun."

Matt didn't respond as he opened his door. Lili waited until Matt and Manny surveyed the area, then Matt opened her door and motioned her out. He covered her as she exited, shielding her with his body. Manny moved into position, and they walked swiftly along the dimly lit walkway toward the plaza, with its wide steps leading up to the elegant columns and portico outside the second floor.

From the car, she'd seen tables set up on the plaza; the gala's organizers had taken advantage of the unseasonably warm October weather to let guests mingle outside as well as inside.

At the moment, though, Lili couldn't see anything except Manny's back. Between the two men, they effectively covered her, and it made walking a little tricky. She had to take shorter steps to keep from tromping on the back of Manny's shoes.

An armed security guard met them halfway to the building, and escorted them the rest of the distance. Through a box of broad male shoulders, Lili glimpsed a number of people already gathered on the plaza, drifting amid tables set with la-di-da munchies, white tablecloths fluttering in the breeze. Formally dressed waiters with drink trays moved among the costumed guests.

A number of people wore detailed historical costumes that looked like something right out of a Shakespearean play, while others had dressed up as celebrities, or characters from popular movies and books. But Matt didn't give her time to linger. He ushered her quickly up the steps, his hand on the small of her back. Lili flashed her invitation and passed through the glass doors and into the East Lobby, the heels of Rose's shoes *click-clacking* on the black-and-white marble floor.

That five-minute walk had seemed to take half a life-time, and she became aware of a faint trembling in her hands.

God, she was tired of living with this constant fear!

As she took a long, calming breath, Matt thanked the security guard, who nodded and headed back the way he'd come. Looking out the doors, she glimpsed the statue of a seated Abraham Lincoln in the distance, and the headlights of passing cars on the streets beyond that.

"Stay here," Matt told Manny. "Nobody gets in without an invitation."

Manny nodded. He positioned himself by the main doors in a wide-legged stance, hands clasped before him. As she and Matt walked away, Lili smiled and waved. Manny grinned back briefly, then returned to bodyguard mode.

Chatting and smiling, shaking hands in introductions, Lili slowly worked her way through the crowd of people and down the steps toward the North Atrium. She slowed as she passed under the graceful curve of a marble staircase—festooned with garlands of white roses, ivory ribbons, and gauzy golden bows—and lit from above by a softly glowing crystal chandelier.

The atrium was lovely, and she smiled with delight at the pale white columns of the two-story loggias. The walls were adorned with elaborately framed watercolor scenes from the Chicago World's Fair of 1893, and dozens of circular tables with white linen tablecloths dotted the floor, each table boasting a lush floral arrangement of white and gold, and set with china and silver and crystal.

"Look at the ceiling, Lil."

Matt stood beside her, his hand at her back—but his touch tonight felt possessive; the touch of a lover, not a guardian.

Smiling, oddly warm of a sudden, Lili looked up at what appeared to be a night sky with stars twinkling away. It wasn't real, of course, but it added that final, magical touch—perfect for the night's mood of make-believe.

"I feel like I'm in a fairy tale," she murmured, and when she looked down again, Matt's gaze was on hers and his mouth so close that she almost stopped breathing.

But he only smiled, glanced up again, and slowly shook his head as if he couldn't quite believe the ceiling, either.

Or maybe it was that he'd come awfully close to kissing her that he couldn't believe.

Ever optimistic, Lili latched on to the latter, and as they went in to dinner together, he crooked his elbow at her with a half-smile. Lighthearted, trying not to be too hopeful, she took his arm and let him lead her to their table.

The dinner passed smoothly. Matt sat on her left, and to her right was one of the dozen or so Phantoms of the Opera—just as she wasn't the only flapper, or Matt the only gangster. Still, in her opinion, her dress was the prettiest and Matt was by far the sexiest gangster in the crowd.

Lili did most of the talking, chatting up her business and showing off Rose's shoes whenever asked to do so—which was often, as a number of guests had attended her earlier lecture at the society.

Barely an hour had passed before she'd handed out all her business cards, and resorted to jotting down notes, names, and numbers on cocktail napkins. Then, on her way back from a trip to the ladies' room, Matt at her side, she cornered the columnist who wrote for the art section of the *Chicago Tribune*. Naturally the columnist had a photographer with her, and Lili charmed and schmoozed until she finagled a picture of herself, draped in a dramatic pose along the marble staircase.

Lili caught Matt's eye and winked just before the photographer snapped the picture.

Surprising her, he threw back his head and laughed, the sound echoing through the high-ceilinged room and filling her with a warm delight—and the most powerful pull of desire she'd ever experienced.

Now, as Lili delicately licked the last bit of chocolate mousse off her spoon, the Phantom sitting beside her leaned close—too close, again—and said, "Here's a good one. There's this blond, see, and she's driving through a park . . ."

Tired of the man's endlessly tasteless jokes, and annoyed at how he was practically breathing down her neckline, Lili scooted her chair closer to Matt. Lili hoped the Phantom would take the hint before Matt caught on, because she didn't want a repeat performance of the Redhead Piano Bar incident.

As she bumped her chair a fraction of an inch closer, her thigh brushed Matt's, but he made no effort to shift away. After a moment, she glanced at him over her coffee cup.

"Is something wrong?" he murmured, leaning toward her so that his shoulder pressed intimately against her arm.

Heat washed over her, and she managed to shake her head. "Not at all."

He smiled—not that polite, working-on-the-clock smile, but one of rare warmth, and Lili couldn't help reading encouragement in it.

As the meal wound to its close, she and Matt gradually leaned nearer and nearer into each other. Her feminine instincts warned that he was putting the moves on her in his own understated—yet very effective—way. In a way that meant he would create the opportunity, but she had to take the next step.

While the waiters cleared their plates away, Lili caught him watching her with a quiet, almost expectant, intensity. Quickly, before giving herself a chance to think twice, she slid her hand over to his lap, taking his hand in hers.

His mouth tightened and his muscles stiffened. She went still, worrying that she'd somehow misread him, despite this unmistakable heat of attraction tingling between them.

No. Absolutely no way had she misread him—more than likely, it was his blasted professionalism suddenly warring with his very human needs.

"You think too much," Lili whispered, leaning against him. When a look of wry amusement crossed his face, she added, "That wasn't a joke, you know."

"I know. It's just that getting accused of thinking too much isn't something that happens a lot to guys like me."

Lili sent him a speculative glance, part curiosity, part disbelief. Was he saying people didn't think he was smart? Ridiculous; the man had "intelligence" and "capability" written all over him. "Well, you *do* think too much. And you give yourself too many rules."

"This particular rule is a good one," he said, not pretending to misunderstand her unspoken meaning.

Yet he hadn't slipped his hand from hers.

"You're here as my date. You can act the part as much as you want."

The look he gave her said he found the excuse as weak as it sounded to her own ears. A scant second later, his gaze slowly tracked downward over the low neckline of her dress and the flimsy silk chiffon that skimmed her curves. She could almost imagine his fingers touching her with the same lingering slowness as his gaze, and she grew warm again under his scrutiny.

Then, with a brief squeeze, he pulled his hand from

hers. He looked away, surveyed the room, and checked in with Dal and Manny.

Lili stared down at the tablecloth. She shouldn't be frustrated or disappointed; he was doing what he needed to do, and distracting him wasn't a good idea. Still, she recognized half the people in this room, and the rest hardly looked menacing. They looked and acted as if they belonged. No one seemed as if they'd crashed the party. If she could see this, then certainly Matt could.

Quickly draining the last of her coffee, Lili put the cup down and, before she lost her nerve, touched Matt's shoulder. He turned to her, brow raised in question.

"I know I've been a pain in the ass this week, but I do want to thank you for what you've done for me. You, Manny, and Dal have helped make a very frightening and difficult time much easier to deal with."

"It's my—"

"Please." She held up her hand to silence him. "I know it's your job, but I still want to thank you. Didn't they teach you in bodyguard school how to accept a compliment with grace?"

A reluctant smile curved his mouth. "Yes."

Still watching him, she said abruptly, "I've been doing some thinking myself lately."

The muscles of his arm, still pressed against hers, went taut, and a sudden wariness hardened his face.

In the same quiet voice, she added, "It's not as if I think I'm in any real danger, because I trust you to keep me safe, but this week I've realized how easily someone *could* take my life away. It made me see that I take too much for granted, and I'd be happier if I changed a few things in my life."

He took a long breath, tension easing away from him. "Such as?"

"For one, I let people do too much for me. It's not because I'm scatterbrained or disorganized. I know I'm not . . . but people have been telling me that for so long, I've let myself believe it, and lived up to everybody's expectations of Lili the dreamer, the butterfly." She frowned. "I guess, more accurately, I've lived *down* to expectations."

"Lili, I've watched you tonight. You charm people, and you're smart and talented. You're being too hard on yourself."

"I'm satisfied with what I've accomplished, but what I mean is that I've really never had to depend on *me*. Somebody's always there to bail me out: my parents, Jared, my friends. You."

"But—"

"I know, I know. Don't say it." She grinned at him, to take away the sting of sarcasm in her voice. "I'm serious, Matt. I've never really had to take a chance without the cushion of family or friends to fall back on, and now I'm feeling a need to take a few risks. To get out of a rut. To do something just for *me*."

His wariness returned, and she supposed he had cause. The risks she was talking about included him, in letting the night's events unwind as they may, and going where they'd take her.

She glanced away, watching guests head toward the East Lobby and hearing the drifting strains of violins and cellos.

Seized with a sudden uncertainty, she stared down at her hands, folded in her lap. She wanted to ask him to dance, but maybe she should slow down, spend time talking, think things through—

"Lili."

At the touch of Matt's hand on her bare arm, she looked up, her senses acutely alive to his touch, the sound of his voice, his scent.

"So whaddya say, dollface?" He tipped back the fedora, smiling an irresistible half-smile, humor sparkling in his gray eyes—and looking so handsome that a sweet, aching pang spread through her. "You wanna dance?"

God, she wanted him. It was that simple.

With far more nonchalance than she felt, Lili reached up and tucked his boutonniere in his pocket, letting her fingers linger on his chest, and flashed him a smile.

"Sure, mister." She tried to sound tough, languorous, like a Hollywood glamour bad girl—Mae West, or Jean Harlow. "You look like the kind of guy who can show a girl a good time."

She pronounced "girl" as "goil."

Matt stood, laughing, and helped her to her feet. He crooked his elbow, and she took it, smiling. Slowly, they walked toward the curving staircase.

Before they reached it, Lili stopped. "One last look," she said, tipping her head back to admire the faux night sky above the pale, elegant room. "Humor me, okay? I'm such a damn hopeless romantic."

"It's what I like about you, Lili." His voice was quiet. "Maybe I could use a little more romance in my life."

She felt him ease closer, his arm slide around her waist, and her breath caught. She blinked several times, rapidly, before looking down.

His face wasn't even an inch from hers, his lids half-closed, and she was suddenly struck by how long and thick his lashes were, and she had a sudden urge to lean forward and kiss those lashes, letting them tickle her lips.

Come on, come on . . . kiss me . . .

Lili hesitated for what seemed forever and a second, then instinctively leaned forward. As she did so, Matt brought his mouth down on hers: a soft, press of warm, dry lips, more of a question than a kiss.

She answered his question by sliding her hands upward along his chest, over the bump of his holster, and twined them around his neck, bringing him full against her.

It was the answer he wanted, and his kiss turned more demanding. His hands skimmed down the curve of her back to her bottom, lightly caressing her for a moment before his fingers tightened and he pulled her against his hips.

At the unmistakable press of his erection, Lili drew back. Looking past the shadows, she saw the need in his eyes—and the uncertainty.

So she closed her eyes and kissed him again before he could change his mind.

Her senses filled, soaking in the waxy-sweet smell of fresh-cut flowers around her, the echo of laughter and voices shot through with the taut, longing strains of violins, the clink of silverware on china, and the dim glow of the chandelier.

And, above it all, her awareness of Matt: the taste of coffee on his lips, the strength of arms and chest and legs beneath his suit, his warmth, the firm feel of his lips, that scent so uniquely his own . . . what his hands were doing to her, moving ever so slowly across her bottom.

Matt let out his breath, murmuring her name as he broke the kiss, and he trailed his mouth to her chin, to the tender and sensitive place just below her ear. She shivered, her fingers tightening on his shoulders, and her body arched against him, wanting more.

At her urgent and wordless appeal, Matt pulled away.

Flushed and frustrated, Lili observed his own rapid breathing, how he touched the back of his hand to his upper lip.

By habit, his gaze quickly swept their surroundings. Checking for danger, she thought—but what if he felt guilty, and was checking to make sure no one had caught him feeling up his client under the stairway?

Oh, God. If he pushed her away again, she'd die of embarrassment. If he said anything, if those eyes of his went cold—

Matt reached a hand above her head, and Lili went still. A slow smile crossed his face as he pilfered a white rose from the stairway swag. Carefully, he slid the stem into her chignon.

Then, his fingers lingering in her hair, he slid his hands gently down to cup her face, his thumbs caressing her cheekbones. "You have beautiful hair," he murmured, then leaned forward and kissed her again.

She returned his kiss, sliding her hands beneath his coat and up his broad back, delighting in the play of his muscles beneath her fingertips. When his tongue touched hers, she sighed and parted her lips to let him in, tasting his hot warmth.

Matt made a low sound deep in his throat, and eased his hands down to the bare skin of her shoulders. He gathered her to his chest, slanting his head to better fit her against him. All his warmth, safety, and power enveloped her, arousing and yet oddly comfortable, as if no other arms, no other mouth, could ever fit her as well as his.

Pressed against the length of his body, she couldn't miss the urgency of his body's needs.

The sound of a woman's laughter sounded nearby. Matt broke the embrace first, stepping away, and Lili raised a not very steady hand to tuck away the tendrils of hair that had come loose from her chignon.

"Lovebirds," murmured the woman's companion, chuckling. "Kids these days will do anything anywhere . . ."

A blush heating her cheeks, Lili darted a glance at Matt. He was finger-smoothing his hair, straightening his tie, looking anywhere but at her. The seconds stretched on, edgy and awkward.

Finally Lili cleared her throat. "You'd said something about dancing?"

Matt looked up, and as he did so, tipped the fedora downward, hiding his eyes. "I gotta check in with my team first."

Lili forced back the twinge of resentment. After all, it was The Job that was keeping her safe. She just wished . . .

Well, wishing was pointless; after tonight, it would be over between them. Repressing a sigh, she waited as Matt checked in with Manny first, then with Dal, and heard him say: "You stay in the car. Yeah, I know . . . you can talk through the window if you have to, but don't get out of that vehicle. That's standard procedure."

"What was that about?" Lili asked, curious.

Matt glanced at her, and when his eyes met hers, the memory of what they'd been doing scant seconds before came rushing back and she wanted to ask: *Did they teach you to kiss like that in bodyguard school?*

"A couple other limo drivers are hanging out, talking. I'm just reminding him to stay put."

"That must be an awfully boring job," Lili murmured as they began walking toward the steps. She held her hands clasped before her, and every time her body brushed his, her nerves skittered.

"I know it's boring. That's how I started out in the business. And I don't mind if he talks to the other drivers, but he has to stay in the car." At the stairs leading up to the East Lobby, he held out his arm. "Dal's good. Smart, reliable, and dedicated. You don't have to worry about him screwing up."

"It's not Dal I'm thinking about," she said, slipping her arm through his.

At her arch comment Matt sent her a quick, unreadable glance, and they climbed the broad steps toward the upper story where the orchestra was playing.

The East Lobby was small, with marble floors and a row of high glass doors that opened to the portico and plaza. Lyrical music, mostly strings, thrummed through the night air like a heartbeat, and the lights were dim and soft—the perfect mood for a little romance.

The more forbidden, the better. And something about the darkness made intimacy—not to mention taking risks—impossible to resist.

Manny was still standing where she and Matt had left him. When he saw her, he nodded an acknowledgment and even cracked a lopsided, endearing smile. It struck her how much she'd miss Manny and Dal, too.

Lili expected to join the other dancers in front of the glass doors, but Matt stayed toward the back. When she sent him a questioning look, he said, "I don't want you standing in front of any windows at night. You might as well be a target with a neon arrow pointing toward you."

"I would never think of something like that." She took in a long breath. "God, Matt, I hate feeling this helpless."

"Give yourself a break. You're a shoe designer. Nobody expects you to know how to handle stalkers, or how twisted minds work."

True enough, and his words made her feel a little better. "Well, I'm still desperately grateful to have you watching over me."

"It's been my pleasure," he said quietly, meeting her eyes. "Do you still want to dance?"

She moved against him without hesitation. "It's a lovely night," she murmured. "It would be a shame not to enjoy it."

He looked as if he wanted to say something, but instead he took her in his arms. This time, though, Matt slid his right arm around her waist and pulled her close.

Looking out over his shoulder, Lili saw the moment Manny noticed them. If it were possible, he stood even straighter, his gaze sharpening, and a frown creased his forehead before he looked away, as if he refused to let himself see anything at all.

Uh-oh. Trouble.

"I feel like I should say something," Matt said tightly, bringing her attention back to his shadowed face.

"We're both adults, we both know what we want, and we both know I'm leaving tomorrow." Lili met his gaze. "What's there to say?"

"When you put it that way, not much."

"I'm very attracted to you," Lili added, as Matt swung her around. "I don't think there's anything wrong with that—or with doing something about it."

Several emotions played across his usually unreadable face: wariness and anger, hope—and a healthy, hot desire. "I messed up."

"That's not what a girl likes to hear, Matt," she teased. "You didn't mess up; all you did was kiss me." Stepping onto the toes of his shoes, forcing him to stop, she went on tiptoe and whispered in his ear: "And I liked it."

A tremor rippled through his tensed muscles before he started moving again. They danced for another fifteen or twenty minutes, and Lili allowed herself the luxury of losing herself completely in his embrace. She loved the feel of him against her, his warmth, the touch of his hands. She loved how the shadows deepened the cleft in his chin, hollowed his cheeks, and made him look dark and sexy and strong.

As the minutes waltzed along, his hand at her waist slowly slid lower, possessively cupping her bottom. In encouragement, she ran her fingers over the muscles of his arms and pressed against him. She hardly registered anybody else at all, although there must have been at least two dozen other couples dancing. The music became a mere accompaniment to the beating of her heart and her rapid breathing.

Finally, she couldn't stand the tantalizing closeness any longer. If she rubbed against him for one second more, she'd have to drag him into the nearest dark corner and risk scandalizing half of Chicago's cultural elite.

"I want to go back to the hotel now."

Matt held her gaze long enough for Lili to know he'd understood her meaning. Awareness hummed between them, rich with anticipation and uncertainty.

He nodded, drawing her away from the other dancers, and spoke into his radio. "We're heading out. Get the car over here."

Dal must've said something amusing, because Matt smiled a little. When he looked back at Lili, he said, "Dal's on the way. Let's go."

Matt retrieved her wrap and guided Lili toward the glass doors as she thanked their hosts, then said a few good-byes. Manny met them at the door, along with another security guard.

"Having a nice time?" Manny asked, dark eyes snapping with anger.

Matt's mouth tightened to a thin line, but he said nothing.

Worried, Lili glanced between the two men. She hadn't given a thought to what Matt's team would think about this, and while part of her felt guilty, she mostly wanted to tell Manny to mind his own damn business.

Now, however, was not the time or the place for an argument.

"Let's go," Matt said tersely.

Once again, Lili found herself outside and boxed in by broad masculine shoulders and chests. The night was brisk and she gathered the wrap more closely around her with a lightness in her step, even as she scolded herself for being so hopeful, as giddy and nervous as a teenager on a first date.

Maybe nothing more would happen between her and Matt, especially now with Manny's disapproval hanging heavy between them, but the night was young. Selfish or not, she wanted nothing more than to get him out of that suit and to leisurely examine all those wonderful muscles she'd run her fingers over all night long.

"Isn't your car supposed to be waiting here?" the security guard asked.

The abrupt question yanked Lili from her thoughts, and Manny, walking in front of her, stopped short. She ran up hard against his back, and winced.

"The car's not here," Manny snapped. He moved, and Lili saw a sudden gleam of metal in his hand. "Where the hell is Dal?"

Aware that something was wrong—terribly wrong— Lili turned toward Matt just as Manny made a short, hoarse sound and slammed back into her.

Lili stumbled under his weight, trying to catch him. She'd have fallen if Matt hadn't wedged his body between her and Manny, and shoved her away.

Manny stumbled again, and as he dropped to the ground, Matt lunged in front of her, pushing her down as he shouted, "Stay low!"

Hunched over, cold with dawning understanding, Lili saw Manny rocking from side to side, his knee drawn upward, his hands clutched over it. Even in the dim light, she could see a dark stain on his hands.

Blood.

9

"Get her out of here," Manny gasped. "Go, go!"

Matt had already grabbed Lili by the waist, shielding her with his body as he roughly shoved her head downward, making her as small a target as possible. He ran them both toward cover, pushing her ahead of him.

From the corner of his eye, he glimpsed the security guard dive behind a row of hedges.

"Manny! Oh, God, Matt, we can't leave him, he—"

"Goddammit, Lili, run!"

Hands still locked around her waist, he hauled her out of the line of fire and toward a copse of bushes and trees. He could hear the rapid sound of her breathing, feel her every stumble.

God, Manny was down . . .

Slivers of tree bark suddenly exploded near his face. He reflexively jerked his head back, cursing.

Too damn close. Where was the bastard?

Ducking behind nearby bushes, he crouched beside Lili. In the darkness, her face was a pale blur, her eyes dark and wide. He swore under his breath again.

They'd been set up, by at least two gunmen, maybe more. One must've taken out Dal within seconds after he'd talked to Matt. A sniper with a rifle and silencer had dropped Manny with a disabling hit to the knee—most likely thinking Manny wore body armor—but none of the shots was directed at Lili.

So much for his stalker theory.

As he looked around, searching for a way out, a line of cars parked a short distance away snagged his attention. Not a great way out, but it wasn't like he had a lot of options.

"Lil, I want you to go to those parked cars . . . the big white one. See it?"

Too scared to talk, she only nodded.

Matt squeezed her shoulder, then gave her a push out of the bushes. He stood before her, retreating backward to cover her as she darted toward the parked cars.

The instant he stepped onto the sidewalk, the shooter opened fire again. Pain burned in his arm as he dived toward the curb. Ignoring it, he rolled behind the car. Crouched over, hugging the line of cars, he grabbed Lili by the waist and ran a short distance down the road before steering her between a van and a Mercedes-Benz.

Lili huddled between the bumpers, the dark fabric of her wrap keeping her in the shadows.

What the hell was this about? There was something here he wasn't seeing. An answer, a clue, *something*.

"What are we going to do?" Lili whispered.

"We're going to try to slip past the shooter. The darkness keeping him hidden from us also gives us the advantage of cover. We're all running blind."

"Manny—"

"Forget Manny! I'm doing what I need to do and he knows that. Getting you to safety is the only concern."

"How can you just leave him lying back there? What if—"

"Don't talk," he snapped. He wouldn't let her finish the sentence. He forced himself to ignore the memory of Manny falling, the twisted look of pain on his face. "You do what I tell you to do. Got that?"

She flinched at the harshness of his voice, but he couldn't do anything about that now, either.

Jesus. He was trapped, and on foot with a vulnerable client.

"We're going to run across the street, and I'll stay between you and the shooter. You ready?" When she nodded, he got into position to cover her, muscles tensing, then barked, "Go!"

They darted across the street, bullets slamming into the pavement behind them as they made the sidewalk. "Keep going!" he shouted, yanking her along down the darkened, residential street.

Headlights unexpectedly split the darkness, and Matt slowed, staring at the car slowly coming toward him.

Perfect. Or as perfect as he was going to get.

"Stay put," he said, pushing Lili down behind a parked Blazer. "Don't even move until I tell you to."

Before she could question him, Matt stepped out into the street and raised his gun at the dark Lexus coming his way.

The headlights flared across his face, and the car squealed to a halt. Through the windshield, Matt could see the frightened face of a young man, both hands tightly gripping the steering wheel.

Matt aimed the gun at the man's head. "Do exactly what I tell you, and you won't get hurt."

The man stared, mouth agape, frozen in place.

"Put the car in park. Now!"

Jumping at the harsh tone of Matt's order, the man did as ordered.

"Open your door."

The driver's side door swung wide, and as Matt moved toward it the skin between his shoulder blades twitched, as if waiting for a bullet to hit. He ducked down and stared at the driver.

The man raised his hands in defense. "Jesus, don't shoot me. You can take my money—"

"I don't want your money. I want your car. You'll get it back." Matt kept his voice calm, but didn't lower the Glock. "Get out."

"Okay . . . okay," the man said, his breathing rapid, perspiration glistening on his face as he eased past Matt and stumbled onto the street, then ran.

Matt climbed in the car, shutting the door and cutting the headlights. With one eye still on the driver's retreating back, Matt reached over, opened the passenger side door, and yelled, "Lili, get in!"

At his order, she darted forward, and all but dived onto the front seat.

"Shut the door, buckle up, and get down," Matt said. Ahead, he glimpsed lights coming toward him—fast. Too fast. Grimly, he added, "And hang on."

With a quick check to the mirrors, Matt rammed the transmission into reverse and floored the accelerator. The car shot backward along the street.

Lili yelped in surprise and grabbed on to the seat, her head pressed against the upholstery.

Keeping one eye on his mirrors and one eye on the car in front of him, closing fast, Matt swung the steering wheel hard to the left, careening around a corner onto another residential street lined on either side with cars and trucks. He was distantly aware of Lili's muffled gasps, but kept his focus on the mirrors and the narrow street he was speeding through in reverse. Streetlights flashed as he sped past them, sudden and intense, like strobes.

This late, the streets were quiet, but if another car turned onto this street he was screwed.

"Hold on," he warned again, and turned sharply, just as bright headlights arced toward him.

He braked, tires squealing, and backed onto yet another street. He floored the accelerator for several blocks. Eyes on the rearview mirror, he looked for the next intersection.

Spotting it, he aimed for the wider street space of the intersection and shoved back on the emergency brake. As the rear wheels locked, he swung the steering wheel hard, spinning the car with sickening speed in a near one-hundred-eighty-degree turn. Lili cried out as her head banged against the dashboard.

Hands working fast on the wheel, Matt steadied the car, released the emergency brake, and accelerated forward down the street at twice the speed limit and with the lights off.

And he could still glimpse those bright headlights, close on his ass.

Flying along the warren of small streets and driveways, he kept turning, braking, speeding, and turning again.

He glanced quickly at Lili, huddled silently in her sparkling finery, her face white. Matt looked away, and as he did so, spied a construction-sized Dumpster sitting in the driveway of a house under renovation. He braked hard and turned, the car jostling from side to side as he jumped the sidewalk, and then he drove behind the Dumpster, parked, and killed the engine.

"What are you doing?" Lili whispered.

"Waiting. I think I lost them at the last turn."

Not far away, he heard the sound of squealing tires and furious honking—and over that, the wail of sirens. Many sirens.

"The police, thank God," Lili murmured. "We can go back and—"

"We're not going back," Matt interrupted, turning to her. Their eyes locked and held, and the terror in her eyes left him with a sinking feeling in his stomach. "No talking."

They sat in tense, uneasy silence as the minutes crawled by, and when Matt felt certain it was safe, he put the car in gear and quietly rolled back out onto the street. Then he switched on the lights, and drove away.

Just another guy out for a late Saturday night drive with his girl.

He glanced at Lili. "You okay?"

"I think so." She swallowed, gaze searching his, then added in a shaky voice, "You never even lost your hat."

Matt brought his hand up by reflex, and touched the brim. Sure enough, the damn fedora was still on his head.

"That was some pretty fancy driving," she said after several seconds had passed. "I suppose you learned that in bodyguard school, too."

She was trying for humor, but it fell flat.

"Evasive Driving 101." Regretting what he'd just put her through, he added, as if it would help, "That was what we call a J-turn."

"A J-turn," she repeated, then let out a sigh. "I thought I was going to throw up."

"Sorry." What else could he say?

"It's all right. You did what you had to."

Silence fell over the car as he drove, checking street signs and getting his bearings—and trying not to think of his team. He knew he had to stay focused on the here and now, because Lili wasn't out of danger yet.

"What happened back there, Matt?"

"They took out Dal at the last possible minute so they wouldn't tip us off, and then dropped Manny." In a voice tight with a sudden, cold fury, he added, "A sniper, dammit . . . I didn't see that one coming at all."

With the immediate danger past, he spared a thought for his arm. He could feel the sting where the bullet had grazed him, and the warm, sticky wetness of blood. But it was nothing compared to Manny's injuries. And God knew what had happened to Dal . . .

"But *why?* I don't understand."

"I don't know," he said, keeping his voice even as he tried to catch his breath. His heart pounded in his ears. "But somebody wants you, and they were willing to kill me and my team to get you."

Matt looked at her, huddled against the seat, still wide-eyed. Why, indeed? There had to be a reason. What was he missing? The attack at the auditorium, the attempt to get into her room, the shots tonight that weren't aimed at her, but at her protection. What did they all have in common?

Think, think, dammit.

He glanced at her again, and as they passed a streetlight, her dress sparkled in the darkness, and her shoes—

Oh, Christ, her shoes!

It clicked, just like that—Matt could've sworn he even heard the sound of it in his head. It had to be those shoes; nothing else made sense. He didn't know how, or why, but he'd bet his balls they were the key to what was going on. She'd had them at the auditorium, in her room, and on her feet tonight.

He was furious with himself for not seeing it earlier. They'd been there all along, right under his nose. He'd even briefly wondered if they might've been the motive, but he'd dismissed it as too far-fetched.

Mind racing, he stared out ahead as the headlights cut through the darkness, illuminating quiet townhouses and condos and expensive cars.

Knowing the cops would be looking for the car he'd "borrowed," he stayed to the side streets, keeping an eye out for patrol cruisers. He had to ditch it, but he couldn't go back for his own car. These bastards probably knew who he was by now, but even if no one was watching his house, his plates were too easily traced.

Like it or not, he needed help. Reluctantly, he reached inside his jacket, pulled out his cell phone, and dialed.

"Who are you calling?" Lili asked, watching him.

"Police dispatch. I have a friend with the Chicago PD."

Within a few minutes, they'd patched him through and he heard her voice, crisp, professional and a little guarded: "Hawkins? Are you still there?"

"Yeah, Espinosa, I'm here, and I'm calling in that favor you owe me." Monica Espinosa would know what was up, no need for chitchat or lengthy explanations. "I need a car, and I need some cash, and I need both fast."

Silence. "Dammit, they're looking all over for you and the Kavanaugh woman. Are you okay?"

"She's okay. I took one in the arm." He glanced at Lili, and her eyes widened as she looked at his arm, where the blood had darkened the fabric of his coat. She hadn't known he'd been shot. More for Lili's sake than Monica's, he added, "It's not bad. Just a scratch."

He didn't ask what he wanted to know: *My team . . . how bad are they?*

"You have a good reason for what you're doing, right?"

"I do."

A heavy sigh sounded on the other end of the phone. "Where?"

"A little restaurant in Chinatown . . . you know the one I'm talking about."

Another brief silence. "I'll be there in thirty minutes."

The line disconnected with a click, and Matt slipped the phone back into his pocket. "Keep that dark wrap over your dress."

Lili pulled it more tightly around her. "We're going to Chinatown?"

Matt nodded.

"Are you going to tell me what's going on?"

He didn't look away from the street. "Once I figure it all out, you'll be the first to know."

He avoided the main thoroughfares as he drove, stopping at a couple of out-of-the-way ATM machines to withdraw as much money as possible, and finally turned into a seedier part of Chinatown. Storefront signs were lettered in Chinese, with haphazard English here and there. From Yuppie Town to Chinatown, in just thirty minutes.

He pulled up behind a small restaurant housed in a squat, square building, and spotted the unmarked car and squad car at once. He turned off the engine and lights. Three people were leaning against the unmarked car, a woman in a suit and two men in uniform, one tall and one short. As the trio walked toward them, Lili asked, "Which one is your friend?"

"The woman." Matt opened the door, and glanced at Lili. "Stay put for a minute or two, please."

The tall, dark-haired woman came to a stop before him, arms folded across her chest. Monica Espinosa—as pretty as ever, if a little hard-looking around the eyes and mouth.

"Hello, Matt. Long time no see."

"Monica," he said, a shade wary.

"I thought you'd given up carjacking."

"Please make sure the car gets back to its owner," he said, holding back the spurt of anger she was always so good at rousing. He looked over her shoulder at the uniforms. "Who're they?"

"Guys I can trust to keep their mouths shut. The tall one's Mark Ward, my niece's husband. The other is a cousin. Johnny Degas."

Matt nodded a greeting at the uniforms, then asked, "You brought a car?"

"I guess you can call it a car." She motioned behind her, and he leaned sideways to glimpse a big Olds Royale, badly rusted out, but with brand spanking new wheels and hubcaps.

"It's a damn boat," Matt muttered.

"It was the best I could do on short notice," Monica said dryly. "It's Ricky's. It may be a piece of shit to you, but it's his pride and joy."

"Ricky's old enough to drive already?" Matt stared at her, surprised—and a little guilty, too. He'd meant to stay in touch better than he had.

"It's been that long," she said, her tone going cool. "You care to tell me what the hell is going on?"

"In a minute. First, I need to know about my team. Are they—" He couldn't bring himself to finish the sentence.

Her face softened. "Manny took a hit to his knee and hand. The knee's busted up pretty bad, and he lost a lot of blood, but he's okay."

"What about my driver? Farrell?"

Her gaze shifted briefly, but enough to send a cold dread lancing through his body.

"He's not so good," Monica said quietly. "I'm sorry. The best news I can give you is that he was still breathing when the EMTs arrived on the scene. They found him sitting in the parked car. The driver's side window was rolled down a couple inches. The best guess is that he was talking to somebody who slipped a gun barrel in the opening and shot him in the head."

"Jesus," Matt whispered. He raised a hand, as if doing so could hold back the ugly truth, then lowered it again. "Oh, Jesus."

Turning away, he rested his fists against the roof of the car and closed his eyes.

Shot him in the head . . .

"He has a wife," he muttered, eyes still closed. Rage swept over him, white-hot in its intensity. "Her name is Jodie. Somebody should—"

"They already got that information from Manny. There's an officer on the way to her now."

The rage built, pushing outward.

"They got married three months ago." Matt straightened, opening his eyes. Lili was out of the car, watching him over the roof. He hadn't even heard her door open. "I should've told him to keep the window shut. My fault. I should've—"

His control snapped, and he slammed his fists down on the car roof, savagely glad for the pain.

"I'll kill them . . . I'll fucking kill every one of them," he shouted, not caring who could hear. Distantly, he was aware of moving his arm back, above the car window. "I'm going to take them down!"

A sudden, sharp pain radiated upward along his arm. Matt looked down, realizing he'd punched the window. Breathing hard, he stared at the blood beading across his scraped knuckles.

The short cop, Degas, grabbed his arm. "Hey, take it easy."

Matt pulled free, dropping Degas with a sharp elbow jab to the belly.

"Dammit, Matt!"

Monica grabbed his uninjured arm as the tall cop

moved in, getting a hold on Matt's other arm and twisting it painfully behind his back. Matt bucked and twisted, not caring if he snapped the bone—and suddenly Lili was standing in front of him, cupping his face in her hands, her blue eyes locked on his.

Everything around him faded; nothing else registered but the intensity of her eyes, the paleness of her face. Her fear.

Fear of him.

"Stop this," she said quietly, unblinking. Her voice reached deep inside him, soothing and calming. Hooking sanity, and dragging it back to the surface. "You're not going to kill anybody. No more talk like that. Look at me, Matt!"

He stared into her eyes, as his rage slowly ebbed. Sensations and sounds returned, and he heard the harsh sound of his breathing. His hand hurt.

God, but it hurt . . .

"I want the bastards dead, Lili," he whispered, his voice ragged, and something hot stung the back of his eyes.

Her hands, so slender, so soft and warm, closed over his jaw with amazing strength. "Killing them won't change what happened, or help Manny and Dal." Her eyes gleamed with a sudden sheen of tears. "Stay with me, Matt . . . stay with me."

"I'd never leave you now, Lil."

"I know." She still hadn't broken eye contact—as if she were afraid that by doing so, she'd lose him. "But that's not what I meant."

Slowly her meaning sank in, and as it did, the last of the rage vanished as suddenly as it had come.

Shame washed over him for his loss of control, his useless anger, his stupid talk of killing. Rage, threats, violence—that was a way of life he'd put behind him a long, long time ago, and it chilled him how quickly and easily he'd fallen back on it.

"I'm so sorry," he whispered.

Taking her hands in his, he lowered them from his face. He squeezed her hands in a silent gesture of gratitude he hoped she'd understand.

Then he looked around, seeing Monica's grim expression, and how both Degas and Ward had their hands on their gun belts in a defensive stance.

Before he could offer any apology, headlights flashed down the narrow back street. Another patrol car; slowing as the driver peered out, sensing trouble. The car stopped.

"Shit," Monica said in disgust. "Ward, get rid of them. Tell them to move on, that we've got everything under control."

As the tall cop trotted off to shoo away the patrol car, Monica turned back to Matt and Lili. Her gaze briefly touched on Lili, and a small frown settled between her brows. "I'm Detective Monica Espinosa. Homicide. Pleased to meet you."

Lili appeared a little taken aback, but managed a smile and shook Monica's hand. "Lili Kavanaugh. Shoe designer. Thanks for your help."

"You're welcome." Monica looked Lili over with frank curiosity. "I never met a shoe designer before."

"Well, I never met a homicide cop before." Lili blew out a shaky breath. "It's been a hell of a night."

The patrol car slowly drove away, and Monica turned again to Matt. "Every cop in the city is looking for you two, and I don't think those guys in the squad are going to keep quiet for long. You'd better go."

Matt nodded, and glanced at Lili. "Wait in the car for a second. I need to talk to Monica alone."

Lili merely nodded, and went back to the car. Her silent trust brought him back to his purpose, sharpened his concentration. He had work to do; there'd be time later for grief.

"Something tells me your interest in the lady is more than a little personal," Monica said, watching him carefully.

Matt shrugged, unwilling to discuss it, but not denying it, either. Monica knew him too well.

After a moment, Monica tightened her lips. "So what are you going to do?"

"I'm going to take her into hiding until you catch these guys. I don't want anybody knowing where I am. Not even you."

"I don't like that."

"Too bad. I'm not risking her life to keep the Chicago PD happy," Matt said bluntly. "Secrets have a way of leaking out in a police department. I know it. You know it."

"You're both witnesses to a crime. We need to talk to you about that."

Matt snorted. "Nice try, but Manny and the security guard can tell you just as much as I can." He paused. "Was the guard hurt?"

"He's fine. Unlike you, he's trained to take cover when the shooting starts. He's not a bullet catcher." Her gaze flicked to his blood-darkened sleeve. "You need a doctor?"

"No." Matt held on to his temper with an effort. "Look, going into hiding is the only way to keep her safe. That was a professional hit, and you know what we're up against. It's personal with me now, Monica. Nobody gets to her unless it's through me."

"You'll call? Keep me updated?" Monica demanded, a shade suspicious.

"I swear it. You know I always keep my word."

"Are you armed?" she asked after a moment. When he gave a short nod, she glared. "I figured you were when I heard about Manny. Luckily for him, his gun seems to have disappeared."

Despite the tension vibrating through him, Matt smiled faintly. "I wonder how that happened."

"It helps if you're related to half the cops in Chicago. They'll look after him." Manny was Monica's cousin, and had introduced her to Matt years ago. "Manny may be hurt, but I swear I'm gonna kick his ass for this." She paused, then asked, "Does your client have any idea what you're doing?"

Matt shook his head.

"So she doesn't know I could bust you for carrying concealed."

"I don't give a shit," he retorted.

"You should. It's the law."

"I feel that law doesn't apply to my situation right now."

Monica's eyes narrowed. "If I had a nickel for every time I heard that excuse, I'd be a rich woman."

"The bad guys aren't playing by your rules, either. They put a fucking bullet through the brain of my twenty-five-year-old driver, and if I have to break every law in the book to keep Lili safe, I'll do it."

"Same old Matt," Monica said, her quiet voice threaded with bitterness. Or maybe it was disappointment—he didn't care to look too closely. "One of these days, you're going to cross a line that can't be uncrossed. I just pray I'm not there to have to see it, or to pick up the pieces."

And same old Monica; some things never changed.

"Are you going to help me or not?" Matt didn't look away from her dark, searching gaze, and finally Monica sighed in resignation.

"You're making this really hard for me." After a brief

silence, she added, "If you get caught, I may not be able to help you. And if word leaks out about what I'm doing, it could mean trouble for me."

"I know."

"Then you'd better not shoot anybody unless you have to." She sounded pissed. "And we didn't have this conversation."

"Thanks . . . I owe you."

"The keys are in the ignition. Money's in a bag on the floor," she said, brisk and businesslike again. "It's not much. I stopped at two ATM machines on the way here. Only four hundred bucks."

"It's enough."

She eyed him critically. "You should've asked for clothes. You'll have a hard time going unnoticed wearing that, especially since you bled all over it."

Damn. "I didn't think of that."

"Do you want me to—"

Matt shook his head, impatient. "We don't have time. I'll deal with it later. There's one more thing I need from you before I go."

"Matt—"

"This is important. I need everything you can find on Joey Mancuso and Rose McIntyre. I'll call for it in two days."

Monica stared. "You mean the outlaws killed back in the thirties? Why?"

"What do you know about the stolen money that was never found?"

"I asked you a question first."

Matt glanced over his shoulder at Lili, sitting in the car, watching him. "I don't have time to explain everything now, but I think all this is about a pair of shoes that belonged to Rose McIntyre. Lili owns the shoes . . . she's wearing them. The only reason I can figure anybody wants her this bad is because her shoes have something to do with the money Joey Mancuso stole in 1933."

"That's way, *way* out there, Matt."

"Nothing else fits. My team and I were set up, Monica. We never stood a chance."

She still looked skeptical, but she was listening. She was too good a cop not to. "I don't know much about Joey and Rose beyond that they were crooks, he double-crossed a mobster, and got whacked, but I'll see what I can dig up. It might take me more than a couple days."

"Get me what you can. Do you remember where they were killed?"

"Somewhere in Wisconsin, right?"

"Big Moccasin Lake Lodge," said the tall cop from behind Monica. "It's in northern Wisconsin, about a half hour from the Michigan border, just off Highway 45. I go up that way every summer. Good fishing."

Fishing. Matt almost smiled. That pretty much summed up his plans.

Matt nodded his thanks at the cop, then turned back to Monica. "I need your help on this. It was a long time ago, but there may be people around who remember, and might know why the shoes are important."

She nodded, her expression thoughtful. "Who's working on Kavanaugh's assault case?"

"Mike Payton."

"Payton's good. I'll talk to him and see if they turned up any leads. I know a few other people I can talk to." She smiled faintly, and said, "Your instincts are good, Matt. You shoulda been a cop."

He snorted. "With my history? I don't think so."

"Sometimes reformed troublemakers make the best cops." When he didn't respond, she asked, "Are you going where I think you're going?"

"I can't tell you exactly where I'm headed." It was mostly true—until he bought a map, he didn't know. "Trust me, okay? And there's one more thing . . . I'll also need everything you can find on Willis Conroy."

10

Matt's stony reticence, combined with the dark confines of the car, her still raw nerves, and the fact she had no idea where he was taking her, filled Lili with anxiety.

Finally, to break the long silence, she said, "I'm sorry about Dal."

He didn't respond, driving with such a focused intensity that she wondered if he even knew she sat beside him. She wanted to hear his calm voice, feel his reassuring touch—but he had problems enough to deal with, and didn't have time to hold her hand and tell her everything was hunky-dory.

"He'll be okay," she added firmly.

His mouth thinned. "You really believe that?"

Taken by surprise, she hesitated, then said, "I need to believe that." After a moment, she raised her hands, staring at them. "I can't seem to stop shaking."

He glanced at her, then back to the road. Traffic had

thinned after they left Chicago, but there were still a lot of cars and trucks on the highway, considering it was after midnight.

"Adrenaline crash," he said quietly. "It'll pass."

He sounded as if he knew what he was talking about, so she settled back in her seat, watching the headlights flash by, and after a while noticed he never exceeded the speed limit by more than five miles per hour.

No need to catch the attention of any state troopers, she supposed. They'd have a tough time explaining why a bloodied gangster and a shell-shocked flapper were driving in a heap of a car in the dead of night.

The road hummed beneath the tires, numbing in its monotony. Now and then a hint of greasy french fries tickled her nose, mingled with the stale odor of cigarette smoke.

Lili glanced at Matt, taking in the uncompromising lines of his face, shadowed by darkness, and the large, powerful hands gripping the steering wheel.

"How's your arm?" she asked.

"It's nothing. Don't worry about it."

Right; he'd been shot, and she wasn't to worry. Lili studied his tense face a moment longer, then asked abruptly, "You and that detective were lovers?"

"It was a long time ago."

From the start, she'd known there'd once been something between them—from the way they'd moved warily around each other, a hesitation hinting at history, at old hurts—and now curiosity warred with a sharp, unexpected jab of jealousy.

Monica Espinosa was attractive and gutsy. She wouldn't have shaky hands or feel like throwing up during car chases—Monica probably thrived on that kind of action. The woman seemed much more Matt's type. Lili didn't like the thought, or the mental image of Matt's long fingers running down Monica's skin, palming her breasts, making love to her . . .

Shaken by the force of her animosity, and unable to deny her feelings for Matt were running way, way beyond simple lust, Lili curled her fingers in her lap. "So what happened? Why'd you split up?"

Matt shrugged, pressing back in the seat to stretch. He slid his hands lower on the steering wheel. "She had problems with my job."

"A woman who deals with murder on a daily basis had a problem with *your* job?"

"It's a long story." He shifted his gaze toward her. "I don't want to talk about it."

Fair enough. It wasn't any of her business, anyway. She looked back out the window, although there was nothing to see except for the occasional glare of passing headlights.

"Why did she help us? And those two officers?" she asked, changing the subject. "I don't know much about police work, but I don't think what they did tonight was by the book."

"Are you complaining?"

At the flat tone of his voice, she looked away from the window. It almost seemed as if he were angry with her, and this was the absolute last thing she needed to deal with tonight.

"No, but I have a feeling she's bending a few laws on our account, and—"

"You let me worry about that."

Resentment spurted that he was treating her like some brainless bimbo, but she forced herself to hold it back. He'd been through a lot tonight, and she suspected all that careful professionalism had thinned to a gossamer veneer—and she had no desire to see it crack.

Not again. The last time had been frightening enough.

"Where are we going?" she asked instead.

"North."

Lili opened her mouth to snap back, but clamped her lips closed and turned back to the window.

Obviously he was in a mood, and she'd be better off trying to get answers out of him later. Probably he needed time to regroup or whatever it was guys like him did when things went all to hell.

Her own guilt threatened to overwhelm her if she dwelt too long on what had happened. Her head knew it wasn't her fault Manny and Dal had been shot, but in her heart beat a sickening guilt that Dal might die because of her.

What made it even worse was that she didn't know *why*.

"That was a trap back there, wasn't it?" She couldn't keep her questions bottled up inside any longer. At his curt nod, she said, "It sounds more like assassins than stalkers."

He briefly met her gaze. "That's what I'm thinking."

"I can't believe it," she burst out in frustration. "There has to be a reason! I live the most boring life you can imagine—working or traveling day after day, month after month. Do you think I've been mistaken for somebody else? Somebody rich, or important?"

"Who says you're not important?"

"Come on, Matt, you know what I mean."

"The shooters were too professional to make a mistake like that." He let out his breath, and said tightly, "I never thought to warn Dal about opening the window. I told him to stay in the car, and he did. Maybe if he'd been out of the car, they just would've knocked him out cold—"

"Matt, don't. It's not your fault."

"The hell it isn't! I'm the team leader. When something goes wrong, it's my fault. If I'd been paying more attention to the situation instead of getting in your pants, maybe they'd be okay now."

She flinched from the anger in his voice, hurt and offended by his crudity, especially after his earlier tenderness. It was all she could do not to snap back at him—and she would've, had she not sensed his anger, his need to hurt, was directed at himself, not her. "You're not superhuman. You weren't expecting a sniper, just a stalker. They'd have shot him through the window, anyway. There wasn't anything you could've done to stop that."

"It was bullet-resistant glass, Lili, and I *knew* I wasn't dealing with an average stalker. I should've been more alert."

There was little else for her to say; protests would do no good if he was determined to punish himself for being human rather than omnipotent.

After a lengthy silence, he said, "The shooter could've easily killed Manny, but didn't, and that's one more thing about this damn mess that makes no sense. Why go to the trouble of disabling one, then shoot the other in the head?"

Even hearing him say the words left her cold with fear and dread. Lili reached over and touched his arm. He tensed, but only for a moment, then took one hand off the steering wheel to briefly squeeze her hand.

That one little touch sent a spurt of relief through her, and a welcome comfort.

"There had to be two shooters, in two different positions," Matt added. "One must've been following orders, and the other not. The question is, were they ordered to maim, or kill?"

"So what's our plan? Are you going to tell me, or don't I have any choice but to tag along?"

A twinge of what looked like guilt crossed his face.

"I'm still working out the details, but we're hiding out until the cops catch these guys, or until we figure out why they're after you and how to stop them."

"Maybe I could go back home," she said, even knowing it was impossible. "I have a job, and a family . . . I can't just up and disappear."

"You can call your parents and work later. Going home isn't a good idea. If they can get to you in Chicago, they can get to you in New York."

"And who are 'they'?" she asked, pulling the wrap more tightly around her. Cold . . . she was so cold.

"I have a feeling we're dealing with organized crime here."

"Organized crime," Lili repeated, the chill seeping ever deeper. "My God."

"What's bugging the shit out of me is that these people kill each other all the time, but generally don't go after ordinary citizens. It's bad for business, and above all else, these guys consider themselves businessmen."

Lili studied him, a sudden suspicion dawning. "You know what's going on, don't you?" When he raised his shoulders in an evasive gesture, she added, "Tell me, Matt. Right now."

"It has to be the shoes." He didn't look away from the highway. "Joey Mancuso stole something he shouldn't have, and those shoes are the key to finding it."

Whatever she'd expected him to say, this wasn't it. Lili stared down at her shoes. "But how?"

"I don't have an answer, but we're heading north to find the one man who might."

"Who?" she asked, thoroughly confused. How the hell had he come up with all this?

"Joey's partner, Willis Conroy. You said he's still alive, and if there's anybody who can tell us what's up with these shoes, it'll be Conroy."

The impact of his answer shocked her . . . yet, as far-fetched as it sounded, it also carried a ring of truth.

"The hit tonight wasn't directed at you, Lili. They were trying to take out your protection, which tells me you have something they want. The only thing I can come up with are the shoes."

Again, Lili looked down. Acquiring Rose McIntyre's dancing shoes had been an indulgence, a guaranteed attention-getter, and the big draw for both her public Chicago lectures—

The lectures . . .

That was how they'd known; it had to be.

"Your lectures were advertised in advance," Matt said, as if he'd read her mind. "The shoes were featured in campus bulletins and newspaper publicity ads—I checked that first day. You had the shoes with you at the Art Institute, and your attackers knew it. Once they realized you'd hired bodyguards, they decided to try for them at your suite."

Lili turned, staring out at the blackness of night, seeing nothing but the pale reflection of her own face, her eyes wide, her mouth pulled into a tight line.

Publicity was a given in her work; she used it whenever possible, but had never once considered how it could be used against her.

"They could've gotten past the hotel security guard if they'd wanted to," Matt said. "These guys were working with orders not to kill unless necessary, and when they didn't get into your suite, they waited until the fund-raiser. After failing twice, they decided not to play nice anymore. The plan was to get rid of your bodyguards and grab you, just in case you knew something."

"At that first attack, if I'd just dropped the shoebox, then none of this would've happened. Manny and Dal wouldn't have been hurt."

Hurt. What a weak euphemism. The thought of Dal made her sick all over again. Was he even still alive? Lili wondered about his wife—Jodie, she now had a name—and how she was dealing with it all.

When Lili turned back to Matt, waiting for his answer, she saw his expression had turned hard, bleak.

"Maybe," he said. "I don't know for sure. This is just a guess."

A pretty good one, and on a sudden inspiration, Lili clicked on the dome light and then slipped off both shoes. She intently examined them, and ran her fingers along the insoles, the leather still warm from her skin.

"What are you doing?"

"Feeling for a false bottom . . . these *were* custom-made shoes. I didn't notice anything when I first bought them, but I wasn't looking for anything beyond damage." She ran her fingers along the seams, pinched the outside and soles, feeling for any strange thickness, but found nothing. Turning the shoes over, she examined the caps of the blocky heels. "The heels are hollow, I think. Maybe Joey pried off a cap and hid a piece of paper inside the heel."

"A treasure map," Matt said, his tone wry. "Christ."

Lili shrugged. It did sound a bit melodramatic. "Maybe he stashed the money, planning to come back for it later when it was safe. Who knows? It seems like an awful lot of trouble to go through for a bag of old money, though."

Matt glanced at her, looking as if he might say something more, but instead motioned to the shoes in her lap. "Were the heels tampered with?"

"I can't tell in this light. There's a lot of wear on these, but once we stop and find a knife or screwdriver, I'll know for certain." She switched off the light and regarded him, still amazed by his quick thinking. "When did you figure out the shoe part?"

"Before we met up with Monica."

While she'd huddled in the car, willing herself not to throw up or scream, he'd been saving their bacon *and* solving puzzles. That left her feeling more helpless than she liked.

"I never would've figured any of this out . . . I am so glad Jared hired me a genius bodyguard."

"I'm no genius, Lili. It's the most obvious answer."

"Not so obvious to *me*." She sensed something else behind his dismissive response—and it wasn't modesty. "You shouldn't sell yourself short, Matt. Why do I get the feeling you think you're only some grunt who operates with brute force, and not smarts?"

He was silent for so long that she thought he wouldn't answer. Finally, he said, "It's not genius, just street sense."

"What difference does that make? I—"

"I'm not going to argue with you," he said, his tone irritable. "Drop it."

Not wanting to provoke a fight, she again forced back her anger. "Willis Conroy has to be well into his nineties by now. His mind could be gone."

"It's worth a shot."

"And if Conroy gives you the answers you're after, then what?"

He paused. "I haven't thought that far ahead."

Lili watched him, not missing his closed expression. "I don't believe you."

Matt stared at her, but she didn't back down before his chilly glare. She was on to his tricks by now, how he worked this whole intimidation business.

Unexpectedly, a rueful smile curved his mouth. "Okay, you're right. I wasn't going to say anything yet because I don't want to scare you, but I swore I wouldn't coddle you like everybody else—"

"*Coddle*?" she repeated, offended.

"Your family and friends baby you along, Lili, and you know it. You said so yourself at dinner."

Her pride demanded she deny it, but she sighed and said, "Sometimes I'm not the bravest woman on the planet, I admit that, but I can handle the truth."

"I should've told you right away," he said at length. "Sorry."

The apology helped soothe her bruised pride. "So what's your plan?"

"If this is about Joey Mancuso's last heist, and if we can find his missing bag and turn it over to the police, along with the shoes, we neutralize the problem. Then these goons have no reason to come after you anymore."

"Oh." A sick feeling settled in the pit of her stomach. "I think I see a problem with this."

"I figured you would."

"Those goons might put two and two together and come up with Willis Conroy, too."

"They probably will. That's why I waited to tell you. I wanted to think it over first, get everything straight in my head. Finding Joey's bag, instead of just holing up in a room somewhere in the sticks, could be dangerous. I don't want to risk your safety without your consent."

"And you're afraid I might turn into a shrieking idiot in a crisis moment."

He arched a brow at her, his expression doubtful. "You're stronger than you think you are, Lili."

"Thank you," she said, as a warmth of surprise and gratitude spread through her at this unexpected compliment. "Nobody's ever said that to me before."

Their eyes met, and a corner of his mouth tipped upward. "Follow your own advice—don't sell yourself short."

She blinked back a sudden sting of tears, and told herself not to make too much of it.

"Why not tell the police about your suspicions?"

Matt stretched in the seat, and rolled his shoulders. "Not a good idea. Crime syndicates have access to information in places you wouldn't believe, and no police department is leak-free. There's always somebody who'll talk—either because they're stupid, or because they're greedy."

Lili weighed the risks. She didn't much like his plan, but it had a certain simplicity that told her it might work. "Well . . . sign me up for the treasure hunt. I'm sick and tired of these creeps messing with my life."

The fierceness of her voice startled even her, and when Matt looked at her, he smiled. "That's my Lili."

My Lili . . .

She smiled back before turning her attention to the window, staring out at the blackness. She shouldn't make too much of that, either. It wasn't like they had something permanent going on here. The sooner they found that stupid bag—if it existed at all—the better. She had a life to get back to, and so did Matt.

The thought thoroughly depressed her.

After they passed through a toll booth, Matt turned the radio to an oldies station, keeping the volume low. He drove with intense concentration, and Lili assumed he was busy making more plans. She didn't disturb him.

Shortly after passing through Rockford, however, disturbing him became a moot point. She shifted uncomfortably in her seat, sighed, and tapped Matt on his arm. "I really have to use the restroom."

He nodded, and then yawned widely. "There's a wayside coming up. We can stop there. I need to walk around, anyway."

She glanced down. "Even with the wrap on, I can't hide all of the dress, much less the shoes. We'll be noticed."

"It's either the wayside, or I pull over on the side of the road and you take your chances in a ditch. Can't guarantee you won't find anything nasty in all that long grass, though."

"No ditches," she said hastily. "Have you decided yet where we're going?"

He gave her a brief, considering look. "I'll need to gas up the car by the time we cross the Wisconsin border. After that, we drive up to Big Moccasin Lake."

Where Rose and Joey had died all those years ago. She shivered, finding the whole notion creepy.

"I figure we have a few days before they figure out where we went, but I'm not planning on hiding out at the old lodge, just close by. I'll decide exactly where when we get there, after I've looked around."

"How long do you think we'll have to stay in hiding?"

"As long as it takes." He glanced at her when she groaned with frustration. "I know it's an inconvenience, Lili, but it's for the best."

"I'm not arguing, but I'm tired . . . of the fear, of wondering where the next attack is coming from. And I am so afraid for you," she admitted softly.

His jaw tensed. "I don't plan on making myself a convenient target again."

Not as certain of his invincibility as he was, and knowing he wouldn't appreciate her saying so, Lili fell silent. A short time later, after crossing the Wisconsin border, Matt pulled into the welcome rest stop. The place was mostly empty, although a number of RVs and semis were parked nearby, some silent and dark, others with their running lights on and engines idling.

Lili looked around, suddenly uneasy despite the urgency of her needs. "I'm not sure this is a good idea."

"I don't see anybody except two people talking by the

Trams Am. Could be worse: could be daylight, with this place packed, a state trooper or two hanging out. The bathrooms are inside the building. I'll come with you."

She nodded, opening the door. It creaked loudly, and the young couple cuddling on the hood of their red Trans Am glanced over at the noise.

Matt hesitated, then reached behind him for the fedora. He put it on with a grimace, and pulled the brim low over his face. "If anybody asks, we're on our way back from a Halloween party."

Again, Lili nodded. More little details she'd never have considered. Thank God she had Matt between her and this ever-present shadow of danger.

The young couple swiveled around to stare when she passed by, the hem of her skirt sparkling. But their astonishment turned to unease when they caught sight of Matt.

Maybe he should've left the fedora in the car; obviously he looked a little too much the part. Then again, maybe it was the blood.

"Halloween costumes," Matt muttered. "Bonnie and Clyde."

"Okay," said the man, moving protectively in front of his girlfriend. "Except Halloween's not for a couple weeks, man."

"It was an early party," Matt retorted, and the girl flinched at the tone of his voice.

Lili gave the couple a forced smile as she grabbed Matt's arm and yanked him forward. Thankfully, no one was in the rest stop building, so there were no more awkward questions. After she'd finished up and he'd cleaned himself off as best he could, they walked back to the car. Lili wasn't surprised to see the Trans Am gone.

Within minutes, they were on the road again. The next half hour passed in a tense blur before Matt drove into a sleepy little town and pulled up at a mini-mart gas station.

After filling up the car, he motioned her to follow him inside.

"Shouldn't I stay in the car?" she asked, uneasy.

"I want you where I can see you. And it's not like you'll be any less conspicuous sitting out here under the lights, in full view of the attendant. He's already staring," Matt said. "Just play the Halloween party angle."

Once inside, he piled a Wisconsin map, two cups of thick black coffee, and two sub sandwiches on the counter, all under the uneasy gaze of the young attendant.

"Had an interesting night, huh?" His voice cracked, and he eyed the dark stain on Matt's coat sleeve.

"A shoot-out." Matt fixed him with that flat, steely stare from beneath the brim of the fedora. "That's all."

Lili darted a glance at Matt, then caught the attendant's nervous gaze. The poor guy probably expected to be robbed at gunpoint at any second.

"Just a joke," Matt said, as he headed toward an aisle. "Halloween party."

Lili stayed by the register, and smiled. The attendant didn't smile back.

Matt returned with a roll of gauze, antibiotic ointment, Tylenol, and bandage tape. The young man looked at the first aid supplies, then at Matt's sleeve—and went absolutely white when Matt reached inside his coat.

"Ring it up," Matt said, taking out his wallet. "And twenty bucks in gas."

Lili let out a soft sigh of relief when they left the gas station and staring attendant. By the time Matt pointed the rumbling jalopy north, the dashboard clock read 2:02 A.M.

"That kid thought you were going to rob him."

"I know. I was waiting for him to hit the alarm."

Lili wondered what Matt's response to that might've been, and was glad she hadn't had to find out. "Do you think he believed your party story?"

"People tend to believe what makes sense, and selling gas and coffee to two people in costume who'd been in a shoot-out doesn't make much sense."

"Well, I think you could've got by without telling him about the shoot-out part." Lili sipped at the coffee, frowning. "That's just tempting fate."

"Look, I need to catch some sleep," Matt said, his tone suddenly weary. "The map shows a rest stop outside Briggsville, about an hour away. We'll stop there. It should be more secluded than the last place we were at."

A little more than an hour later, Matt spotted the rest stop sign and suppressed a groan of relief. If he didn't pull over soon, he'd probably drive the car into a ditch.

"Strange, isn't it?" Lili said abruptly, as a huge semi truck blew past, its outlining rows of orange runner lights making it look like a carnival ride. "It all seems so unreal, like a dream. Not so long ago you were kissing me, and now . . ."

She trailed off, as if she had no idea what she meant to say, and this time, Matt did sigh. He'd kept her at a distance, his temper too brittle to deal with anything but the most immediate problems at hand. Now, it was time to face the consequences of that kiss.

Even if he'd knowingly, deliberately, discarded ten years' worth of training and his own code of ethics, it didn't make dealing with it any easier. Maybe if he hadn't been so wrapped up in Lili, if he'd been more on top of things, he might've realized what was going on. He might've saved his team.

Christ. He couldn't have picked a worse time to go all romantic like this. "About that kiss—"

"If you say you shouldn't have done it," Lili cut in sharply, "I swear I'll take your gun and shoot you."

Matt eyed her warily as he turned off the highway. She

looked pissed-off. "Forget it. We can talk later. I really need to get some sleep, Lili."

She sighed, then slumped back against the seat as he parked and turned off the car. "I know. I'm tired, too." She sent him a look from beneath her lashes, and in the low light, he could see the shadows of exhaustion marking her face. "And I'm sorry for snapping at you like that."

"It's okay. We're both wound a little tight." He glanced away, resisting the need to touch those tired lines on her face and smooth them away. What they both needed was sleep, not messing around. "You can stretch out in the back. You'll be more comfortable there."

"What about you?"

"I'll stay up front."

He wasn't sure he trusted himself, despite his exhaustion, but he also needed to be alone, shielded from her watchful glances, her questions. Just for a little while.

Not that he could tell her this—she'd only misunderstand, and feel hurt. Matt got out of the car and helped her from the front seat to the back. He returned to his seat, locking all the doors, then surveyed the situation. It wouldn't be comfortable, but he'd make do. Bench seats came in handy, after all.

He watched her from the rearview mirror as she fussed and shifted, then finally settled, curled tightly for warmth. He wished he had a blanket for her.

Turning, he asked, "You want my coat?"

She shook her head. "I'm all right, thanks."

She looked so forlorn, curled up back there—but a goodnight kiss didn't seem right just now. His friends were shot up and hurting—what right did he have to think of kissing a pretty woman, or even expect to sleep comfortably?

Enough of that. He couldn't afford the distraction of

what-ifs or guilt. He couldn't protect Lili if he was half-dead from lack of sleep.

He faced forward again, and searched for the handle to recline his seat. Finding it, he eased the back down a few inches, rested his hands across his belly, fingers laced, and closed his eyes.

Minutes passed, but sleep didn't come. His arm ached like hell, but he'd already done everything he could for it, and as he listened to Lili shifting restlessly behind him, the vinyl upholstery creaking with her every movement, images played in his mind again and again: kissing Lili under the staircase, fixing the rose in her hair, the grin Dal must've had on his face when he made that last smart-ass comment, and Manny's blood, so dark against the pale concrete sidewalk.

He slowly breathed in, rubbing the heels of his palms against his closed eyes as if that could wipe away the bad memories, and all the while the grim images whirled around in his mind, jumbled thoughts plagued him.

Those damn shoes—he couldn't stop thinking about them, or about Joey Mancuso and his missing bag. The risks he was taking troubled him, along with doubts that a geriatric ex-gangster would be any help at all, or that after so many years, even Monica's pit bull stubbornness would turn up anything helpful.

After nearly seventy years, what the hell could be in that missing bag worth all this trouble? Lili was right; it had to be more than money.

The backseat creaked again, and Lili whispered, "Matt?"

Slowly, he opened eyes to the black sky above, filled with billions of tiny dots of light, and his senses slowly registered his cold hands and the sting of pain, his stiff muscles, and a dull throb behind his eyes from stress and exhaustion.

"Yeah?"

"I'm cold."

"You want me to turn on the car heater?" he asked, but he knew what she really wanted.

He wanted it too, thinking Lili could chase away this dark, bone-deep chill in a way that no blanket or heater could. At least for a little while.

"No. I thought you might be cold, too." She hesitated, then said, "I was wondering if we could share a little body heat. That's all."

Her coldness wasn't anything like his, he knew, but the night had a nip to it—he could smell fall in the air, hear the dry rustle of dead leaves, and almost taste the edge of frost in the wind.

"So you want me to come back there with you?" He still hadn't turned to look at her, only continued to stare up at the stars. Sometimes it amazed him, how bright they were. And how many, many, many . . .

Eternity, right there above him, and no limits. Facing such vastness, it seemed stupid beyond belief to turn away from her comfort. How could being with her even matter in the greater scheme of things? Tonight, with his mood brittle and dark, he couldn't help wondering if everything he'd struggled with his whole life mattered at all.

Maybe life was nothing more than grabbing whatever came your way, as fast as possible, because you never knew if the next minute somebody might put a bullet through your brain.

Realizing Lili hadn't answered, Matt glanced over his shoulder at her. She still huddled in the corner of the seat, covered in her wrap, watching him with those wide, all-seeing eyes—as if she understood what was going through his mind.

"Is that what you want, Lili?" he repeated softly.

She nodded and whispered, "Yes."

Matt climbed into the backseat, cursing under his breath when he bumped his head, then angled himself into the seat beside her. Staring at his hands, clasped loosely between his knees, he wondered what to do next.

She must've sensed his discomfort, because she took his hand in hers. The coolness of her skin surprised him.

"You're still with me, right?" she asked, angling her head to one side, studying him intently. "I have a feeling your mood's pretty dark right now."

He looked at her, more curious than surprised. "How do you know?"

"Must be one of those women's intuition things." She squeezed his hand. "You don't have to deal with it alone."

Her words were so simple and her voice so quiet—and yet a sharp grief ripped through him, wound tight with a need to salvage some softness from the night's harsh reality, to seek warmth from the cold, maybe find some peace of mind . . . and reach out for a woman's touch, to ease that deep hurt inside.

"Come over here, Matt, and hold me. I don't want to be alone, either. Only I don't do this macho bullshit, so I can ask for what I need."

Matt smiled, desperately grateful for the gentle humor that kept him from spinning off into the darkness pushing at the edge of his consciousness.

Taking her place in the corner, he drew her onto his lap and wrapped her in his arms against his chest, where she snuggled against him like a kitten. She was shivering; he could feel the faint vibrations and he tightened his arms.

Taking in a deep breath, he whispered, "I love the way you smell. Like incense inside a church . . . like you're holy."

She looked up and smiled. "I may be a good girl, but I'm not *that* good."

The faint, musky scent of woman lingered beneath that

exotic, smoky perfume. It aroused him more than he expected, coupled with the softness of her body in his arms, and he reacted without thinking, lowering his head to her upturned face, and kissed her.

Lili made a low sound and grasped his lapels, pulling him closer. Her response was all Matt needed to coax her lips open and slide his tongue inside her hot, smooth mouth. He gave a growl of satisfaction as he tasted her.

She opened to him, her tongue stroking his own, pressing urgently against him, and making soft, needful sounds. He tilted his hips against her to ease the ache, shifting her on his lap until the soft roundness of her bottom rested over his erection.

Sliding his hands slowly upward, he pulled the pins out of her chignon, one by one, until he'd freed her hair and it filled his hands, heavy and warm and silky.

"I've wanted to do that for a long time," he murmured, spreading his hands wide and letting her hair fall, rippling and black, through his fingers.

She smiled, a flash of white in the darkness, before cupping his face in her hands and kissing him again, hard and hungry.

Her intensity took him by surprise, then he kissed her back as hungrily, as demandingly. She shifted, bracing a knee on one side of his legs, her other foot on the floorboard beside his, her hips moving against him in an insistent rhythm that totally fried clear thinking.

All exhaustion fled. Matt slid his hands to her hips, and then lower, easing the heavy beaded fabric of her skirt upward along her legs. His questing fingers found silky stockings, the lacy elastic of a garter belt, and, above that, the smooth warmth of her thigh.

"Jesus," he muttered, kissing the side of her neck as he pushed the wrap down her shoulders. Her arms were warm, yet he could feel goose bumps all along her skin.

Lili made a contented sound as she ran her hands up and down his chest, then whispered, "You have on more clothes than I do. No fair."

Matt kissed his way along the swell of her breasts, up the line of her neck to her chin, and met her heavy-lidded gaze. She wore a half-smile on her shadowed face, and he said, "Easy enough to fix."

As Lili watched, he eased out of his suit coat and shoulder rig. Frowning, she touched the bloodied sleeve. "You're hurt. Maybe we shouldn't—"

"Don't worry about it." Like he'd let a little blood stop this.

"You're sure?" she asked, and when he nodded, she began unbuttoning his vest. After she tossed it aside, he leaned back toward the door so they could stretch out. Ignoring the window handle jabbing him between the shoulder blades, he reached for his shirt buttons, but Lili pushed his hands away.

"Let me . . . I've wanted to do this for a long time."

He sat absolutely still as the deliberate progress of her fingers, lower and lower toward his erection, knotted his gut. He welcomed the cool night air on his chest. God, he was perspiring like some nervous kid with his first girl.

His exhaustion left him hypersensitive, and he was very aware of Lili's long nails trailing down the skin of his belly, her breath tickling his cheek, and the faint swish-swish sound the beaded skirt made as she moved.

A quick glance showed all the windows were steamed up. *Good.*

Lili had pushed his shirt open and started working on his belt buckle when Matt grabbed her hands, and murmured, "Hold on. It's my turn."

Without protest, she let him press her back on the opposite side of the seat, and he slid his folded coat behind her head as a pillow. The parking lot lights—a pale smear through the fogged windows—provided just enough illumination for her beads to glisten as he pushed her skirt upward, revealing a white garter belt and her stockings.

"I've always had a thing for garter belts," he said, and his muscles tensed with anticipation. God, there was nothing sexier than a woman in stockings.

"I was aiming for authenticity." Her breath caught as he ran his finger up along her thigh and traced the elastic of her white lace panties.

"As if anybody was going to know."

She sighed, her hips rising to meet his fingers. "I was hoping at least one body in particular would notice."

Matt's fingers stilled their soft stroking. "You mean me?"

"Don't be dense, Matt. I've wanted to get you down to your underwear for days."

Her admission filled him with fierce satisfaction, and he smiled as he slid the tip of his index fingers inside the elastic of her panties, brushing against the soft hair there, feeling her moist heat. Lili's eyes fluttered closed, and her lips parted.

Watching her response aroused him almost to the point of pain, and he couldn't wait one second longer. Matt leaned forward and kissed her as his finger traced her sex, dipping lower.

"God, I want to make love to you," he murmured against her mouth as she let out a soft "oh" of pleasure. "I want to be inside you. Right now."

"Yes," she said, more a moan than a word. "Oh, please . . . I swear I'll start screaming if you don't do something really fast."

"You don't want fast."

"Yes I do! I do . . ."

"Whatever the lady wants," he whispered, raising his chest and hips so that she could unfasten his belt and open the zipper of his trousers. "She gets."

The next thing he knew, her soft, warm hands were on him, stroking his erection with an unmistakable urgency.

"That feels so good," he managed to say, eyes closed, totally focused on the touch of her hands, on the tight desire and obliterating need sweeping over him.

"Mmmm," she sighed, her hips again rising against his hand. This time, as he slipped his hand below her panties, he pushed his finger into her and heard her gasp.

He nearly lost it right then and there. The hot, moist feel of her was too much. Too much.

Lili made a soft mew of protest when he slid his finger out, but he deftly unfastened the stockings from the garter belt. Then he eased her panties down, along with the stockings and shoes, and tossed all the soft, feminine things aside.

His only thought was to be inside her, to find release and ease in her body and the soft comfort of her arms—and to give her the same, to show her, better than words ever could, how he wanted to care for her.

Matt pushed the dress up past her hips and moved over her, his erection nudging her. He braced a hand above her head and slid the other upward, over her belly and beneath her bra, and cupped the soft roundness of her breast. Her nipple was taut and hard against his palm. He rubbed his thumb over the tip, and she arched beneath him.

"Now," she whispered. "Matt, don't make me wait . . ."

"Okay," he breathed, angling his hips against her, feeling himself slide inward—until a sudden realization stopped him cold. "Ah, damn . . . Lili, I don't have a condom. Please tell me you're on the pill . . . on something, anything."

Lili went still, and her eyes snapped wide. "Oh, God," she moaned, and he heard the answer in her voice, thick with frustration.

Matt rested his forehead on hers, struggling to get his breathing under control—as well as the urge to bang his fist against the side of the car.

"Shit," he snarled, as he pulled out of her.

She wriggled, clearly as frustrated as he was. "Maybe if you—"

"No," he cut her off, his voice roughened with the need hammering away at him. "I won't risk that."

To his surprise, Lili burst out laughing. Disgruntled, Matt stared at her, not finding the situation at all amusing. At this rate, he'd have to lock himself in a bathroom and take his hand to himself before he went crazy.

"I'm sorry," she said with a soft chuckle. "It just struck me as kind of funny . . . tonight you were shot at, saw your friends nearly killed, and you stole a car. But you won't make love to me without protection because it's too risky."

Put that way, his refusal sounded pretty damn lame. His anger faded. "I'm supposed to be protecting you, Lili, not knocking you up."

She frowned. "Don't be crude."

Matt moved away to sit next to her, and dropped his head back against the seat. He cleared a small space in the back window, and the stars twinkled merrily down on him. "I'm not feeling very happy right now."

He hiked up his trousers while Lili groped around the floor for her underwear. She found them, and with a biting disappointment, he watched her slip them back on.

"I'm not exactly happy, either," she retorted a shade grumpily.

"If you want, I could . . . you know, take care of that," Matt offered.

A sudden heat flushed his face. What the hell was the matter with him? He'd never acted so knotted up or clumsy around a woman before—or felt even a twinge of embarrassment at discussing a basic sex act.

Lili smiled—which kind of pissed him off—and leaned over to kiss his cheek. "That's sweet of you, but I prefer a joint event. I can wait."

He rubbed at his jaw, feeling the rough beard stubble. No razor. No clothes. No condoms. Sure, he was in total control of the situation.

"I guess we should just sleep," she said, and snuggled against him. "Good night, Matt."

"Yeah," he murmured, and smiled ruefully into her softly mussed hair. "Sweet dreams."

Matt tucked the wrinkled wrap around her, and a lump rose in his throat at the sight of her lying trustingly against his chest. No matter the cost, no matter the risk to himself, he had to keep her safe.

For a long while he remained still, listening to Lili's breathing grow slower and deeper. Her heat soothed him, soaking all the way into him, lulling him. He closed his eyes, unable to keep them open any longer, and, amazingly, fell sound sleep.

11

Conroy Cove Resort
Little Moccasin Lake, Wisconsin

Willis Conroy never wasted any more time than necessary on sleep. Figuring his number would be up soon enough, he might as well pass what time he had left doing something more exciting than snoring.

Not that he could do a hell of a lot, anymore. His niece Susie—grandniece, if a body wanted to get picky—wouldn't let him drink, and he hadn't had any nice juicy romance in over twenty-five years. These days he had to watch damn near everything he put in his mouth, and just walking down the road to the mailbox tuckered him out. What he could do was play cards, take short walks, and watch TV.

So here he was, at six in the morning, parked in front of the tube in the resort's lobby watching CNN. Behind him, the clattering racket and smells of frying eggs and bacon and percolating coffee told him Susie and her husband, Frank, were busy serving breakfast to the handful of guests who were hell-bent on squeezing in one more fishing trip before the lakes froze over. The Moccasin Lake chain was known for the best bass fishing in Wisconsin, and Susie and Frank did good business.

Over the drone of the TV and the buzz of voices, he heard the *clomp-clomp* of shoes coming his way.

"You're up early today, Uncle Willis. You want anything to eat? Coffee?"

Willis looked up at Susie. Sixty-something, thin as a rail, with short iron-gray hair and tanned skin weathered by years in the sun and wind, she was no beauty. But she always had a smile—even for him, the family embarrassment.

"Getting up early every day is what keeps me so young and good-looking." At her grin, he added, "Coffee'd be good."

"You got it. I'll be right back."

When Susie returned, she set a cup on the table beside him and said, "I don't know how you can watch the news all day. I think it's depressing. Wars here, plagues there, planes dropping out of the sky, kids killing kids . . . makes me afraid to walk out my front door."

Ignoring the palsy he couldn't do anything about, Willis had just raised the cup to his lips as Susie chattered on, when the anchorman said, "And in other news this morning, police in Chicago are baffled by a shooting at a fund-raiser late last night, involving fashion designer Lilianne Kavanaugh—"

"Quiet," he barked.

At once Susie stopped her yammering.

"—the second attempted assault on Ms. Kavanaugh this week. Few details are available, but two of Ms. Kavanaugh's security escort were wounded, one of them critically. Police have confirmed that Ms. Kavanaugh and the third member of her security escort were unharmed, but sources say that the police are unaware of Ms. Kavanaugh's exact whereabouts at this time. Angela Darling is on scene with the latest update . . ."

Slowly, Willis returned the cup to the table, his hands shaking so badly that he spilled the coffee.

"Don't worry, I got it." Susie whipped out her dishrag, which she always carried in her apron pocket, and wiped away the spill. She bent down, her expression concerned. "You okay?"

"Yeah. Damn shakes," he muttered. "It's hell, getting old."

Willis stared blindly at the screen, lost in old memories and a helpless frustration that he could do nothing but wait.

The last thing he wanted was to see anybody in trouble because of those shoes, or let another innocent girl die on account of his damn fool pride. He'd thought of calling the gal, this Lilianne, but knew he'd never find her. She was probably staying in some swanky hotel, and Chicago was full of swanky hotels with people who asked too many questions when they answered phones.

But one thing Willis knew for sure: Crazy Tony wanted Rosie's shoes, and he wouldn't give up. For years, the man had searched for the bag, and had questioned Willis more than once. It didn't sound like Tony had managed to get his hands on the shoes yet—and it sounded like the girl had been smart enough to make herself disappear. Maybe her hired gun had more brains than usual.

Once that designer gal or her bodyguard figured out it was all about Rosie's shoes, though, the old shit would hit the fan.

Goddamn, he'd thought for sure those shoes were lost for good.

"See what I mean?" Susie said in disgust. "Now they're shooting each other in *museums* . . . I don't know what this country is coming to."

"It's a shame people can't even have a little party without somebody getting shot. The trouble, see, is that nobody's got respect for nothing these days. In my day, I never killed nobody that didn't deserve it."

Not true; and he remembered bewildered eyes in a face not much older than his own, the badge shiny and new on the blue uniform. So puzzled, not understanding that what he was feeling was his own dying.

Susie frowned. "Don't talk about that. You know I don't like it."

His niece liked to keep her head in the sand about what he was. She didn't mind the many nights he'd spent entertaining her guests with the stories of his wild old days in Chicago—it was part of the draw of her place, and he was something of a local celebrity—but the men he'd killed were never, ever mentioned.

Ghosts were better suffered in silence. That way a man couldn't share the pain of it; he had to take the burden all on himself right to the end of his days.

12

"Have you decided yet what to do about our clothes?"

"I'm working on it right now," Matt answered, peering intently through the car window as they drove down a narrow country road out in the middle of what appeared to be endless miles of farmland.

Everywhere she looked, Lili saw red barns, herds of cows, and acres and acres of tall stalks of drying corn looking golden in the morning light. She had no idea where they were, or why Matt had turned off the main highway.

"I hate to break this to you, but I don't see any shopping malls," she said dryly.

"Forget malls." He slowed the car, his gaze sharpening. "The fewer people who see us the better."

Curious about what had caught his attention, Lili glanced out the window but saw nothing except another neat, square white farmhouse, with a red tractor parked outside the garage, bedsheets and clothing on a clothesline, flapping in the breeze—

She jerked straight in alarm. "Oh, no. Absolutely not. You are *not* stealing any clothes!"

Matt stopped the car, put it in reverse for a short distance, and pulled off the road by a copse of trees along a lazy little creek, hiding them from the farmhouse.

"It won't be stealing," he said, looking at her. "I'll leave more than enough money to cover the cost of overalls and old flannel shirts."

Lili shook her head. "It's a bad idea. We can just go to a store and—"

"No stores," he interrupted, his tone uncompromising. "I've got blood on my clothes, and by now the shooting will have made the news. The papers and news stations probably ran your photo, and I'm pretty sure the cops will know we're in Wisconsin. People may or may not make the connection if they see us, but I'm not taking that chance, dressed like this. The people after you will not hesitate to kill, Lili."

"What about staying at Moccasin Lake? People up there read the papers and watch the news, too."

"I know, but I'm trying to give us as much of a head start as possible. If Conroy can tell us where the bag is, we'll be in and out before anybody realizes what's happening. Then the local police can step in. At that point it won't matter if the cops, or anybody else, knows where we are."

She tried one last argument. "You could go to the door and offer to pay."

He shook his head. "They'll remember us, and word spreads fast in small towns."

"You still can't be sure they won't report a bunch of missing laundry to the cops, Matt."

"Maybe, but there'll be no way to connect it to us. They'll probably just assume some kids pulled a prank."

"Fine." She glared at him, letting him know she wasn't happy about his idea. "So how do you intend to do this without getting caught? And what am I doing while you're off stealing overalls and flannel shirts?"

For an answer, he popped the hood on the jalopy and turned on the hazard lights. "Keep the doors locked and windows shut while I'm gone. I'll leave the keys in the ignition in case you need to leave in a hurry." He slipped his cell phone out of his pocket and gave it to her. "If that happens, just park and wait. I'll find a phone and call to tell you where to meet me."

Obviously he'd thought this through.

"If someone stops, say you're having engine trouble," he added, "but you don't need help because your boyfriend's gone up the farm to use the phone to call for a tow truck. So keep the cell phone out of sight."

Lili arched a brow. "Boyfriend?"

"You gotta call me something." A faint red tinged his cheekbones, despite his even tone of voice. "I'm going through the woods, which come up against the back of the barn. I'll follow the barn around to the clothesline. The big tree up to the left will hide me from the house, and all the bedsheets are to the front of the clothesline, which will help keep me out of sight."

She stared at him in astonishment. "Is this something else they taught you in bodyguard school? How to rip off farms?"

"No." A sudden coolness settled over his face. "Quickly sizing up situations for points of entry and exit, potential areas of concealment, where trouble might come from and how to avoid it, is what I do for a living." He reached for the bag of money he'd hidden under the seat. "And for the last time, I'm not ripping anybody off."

"What if there's somebody in the barn?"

"Then I'll come back and we'll try some other place."

He watched her lock the door behind him, then disappeared into the woods.

Lili sighed and closed her eyes, dropping her head back against the neck rest. She didn't like this, even if she couldn't find much fault with his logic.

The hazard lights made an annoyingly rhythmic *tink-tink* sound as they blinked away, breaking through her attempt to relax, so she opened her eyes. The car keys dangling from the ignition caught her attention, and she noticed for the first time that the key chain was in the shape of a naked woman.

Smiling, she wondered what Mama Espinosa thought of her son's taste in key chains.

Her butt had gone numb hours ago, and she stretched, trying to ease her cramped muscles. How long would Matt take to do his thing? She wanted it over and done with already. She checked her watch, and sighed. He'd been gone for only five minutes.

She stared out at the woods and creek, her head resting on the seat. Without the distractions of the passing countryside and Matt's conversation, she couldn't stop thinking over what had happened earlier that morning.

Warmth flooded her as she recalled what Matt had done to her. Sometimes she wondered if it was all a dream, a delirium brought on by exhaustion—except patches of beard burn on her face, not to mention a lingering, aching frustration, told her otherwise.

She looked down at her tightly clasped hands, smiling ruefully. She'd daydreamed of what their first time would be like, of taking him back to her suite at the Drake and slowly seducing him, all sleek and sophisticated—nothing

about this morning had been sleek or sophisticated, just a
lot of heat and urgent need, like teenagers making out in
the backseat.

Not that it had been any kind of a disappointment;
God, not at all. Matt Hawkins kissed like a dream, and his
tongue and fingers had found all her hot spots, and he'd
known exactly what to do with them to make her mindless of anything else but making love with him and easing
that tight, delicious cord of tension. The touch of his
thumb on her breast had almost been enough to plunge
her into the shivery release of an orgasm.

If a little kissing and foreplay could do that, making
love with him would be absolutely wonderful. She had no
doubt he'd be an incredible lover—and despite the danger
and worry hanging over them, she couldn't wait to find
out just how incredible.

Lili shifted in discomfort, grimacing. Great; now she'd
worked herself into a state again.

She looked out toward the woods, thinking Matt had to
be as frustrated as she was, and wouldn't protest too
much if she dragged him into the trees. Maybe getting it
out of the way would make the long ride a little more tol-
erable. The lack of condoms was inconvenient, but there
were ways to get around that—

BAM!

The report of a gun cracked across the silence. With a
sharp inhalation, Lili froze—until a second shot galva-
nized her into action.

Her fingers shaking, Lili turned off the hazard lights
and unlocked the doors. She scrambled out of the car, ran
to the front, and dropped the hood with a loud clang.
After sliding back inside, she cranked the ignition and
shoved the passenger side door open, ready to go the instant Matt appeared.

If he appeared.

"Dammit," she hissed. "I told you it was a bad idea!"

She shifted the automatic transition into drive, one foot on the brake, the other on the accelerator, and through it all her anger grew—but beneath that pulsed a cold fear for Matt.

A split second later, he came crashing through the woods at a run, a bundle of clothes crushed against his chest and a grim expression on his face.

Throwing the clothes into the car, he jumped on the floorboard, grabbed onto the open door, and yelled, "Go, go!"

Lili hit the accelerator. The jalopy shot onto the road, tires spinning and spitting gravel. Matt, dangling half out of the car, slammed back against the door frame.

"What happened?"

"Just drive!"

Tightening her mouth to keep from screaming at him, Lili sped down the road and past the farmhouse. From the corner of her eye, she glimpsed a tall, paunchy man with a rifle. As he ran toward the road and their car, he fired again.

Cursing, hanging precariously with one hand on to the wildly swinging car door in a white-knuckled grip, Matt pulled his gun.

"What are you doing? Put that down!"

Ignoring her, Matt fired his gun into the air. Lili flinched at the noise, then twisted, looking back over her shoulder. The farmer had dropped into the ditch for cover.

"Lili, slow down so I can get in!"

She mashed the brake. The car jerked to a stop, the open door swung inward, and Matt yelped.

"Ow! Dammit, I said slow down, not stop!" He ducked into the car, his hair mussed, clothing askew, face damp with perspiration, and pulled the door shut. Glaring, he said, "Driving like that'll get you killed."

Through clenched teeth, she said "I live in New York *City*—I don't own a car! I take cabs, trains, or buses. Okay?"

"Okay." He eyed her for a long moment, his expression oddly tight. "So when was the last time you drove a car?"

Lili scowled, stomped on the accelerator, and roared back onto the road. Matt slapped a bracing hand on the dashboard.

"A while."

"Ah." A pause, then, "You do have a driver's license, right?"

"Yes!"

His face reddened, his pinched look deepening—and suddenly he burst into laughter. Loud, rolling belly laughter that engulfed the car as he sprawled in the seat, his head thrown back.

Lili darted a glance his way, torn between irritation and alarm at his lunatic response. "I don't find any of this amusing, Matt."

His broad grin, flushed face, and bright eyes—adrenaline obviously still running high—made it impossible for her to stay angry, despite her urge to throttle him for scaring her half to death.

"Yes, it is: My getaway driver doesn't *drive*!" Another spasm of laughter shook him. She glared, and he held up his hand. "Sorry. Really."

"You don't look it," she retorted and, catching sight of the speedometer, applied the brakes. Not with such a heavy foot this time, but she and Matt still snapped forward, then back against the seat. She winced. "Touchy brakes."

Matt rubbed a hand over his jaw, wiping the smile away. Mostly. "Pull over; I'll take it from here."

Lili did so, carefully bringing the car to a rolling stop.

"I'll squeeze over you while you slide to this side. I don't want to get caught out of the car in case our farmer friend decided to come after us."

After putting the car into park, Lili slid across the seat while Matt arched over her, brushing her breasts.

For a moment, they both went still. He glanced over his shoulder and caught her gaze. As a blush heated her cheeks, Lili looked away, focusing on the purloined clothes, well-worn denim and faded flannel, strewn across the floorboard.

"Nothing worth getting nearly shot for," she said, annoyed all over again. "What happened?"

"Bad break, that's all." Matt put the car in gear and drove back onto the road, not sounding at all upset. "That guy must have eyes like a hawk, because I swear nobody could see me from the house. I'd just pinned the money to the line when he fired. I didn't even know he was there. I grabbed the clothes and ran for it. I'm lucky I didn't catch a load of buckshot in my ass."

"So much for our low profile. Between this and the gas station caper last night, we may as well have walked into a Wal-Mart—it would've caused less attention." She glanced at him. "Do you think he'll call the police?"

"Hard to say. The money should keep him quiet, and I don't think the police would be too happy to hear he fired at me. On the other hand, I fired back, and he could be pissed-off enough to report what happened. The quicker we get out of here the better. Give me that map, would you?"

Lili handed him the folded map. He studied it as he drove, grunted, and put it aside.

"What?" she said, exasperated. "I'm not fluent in grunt. Is something wrong?"

"Nothing's wrong. I'm just thinking I should take the

back way north. We're more likely to avoid the highway patrol that way."

"Oh, great—now we're running from the police. If I get arrested, don't expect me to handle it with grace." She glared again at the pile of clothes on the floor. "Especially over a bunch of ugly clothes."

Wisely, Matt kept his mouth shut and drove along a route consisting of winding little country roads through more farmland. A half hour later, when he was sure they hadn't been followed, Matt turned onto a gravel road, and the car slowly rolled and bounced along until he stopped just below the crest of a hill, out of sight of the main road.

"Now what?" she asked.

"Now we change."

Lili looked around. Nothing much to see beyond a lot of rolling fields gone wild with tall grasses, wildflowers, and scrubby bushes. No handy buildings to duck into. No big trees to scurry behind for modesty's sake.

As if modesty mattered, considering what they'd already done. Still, daylight made things so much more awkward.

Oh, screw it.

Lili slipped out of her wrap and threw it in the backseat. Ignoring Matt, she grabbed the hem of her dress, raised her hips from the seat, and pulled the dress up and over her head. She gently tossed it over her shoulder, and heard it land with a soft *whump* on the seat.

Bared to the cool air, in nothing but a white lace bra and panties—the stockings and garter belt were still somewhere in the backseat—she shivered and pulled the scattered clothing onto her lap.

Then she risked a quick peek at Matt. He was looking at her breasts, and she cleared her throat, bringing his attention back to her face.

He didn't appear at all happy.

With a deliberate calmness, Lili said, "There's not much of a choice here. The overalls look way too big for me, so I'll take the jeans."

She dropped the overalls, plain white Hanes T-shirt, and a red-and-black buffalo-check flannel shirt on his lap. She slipped on the other flannel shirt, a basic blue-and-green Campbell plaid. Old and worn from many washings, it was soft on her skin and smelled of sunshine and fresh air. The shirttails nearly reached her knees, and she rolled up the sleeves so they didn't dangle past her hands. She pulled on the jeans, sighing when she saw how badly they gaped around her waist.

Matt was still staring at her. "I can't believe you just stripped in front of me. I was going to offer to step outside and turn my back to give you some privacy."

"Oh." So much for acting tough. "Well, I'm not showing anything you haven't already seen."

"True," he admitted, and took a long breath. "Except it was pretty dark, I was in a hurry, and I didn't get that good a look."

Flustered, Lili dropped her gaze. Without really thinking about what she was doing, she pushed his coat aside and poked at his belt. "I need this."

Silence, then, "My belt, you mean?"

She jerked her head back up and said tartly, "Don't get cute. After that stunt you pulled, I'm tempted to shoot you myself."

He grinned. "And I thought you were such a nice girl."

An answering smile almost eked past her guard, but she held it back and looked down again at his belt. "Be that way. I'll just take it off myself."

Ignoring his amusement, she began unbuckling his belt—only to stop when one of his large, tanned hands covered hers, holding her palm down over him.

He was aroused, and deep inside, her body answered with a sweet ache to the feel of him beneath her hand.

"I can unbuckle my own belt, Lil."

She looked at him through her lashes. "So you want me to stop?"

He arched a brow, all cool and controlled, but the expression in his eyes was rueful. "I'll take anything I can get right now. Even cheap thrills."

Lili laughed; she couldn't help it—but when his thumb caressed her, her laughter faded. Beneath her hand, he was hot and hard, and as she circled her palm tentatively over his erection, he sucked in his breath.

"Right." He abruptly removed her hand from his lap. "As good as that feels, we don't have time for it, and I've gotta change."

He removed his belt and handed it to her, then climbed out of the car. "Maybe some cool air will clear my head."

Lili considered doing the decent thing and not watching, but to hell with that. She wanted to get a better look at what she hadn't been able to see in the darkness, either.

She turned and looked through the rear window. He'd moved to the back of the car and was busy peeling away his clothes: coat, gun, vest, and shirt. When he dropped his pants, she smiled.

Black silk boxers. She *knew* it.

Opening the door, she slipped her feet into Rose's shoes, and then stepped out. When she moved into his view, he snatched up his trousers and held them in front of him, cheeks flushing darkly.

Enchanted by this unexpected show of shyness, Lili grinned and said, "Hi. Nice boxers."

"What are you doing?"

"What does it look like? I'm watching." Folding her arms over her floppy shirt, she tipped her head to one side and unabashedly enjoyed the view.

He had a body that showed exactly what was beautiful about a man. Muscular, but not overly so—broad-shouldered and narrow-hipped, he had a lean power she found irresistible. She liked the light dusting of dark hair that fanned across his chest, and how his ridged muscles flowed seamlessly as he moved. The bandage on his arm looked startlingly white against his tanned skin. He might not have the thick, blocky build of a Hollywood-style bodyguard, but she didn't doubt for a minute he'd move fast, and lethally, if the need arose.

Obviously uncomfortable, Matt shifted, but a small smile played at the corner of his mouth. "Can I get dressed yet?"

Lili gave an exaggerated sigh. "I suppose."

He hesitated, then tossed aside his trousers, and Lili noticed that while her presence might embarrass him, he didn't mind *that* much. Probably why he was holding his trousers to begin with, considering his state.

As she watched, he pulled a plain white T-shirt over his head. It was too small through the shoulders and chest, but she couldn't complain, considering how it looked on him. He pulled up the overalls, and fumbled with the unfamiliar contraption of buckles and straps. The scabbed wound still hurt him, and he moved his arm gingerly.

"A little short in the crotch," he said.

"You can make the straps longer. Here, let me help." She extended both straps as far as possible, then fastened them. Moving back, she gave him a critical once-over, and smiled slowly.

The bib rode low across his broad chest, and the baggy cut of the overalls only emphasized the fabulous muscles beneath the old T-shirt.

"My God," she said, and whistled in appreciation. "I never considered overalls sexy. I think I need to broaden my fashion horizons a little."

A flush marked his high cheekbones as he gathered his suit, folding it neatly before stashing it on the backseat. He folded her dress as well, and hid all the clothes beneath the wrap. A Chicago Bulls ball cap sat below the back window and he pulled it out, looked it over, and put it on, bill backward. Then he retrieved the cheap pair of sunglasses he'd found earlier in the glove box—black, with oval lenses—and slipped them on.

When he grinned at her, Lili stared back, dumbfounded by the transformation from grim-faced bodyguard to cute guy who, if he were ten years younger, would fit right in on any college campus.

"At least now we look like we belong in this car," he said.

Lili glanced behind him at the mud-brown, rusted-out jalopy with its big wheels and shiny hubcaps. He had a point.

His wing tip shoes suddenly snared her attention, and she grinned. "Houston, we have a problem."

"I know. There wasn't much I could do about the shoe situation." He lifted his shoulder rig from on top of the trunk. "We'll have to find a Wal-Mart or Kmart and buy a few decent clothes and shoes. And I need to call Monica to check on Manny and Dal."

Lili felt her smile fade. She'd been trying not to dwell on her worry and guilt; now it all came rushing back. What was wrong with her? How could she even think of flirting with Matt like this, after what had happened?

Her mood darkened, a shadowy foreboding fluttering at the back of her mind as she watched Matt check his gun and then slip on his holster. He pulled on the flannel shirt and buttoned it to hide the gun.

Matt caught her gaze over the top of his sunglasses. Lili didn't miss the sudden anger, the grim determination in his eyes, and a cold fear wrapped around her.

"You could've been killed back there," she whispered. Despite her efforts to stay strong, to be as cool and unemotional as he was, a tear rolled down her cheek.

"C'mon, don't do that," Matt said, grimacing. "Nothing happened to me. You don't have anything to worry about."

"It's not me I'm worrying about! I'm crying because I'm scared *you* will be hurt," she snapped, angrily wiping away the tear. "I feel so stupid. I want to be tough for you, and not drag you down—"

"Lili, you're not dragging me down. And what makes you think I need you to be tough?" he interrupted. "I don't need you to be like that, I need you to be—"

He caught her hand and pulled her against him, leaning back against the trunk for support. After removing the sunglasses, he cupped her face in his hands and looked directly into her eyes.

"I like your mile-wide romantic streak," he said with a quiet intensity. "And I like how you throw yourself into everything you do. Okay?"

Still embarrassed—and feeling a tingle of pleasure at his words—she buried her face against the warmth of his chest.

"I have enough hard people in my life," he said as he moved his hands to her back, cradling her. "I don't need any more."

Lili wound her arms around his waist and, for a brief moment, it seemed he held on to her as tightly.

Squeezing her eyes shut, she said into his chest, "I hate your job, Matt."

His body stiffened, and she gathered his shirt in her fists, half-afraid he would try to push her away—and she wouldn't let him do that.

"Yeah, I know, but I do all right at it, and there's not a lot of jobs out there for guys with résumés like mine." His voice was cool, but she detected no bitterness, sensed no shame or apology—just a flat statement. "I don't see that you've got much to complain about. I'm keeping you safe."

Lili shifted, looking up into his dark, grim face. "But at what cost?"

His eyes were shuttered to her, and she couldn't read him at all. "Most of the time, the job is boring. Most of the time, I don't even carry a gun."

Not exactly the answer to her question.

"Try telling that to Jodie Farrell and see if it makes her feel any better."

Anger suffused his face. "Dammit, Lili, that's not—"

"What? Not fair?" she cut him off, narrowing her gaze. "What happened to Dal wasn't fair, either, was it? And for what, money? Was it enough to risk dying for, or having his entire life altered in a split second?"

He regarded her for a moment. "It's not that clear-cut. What I do isn't pretty or nice, but people like me are all that stands between the monsters and people like you. I make the monsters invisible, so you don't have to think about them."

"I know that, but I still don't like it." She took a deep breath, and even knowing it was impulsive and illogical, added in a rush, "I care about you, Matt. A lot."

He didn't respond, and with his lids lowered, she couldn't tell if he was pleased or angry or surprised.

"Thank you," he said, his tone almost painfully careful. "I appreciate your concern—" He broke off, as if searching for what else to say, and a sinking feeling settled in the pit of her stomach.

How embarrassing. She'd revealed her innermost feelings to him, and for all she knew, he was just looking to her for a good time.

"But it's not something you need to worry about," he

continued. "Once your life gets back to normal, you'll forget about me, and what happened between us won't seem important anymore."

A sudden, icy anger washed over her. "Is that supposed to be comforting?"

"It's the truth. I'm not denying there's an attraction between us, Lili, but it won't last. And it shouldn't . . . you and me, we don't exactly move in the same circles. After you're home, after you've put some distance between us and had time to think, you'll see I'm right."

"What if you're wrong?" His words hurt; he made it sound so trivial, and her feelings for him were anything but trivial.

"I'm not. Not about this."

He sounded tired, and for an instant she glimpsed a weariness in him, an old and long-standing weariness that triggered an instinctual need to comfort and protect, and she ached to hold him in her arms.

"A threat to your safety is all that's keeping us together," Matt said, avoiding her gaze. "Once the threat is eliminated, we move on."

Lili watched him, torn between accepting his answer and her certainty that their deepening feelings for each other weren't as temporary as he wanted her to think.

She also wondered if perhaps he wasn't as certain of himself as he'd led her to believe. He'd seen Manny shot, was grappling with the possibility that Dal might die—and the undeniable fact that it could just as easily happen to him.

The thought made her shiver, and she pressed closer against his warmth. He cupped her face again, tipping it toward him, and he stared at her—and this time, she couldn't miss the turmoil in his gray eyes.

"Ah, damn," he whispered, and kissed her.

Hard this time—no gentleness at all—and angry. At

her, at himself, it didn't matter, not now. She returned his kiss with the same anxious, angry intensity, gripping his shirt in her fists.

Matt slid his hands downward, and under her shirt. His hands were warm and rough, and rested a moment on her belly before moving up to her breasts. He cupped her breasts in his hands, rubbing her aroused nipples through the lace, and then he slipped his fingers beneath her bra.

Lili sighed with the pleasure, wanting it, and guilty for wanting it, but not protesting as he lifted her and set her on the trunk.

He moved between her legs and pressed her down against the sun-warmed metal, still kissing her, his hands on her breasts, teasing and promising. Desire wound through her, aching and taut.

She didn't even realize she was crying again until he kissed the tears from her cheeks, murmuring her name, his kisses and touch suddenly gentled. He kissed her eyelids, her nose, chin, and neck, as he pushed up her shirt, then her bra, and finally the hot, wet heat of his mouth closed over her breast, teasing, before moving to the other. His tongue caressed her nipples, and the need to have him inside her, moving hard and deep and strong, swept through her.

Damn him, damn . . . damn . . .

"Don't," she whispered.

He looked up at her, his face dark against the paler skin of her breasts. "You want me to stop?"

"No," she said on a long sigh. "But don't try to distract me like this. It won't work, Matt . . . I won't forget."

He gave a low, frustrated groan and pulled away.

"You're going to drive me crazy," he said, sounding more resigned than angry. "You'd better get in the car before I do something stupid."

13

Lili waited in the car as Matt stashed their Wal-Mart bags—full of clothes, shoes, toiletries, bags of munchies, various odds and ends, a couple boxes of Trojans, and two cheap gold wedding bands—in the backseat.

The wedding rings had startled her badly; though she'd managed to quip dryly, "Hey, you don't have to marry me to have sex with me."

The elderly counter clerk hadn't been amused and Matt had flushed that telltale dark red color, but he hadn't said a word.

Now, as he got into the car, a more serious problem concerned her. "What did Monica say? How are they doing?"

"Manny's in surgery," he said, slipping on the sunglasses. He took a long breath. "Dal's doing the same."

She looked down, fighting the disappointment. It

would be too much to hope for, that he'd come out of his coma this soon.

"But it's not all bad news," he added, and cranked the ignition. "Monica gave me an address and number for Willis Conroy. Pine Lake Retirement Park, about an hour away from Big Moccasin Lake Lodge."

"Are we going there next?"

"Nope." Matt pulled out of the parking lot, and headed for the highway on ramp. "I called. He's gone to visit his niece." He smiled humorlessly. "Willis is back at the family resort, next door to where Mancuso died."

"Well, that's convenient."

"Yeah, it sure is."

"So we're going to the resort?"

"You got it."

He said it in a nonchalant tone, but a sudden fear fluttered in her stomach. "Are we staying there?"

"I don't know yet."

She shot him a glare, but he didn't notice, once again fixated on the road, on his inner thoughts, and on planning his moves. Unbuckling her seat belt, she reached over to the back and rummaged through the shopping bags until she found the screwdriver, penlight, and pocket knife.

"What are you doing?" Matt asked as she buckled up again.

"Looking to see if Joey Mancuso left us a handy set of instructions." She turned over one of Rose's shoes, and winced. "I hate this, though. It's like defacing a Leonardo da Vinci or something."

"People have been shot on account of those shoes."

"I know, but it's still hard." As carefully as possible, she pried off the heel cap, then took the penlight and peered inside. "It's hollow, all right."

"See anything?"

"No," she said, disappointed. "Maybe we'll get lucky with the other one."

Soon after, she had the other heel cap off and she sighed. "No luck. Nothing. Nada. Zilch."

"I guess a map would've been too easy."

"We could use a break," Lili said irritably. "Joey Mancuso was just a two-bit bank robber, not Einstein. Why is it we can't figure this out?"

"We work backward. Once we know what was in the bag, then we'll know how the shoes fit into it."

With some disgust, Lili stared at the shoes on her lap. "It's only money."

"There has to be something more," he said after a moment. "Gotta be."

"But what? Mike Riley was a bootlegger. He dabbled in prostitution, extortion, and gambling . . . all the usual vices, but that would've brought in nothing but cash. Maybe Joey made off with a lot more money than Mike Riley was willing to admit to."

"Maybe the money wasn't in bills."

Intrigued, Lili stared at Matt. "I hadn't thought of that. You mean like gold bullion or something?"

"Could be. It would hold up better over seventy years, too."

She frowned, turning to look outside, where the farms had given way to trees, mostly pines. "Where would Riley get hold of gold bullion during the Depression? Banks were failing left and right, and I can't see anybody stashing gold bars at speakeasies or next to the stills while they were brewing hooch."

"It's a long shot. Maybe Joey's boss didn't tell the truth. It wouldn't be the first time the crooks held back on the cops."

Lili sighed. "I hope Monica turns up a few answers fast."

"Conroy's gotta know something." He glanced at Lili. "What can you tell me about him?"

"Not much," she admitted. "I did most of my research on Rose. Willis worked for Mike Riley and met Rose when she was sixteen, probably through her mother's brothel, and was briefly involved with her. After Willis hooked up with Joey, he introduced him to Rose, and it was love at first sight."

Matt arched a brow in interest. "Joey poached his own partner's girl? Little bastard. How come Conroy didn't kill him for that?"

Lili shrugged. "Maybe he didn't care. Willis never lacked for lady friends. Later, when they started pulling bank jobs, Joey was the brains, and maybe Willis stuck by him as long as it was in his best interest to do so."

"How did Conroy know Mancuso was at the lodge?"

"They'd made plans to go to Canada together, and start over clean."

Matt looked at her, his expression skeptical.

"Well, that's what the book said, and apparently they split up to make hiding out easier. They intended to hook up again in Canada, and kept in touch by phone." The open windows admitted a breeze sharp with the tang of pine and loam, and Lili inhaled deeply. "When Willis was caught in Minneapolis, he bargained for a reduced sentence by giving away his partner to the police."

He peered over the top of his sunglasses. "Riley's men killed Joey, right?"

"Right. Half the cops and politicians in Chicago were on some mobster's payroll, and once the word was out, it was just a matter of who got to Joey first. Riley's men had the advantage because they didn't have to go through local red tape, like the bureau agents from Chicago did."

The wind whipped a lock of hair from her ponytail, and Lili tucked it back behind her ears. "The old couple who owned the lodge claimed Joey got a late night call the day after Willis was arrested in Minneapolis. Somebody must've tipped Joey off that he was in trouble, because the police said the getaway car was packed and it looked as if they were getting ready to run."

"But they never made it out."

"Riley's gunmen arrived first. Joey never stood a chance."

"What happened after Mancuso was killed?"

"The bureau agents and local deputies caught Riley's gunmen on the road, and there was another shoot-out," Lili answered. "The cops found the lodge's blood-stained outboard drifting on the lake, and later sent divers down to look for the bodies. They didn't have any luck, so Riley got away clean on the Mancuso killing. No bodies, no crime."

"What about Riley? And Conroy, what did he get?"

"Riley was gunned down a year later by bureau agents. Willis got life for armed robbery and murder, but his sentence was eventually reduced and he was released in 1978." She paused. "Does any of this help?"

"It sounds like a typical heist gone bad, with a bunch of greedy bastards double-crossing each other, and it tells me Joey wasn't very smart."

"He was smart enough to hide that bag," Lili said wryly. "And smart enough that nobody ever found it. People have looked, you can bet on that."

Matt didn't answer, and after a while Lili settled back in the seat. She yawned.

"Get some sleep," he said, glancing at her. "We've got a couple more hours to drive yet."

"As much as I'd like to, I don't think I can." She shifted, trying to ease the tight muscles of her legs and back.

"I could turn on the radio. Can't say we'll get much of a selection way up here, but it might help you relax."

She shook her head. "No, that's okay. I'd prefer to listen to you talk. I love your voice, I could listen to you talk for hours and hours."

Matt shot her a startled look. "You want me to *talk* you to sleep?"

"Something like that." Lili smiled at the incredulity in his voice. "If you don't mind, that is."

"What do you want me to talk about?"

"I don't care, as long as it's not depressing, or doesn't have anything to do with these stupid shoes."

"How about something guaranteed to put you to sleep?"

"Sounds good," she said, and closed her eyes, still smiling.

A moment later, Matt started talking quietly. His deep, even voice washed over her, comforting and familiar. And sexy. God, he had the sexiest voice.

When the actual meaning of his words penetrated, she almost opened her eyes. What was this? He was talking stocks and bonds, business plans, mission statements . . . it sounded like the sort of talk she'd heard from Jared.

Instead of putting her to sleep, it intrigued her. Finally she opened her eyes, watching him through lowered lashes.

"Are you thinking of starting your own business?" she asked, unable to hold back a wisp of hope that maybe, despite his repeated comments to the contrary, he wanted to ditch his dangerous job.

"I've reached a point in my life where I need to be doing more. I'll be leaving Armistead and Flannery to start my own agency." He didn't look away from the winding road. "You're my last assignment."

A sudden chill—and a dark premonition—swept over her at his words. To distract herself, she looked out the window. It was pretty, the fall colors just past their peak. In another week or so the trees would be bare, and the ground covered with brown, brittle leaves.

"You hungry?" he asked.

"A little."

"There's a restaurant coming up. I need something to eat, too."

The restaurant barely qualified as one. The first thing she saw was a crude, hand-lettered sign that proclaimed FOOD, and beneath that were the words: ARLENE'S EATERY.

Matt pulled to a stop and they both surveyed the tiny building. Its yellow, weatherworn plank siding needed a new coat of paint, and the gravel parking lot was uneven and riddled with potholes.

"There's cars in the lot," Matt said. "Maybe the food's not so bad."

A few minutes later, they were seated at a small table with a chipped Formica top. The linoleum floor was worn and old, and the faded papered walls were decorated with dime store pictures of country scenes. Arlene hadn't invested much in the decor, but at least the place looked clean.

A young waitress wearing an apron over her jeans and T-shirt took their order, then Lili and Matt sat back to stretch their legs and relax. A dozen or so people were in the diner, and a young family of four sat next to them. The mother was feeding and entertaining a baby in a high chair, her own plate of food untouched, while the father repeatedly told the little girl to sit still, for God's sake, and eat her food, not play with it.

From his high chair, the baby could easily see Matt. A new face was more interesting than the hot dog chunks on his tray, so he smiled at Matt, showing neat rows of little white baby teeth.

Matt smiled back, and waggled his fingers. Excited, the baby banged his fists on the tray, squashing the hot dog chunks—and earning a scolding from his mother. He retaliated by bursting into tears.

Matt turned away, rubbing the back of his neck as he looked at Lili. "Uh-oh. Guess I shouldn't have done that."

She smiled, finding his discomfort endearing in a rough sort of male way. "You don't hang around too many kids, I take it?"

"Nope."

"My sister Lauren has two kids, and I see them often. Kids are adorable, but they're a lot of work, too."

Matt peeled the wrapper from his straw and stuck it in his glass of Coke, his lack of comment conspicuous in itself.

A few seconds passed, and she asked, "Do you have any family?"

"Not anymore."

"Oh." His blunt answer left Lili momentarily startled. "I'm sorry."

"Don't be. I'm not."

"Okay," she said slowly. "My guess is that this is one of those subjects you don't want to talk about."

He watched her, sipping his drink. "You got it."

"Do you like kids?"

His brows lowered. "Yeah, I like kids."

"I'd like to have a couple, eventually. I don't think I'm ready for the whole motherhood thing just yet—much to my mother's despair. I'm her last hope for more grand-kids, because I think she's given up on Olivia."

"Olivia's the sister who keeps your business manager on a short leash?"

Lili laughed. "That's one way of looking at it. She's certain marriage will wreck her routines and nice, tidy lifestyle."

"So how come Sayers keeps chasing after her?"

"I guess he loves her. Between you and me, I think he should get a little more aggressive and show Olivia he means business."

"Sounds like your sister is playing hard to get."

"Of course she is. That's the way the rules of courtship work. A girl doesn't want to make it too easy on a guy." A sudden heat warmed her cheeks as she realized what she was saying—and how he might interpret it. Hastily, she added, "Unless there's a reason to make it easy, like extenuating circumstances." And being chased by ugly thugs with guns. "There's always an exception to a rule. But I'm sure you know that, since you're so big on rules."

Matt smiled, a slow, wolfish smile. "You better quit while you're ahead."

"Good idea." Relieved, she saw the waitress heading their way. Saved by a house salad.

They ate in silence, and while Matt seemed totally focused on his food, she still had dozens of questions plaguing her. Maybe if she asked often enough, she'd catch him off guard or wear him down so that he'd answer at least one or two.

"Tell me about this business you want to start," she said.

"Not much to tell. I want to start my own agency. That's pretty much it."

"A security agency?"

He nodded, popping a cherry tomato in his mouth. "That's where my experience and skills are. Security's the only thing I know how to do."

"I don't know about that. I was listening to you rattle

on about stocks and bonds, profitability assessment, cash flows, legal liabilities, and business plans." She dabbed a bit of salad dressing off her mouth with a paper napkin. "You have plenty of other skills and experiences you could put to use in something besides security. Starting your own business—"

"—is something a lot of people do, all the time. It's not a big deal, Lili. You have your own business."

"Except I'm not very good at the business end of things," she said as she watched him polish off the rest of his salad—and avoid her eyes "But I'd like to learn. Maybe you could teach me."

He snapped his head up in surprise. "Me?"

"Why not? What you were talking about earlier applies to me, too. That whole thing about market assessment . . . that's what Jared means when he talks about diversifying. The problem is, I'm not sure I want to." Warming to her subject, she leaned forward. "I design bridal shoes, so I'm always going to have a market. Brides and weddings will never go out of style, and while it's not as high profile as haute couture fashion, I don't care. I *love* designing bridal shoes."

He smiled. "I never would've guessed."

"Hey, I'm serious," she said, but smiled at his teasing. "In my line of work, you either get hired into a big name designer stable, or you strike out on your own. Most people who strike out on their own don't make it. That's why I set my sights on a very specific target market and started out small with local, privately owned boutiques, specialty shops, things like that. But I did well, and word-of-mouth started spreading, and now my designs are carried by the big department store and bridal chains. Rather than diversify, I'm thinking I should expand what I'm already doing. What do you think?"

She waited, nervous—and a little embarrassed at how hesitant she'd sounded to her own ears. She should've spoken up on her own behalf ages ago and dug her heels in with Jared, who could be quite persuasive when he wanted.

"Makes sense to me. If you're building momentum, capitalize on it. Changing direction might not be the best thing for you right now. In a couple of years you can reassess. I think you're right, and if somebody's trying to tell you differently, stick to your instincts."

Lili nodded, regarding him thoughtfully. "I will, thanks."

Their meal arrived, putting an end to further conversation. She cleaned her plate, and even ordered dessert—apple pie, with French vanilla ice cream. She hadn't realized she was so hungry.

Matt packed away half a baked chicken, mashed potatoes and gravy, green beans, and a roll. He declined dessert, but she did persuade him to eat a bite of pie and ice cream off her spoon.

Laughing, she tried to aim the heaping spoonful of pie into his mouth, and finally leaned across the table and slid her hand under his chin to hold him where she wanted him—and their gazes locked.

An unexpectedly intimate gesture, possessive, as if she had every right to touch this man, as if they shared a bond as close and private as that young couple with the children.

Lili put the spoon aside and, not caring what anybody thought, leaned over and kissed him, tasting apple and vanilla and cinnamon. She sat back down and licked her lips, still tasting him.

He looked mildly alarmed—but then, he'd looked like that for most of the day. He didn't think their attraction would last—but she wasn't so sure. What she felt for Matt had deepened, going way beyond that initial physical attraction. In only a few days, she'd begun to feel such a part of this man that she could read his thoughts and emotions from silences, from a tone of voice, a gesture.

He sensed it as well; he had to. Maybe he didn't realize the full extent of her feelings for him yet, but if she had anything to do about it, he'd soon see that they had a lot more to offer each other than just sex.

After the waitress brought the check, Lili made a quick stop in the restroom and then headed back to the car. Matt was already waiting for her, sitting on the hood. All over again, she was struck by his lean strength, his dark good looks—and how his gaze followed her. Always.

Being the center of attention of a man like this was empowering in a way she couldn't precisely identify . . . but very much liked.

Matt drove back onto the highway, and between the warm sun, her full stomach, and the flat ribbon of road surrounded by trees, she couldn't seem to keep her eyes open.

"Quit fighting it. Close your eyes and sleep," Matt said, his tone amused.

"You don't mind?"

"Not at all. I like watching you sleep."

Again, their gazes held, then he returned his attention to the road. With a small sigh, Lili reclined her seat and settled back, feeling completely safe, knowing that Matt was watching over her.

Lulled by the hum of the road beneath the tires, the gentle swaying of the car, Lili must've dozed off, because the next thing she knew, Matt was shaking her shoulder.

"Wake up, Lil. We're here."

Here.

She opened her eyes, blinking against the late afternoon sun, and stared at a weather-beaten sign: CONROY COVE RESORT . . . WORLD'S BEST BASS FISHING.

She faced Matt, who was again watching her over the top of his sunglasses, in need of a shave and looking incredibly sexy. "Well, what are we waiting for?" she asked. "Let's go find Willis Conroy."

14

"**H**old on." Matt grabbed Lili's arm as she made to leave the car. "Before we go in, we need to decide what to call each other. So far, I'm just the 'unidentified security escort,' but you've been named."

"So we use fake names."

"Two potential problems with that." He released her and sat back. "First, if we stay here, the manager may require a driver's license before giving us a room. That's standard practice. Second, if you slip up and call me by my real name, or forget to answer to your fake one, it'll raise suspicions."

She sighed. "I never thought of that. Okay, then we should use our real names?"

"I didn't say that, either. These guys after you probably know who I am. If they figure out we're up here, all they have to do is call around until they find out where I'm registered."

She looked confused, then understanding dawned. "You want me to make the decision."

"It's your neck as well as mine."

For a moment, she was silent, then said quietly, "Thank you."

Matt only nodded, and waited as she worked out the details for herself.

"Do you think we should stay here?" she asked.

"I drove around while you were sleeping. There's not much to choose from. This place is isolated, not to mention that Conroy is here. I'd like to stay, if you're all right with that. I think we have a few days before anybody catches on to where we went."

"But they might not catch on at all."

Matt searched her eyes for fear, but saw only determination—and was struck by sudden, unexpected pride that Lili, always worrying about being "tough," was holding her own with no help from him.

"It's a possibility. Not one I'd place any bets on."

"No, but you're the paranoid one."

Matt smiled. "I'd prefer 'prepared' over 'paranoid.' "

"Prepared . . . like buying those rings so we could pretend to be married." When he nodded, she rubbed at her brows. "You have a devious mind. Okay, I say we register as Matt and Lili Hawkins. The newspapers call me 'Lilianne,' and even if there's not much difference between Lili and Lilianne, it might be enough that nobody will notice, especially if we register as husband and wife. If those goons figure out where I am, they're going to find me, no matter how hard we try to hide."

"Exactly. It's more difficult to disappear than people think."

"So did I do well? Was that the right answer?"

"As right as it can be." He hesitated, studying her. "You're okay with this? Because I could turn the car around and drive you to Milwaukee, or right back to Chicago and let the police put you in a safe house."

"I won't be safe until we find out what's up with Rose's shoes. You're doing everything you can to protect me, and the police in Chicago are doing everything possible to find these guys. It's my turn to do my part in saving my own butt. So let's go and find Conroy."

Matt held up his hand. "One more thing. When did we get married?"

Lili rolled her eyes. "Last Saturday, of course. It's when you walked into my life, and it's not like I'll ever forget that."

He pulled out the rings he'd bought at Wal-Mart. He slipped on his ring first, then took her hand and slid the narrow gold band on her finger. He looked up. She was chewing on her lip, looking as uncomfortable about this ring business as he felt.

He let go of her hand. "Let me do most of the talking. I've more experience in bluffing than you do."

"You mean lying." She cast an arch look over her shoulder as she got out of the car and headed toward the scruffy log building with a sign marked OFFICE over the red door.

"It's not lying if it saves our butts," he retorted, placing his hand on her back. Again, his gaze lingered on the gold band. It felt strange—in a way he wasn't too sure he wanted to pursue.

Then they were through the door and facing a middle-aged man in jeans and a flannel shirt, his belly hanging over his belt. He had a round-cheeked, florid face, thinning gray hair, and a friendly smile.

"Hello! How can I help you folks today?"

With his arm around Lili, Matt stepped up to the desk and smiled back. "We're looking for a room."

"That's something I can help with. I'm Frank Sajcek, and I run the place."

"We just got married last week and—"

"Congratulations," Sajcek interrupted cheerfully. "We love newlyweds around here."

"Thanks." Matt gave Lili a squeeze to make the story look good—and it didn't hurt to have a reason to press her breasts against him. She blushed like a bride. "For our honeymoon, we decided to go hiking and fishing, and a friend of mine said there's good fishing up this way. Do you have any rooms?"

"Sure do. At this time of year, the main tourist rush is over. You kids want the honeymoon cabin? It has a fireplace and a whirlpool tub." The man's smile widened. "And it's a little more private from the other cabins."

Secluded was far better than he'd expected. "We'll take it."

"Four-fifty a week. And I need to see a driver's license and a credit card."

Four-fifty was reasonable, and shouldn't put too big a dent in his cash until he could get more. Matt hauled out his wallet and held it up, driver's license visible—and casually watched for any sign of recognition.

"All the way from Chicago, eh?"

Matt nodded, but didn't answer, not wanting to encourage conversation.

His lack of response didn't hinder Sajcek, though. "We get a lot of people from Chicago. Weekend refugees from the urban jungle, we call 'em. Without you flatlanders, I'd do a lot less business . . . and no offense by the flatlander remark," Sajcek added, grinning. "We love you Illinois people. I've got people in Illinois myself, and I'll tell you . . ."

Sajcek rattled on. The check-in didn't take long, and while Matt answered questions and fielded the ones he didn't want to answer, Lili slipped away and wandered toward the spacious lobby. To one side was a dining area with a large serving table toward the back. A lone man sat at a table, reading a newspaper and drinking coffee. Overstuffed sofas and chairs filled the other part of the room—along with a large TV, currently blaring the news.

Matt spotted the old man, sitting in a red plaid chair across from the TV, at almost the same time Lili did.

Shit!

"I'll need your signature right here, Mr. Hawkins," Sajcek said, forcing Matt's attention away from Lili.

He didn't really think she'd do anything stupid—like ask if he was Willis Conroy and if he knew Joey Mancuso—but having her over there, alone, made him nervous as hell. Quickly, he scrawled his signature, half listening to Sajcek's directions to the cabin.

Lili stopped beside the old man, and he looked up.

A shock of white hair and bushy white brows topped a face creased with age—the man easily looked ninety, and then some. Thin, frail . . . nobody would know from looking at him now that he'd been a killer, or the kind of man who'd double-cross a partner.

"If you need anything," Sajcek said, "all you have to—"

"Thanks. I've got it," Matt interrupted, with a quick nod at the man to keep up a polite appearance, and walked toward Lili. The old man saw him coming and he went stiff.

"What's your name, little gal?" the old man asked, but he was intently watching Matt.

Lili glanced at Matt, then smiled and said, "Lili Hawkins."

"Nice to meet you." The old man paused. "Lili, huh? Now that's a pretty name. Old-fashioned. You don't hear many names like that these days."

Matt met the old man's gaze, letting nothing of his unease show. Paranoia or not, his instincts for self-preservation made him wonder if there was something more to the man's words.

Lili didn't bat an eyelash as she flashed her warmest, widest smile. "I was named for my grandmother. And it's nice to meet you, too, Mr.—?"

"Conroy. Willis Conroy. My niece and her husband own the place. Hope you don't mind that I don't get up. The joints ain't what they used to be."

"Oh, that's quite all right," Lili said, and Matt could tell she was trying not to stare. Or, at least, trying not to be too obvious about it.

"We have to get going," Matt said, seizing his chance to draw Lili away. With his hand at her back, he gave her a slight push. She frowned at him.

A grin cut across the wrinkles of Conroy's face, then he gave an exaggerated wink. "Can't wait to get her alone, eh?"

Lili blushed. Matt smiled tightly, then propelled her out the door and down the walk to the car.

"What the hell were you doing?" he demanded through clenched teeth as he opened her door and helped her into her seat.

"What do you think? My God . . . Willis Conroy," she said softly. "He doesn't look very dangerous now, but I'd say his mind is still pretty sharp."

That had been Matt's impression as well, after he'd calmed down enough to catalog details. "I'd appreciate it if you didn't walk off like that again, please. I'm still your bodyguard."

Matt started the car and set off down the narrow dirt road. Several minutes later, he pulled up before a little log cabin set apart from the others, nestled up against the woods. Not the easiest place to secure, but with any luck, he and Lili would be out of here in a few days.

"Is this it?" Lili asked. When he nodded, she added, "It's kinda cute."

He thought it looked small. "I don't care if it's cute or not. All I want is to lie down, on a bed, for an hour."

"A bed sounds like paradise about now. And so does that tub. My butt's been numb for hours."

She swung out of the car after he parked, and Matt eyed her flannel-clad back and bottom, and her black hair hanging long and straight, swaying from side to side as she climbed the stairs.

I could do something to get your blood pumping . . .

Letting out his breath, he pushed the thought away. He stepped out of the car and followed her to the cabin door, unlocked it, and pushed it open.

He'd have to talk with her about this bed business. Just yesterday, he'd have grabbed the chance to roll in the sheets with Lili Kavanaugh. Now he wasn't sure pushing for further intimacy was a good idea.

God, he wanted her, and badly—but when he'd given her the silent go-ahead Saturday night, it had been with the expectation that whatever happened would be for a night only, and she'd be on her way home, safe, the next day.

And all that had changed.

I care for you, Matt. A lot . . .

He cared for her, too, and the last thing he wanted was to hurt her. She wasn't looking at this with her head, and wanted to believe a New York designer could fall in love with a bodyguard from Chicago, complete with some kind of damn fairy tale ending. But he knew better.

"Look," Lili exclaimed after she switched on the lights. "This cabin is absolutely adorable."

It seemed the sort of place a woman would get excited about. It was small but open, and decorated with a backwoods theme right down to the rough-hewn tables and dark plaid furniture. No sofa, just a love seat and two chairs. The exposed beams of the walls and ceiling, and the polished hardwood floor added to the homey look. A fieldstone fireplace dominated one wall, with a round braided rug in front of it. Detailed botanical and wildlife prints crowded the walls, and the table lamps appeared to be birch logs, topped by leatherlike lampshades with whip-stitched edges.

Off the main room was a short hall leading to a tiny galley kitchen on the right—plain pine cupboards, with what looked like ceramic antler drawer knobs, and a small farm table surrounded by spindle-back chairs—and what he figured was the bedroom and bathroom to the left.

Lili disappeared inside the bedroom, and Matt heard squeals of feminine delight. It made him smile, despite his steadily increasing tension.

"Hey, Lil," he called. "I'm going to bring in our bags from the car."

"Okay," she hollered back, over the unmistakable sound of squeaking bedsprings, followed by a loud sigh of contentment. "Oh, Matt, this is *heaven*. The bed is huge! And it's so soft . . ."

Matt briefly squeezed his eyes shut, trying to hold back the image of Lili in that bed, soft and bare and waiting for him, arms open. Failing that, he went out to the car and retrieved the bags. He made his way back to the bedroom, and found Lili flopped back on the bed crosswise, her feet dangling off the floor, arms spread wide, and her hair spilling across a colorful quilt and over the side of the bed.

And what a bed it was.

"You weren't kidding when you said it was big," he said, staring.

The headboard looked like a purloined piece of church architecture, and the mattress sat high off the floor. Dried flower wreaths decorated the wooden walls, and delicate lace curtains covered the window overlooking Little Moccasin Lake. The quilt was the focal point of the room, and a fake bearskin rug covered the plank flooring.

Cozy. Intimate. The sort of bedroom that encouraged a couple to dally inside, no matter how good the fishing or how pretty the scenery outside.

Lili patted the bed beside her. "Dump those bags and come here."

Too tempted to pass on her offer, Matt dropped the Wal-Mart bags and fell back onto the bed, making it bounce and creak. He closed his eyes and groaned. "God, this feels good."

"Mmmm, that it does."

For several minutes he stared up at the ceiling beams, enjoying the enveloping softness of the bed, the secluded quiet of the room. If it hadn't been for that taut physical awareness of Lili so close to him, and on a bed, he might've drifted off to sleep.

As it was, his entire body had gone tense from head to toe, and he was aware of her heat beside him, her scent, and the soft, even sound of her breathing.

"You can have the bed. I'll sleep on the love seat," he said abruptly. Although he didn't look at her, he could feel her sudden stillness.

"Why?"

Rolling over to his side, he said, "What happened between you and me on Saturday . . . neither of us expected anything to go beyond the night."

"What difference does that make?"

"Everything's changed, Lili. You know that."

She also rolled over to her side, mimicking his pose, her face inches away, and her gaze steady. "Can you define 'everything'? That's pretty broad."

A hundred reasons pressed in upon him, none of them clear enough or good enough. It was as if all the words—all the *right* words—hung just out of his reach.

"There are complications . . . and getting involved with a client goes against all my training, against everything I try to be."

"It's a little late for doubts now, isn't it?" she asked sharply.

"It's not that I don't want to, Lili, because I do. But just because I want to doesn't mean I should, or that it's right."

"It felt pretty damn right to me in the backseat of that car," she snapped. "And on the trunk this afternoon."

He took in a long, steadying breath. "Yes," he said. "It did."

"Matt, I want you to make love to me."

He was speechless, though Lili never did anything he expected. But to actually hear her say it . . . God, he'd fantasized for hours about her saying those words to him.

"It would be wrong of me to take advantage of your trust or vulnerability. I've told you before that danger can make people act in ways they ordinarily wouldn't. I can't be sure that's not what's happening here. As much as I want to push you back on this bed, rip off your clothes, and make love to you until we can't walk," he said with low intensity, "I can't be sure it's what you really want."

She sat up, anger blazing in her eyes. "So what you're saying is that, for my own good, you won't touch me."

Uneasily, Matt pushed up as well. "I guess, yeah." Even as he spoke, he was aware that he'd made a very big mistake—he just wasn't sure what it was, exactly.

"Get out."

"What are you mad about?" Matt asked, staring at her pale, angry face. "I'm trying to do what's right for you, and—"

"I said, get out!" she shouted, and shoved him.

He opened his mouth to try and reason with her, but seeing the tears brimming in her eyes, he clamped his mouth shut, stood, then turned on his heel and left.

Lili watched as Matt disappeared through the door, and a white-hot fury ripped through her. After everything they'd been through, everything they'd shared—and after he'd had his hands and mouth all over her *twice* today— he had the nerve to go all noble on her like this.

"You jerk!" she yelled, and hurled one of the decorative bed pillows against the wall.

Squeezing her eyes shut, Lili struggled to hold back her tears. That she was crying over a big, dumb prick like Matt Hawkins just made her all the more angry.

She stood abruptly, gathering the heavy quilt toward her. What did she care if he spent a miserable night on the love seat? It'd serve him right if he got the world's worst crick in his selfish, stubborn neck.

"Thank you so much for assuming you know what's right for me." She scowled at the empty doorway. "It's *such* a relief, not to have to think for myself."

Lugging the quilt, she marched into the living room, pointedly ignoring the fireplace, because it would only remind her of the decidedly erotic plans she'd been making only moments before.

His expression wary, Matt stood next to the love seat in a loose-limbed stance that told her he didn't know whether to come toward her or back away.

"You made me think you were different." She glared as she threw the quilt at him. "That you wouldn't treat me like I was helpless, or—"

"Lili," he interrupted, swatting the quilt aside. "Stop this."

Lili spun and stomped back to the bedroom. She couldn't hold back all her bottled-up frustrations and fears, even if she wanted to.

To hell with losing with dignity, or acting like a good sport!

Grabbing one of the bed pillows, she whirled and headed back to the sitting room. Matt was standing where she'd left him, still looking baffled—and a little angry.

He didn't get it. He honestly didn't understand why she was so angry, so hurt—and that just made everything worse.

"Go ahead and sleep out here; I don't give a shit!"

Dark satisfaction spurted through her at his stunned expression, and with all her strength, she swung the pillow and smacked him in the chest.

Whomp! Matt went down and landed—hard—on his back.

Lili stared at him in amazement. This she hadn't expected: the mighty bodyguard, brought low by a feather pillow.

Why wasn't he moving? She hadn't meant to knock him down, and she *really* hadn't meant to hurt him.

Her anger fading, she bent over him, still clutching the pillow. "Matt? Are you okay? I didn't—"

Matt's hand shot out, nearly snatching the pillow from her. Quick as he was, she managed to yank the pillow free of his grip and scoot back.

With a smooth, fluid grace, he rolled and came to his feet, face flushed, eyes hot. He reached for her and Lili, thinking that maybe she'd pushed him far enough, smacked him again with the pillow to keep him away from her.

"Lili, I'm not going to hurt you, for God's sake. Now give me that pillow!"

The rational part of her told her to do as he said, but the contrary, emotional part of her wasn't having any part of his ordering her around.

She swung the pillow toward his head, but this time he ducked. When he straightened again, she froze at the furious expression on his face.

"That," he said through his teeth, "is it."

Lili turned and ran for the bedroom. She'd made him lose his temper, and there was no way his male pride would let her get away with that.

Inside, she whirled to shut the door, but he was already there. He shoved against it with such force that she stumbled back against the thick mattress. Quickly, she rolled to the other side to keep the bed between them, her pillow raised and ready.

"Give that to me," he repeated, and suddenly lunged, grabbing the pillow and yanking it out of her hands.

Immediately she snatched the second pillow, and as she looked up again, she caught the wicked gleam lighting his eyes.

"Okay, Lil," he said. "Have it your way. But I'll win."

A unexpected tickle of pleasure—and anticipation—cracked through her anger. "In your dreams," she said in a low growl, and swung the pillow.

She missed him by inches but forced him to move back, giving her the chance she needed to dash around the bed and pummel him again.

"You are so arrogant!"

Whomp!

"I do *not* need you to think for me!"

Whomp, whomp . . .

"Ow! Lili, cut it out," he said, but he was laughing.

Laughing!

With all the force of her temper behind her, she swung her pillow again. Ducking neatly, Matt pitched his own pillow at her as if it were a Frisbee.

It hit her in the stomach, knocking her back on the bed with an *ooph!* Matt followed, the weight of his body pressing her down into the soft mattress. His fingers closed over her wrists and pinned them above her head, trapping her beneath him.

Panting from exertion and ire, she stared up into his face, absurdly pleased to see he looked more than a little ruffled himself.

"What a typically male response," she grumbled. "When all else fails, overpower." She narrowed her eyes at him, chest still heaving. "Of course, manhandling people is your *job*."

Matt exhaled, loudly and forcefully. "You can be a real bitch when you want to be, you know that?"

"You bet," she retorted, still glaring. "And you can be a real bastard."

His face was only inches from her, his pupils dilated so much that his eyes looked almost black.

In that moment, she realized he had her on her back on a bed, his body against hers. Her temper ebbed as her need for him—which had been there all along, even in her anger—swept over her in a hot, liquid rush.

In his eyes, half-hidden by his long lashes, she recognized that same awareness and desire. Her muscles softened, and she relaxed back onto the mattress.

"You like to play a little rough?" he murmured, and his hips moved against hers, just enough to make his point—that he was about as aroused as a man could get.

"I don't know," Lili whispered, not sure what to make of the question, much less how to answer.

Did *he* like to play a little rough?

For a long moment he studied her, his gaze moving across her face, her mouth, then lower. When he returned to her eyes she saw his indecision, but also a raw need he couldn't hide.

"You'll regret this," he said quietly.

"That's my problem."

"And I'll regret it. Later."

"Not if you do it right."

He suddenly laughed, a low, wonderful sound that made her smile. "Nothing like putting a little performance pressure on a guy."

Matt released her wrists and slid his hands downward. He rested one against her cheek, his thumb brushing her skin lightly, and his other hand cupped her breast through the old flannel shirt.

She sighed at the warmth of his hand on her, the tingles of pleasure. Reluctantly she drew his hands away, smiling as she sat up, then kissed him with enough heat to keep his attention right where she wanted it—on her.

Lili slid off the bed and unbuttoned her shirt. Matt rolled to his side, his gaze following her every movement as she tossed the shirt aside, then began on the buckle. Since the jeans were so large, all she had to do was wiggle her hips a little, and they fell in a heap of faded denim at her feet. She stepped out of the jeans and kicked off her shoes, standing before him in her bra and underwear.

Matt sat up, his gaze moving downward, then back to her face. "Most women are shy. I like it that you're not."

After unlacing his boots and removing his socks, he stood and unhooked his overall straps, then stripped them off. He pulled his T-shirt over his head, leaving him only in his boxers.

Lili pressed close against him, her white lace and fair skin pale against his darker skin and black silk. She tipped her head for his kiss, and he responded with surprising gentleness.

After a moment, Lili broke the kiss so they could both come up for air—and it was then she noticed a strange, puckered scar on his left pectoral muscle, almost hidden by his dark chest hair.

"What's this?" she asked, touching it—and understanding jolted her. "Is that what I think it is?"

"Yes." He caught her hand, pulling it away. "It's a bullet scar, and it happened a long, long time ago, Lili. Don't worry about it."

Easy for him to say. She leaned forward, and kissed the scar. "To make it better, even if it was a long time ago. I bet it hurt."

He shrugged, as if it didn't matter, but looked away. Lili hesitated, then took his hand, and pulled him after her toward the bathroom. The whirlpool tub and shower dominated the room, which was decorated in the same quaint woodsy theme as the rest of the cabin. A pile of thick white towels rested on a small table, beside the pedestal sink topped by a mirror with a twig frame.

The room was small, with barely enough room for the two of them to move without bumping into each other—not that Matt appeared to mind her brushing against him as she started the shower and pulled the curtain closed.

As steam began to rise in the room, Lili turned and met his gaze. The blue-black stubble made him look dark and sexy, and his teeth gleamed white as he smiled.

"Come here," he murmured, sending shivers through her, just like the first time he'd said those words to her. Without hesitation, she did.

He slipped the bra straps from her shoulders, then reached behind her and unhooked its fasteners. He let the bra fall to the floor, watching her face. He rubbed his hands down her back, across her shoulders—and eased her away for a better view of her breasts.

"Beautiful," he said softly. "God, you're beautiful."

Going warm with pleasure, Lili took her time surveying his bare body as well, from his chest down to his narrow hips—and lingering, again, on that troublesome bullet scar.

"You're not too bad yourself."

She was a little nervous under his intense regard, jittery with anticipation, yet aroused, too. She wanted to make love with him so much, to do everything right and perfect, but what if she screwed up? What if she disappointed him, or—

"Lili, stop worrying," Matt said, his smile widening.

"I'm not . . . all right, I'm a little nervous," she admitted. "It's just that I want this to be special."

"It will be," Matt assured her as he slipped off her panties. He kissed her again, hungrily.

His reassurance warmed her and chased away her lingering doubts.

"Just touch me," he said. "We can get used to each other. No rush."

The tiny bathroom gradually filled with steam, wisps of it floating around them, making the air thick and moist. She met his eyes, still dark and dilated, and touched him. Her finger slowly traced the powerful muscles of his arms, his collarbone, the crisp dark hair fanning his chest—even that scar—then the warm, smooth skin of his belly, and finally the tight feel of his rear through the soft silk.

Catching her bottom lip between her teeth, she hooked her thumbs in his waistband and slowly pulled the boxers down, revealing his erection. She lightly touched the hard, hot flesh, and Matt sucked in his breath.

"The condoms are in the other room," he said, and she wasn't sure if it was a reminder or warning.

"Then we'll have to keep this a clean shower," she said, and winked.

Wink? Had she just actually *winked*?

Matt laughed and cupped her face in his hands. "What I love about you is how you always find humor in a situation."

Love . . .

She went still, feeling her eyes widen in surprise, and Matt must've realized what he'd said—but did he mean it in *that* way, or only that he thought she was good for a few laughs? "Love" was a word thrown about so casually: *I love your hair, I love this car, I love this movie* . . .

Too chicken to ask what she really wanted to know, she said instead, "Let's get in the shower."

An awkward moment followed as they both tried to stand aside to let the other into the shower first. Self-conscious, Lili stepped in, and Matt climbed in beside her.

"You wash up first," he said.

Leaning back into the spray, eyes closed, Lili let the hot water soothe away her anxieties. Small bottles of guest shampoo were in the bathroom, and she used a palm-sized bit to wash her hair while Matt watched, the spray slowly dampening his skin and hair.

Blinking rapidly so she wouldn't get shampoo in her eyes, Lili shamelessly enjoyed the view of his hard, wet body, and she couldn't wait to run her hands along all those slick hollows and broad planes.

After she'd rinsed her hair, Matt moved closer, a bar of soap in his hands. He worked it into a rich, white lather and slowly spread the soap over her—first her arms and shoulders, then her back and bottom, his fingers lingering and teasing, making her go achy and shivery at once. He kissed each bruise on her arms, then soaped her chest and breasts, smiling and watching her face as he played with her aroused nipples.

Pleasure rippled through her, building, and she had to close her eyes and take a deep, controlling breath. But her eyes snapped open again when Matt went down on one knee, soaping her stomach and legs.

Knowing what was coming, she leaned back against the slick tiled wall, and the instant his fingers touched her, stroking gently, she came in a matter of seconds with tremors that left her feeling weak and hot.

Matt straightened, his expression tight, eyes dark with hunger, and kissed her; another hard, demanding kiss as his erection pushed against her belly. His kiss deepened, his tongue touching hers, caressing lightly. Lili sighed deep in her throat, and leaned into his warm, wet body, her breasts pressed against his chest hair.

His kisses turned leisurely, and she met his mouth and tongue, kiss for kiss, stroke for stroke.

Only when she became aware of the cooling temperature of the water did she realize how long they'd been kissing, and she broke away.

"You better wash up before we run out of hot water."

"I didn't even notice," he said with a grin, and tossed her the soap.

When she looked up at him as he washed his hair—head back, eyes closed—a sudden and powerful feeling of possessiveness seized her.

I'm not letting you go.

The intensity of the thought left her momentarily shaken, but she managed to smile at him as she washed his body, careful of his healing arm, taking pleasure in how his stomach muscles tightened when she touched him, how he breathed more rapidly, and never took his gaze from her.

"I love touching you," she murmured, rubbing her fingers along his skin, delighting in the contrast of coarse hair and slippery skin, smooth to touch, even giving, until she reached the powerful muscles beneath.

With something almost like wonder, she ran her hands along the breadth of his shoulders, then down the length of his arms, and up again. Finally, she coaxed him around to soap his back.

A masterpiece of beauty and power, a man's body, and so different from hers—straight where she curved, hard where she was soft. She ran a finger down the valley of his spine to his rear with a low sound of approval.

He turned back, meeting her gaze. The water was growing steadily cooler, and she quickly peeked south to assure herself that Matt hadn't lost any interest.

He hadn't.

Lili leisurely soaped his penis, every marvelous inch of it, and grinned at his sharp intake of breath.

"You're driving me crazy," he muttered.

"Good," she whispered, sliding her hand along his erection, slippery and silky smooth with soap. She ached to have him inside her, to connect with him in the most intimate way, and couldn't resist teasing him a little, rubbing his erection against her sex.

Matt caught her hand and pulled it away. "We're done in here."

A little abrupt, but she didn't protest.

He shut off the water, helped her out of the tub, and tossed her a towel. When he stepped out, he grabbed her by the arm and steered her toward the bedroom, dripping water along the way.

She was still holding the towel against her, more out of surprise than modesty, when he let her go. He plucked the towel from her fingers, threw it aside, and with his hands on her shoulders, pressed her down on the bed.

"I'm still wet!"

"I don't give a damn."

Goose bumps prickled her skin, and her nipples tightened in the cooler air. Matt made a low sound and his jaw clenched. He gave her a hard, quick kiss, then walked to the Wal-Mart bags on the floor. He quickly rummaged around until he grunted in triumph and returned with a box of condoms.

"This ought to last the night," he said. She stared at him, not sure what to say, and he suddenly grinned, eyes crinkling in that sweet, almost boyish way of his. "Just joking. I do have a sense of humor, you know."

Turning away, Matt took care of business with an efficiency that sobered her. She sucked in a long, shaky breath. *This is it . . . no turning back now.*

He faced her again, his gaze probing, as if checking to make sure she hadn't changed her mind—and his care for her swept aside her few remaining doubts. She opened her arms to him, smiling.

Matt moved over her, his heat blanketing her, stoking her desire until it was deliciously taut and sweetly sharp.

His kisses were still urgent, but not as rough as before. She expected him to move fast—a kiss here, a fondle there, and then push inside her—but Matt had other ideas. She already felt as if she were about to explode, and it amazed her that he could hold back like this.

He was on his knees, looming above her in the fading light of an October evening. He placed his palms on her hips, and slowly glided them upward until he covered her breasts.

She sighed, and he smiled. "You like that?"

"Oh, yes," she whispered.

His thumbs played with her, making her squirm and arch her hips. He bent, his mouth brushing hers, and he whispered, "Tonight, you're mine."

A sharp thrill shot through her at his husky words, and it stunned her that such a primitive male possessiveness could so arouse her. But an older, female awareness understood—and when his hot mouth closed over her breast, she stopped caring.

Nothing mattered beyond the feel of his mouth, the ache demanding to be eased. Now . . . right now.

"Matt, please," she whispered.

"I know," he murmured, moving to her other breast, kissing and teasing the nipple until she nearly came from the pleasure of that alone.

Sensing how close she was to the edge, he pulled back and kissed her mouth—a deep and devouring kiss. He put all of his need for her in that kiss, holding nothing back. All the intensity, all the tightly leashed passion, all that dark power.

His mouth still on hers, Matt slipped his hand lower, eased her legs farther apart, and touched her. Lightly, slowly at first, and when her breathing grew sharper, more ragged, and her hips rose urgently against him, he fanned her sensitized flesh until the orgasm rocked through her. She stiffened, rising against him, and cried out. Her nails dug into his arm as her other hand closed into a fist on the blankets.

The sweet aftershocks were still pulsing through her when his hands lifted her hips, and the hard flesh of his erection pushed against her. Her eyes flew open as he entered her on a fast, smooth stroke—and Matt went very still for a moment, jaw clenched, eyes locked on her.

"Oh, yeah," he whispered thickly, moving his hips, slowly forward, slowly back. "So good . . . so good."

His low, rough voice excited her, but he didn't say anything else, too intent on going slow for her sake. His eyes glazed over as he focused inward, the corded tendons of his neck standing out, his breathing rapid.

Lili wrapped her legs around his hips, bringing him hard against her—and pleasure shot through her. She gasped, and his attention snapped back to her face. She squeezed his shoulders in a wordless appeal.

At once his rhythm changed, from slow, teasing strokes to a fast, forceful pumping, and that liquid, inner tension wound tighter and tighter and tighter . . .

Resting his forearms on either side of her head, Matt dropped his head on the crook of her neck, and she felt his heated breath, heard his low groans. He kissed her ear, his tongue tracing its shape, and the pleasure snapped free. She came fast and hard, with a sharp, high gasp.

Matt made a sound almost like pain, his hips driving forward a final time, muscles going rigid. A moment later he slumped on top of her, all that tensed urgency transformed to deliciously heavy, warm male.

Lili lay still, eyes closed, soaking in sensations as languor seeped through her. His skin was faintly damp with perspiration, and his beard was rough and scratchy. He was still inside her, and she didn't move, wanting the moment of peace and completeness to last as long as possible.

Gradually, as she held him in her arms, she became aware of an unexpected feeling of protectiveness. Odd, considering that Matt, of all people, hardly needed protecting.

Yet it was there, strong and insistent, and she tightened her arms around him, kissing the bit of chin she could reach, and whispered, "No regrets at all."

15

Lili awoke to birdsong—trills and lilts and cheerful cheeps—and opened her eyes with a contented sigh. It was a much nicer way to wake up than the blaring taxi horns and wailing sirens back home.

Gradually she became aware of a chill breeze, the whisper of a lacy curtain billowing against the windowsill, and the warmth of a body pressed along her back. A warmth all the more welcome because of the room's coolness—they'd forgotten to close the window.

Not that she minded; it was the perfect excuse to cuddle. She turned, careful not to disturb him, and smiled. Waking up with Matt Hawkins in her bed wasn't a bad way to start her day, either.

He was sound asleep, sprawled on his stomach, his head turned toward her. Her gaze traveled along the angles of his face, softened in sleep, across the dark stubble on his jaw, and lingered on those long, thick lashes fanning across his cheekbones. Very carefully, she touched his lashes with her finger tip, both admiring and a little envious.

The curve of his mouth lured her finger downward, and she traced the shape of them, remembering the exquisite feel of his lips over her body during the night.

And here . . . that sexy, intriguing dimple in his chin. She loved how it looked, and how it gentled the hard lines of his face.

Her gaze fell on the plain wedding band on her finger, and she went still. So strange, the feel of it—heavy, almost. She couldn't help but be aware of this unfamiliar weight and all it symbolized. Her thumb played with the ring, twisting it on her finger.

She glanced at Matt's hand, loosely curled on the blanket, where his ring gleamed. She dropped her hand from his face, uncomfortable at how real their pretend "marriage" felt at the moment. Or maybe it was only that a part of her wished it were real, especially after those long, intimate hours that had passed between them.

And not all intense, either. At three in the morning Matt had gone prowling in the kitchen for food, returning with a bag of cheese curls, a bottle of champagne the resort stocked in the fridge for honeymooners, a smile, and a husky, smart-aleck remark: *Am I a classy date or what?*

She'd munched on cheese curls, getting neon-orange crumbs in his chest hair. He complained about that, so she'd tried brushing them away, but was a little tipsy after a couple of glasses of champagne, and the next thing she knew she was lapping champagne off his body, and one thing pretty much led to another.

He'd been gentle with her last night, and rough, too, in a playful way that she'd liked. He'd made love to her twice more after the first time, and despite his care, this morning she was feeling the effects of that last, lengthy bout of athletic lovemaking.

Her face and breasts were tender from beard burn—she'd have to remind him to shave today—and her bottom and leg muscles were a little sore. Her past boyfriends, while considerate and decent men, had mostly taken the steak-and-potatoes approach to sex. The sex had been satisfying and pleasant, but not nearly as vigorous and imaginative as her one night with Matt.

For a moment, she considered why that was—had it been because she'd held back for some reason, or because her other lovers had found basic sex satisfying enough?

Matt certainly hadn't.

Lili liked to think she was comfortable with her sexuality, but when Matt had asked to tie her wrists to the bed, she'd been surprised. Not so much by the suggestion—which greatly intrigued her—but that he'd even *thought* she might enjoy a little playful bondage sex.

Did he see something in her that past lovers hadn't? A rather provocative thought . . .

She propped her head on her palm, studying him, nearly overwhelmed by possessiveness, satisfaction—and other confusing feelings that left her a little panicky.

But even with her impulsiveness, falling in love with her bodyguard would be going too far, and she knew better than to make a mistake like that.

Lili sighed, and shivered a little in the cool air. Her stomach growled—loudly—and she eased out of bed, pulling the covers over Matt. He mumbled in his sleep, and rolled onto his back. She went still, but his eyes didn't open, and he began snoring softly.

It made her smile. She'd never seen him sleep this deeply before. Back at the Drake he'd always been awake when she went to bed, and awake when she rolled out of bed in the morning.

No wonder he looked exhausted. Holding back her

hair so it wouldn't brush against him, she bent and kissed him softly on the forehead.

She shut the window, then tiptoed to the bathroom, closed the door quietly behind her, and took a long, hot shower; working out the soreness and daydreaming under the gentle spray of water.

After she combed out her hair, brushed her teeth, and applied a bit of makeup, she walked back into the bedroom, expecting to find Matt awake. What she found was an empty bed, with the covers pulled up.

"Matt?"

No answer. Frowning, Lili pulled on the nearest flannel shirt—one of the new ones, and apparently Matt's, since it hung nearly to her knees, and went out to the kitchen and living room.

Empty.

Trying to ignore her rising worry—he'd never before left her alone—Lili opened the front door and walked out onto the small porch. Sunlight assaulted her eyes, and she squinted, spotting him immediately.

He was walking from the car toward the cabin, whistling, and holding what looked like a shallow cardboard box with two cups of coffee inside.

Breakfast! God bless the man.

"Hey," she called. "Is that coffee?"

"And donuts," he answered. "There's a continental breakfast in the lobby, but everything's pretty picked over by now."

She bounced on her bare feet, arms wrapped around herself against the chill, as she waited for him to join her.

Matt wore a partially buttoned flannel shirt over a long-sleeved black T-shirt and jeans, and she noted that Wal-Mart's idea of a size large didn't match Matt's needs—especially in the shoulders.

"Good morning," she said, a blush heating her face.

"Morning," he murmured, one corner of his mouth turned up in a smile, and then he kissed her. Not just a little peck on the lips, either, but a hearty kiss that tasted richly of chocolate frosting.

"You look cold. Better go back inside." He poked her toward the door with the box edge, his gaze briefly moving downward. "You wearing underwear?"

"Of course!" Panties, anyway. She hadn't put on a bra.

"Damn. I was getting excited, thinking you didn't have on anything under that shirt." He eyed the shirt. "Isn't that one mine?"

"Not while *I'm* wearing it." She peered inside the box. "Where's the chocolate donut? I tasted it when I kissed you."

The look he gave her was a mixture of exasperation and a guilty dismay. "There was only one chocolate donut, and I ate it. I thought you'd like the custard one better."

"Hmph. Shows what *you* know about women." Custard was all right, just not chocolate. Snatching up the donut, she said around a mouthful, "A pinecone would taste good now, I'm so hungry."

Oh, yes, the best way to handle morning-after jitters was to talk about food or the weather. Or, better yet, just stuff her mouth so she didn't have to talk at all.

Should she touch him? Kiss him?

Sex could be such a neurotic activity—how the species managed to survive, she didn't know.

"Want your coffee?" he asked when they were in the kitchen, standing at opposite ends. He was watching her, holding out the white Styrofoam cup, and it looked like he was trying to coax a skittish animal out of the corner with a tidbit of food.

Disgusted with herself—why on earth was she acting

like she'd never slept with a man before?—Lili walked to him and took the coffee from his hand. After the cloying sweetness of the custard, the bitter coffee tasted good.

"Are you all right?" Matt asked.

Lili forced herself to meet his watchful gaze. "Yes. A little . . . unsure, maybe."

He didn't look away. "Unsure of what?"

Realizing how he might misunderstand her vagueness, she said hastily, "Oh, the usual stuff . . . wondering if you still respect me in the morning." She smiled hesitantly at her joke, then said with more seriousness, "Wondering if I lived up to your expectations."

Matt took a long, slow sip of his coffee, his gaze speculative. "And what did you think I was expecting?"

"That was supposed to be a yes or no answer, Matt."

He took another sip of coffee. "Answer my question."

She blew out a breath in exasperation. "I don't know! Somebody more adventurous, more sexy. More rough and tough—"

"What is it with you and being 'tough'?" he interrupted. "And why don't you think you're attractive and sexy? Christ, Lili, the first thought that popped into my head when I met you was 'sex.' In red capital letters."

"Really?"

He'd certainly done a good job of hiding it.

"Yes," he retorted, rubbing the back of his neck. "And I can tell you, I wasn't at all happy about it. I damn near turned around and walked right back out that door."

"Why didn't you?"

"Because you looked scared . . . I wanted to help, is all."

Suddenly guilty, she said, "And I was so mean to you that first day."

"I understood what was going on with you. I know it bothers you, being afraid of what's happening here, but . . . ah, hell," he muttered. "What I'm trying to say is that we're all afraid of something, Lili. It's nothing to be ashamed about."

She moved closer to him, drawn by his heat, and absurdly happy when he slipped his arms around her. "Even you?"

"Even me."

"What are you afraid of, Matt?"

He looked down at her for a long moment, and finally said, "Failing."

Lili met his gaze, not really surprised by his answer. "It's funny, the things we're afraid of," she murmured. "Failure's never bothered me. I fail a lot. Fall flat on my face, sometimes."

She tipped her head to one side, trying to read his reaction. "I've had designs that I've loved, that I put my heart and soul into, and they've just tanked. I had a string of flops a few years ago, and it was so bad that I seriously considered giving up and getting a job as a cattle herder or something."

He laughed, the chest beneath her cheek shaking.

"But then I'd eat some chocolate and cheesecake, spend a few hours feeling sorry for myself, and get right back to work the next day." She looked up, seeing the suddenly serious look on his face.

"Failing isn't that bad. Sometimes it's good for you. Keeps you humble." She tried a smile, but he didn't smile back. "It would be worse, I think, to *not* try, even if you know there's a chance you might fail."

"So," he said softly. "If I don't take a chance and kiss you now, I might not find out what it's like to make love to you in the morning."

"You're changing the subject," she said, as his fingers moved down the shirt, deftly unbuttoning it. "You do that a lot, whenever I get too personal."

It angered her a little, even though she knew he was guarded by nature, as well by the nature of his work.

"I'm getting personal right now." Matt kissed her, sliding his hands beneath the open shirt, and resting them lightly below her breasts. "I'd like to get even more personal, if you'd let me."

Matt kissed her again, cupping her bare breasts, and all her misgivings, all her frustrations, fractured and scattered.

Somehow he ended up on one of the kitchen chairs, and she was sitting on his lap, her shirt unbuttoned, her panties on the floor. She managed to work his jeans and underwear down to his ankles, all while locked in a hot, wet kiss. There was an awkward moment—spiced by his curses and her low laugh—as he struggled to slide the condom on with her help. The moment he'd finished and she had warm, bare skin beneath her hands, Lili lowered herself, letting out a long, shaky breath as he pushed inside her.

She kissed him again, hungry for the taste of him. He held onto her hips tightly, urging her to move as he arched his hips against her. After several seconds she matched his rhythm, and the pleasure caught like the sudden striking of a match . . . a languorous glow, then a hot, sudden flare.

Her bare breasts rubbed against the soft flannel of his shirt, the pleasure almost painful, and he slanted his mouth against hers demandingly, his tongue stroking hers.

She moved against him, and the feel of him touching her deep inside drove her rapidly to climax. The chair bumped against the table, and she never broke the kiss—wanting to be body to body, skin to skin, sharing the same breath, when he came.

An instant later, Matt made a low moan deep in his throat. His fingers tightened on her hips and he rammed his hips upward, going rigid, tremors shaking his muscles.

It was all Lili needed to join him, and the orgasm, short and intense, left her clinging to him, panting and hot, the fading pleasure pulsing through her.

God . . . even plain vanilla sex with Matt was wonderful.

After a short silence, Matt tipped his head back over the chair and said, "We need to go to the store and buy food. Christ, I'm hungry."

"Woman doth not live on sex alone."

He laughed and kissed her quickly. "Or cheese curls and donuts. I need to call Monica, too."

"Ah, yes. Monica."

Matt eyed her with a hint of humor. "Considering what we just did, don't tell me you're jealous of her."

"I'm not jealous of *her*, precisely," Lili retorted. How awkward, discussing another woman, with her bare bottom resting on his lap. "Just her relationship with you. Did she tie you to the bed, Matt?"

His brows shot upward. "Lili, I don't think—"

"Don't answer. I shouldn't have asked." She took a quick breath. "It's just that she looks like the type of woman who'd be good at tying men into knots."

"You don't know anything about Monica, or my relationship with her."

"You must've been very close once, for her to risk her career for you."

"I helped her out, and she feels she owes me a favor." He hesitated, then said, "Her younger brother was messed up and I helped him get his head straight. Monica's big on family, and she was grateful that I helped him before he ended up dead or in jail."

Intrigued, she asked, "What did you do? To help the brother, I mean."

Matt's gaze went flat. "I talked to him."

"Must've been some talk."

"It worked, that's all I cared about. I need to take a shower."

He looked at her, obviously waiting for her to move. When she didn't, he frowned and said, "What?"

"Who are you?" she blurted.

Surprise flashed across his face, then a sudden wariness, even though he smiled. "Lili—"

"No. I'm serious. Who the hell are you?"

His smile faded, and he held out his hand. "Matt Hawkins. Pleased to meet you." When she didn't smile as he'd likely hoped, he dropped his hand, narrowed his eyes, and said softly, "I figure the part of me still inside you doesn't need an introduction."

She refused to rise to the bait. "Stop evading my questions, Matt. I want to know how you can hold back on me like this, after what we just shared. And I'm sitting here thinking that I know *nothing* about you, not really."

"You don't need my life history. This isn't going to last," he said, his tone cool. "You know it, I know it, and I don't see any reason to make it harder to say good-bye than we need to."

"You really believe that?" she asked, her gaze searching his.

He didn't respond.

After a moment she said, "You know, I don't feel as if I have a gaping hole in my life, and that all I'm missing is a man to fill it. I have friends and family, a job I love, and a life that's pretty good. I'm not looking to fall in love, and even if I were, I'm not entirely sure I want to fall in love with *you*. God, you can be such a pain in the ass!"

She finally stood and buttoned her shirt. Slowly, not taking his gaze from hers, he hiked his pants up and stood as well.

"Do you think you might be falling in love with me?" she asked bluntly.

To his credit, he didn't look away from her. "You're not . . . I've never known a woman like you. You're beautiful and sexy, you have a great laugh, all this energy . . . I like being with you. I like you. But when this is over, you'll still be Lili Kavanaugh, designer, and I'll still be Matt Hawkins, bodyguard. And you hate my job. Remember?"

"So get a different job."

"I can't."

She stared at him, disturbed and angered by his stubbornness. "Of course you can. There's nothing you can't do if you set your mind to it, Matt. I believe in you. Why can't you believe in yourself?"

When he said nothing, Lili gave a loud, gusty sigh. "Never mind. You're right; none of this matters. I'm going to take a shower, too. Are you coming with me?"

He shifted, turning away so she couldn't see his face. "In a minute. You go on."

16

"What have you got for me?" Matt stood at a pay phone outside the small grocery store in the resort town of Eagle River, trying to block out the noisy street traffic as he listened for Monica's answer.

"A warning," she said, her tone grim. "I've heard the brass is issuing a bulletin to all surrounding states to bring you in for questioning. They want you back in Chicago."

"To arrest me?"

"Not exactly, more of a clarifying sort of discussion. There's this issue that you've taken a woman and disappeared with her. She may have gone voluntarily, but only you, me, and Lili know that."

"Shit," Matt said in disgust. He didn't need another complication, not now. His gaze strayed to Lili, sitting in the front seat of the car and reading *Vogue*.

He had his hands full with unexpected complications.

"You better lay low, and stay out of sight of the local law enforcement."

"Will do. What else have you got?"

"A lot, actually. I had Ward copying old files for me off duty, and I went to the library to see what I could find. Care to tell me where you are?"

"Why do you need to know?"

"So I can get everything to you. Most of it's background and history, which doesn't seem all that important, but then I don't know what you're looking for. I figured it'd be easier to give it to you than try and summarize it on the phone."

"You're being straight with me?"

Silence. "There comes a time when you have to trust somebody, Matt."

True, and it wasn't that he didn't trust her—but Monica had always been a cop first, a lover and friend second.

"Who'd be willing to make a long drive up here?" he asked. "I can arrange a meeting away from where Lili and I are staying. That way, if somebody asks, you can say you don't know where I am and it'll be the truth."

"I've got a backlog of vacation time to use. I can get Mom to watch the boys, and drive up myself."

"I don't want you any more involved than you have to be."

"And I'd prefer involving as few people as possible in this mess. I can do it. Just tell me where."

Good point, one he couldn't argue against. "All right. We can meet tomorrow at three, at the gas station in Antigo that's right off the Highway 64 exit."

"Will do."

A patrol car turned the corner, and Matt casually shifted away from the street, looking down.

"I've found something else," Monica said. "I don't know if it means much, but I got one of those feelings."

And Monica's "one of those feelings" almost always translated into something good. "What is it?"

"Do you know who Anthony Graziano is?"

Matt frowned, thinking. "He's that crime boss everybody calls Crazy Tony, right? Involved in some big scandal a few years back, when he got off from racketeering and extortion charges because of an entrapment issue?"

"That's the scumbag."

"What does he have to do with Joey Mancuso?"

"His old man headed the Mancuso hit. Lou Graziano was one of Mike Riley's shooters."

Matt stared ahead, watching cars and trucks go past—and keeping an eye on Lili, still absorbed with her magazine. "Huh," he said.

"Lou Graziano botched the job, since he failed to return the money, and Riley flew into a rage about it. He had Graziano killed a couple weeks later."

"This could be something," Matt said. "What about Graziano's family? Wife, sons, friends? Somebody else who could be involved?"

"I'll check into it further, but it doesn't look promising. Tony's on his third trophy wife, he has three grown daughters, and a bunch of grandkids. None of his immediate family are involved in the business as far as we know, though he has a couple of distant cousins with questionable job histories. Tony was seven when his father died, and his mother, who was an alcoholic, committed suicide two years later. He found her in her bedroom with half her head blown off."

"That could explain why he's called Crazy Tony." Matt shifted the phone to his other ear. "He must be what . . . in his seventies?"

"And still going strong. Tony's a vicious old bastard . . . and the beauty of the mob life is that there's no retirement. You tend to business until the day they put you in the ground." She paused. "I know it's not much to work with, but it's all I have right now."

"It's enough, thanks."

"There's one more thing before you hang up." He heard her sigh over the line. "If you get into trouble, or even *suspect* trouble, notify the local police."

"You just told me to stay clear of them."

"If the kind of trouble you're hiding from comes looking for you and finds you, you're better off in jail. And I really don't want you shooting anybody. There's a lot less trouble and paperwork when cops shoot the bad guys, okay?"

"Sure."

Another sigh. "At least promise you'll call me. I can talk to somebody in the area, try to explain, one cop to another."

He couldn't promise her anything, and didn't answer.

After a moment, she said, "You can come back, you know. Let the police here take care of it."

"No can do, Monica."

"Well, I had to ask. Matt, I understand why you don't trust the cops, but we can keep her safe. Probably safer than if she's with you, if you're doing what I think you are. I'm not going to keep arguing about it, but I'm trusting you to do the right thing. Don't let me down this time."

"I am doing the right thing. I'm protecting my client."

"No matter what," Monica said, her voice weary.

"No matter what," Matt agreed, and then changed the subject before the conversation degenerated into an all-too-familiar argument. "How are Dal and Manny doing?"

"I wish I could give you some good news on Dal, but he's the same. Still hanging on, though. He's a fighter. Manny's out of surgery and doing good. He was asking after you. I told him you were okay. He also went to see Dal, and I think it shook him up pretty bad."

"When you see Manny again, tell him to hang in there. And ask him to tell Jodie I'm . . . sorry."

Sorry didn't sound like much, but he had nothing else to offer beyond the certainty that if the chance presented itself, he'd take down the bastards who'd shot Dal and Manny.

Not something he could tell a cop.

"I'll do that," Monica said. "I have to go. I got an autopsy I have to be at in an hour, and court later this afternoon. I'll see you tomorrow at three. Don't be late."

After hanging up, Matt walked slowly back to the car. Lili had put aside her magazine, her gaze searching his face, trying to figure out if the call had meant good news or bad. She was still a little angry with him, probably; she'd been cool to him in the car.

It was hard to keep his concentration on their danger when she was mad at him—and the reason for it.

Lili wasn't anything like his past lovers; she'd give all of herself, hold nothing back. The problem was, she'd expect the same in return. She needed it. Hell, she deserved it, but he wasn't sure he could ever trust anybody that much—or love a woman so freely.

There's nothing you can't do if you put your mind to it.

Her words had stunned him. After she'd stalked off to the bathroom, he'd stayed in the kitchen, trying not to read too much into her words—and remembering.

As a kid, he'd wanted someone to believe in him. He'd needed it then, whenever he'd looked in a mirror, full of shame for the nobody that had stared back, the boy with the angry eyes and ragged clothes. But he wasn't that kid anymore, and he thought he'd grown beyond that need.

Maybe not.

"Well?" she asked, as he opened the car door and got in, avoiding her gaze. "Did Monica have any information?"

"Not much, which I'd expected, considering it's been nearly seventy years." He cranked the ignition, and the engine roared to life. "Monica's agreed to drop off the information she's copied. We'll meet her down in Antigo."

"Why don't you just corner Willis Conroy and ask him about the shoes? Wouldn't that be easier, not to mention quicker?"

"Because I don't trust him," he said, putting the car in gear and beginning the short drive back to the resort. "Maybe it doesn't mean anything that Conroy's at the resort during the off-season, but every time I see him, he's watching the news. I find it hard to believe he doesn't know about the attack on you, or who wants the shoes. He's old, but who's to say he wouldn't be willing to strike a deal and take a cut if he turns in anybody who comes asking him about Mancuso?"

"Are you serious?" she asked, her voice uneasy.

"Don't forget what he was, Lili."

"It's like a game of chess, what you do."

Matt glanced at her solemn face as he braked at an intersection. "You could look at it that way. It's all about anticipating every possible contingency, and planning for it."

He paused, his jaw tightening at the memory of Manny's blood, dark against the sidewalk. "But sometimes things go wrong, no matter what."

She sighed. "So what's your plan?"

"I'm going to watch Conroy, try to get a read on him, get him to talk."

"He seems harmless enough."

Matt didn't look away from the long, empty stretch of country road. "Trust nobody, Lili."

"What would you do, if you weren't a bodyguard?" she asked abruptly. "Do you ever wonder what it would be like, never having to play mental chess twenty-four hours a day, day after day? Not distrusting every living soul you encounter?"

"Lili, I don't want to get into this again."

She didn't speak for the rest of the drive. The thick, heavy silence of her anger hung over him, and he realized how bone-deep weary he was. What he wouldn't give right now to lie down on a bed and sink into a bottomless, black, and dreamless sleep. Even for just an hour.

When Matt turned onto the road that led to the resort, he finally looked at Lili. She met his gaze and held it— and he saw that concern had replaced her anger.

"I won't change my job," he said wearily. "I make decent money, and I'm good at it."

"There's a difference between being good at a job and liking it."

"Right now you should be glad I'm good, considering I'm the one keeping your pretty ass out of trouble," he said, putting the car in park. He swung open the car door. "Let's get the groceries inside and then we're going for a boat ride."

Lili got out of the car and frowned at him across the sun-faded brown roof. "Boat ride?"

"We're newlyweds here to do some fishing and hiking, remember? So we better make good on it. Besides, I need to talk to you about what Monica told me, and out on the water, there's no ears."

She stared at him for a moment longer, then shook her head, and walked into the cabin without him.

Lili stood on the creaking pier, waiting while Matt untied a rowboat from a sun-bleached wooden post. He'd declined any of the resort's motor boats, telling the owners he and Lili wanted to go for a romantic rowboat ride.

They'd smiled, and bought the lie hook, line, and sinker.

"Careful," he said, and held out his hand to help her in. "It's not too steady."

Once she was settled on the wooden bench seat, Matt climbed in, rocking the boat enough that she grabbed on to the sides. He sat behind her, took both oars, and pushed the boat away from the pier. With amazingly little effort, he rowed out across the wind-rippled waters of Little Moccasin Lake, and past the small island in its middle, covered by scrub brush and scattered trees.

Turning, Lili watched him row. He'd pushed up the sleeves of his T-shirt and rolled up the sleeves of the flannel shirt, and she admired the flexing muscles of his forearms. "You said you have a sailboat."

He nodded. "I keep it at a marina. Sailing is my way of getting away from it all. It's as close to solitude as you can get in Chicago."

Lili smiled, picturing him alone on his boat, shirtless, the breeze ruffling his hair, looking as relaxed and easy as he had last night in her arms.

From her seat at the bow, she surveyed their surroundings. Little Moccasin Lake was part of a wider chain of lakes. The whole area was dotted with small, shallow glacial lakes nestled along the fringes of Nicolet National Forest, and looked almost untouched. She took in a deep breath, smelling pine and lake water, and somewhere in the distance, heard the eerie call of a loon.

"It's beautiful here," she said, breathing in deeply of the cool, fresh air.

"I like being close to the water," Matt said, with another long, slow pull of the oars. "Someday, I'm going to own a house on the ocean."

She held back her surprise at his unexpected confidence. Maybe he was trying, in his own cautious way, to open up to her. So many shades to this man, and she had so little time to discover them.

"If you want a house on the ocean, then I'm sure it'll happen." Lili eased back to get more comfortable and enjoy the ride. It wasn't every day, after all, that she was ferried about by a gorgeous, sexy man. "You strike me as the type that gets whatever you want."

"I do, huh?"

"Most definitely." She gave a long, low sigh of contentment. "I like this. It's romantic."

He was smiling, and she was glad to see that his earlier tension had faded.

"So what's this secret stuff you wanted to talk to me about?"

Matt checked out the few other boaters sharing the lake. There was a group of four fishing boats in the distance, and a couple in a canoe gliding along the far shore.

After pulling the oars into the boat, he sat back. "Monica thinks she's found a connection. It may be nothing, but she's checking into it further."

"Does it have to do with the shoes?"

"No." He tipped his head toward the sun, eyes briefly closing. "The guy in charge of the Mancuso hit was named Lou Graziano. Monica said Graziano's boss had him killed shortly afterward because Graziano blew the job by not bringing back the stolen money."

Lili frowned; the name Graziano didn't ring any bells. "So what's the connection?"

"A Chicago crime boss named Anthony Graziano."

Lili leaned toward him, her attention sharpening. "A son?"

Matt nodded. "He was a kid when Riley whacked his old man, but it makes sense, having somebody like Graziano behind the attacks on you. It feels right, and Graziano would have the resources. What I still don't know is why."

"Would Graziano's son know about Willis Conroy?"

"Mancuso, Conroy, and Lou Graziano all had connections to Mike Riley, and when Conroy turned on Mancuso, it was Graziano who went to take care of the problem. I'm certain the two know of each other. I'd even be willing to bet Tony Graziano has talked to Conroy about the bag, but Conroy doesn't know where it is. He only knows that the shoes have something to do with it."

"That doesn't make sense." Lili scooted closer, frowning at a sudden thought. "Willis and Joey had already split up. There's no way Willis could've known Joey would hide the bag, much less that he'd use Rose's shoes in some way."

Matt swore quietly under his breath. An obvious conflict of established facts, and he'd missed it. "This is starting to feel complicated."

He sat back, staring out across the water as the boat drifted on the gentle waves. "Maybe Conroy doesn't know anything, except that the partner he double-crossed still managed to stiff him before dying. That means the only ones who could've known about the shoes were Graziano and his men."

"How?"

"Joey must've lived long enough to tell them there was a map in the shoes. Or something."

"We didn't find a map," Lili reminded him. "And if that's what happened, why didn't Lou Graziano grab the shoes?"

"Maybe he didn't have time. Or maybe he did, but something happened later, which might be the real reason why Riley ordered him killed. I can't see where Riley could blame Graziano for leaving the money behind. He couldn't do anything about the cops that were hot on his ass."

He frowned. "Do you know how long it was between

the time when Mancuso was killed and when the cops showed up?"

She shook her head. "No, sorry. If there was any mention of it in the books I read, I didn't pay attention. Why?"

"I don't know. Just trying to get all the facts straight." He regarded her a moment longer. "Where did you find Rose's shoes?"

"I bought them at a farm auction in Vermont from some people who had a couple of her things. Their great-uncle worked as a cook at Big Moccasin Lake Lodge during the thirties. Back then, people thought nothing of helping themselves to crime scene souvenirs—including the police. I suspect that's what happened with Rose's shoes, and over the years they were forgotten."

"So if somebody went back looking for Rose's things, he'd have found the shoes missing, and wouldn't know who took them. He'd probably figured the shoes were gone for good."

"Until I showed up in Chicago, waving them around everywhere I went."

"There's something we're missing about those shoes."

"You'll figure it out," Lili said with confidence.

He'd stretched out along the bench, his head against one side and feet dangling over the other, frowning again. "It sure would be a lot easier if Conroy could've pointed out the spot where Mancuso buried that damn bag."

"You think he buried it?"

"It'd be the most obvious answer, except that Joey's turning into something of a puzzle."

Lili had heard enough of dead men and buried loot, and she gave Matt a poke with the tip of her hiking boot.

"Forget Joey . . . all this pretty scenery is making me feel romantic."

Matt looked amused. "We'll end up in the lake if we try to make out in a rowboat."

"Did I say anything about sex?" she retorted. "Maybe I just want a kiss."

She nudged Matt's legs off the bench, then sat down beside him. The boat rocked, but not alarmingly so. She laughed at the look on his face, and leaned down and quickly kissed him.

He made a deep *mmmm* sound, wrapping his arms around her and drawing her down to his chest. He kissed her soundly, thoroughly, leaving her breathless.

"You like to kiss." In the sunlight his eyes were silver-pale, startling in their intensity, and Lili decided she could easily look into his eyes for hours and hours.

The rest of her life, even.

"I do like kissing." He smiled. "Especially you."

She raised a brow.

"Okay, okay . . . *only* you."

"Smart man," Lili purred, and kissed him again, this time running her hands beneath his flannel shirt. While his tongue played with hers, she pulled up his T-shirt until she could touch warm, bare skin.

He made another low sound in his throat, and Lili closed her eyes, letting herself sink into the kiss. She didn't rush it—nor did he. He was getting into it, kissing her on the lips for a long while, then using a little tongue, then moving his lips from one corner of her mouth to the other.

All the while, the boat moving gently beneath her, Lili kept her eyes closed and listened to his breathing—steady at first, then growing faster, less even. Her hands roved over his firm muscles, and the scents of the lake and woods, and Matt's warm skin filled her, arousing her. Especially arousing because the kiss couldn't lead anywhere else.

After several minutes, she began rocking forward and back against him, in time with the rhythm of the waves. The slight friction deepened her languid arousal to something hotter, sharper. Matt's hands moved to her bottom, and cupped her beneath the smooth leggings she wore, his fingers straying closer and closer between her thighs.

Her breathing was as uneven as his, and still he kissed her, biting gently on her lip, letting her do the same to him, rubbing the roughness of his beard against her, peppering kisses on her chin, her ear, her eyelids.

When he kissed her lids, Lili fluttered her lashes against his lips, laughing. She couldn't help smiling as he kissed her. That warm contentment, all that desire and happiness, pushed its way out, even when her predicament was anything but lighthearted.

Finally, Matt broke the kiss. "Enough," he murmured. "You're making me crazy . . . and I've got a hard-on like you wouldn't believe."

She glanced down, then stroked him through the denim. "Maybe we should start rowing back. Fast."

Lili looked around, noticing they'd drifted a bit. Through the trees, she glimpsed a large, unfamiliar building. "What's that?" she asked.

"Must be Big Moccasin Lake Lodge," Matt answered.

Lili's imagination took over, thinking of Joey and Rose, and how their desperate attempt to escape their fate had ended here. It was eerie, in a way. The place was so isolated, she guessed it was mostly unchanged from that night in 1933. If she let her imagination run far enough, she could almost see Joey, his fedora tipped low, his tommy gun in his hand and Rose at his side.

After a moment, Matt said thoughtfully, "It's closer by boat than by car to where we're staying. But I should've figured that, since the two lakes are connected."

"Does it matter?"

He hesitated, then shrugged. "Probably not."

He let her take one of the oars, and together they started rowing back to the resort.

"Will we look around over at the lodge?" Lili asked, working to match her oar speed to his.

"I don't see how we can avoid it, considering its history."

"I can hardly wait." She shuddered, her imagination getting the best of her. "The thought gives me the creeps."

Matt grinned. "I thought you wanted some excitement in your life."

"There's excitement . . . and then there's danger. Unlike you, I don't find them interchangeable."

His grin faded. "Don't make assumptions about me, Lili, and I won't make them about you."

"Are you saying you don't find the danger exciting?" She stared at him. "Please . . . just this once, answer me truthfully."

"There's a rush," he said. "But I don't seek out danger because I get off on it. I told you before, most of the time my job's boring."

"And you prefer it boring."

"Yeah, I do."

There was a tightness in his voice that warned her not to press further. Foolish of her to keep coming back to this, even though it continued to gnaw at her. It accomplished nothing: He ended up angry and defensive, and she never understood him any better.

He liked being a bodyguard; his job scared her—and that was that. Not a hopeful prognosis for a successful relationship, no matter how much she enjoyed being with him, or that the sex was wonderful and sweet.

Maybe she should just accept her time with him for

however long it lasted. That had been her intention to begin with.

It would be the sensible thing to do—except the thought left her completely dissatisfied.

17

As he drove away from his short meeting with Monica—who'd been tired and irritable through it all—Matt kept a constant surveillance in his mirrors, half expecting that someone had followed her, or that she'd arranged a net to take him in. He hated to be suspicious of her, especially after all she'd done for him, but with Lili's safety at stake—not to mention his own ass—he wouldn't take any chances.

He detected nothing unusual, though, and after ten miles of mostly empty road, he relaxed. Lili was engrossed in looking through the accordion file Monica had handed over, stuffed with copies from old arrest records, evidence files, and library books.

"What's it look like?" he asked, eyeing the bulging folder.

"Joey and Willis were never model citizens," Lili said wryly, looking up. "Early on, it was mostly petty theft and assault, some extortion. Willis had a few arrests for running liquor, and Joey did some strong-arm stuff for a mobster in Kansas City before he ended up in Chicago. They didn't get into serious trouble until they started robbing banks, payrolls, and stores. Willis shot and killed a gas station owner in 1931. Joey killed a cop during a bank robbery a few months later . . . and at that point, their fates were pretty much sealed."

Typical gang activity. Poor and angry young men in big cities had few opportunities; it didn't make much difference if the year was 1931 or 2001. Because they grew up with violence and hate and poverty, knowing nothing else, it became a way of life. A short life, and something he knew too much about.

"Anything in there on the murder itself?" he asked after a moment.

Lili thumbed through the papers, then pulled out one. "Monica was right about there not being much of an investigation. Or if there was one, the records disappeared. I guess the police were so happy Joey was dead, they didn't much care how he got that way. There's just a copy of a newspaper article dated the day after Joey and Rose were killed. The headline says *Mancuso and Woman Die in Wisconsin Gun Battle*."

"Can you read it to me?"

"Sure. It's not long." She cleared her throat. " 'The end came in the black of night and in a rain of bullets'—"

"Damn," he interrupted, with a short bark of laughter.

Lili poked him with her elbow to silence him, but she was smiling. "So, reporters back then were fond of their purple prose. 'The end came in the black of night and in a rain of bullets, and when it was all over, Chicago bandit Joseph Mancuso, twenty-five, and his woman accomplice, Rose McIntyre, twenty-two, were dead, killed by fellow mobsters before sheriff's deputies and federal agents could intervene. The deputies and agents engaged the mobsters in a gun battle near Big Moccasin Lake in northern Wisconsin.' ''

"Huh," Matt said, staring out at the road unwinding before him. It nagged at him, this part about the law officials at the scene. What he wouldn't give for an accurate timeline of that night's events.

"What?" Lili asked. "You keep saying 'huh' like it means something."

"Just thinking. Go on. I want to hear about what the cops found at the lodge."

"Okay." Lili paused, looking over the article. "Toward the end it says, 'Deputy Henry Adams reports more than fifty slugs were fired into the lodge, where deputies found a woman's red shoe, soaked in blood.' '' She stopped, grimacing, then continued: " 'A blood trail led from the lodge, and bloody leaves and spent shells were found outside close to the porch. Sheriff's deputies plan to drag the lake today, where they believe the mobsters disposed of the bodies of the slain bandit and his gun moll.' ''

"Is there any speculation as to the motive for Mancuso's murder?"

"It says, 'sources claim the murder was in retaliation over a recent theft of cash and personal belongings from the residence of Chicago mobster Michael Riley, a known associate of Mancuso and his partner, Willis Conroy. Conroy was arrested earlier in Minneapolis, and reportedly tipped off the police as to the whereabouts of his partner and his partner's female companion.' ''

"Personal belongings," Matt murmured. "It *was* more than money. Joey must've taken something Riley valued . . . although that doesn't explain the Graziano connection, dammit."

Going after the money had never made sense, not after seventy years, and whatever cash Mancuso had stolen would be pennies compared to what modern-day drug trafficking, racketeering, gambling, and prostitution would bring in. Something personal, though . . . that made sense. Now all he had to do was figure it out—and where Graziano fit into things.

If he fit into things at all.

Lili had made sandwiches and packed sodas for the trip, and on the way back from the meeting with Monica, they stopped at a small wayside to eat. Still engrossed in the file, she ate her sandwich as Matt sprawled in the grass beside her, apparently dozing.

She'd pulled out photos and copies of personal letters, and the old photographs in particular tugged at her: Joey, with his dark, broody good looks, and Rose, with her long, slender neck and wide-eyed beauty. Not a single picture caught Rose at a bad angle. She looked like a Hollywood starlet, right down to the penciled eyebrows, cupid bow lips defined by a dark lipstick—probably siren red—and finger-waved hair. In every picture, Joey and Rose were touching each other, and it was adoration, plain and simple, on Rose's face when she was wrapped in Joey's arms and looking up at him.

How had such young lives gone so terribly wrong? She couldn't believe Joey had been born heartless and evil; something had made him what he became. And Rose—what had kept her from reaching for more than an ex-con who'd only die young and violently? Had she looked at Joey and seen a way out of her mother's lifestyle? Had he been exciting and handsome, an answer to her boredom? Or had she simply loved him, fatal flaws and all?

After all this time, it was impossible to know the truth.

Lili pulled out the next photo. Careful, almost girlish handwriting on the back identified the two young men decked out in suits and fedoras, looking every inch like "jazz age sheiks."

"Here's a picture of Willis and Joey."

Matt opened his eyes, propped himself on his elbows and looked. "Which one's which?"

Whoever took the picture—Rose, probably—had been standing too far away, and from a distance both men, dark-haired, clean-shaven, and wearing double-breasted suits, looked alike. "I think the one on the left is Joey."

"They look like a couple of arrogant little bastards," Matt said at length, and lay back down.

Surprised, she stared at him, wondering at his reaction. After a moment she continued thumbing through the photos, lingering on one of Joey and Rose hugging each other beside a tree: Rose beaming at the camera, Joey wearing a half-smile, cocky and defiant—yet his grip on Rose looked almost desperate, as if he were afraid to let her go. As if she were all he had in the world.

Then again, that romantic streak of hers was probably seeing things that weren't there.

Putting it aside, she picked up the letters. They were dated long before that fateful night in 1933—so nothing in them would help solve the immediate puzzle of the shoes or missing bag—but she read them anyway. The first, written by Joey from prison, was dated July 12, 1930.

Dear Baby:

How is my sweet girl? I am o.k. Dear, I hope you will come see me soon, for I am lonesome, and thinking about you, often. They took away my picture of you, and it made me mad. But, don't worry, I would not cause no trouble, so I can get out of this joint. You should know, Frank is working on an early release. Honey write soon. I need a sweet let-

ter from my million dollar baby girl. I would die a happy man if I could see you right now.

I love you,
Joey

With a soft sigh, she put the letter down. Tears, irrational and pointless, stung her eyes.

"What's wrong?"

How embarrassing, going weepy like this over two people long since dead, and one of them a killer. "Joey loved Rose. You can tell by reading his letters to her."

She wasn't surprised to see his frown. "Monica told me Mancuso killed at least eight men. Most were scumbags like him, but two were cops and another was a poor farmhand caught in a robbery gone bad. Don't make him into some kind of antihero."

Lili nodded, knowing he was right, yet unable to shake a sense of sadness. She looked over the copies of Rose's letters to Joey, some upbeat and chatty, others moody and dark. Rose was a woman of mercurial moods.

September 20, 1930
Mr. Joseph Mancuso
Illinois State Prison
Joliet, Illinois

Hello Honey:

How is my man tonight? Lonesome and blue as me? I wish you were here to make me laugh like you always do. Darling, I can't find no energy to write. I cry all day, wishing I would die, I miss you so much. All I want is to stay in bed and dream about how

*much better it will be when you are back with your
baby, where you belong, and promise me you won't
work for the mob and stay out of trouble. I know
you can do it, honey, because you are better than
the others. Don't you believe what they say about
you. I would not love you if you were cruel or bad,
and that is the truth. Missing you so much, crying in
my pillow, boo-hoo-hoo, that's me, sugar. Write
soon.*

All my love to you,
Rosie

Lili sighed. "Rose could've benefited from some
Prozac. She was one very depressed young woman."

Matt made a derisive sound. Obviously his opinion of
Rose wasn't any better than his opinion of Joey. He sat up
again, stretching. "I'm going to talk to Conroy today," he
said abruptly. "You up to playing cards?"

"Sure." She glanced at him, puzzled. "Why?"

"I noticed Conroy had a checkerboard and a deck of
cards with him the other day. Probably how he passes the
time when he's not watching TV. I'll ask him to play a
game of cards and get him talking then."

So he hadn't been dozing at all, but plotting. God for-
bid he should just relax.

"Isn't that a little risky?"

"Sweetheart, everything we're doing is risky." His
boyish grin made her heart pound, and he leaned forward
and kissed her nose. "You probably should've gone with
Monica when she asked you to go back."

As if she'd ever have seriously considered it, despite
Monica's persistent arguments. No matter how things
turned out between them, her place was with Matt. She
knew it, with a certainty that went bone deep.

She smiled back. "I probably should've, but it looks like you're stuck with me, Hawkins."

"Lucky me," he said, his tone wry—but the sudden seriousness in his eyes told her he meant it as the absolute truth.

18

Willis sat in front of the lobby television, paying little attention to the late evening news. He couldn't sleep, and nobody was around except for the girl at the desk and Susie, working on the account books. He stared out the window at the full moon hanging low in the sky, a heavy October moon, and yellow-white in color, like old bone.

What to do with those two kids? He'd tagged the boy as hired muscle the moment he'd clapped eyes on him, and when the girl said her name was Lili, it didn't take no genius to figure out who they were and what they wanted.

He glanced down at the crumpled paper in his hand. It was a phone message his niece—totally unaware of its meaning—had given him earlier: *Tony G. called. He says you'll know what it's about. Call back.*

No matter how hard a man tried, there was no escaping some things.

If he didn't call Tony back, the fruitcake would send

his boys up to visit—and Willis didn't want that innocent girl hurt. Her hired gun was on his own; he was no innocent, and could take care of himself . . . and judging from what he'd seen of those two, the boy had gotten under her skirts for real. Not smart, getting involved like that. Tough to keep cool, when your pecker kept you hotheaded.

No use telling them about the shoes. Better to take the problem away from them and onto himself. It was the least he could do, since this was his trouble and nobody else's. It didn't matter if Tony's boys killed him; he'd lived seventy years too long, anyway.

Best to pinch Rose's shoes while the "newlyweds" were out, then call up Crazy Tony, and hand them over. End of story. Maybe no trouble, in the end, and it would all go away.

The bell on the door chimed. Willis turned to see who was up and about at this time of night—and wasn't at all surprised to see pretty black-haired Lili and her muscle walk through the door.

The bodyguard, his arm around Lili, made his way past the front desk, nodding a greeting at the clerk, then settled his gaze on Willis. The sweet young thing smiled, making up for the fact her bodyguard didn't.

So pretty . . . and seeing her made Willis sit up straighter, glad he'd worn his best denims and his red suspenders. He looked right snappy for a fellow his age.

"Well, well, if it isn't our two lovebirds," Willis said. "Decided to come up for air, eh?"

The bodyguard's eyes went flat, edgy as a tomcat caught outside his territory. The girl blushed, and Willis liked how the blush looked on her, soft and pink on her fair skin.

"Something like that," the bodyguard answered, sitting on the love seat next to Willis. Lili sank down beside him, not meeting Willis's eyes. Instead, she looked down at her hands, playing with the wedding band—a plain ring that didn't go with a lady Willis had pegged as all class and flash from the start.

It was a good cover; he'd give them that. Just not good enough.

"Anything on TV?" the bodyguard asked, his tone a shade too casual.

"Nothing much. There never is."

"So how come you watch it all the time?"

Willis gave a dry, near silent laugh. "I ain't got the distractions you do." Jaw set, the bodyguard opened his mouth, but before he could respond Willis said, "What's your name again, boy?"

"Matt Hawkins."

A hesitation—not much, but Willis noted it. A reluctance to be named.

The muscle—*Hawkins*, Willis mentally corrected—motioned to the checkerboard and cards on the table and said, "If you want, break out the deck. We'll play a game with you."

Willis raised his brows, not bothering to hide his amusement. "You just got married, and you wanna play cards?" He leaned toward Lili, trying not to be too stiff about it, and said in a loud whisper, "Don't know what it is with young men today. Back in my day, a fella knew what to do with a pretty gal, and it sure wasn't playing no card games."

Lili smiled, slanting a look at Hawkins, and Willis could've sworn the temperature around him spiked to scorching when their eyes met.

"I've no complaints, Mr. Conroy. Believe me."

Willis laughed, sitting back. "You call me Willis, sweets. 'Mister' makes me sound like an old fart."

Her smiled widened, blue eyes bright, reminding Willis of another girl who'd been a looker, just like this.

He'd always remember Rose as she was the first night he saw her at the opera house: a red-haired girl with a long slender neck wearing a pale silk gown that flirted with her pretty ankles, and sparkling shoes that matched the sparkle in her eyes as she slowly walked down the gilt spiral staircase. All the men, himself included, had stopped to watch her flutter past, soft and delicate as a butterfly.

Always surrounded by men, she was, everywhere she went. If she hadn't picked the wrong man to love, she might've made something of herself.

"Okay, Willis it is," Lili said cheerfully. "Let's play cards."

Her voice brought him back from those faded memories, the pain of it washing over him in a dark wave of grief. Still, he smiled and said, "Sure. How about you take your pretty little self over there and bring us back some coffee first. Can you do that for me?"

Annoyance briefly flashed across her face before she glanced at Hawkins, who nodded. She walked toward the dining area and the large urn of coffee Susie always kept on hand, and greeted Susie with a smile.

Willis looked back at Hawkins, dropping his gaze to the other man's chest—and the unmistakable, if well-hidden, lump beneath his shirt.

"Is there something you wanted to ask me, boy?" he asked quietly.

The bodyguard didn't so much as blink. "Pardon?"

"I know what you are." Willis leaned forward. "I seen enough hired guns in my lifetime to spot one a mile off."

"I'm not a hired gun," Hawkins said, his gaze cold and hard.

"Is that so?" Willis snorted in derision. "Keep telling yourself that, if it helps."

The boy's contempt vibrated outward, despite his attempt to remain civil. Looking at him, Willis could see himself seventy years ago. The same pride and hostility, the same hunger to be something more than he'd been born to.

"I'm old, not stupid," Willis snapped as a sudden, bitter anger took hold of him. "Remember that."

Lili's hired gun remained watchful, considering his answer, and Willis could almost feel the weight of judgment in those pale eyes.

"If you know what I want," Hawkins said, "tell me where to find it."

Good; he was cautious, untrusting.

"Can't," Willis said with regret.

"Give me a reason to believe you."

Willis tipped his head, studying the young man before him. He'd seen a hundred pairs of eyes like these before, a hundred men just like him. All of them dead now, long, long ago. "You don't have a choice but to believe me."

Hawkins leaned forward and said softly, "I always have a choice."

Willis shrugged, although the boy's contempt angered him. This kid ought to take a good, long look in a mirror. "Not if you want to keep her safe, you don't."

At that, both of their gazes swung toward Lili. She was holding a coffee cup and chatting with Susie, who was plainly delighted to have another female around to jaw with.

Turning back to Hawkins, Willis fixed him with a piercing stare. "Those boys that got shot down in Chicago the other night, they were your friends?"

Fury heated the younger man's eyes. "Yes."

As a heavy weariness stole over him, Willis nodded and sagged back. "I know what you're thinking, but it's not worth it, even if they're friends. Don't put her in the middle. No good can come of it." Willis looked toward Lili again, that old sadness biting sharp. "No good at all."

When he turned his attention back to Hawkins, he added, "You won't be safe here for much longer, so you better make up your mind about what's important to you. I know you don't want my advice, but you're getting it anyway. Take that little gal far away from here and make a life with her. Forget the shoes. Forget the bag. Forget revenge."

"I told you, I am not a killer. Unlike you." Hawkins leaned closer and murmured, "You double-crossed your own partner, you sonofabitch."

Willis looked away so Hawkins couldn't see his eyes. "It was me or him."

"And Rose? She'd dumped you for Joey, so maybe you figured if she was killed, it didn't matter. She got what she deserved, is that it?"

Rage filled him, a rage that he hadn't felt in many years. And guilt; oh, dear God, the guilt. "She never done nothing wrong," Willis said, his voice quaking with the effort to hold back his anger. If he lost his temper, no telling what he'd say. "She wasn't supposed to die. I never wanted her hurt."

"Just an accident, right? Like that gas station owner you killed in 1931 . . . he was twenty-eight, and his wife had just had a baby."

Those bewildered eyes, full of pain, flitted across his memory again—and the memory of his own shock, the sick feeling in his gut that had followed the sure knowledge he'd ended the life of a man far better than he'd ever be.

"Listen, boy, I done a lot of things I wish I hadn't, but at the time I had no choice. When you're looking down the barrel of a gun, you don't think. You act. And once you kill a man, there ain't no going back. Ever." Willis paused. "But I'm sorry he died. And the others."

"I bet. You look real broken up about it, Conroy."

Willis looked back up, still shaking with fury. "You ain't no better than me, sitting over there pretending you're not hoping for a shot at those boys who gunned down your pals. Don't try to tell me you won't kill for *her*." Willis tipped his head back toward Lili, still talking with Susie. "I ain't arguing; some men need killing—but killing is still killing, whether they're wearing the black hats or the white ones." Willis hesitated, not looking away from the bodyguard, or the sudden stillness of his face. "You take the killing on your soul, no matter what."

Hawkins glanced over Willis's shoulder, and by the way his lips thinned, Willis guessed pretty Lili—the real wild card in this game her bodyguard was playing—was making her way back to them.

"Can the shoes help me find Joey's bag and the money?"

Willis smiled. He wouldn't answer, for the boy's own good, but he couldn't resist playing with him, either. "Joey always liked a good joke."

Hawkins leaned closer and asked quickly, "What did he take from Riley? I know there's something in the bag more important than money."

Willis stared at him, surprised. Sharp, this boy. Not one to underestimate.

"A wedding ring." Among other things, but Willis kept his mouth shut about it. He motioned to the ring on Matt's hand. "Plain gold, like that one. Not worth much."

Except to one man, now long dead, and that man's son.

Disbelief and astonishment flashed across Hawkins's face, but Lili had returned. Carefully balancing the steaming coffee cups, she set them down and then sat.

Willis waited to see if Hawkins would tell her they'd been made, to see how the boy would play his hand.

When Hawkins said nothing, Willis reached for the deck of cards. "Here's Lili," he said with a forced cheerfulness, like some grandfatherly old codger in a movie. "I sure do like that name . . . Lili. Gets a man's attention."

She smiled, unaware of his meaning, but Hawkins looked mad enough to spit nails.

"Let's play a game. Joker's wild." Willis smiled. "The joker's always wild. Makes for an interesting game. Right?"

Hawkins stared at him. "Right."

19

"Would you care to tell me what happened back there?" Lili demanded once she and Matt were back in their cabin. She rounded on him, fists on her hips. "The entire time we played cards with Willis, something was going on between you two. Do you think maybe you could clue me in?"

He scowled, and in the low light, he looked drawn and exhausted. "Conroy knows who we are."

The shock hit with an almost physical jolt. "Oh, God . . . are you sure?"

Matt nodded. He was upset, trying to hide it—but she knew him too well by now to miss the signs.

"I get the feeling he's been waiting for us to show up. Your name tipped him off. Among other things." He avoided looking her in the eye; and she knew there was more that he wasn't telling her.

"Did you ask him about the bag?"

Matt nodded. "He said he doesn't know where it is. I

also asked him what was in it besides money, and he gave me this look, like he didn't want to tell me, then said it was a plain gold wedding ring."

"A wedding ring." She stared at him, dumfounded. "This whole thing just gets stranger and stranger every day. Whose ring is it?"

"He didn't say. When I asked him what the shoes had to do with it, he said that Mancuso always liked a good joke."

"Joey the Joker. Of course." Slowly, she walked to the love seat and flopped down on it. A slight headache throbbed behind her brows. "Now what?"

"I don't know. I'm still trying to second-guess Conroy's motives."

Lili shivered. "It's cold in here."

"Do you want me to start a fire?"

She glanced at the dark fireplace. "I'd like that, thanks. Then maybe we should go over the papers in the file again. See if there's anything about a ring."

Matt nodded, and went outside to the small pile of firewood stacked beside the cabin. While she waited, Lili stared out across the room, trying to get her thoughts in order.

Willis Conroy had been waiting for them. She could figure out the "how" part—no doubt Matt had as well—but the "why" part troubled her.

A wedding ring?

Mike Riley had been a flashy man with a notorious weakness for women, but going crazy-angry over a gold band was out of character. Faced with a pouting or teary woman, Riley was the type who'd throw his arms out in an expansive gesture, laugh loudly, and offer to buy something gaudy and hideously expensive to replace the missing ring.

Matt walked through the door, shutting it with the heel

of his boot, and then crossed to the fireplace. She curled her legs beneath her on the sofa and watched him build the fire.

Silhouetted against the flickering flames, he looked primal—almost predatory. Something inside her, equally dark and ancient, stirred to the tang of sap and charring wood, the snap and crackle of the fire's dull red glow, the smoke stinging her eyes . . . and the raw physical presence of the man before her, shadowed against the fire, his profile strong, intent, and beautiful.

It was all she could do to drag her gaze away from him, even as she imagined what it would be like to make love with him in front of the fireplace, to the hiss and spitting of the flames, the heat stroking their bare skin.

Reluctantly, she stood and turned up the lights, then pulled the coffee table closer. As she spread out the contents of the file, Matt came to sit beside her, wordlessly taking half of the pile of papers. He felt warm and solid beside her, and smelled of pine and wood smoke. Lili wanted to curl up against his hard chest, and press her nose against the soft flannel of his shirt.

"I bet you anything Mancuso blew off his ex-boss for a personal reason," Matt said. "Look for any mention of shoes, a wedding ring, Graziano . . . Riley, too. Anything in the last year before he and Rose were killed is worth looking at."

"Do you think Conroy was lying about the bag?"

Matt shrugged. "Hard to say. His type wouldn't know the truth if it bit him on the ass. He might not know where Joey ditched the loot, but he knows what the shoes have to do with it. I can feel it."

"Why doesn't he just tell you? What possible good can it do anyone, after all these years, to lie? He has to know the danger we're in."

"I can't figure Conroy's angle, but I know for sure I

don't trust him. From here on out, we take the shoes with us wherever we go."

"Do you think we should stay somewhere else?"

Matt looked up from the paper in his hand. Finally, he said, "No, not yet. I have a feeling Conroy isn't in any hurry to turn us in. But I'm going to be extra cautious."

Lili sighed. "I already thought you were extra-special vigilant. What are you going to do, not sleep?"

"If that's what it takes."

She couldn't tell if he was serious, but wouldn't doubt it. She directed her attention to the mess sprawled over the coffee table. After an hour had passed and she still hadn't found anything useful, Lili put aside her papers and stood, yawning and stretching. Matt glanced up at her briefly before returning his attention to the file.

Lili walked over to the fire and stared at the flickering red-yellow flames. All those words and pictures tumbled in her mind, like the colorful fragments of a kaleidoscope, leaving her edgy, tired. Grim.

"I wonder what Willis meant, about how Joey always liked a good joke."

"I've been thinking about it, too," Matt said from behind her.

She heard him stand and walk toward her. Even by the fire, she could feel his heat behind her.

He rested his hands on her shoulders, thumbs circling the base of her neck, firmly and steadily. Lili's eyes drifted shut.

"But I don't know enough about Mancuso to take any guesses," he added. "I need Conroy for that, and for whatever reason, he's not being helpful."

Sliding his hands around her, he unbuttoned her lowest button, and kissed the side of her neck.

Lili had a fleeting thought that she should protest, tell him they needed to look at the shoes again, but then he unfastened the next button, and the brush of his lips against the sensitive skin just below her ear made her shiver.

"Maybe Joey did the unexpected," she whispered, as his fingers opened the button over her breasts, lingering on their softness.

His movements stilled for a fraction of an instant, then he said, "Forget Joey." Freeing the last button, he slid her shirt off, letting it fall to the braided rug. He turned her.

In the firelight his face was dark, with a reddish cast. A stranger's face, all angles and hollows and eyes lost in shadows. He touched her, running his hands over her bare skin, leaving goose bumps in their wake.

"You have beautiful skin," he murmured. "Soft and smooth. I can't get enough of touching you."

He smiled, almost ruefully—and she was struck again by how lonely he seemed sometimes, and how she ached to protect him, if only from himself.

Wouldn't he laugh, if he knew what she was thinking now.

Lili leaned close and kissed him full on the lips. "I want to make love by the fire."

His smile widened to a grin. "I was hoping you'd get the hint."

"Mmmm. And it was such a subtle hint, too."

He laughed softly, eyes gleaming as he dropped his shirt, shoulder rig, and gun on the rug. "We don't have time for subtle. I want every minute I can have with you before I put you on a plane back to New York."

Despite her sudden chill she managed to smile, even as an inner voice whispered: *We'll see about that . . .*

Three in the morning, and Matt couldn't sleep. Not surprising, considering he'd been operating on pure adrenaline for days. When he came down off this one, he'd crash hard. Once it was over and Lili was safely home again, he'd take out his sailboat despite the choppy October winds, drop anchor off shore, stay put for a few days, and try to forget.

Forget.

Fat chance. A guy didn't just forget a woman like Lili Kavanaugh.

He shifted on the bed, careful not to dislodge Lili, curled up against his back, her bare skin warm against his. In the darkness, he listened to her breathing, slow and even, and tried not to think about never waking up beside her again.

Between the late hour and making love with her, he should be wiped out, but he couldn't forget his talk with Conroy. Too many questions were running through his mind, and every time he drifted toward sleep, another one grabbed him, and shook him back to wakefulness.

Restless, uneasy, he shifted again. Lili sighed in her sleep, and he went still until she settled against him.

What *had* Conroy meant, about Mancuso always liking a good joke? And what was he missing about the shoes? Lili had pulled up the insoles, checked the hollow heels, and found nothing. Joey Mancuso had done something to them, but he and Lili had looked in every possible place—

Matt bolted upright in bed, rolling Lili backward.

"What?" she demanded in a sleepy, anxious voice. She sat up, clutching the sheet against her breasts. "Is something wrong? Is somebody outside?"

"No," Matt muttered. He shoved the sheet back, ignoring the slap of cold air against his bare skin as he stood. "Dammit, we looked at the shoes exactly where Mancuso *expected* us to look."

He snapped on the lights, blinking against the brightness, and pulled the shoes out from where Lili had hidden them under the bed.

"Matt, I have no idea what you're talking about."

He sat on the bed and held up a shoe. "The top, Lili. We didn't look in the *top*."

"The vamp? I never thought . . . damn." All sleepiness fled, she took the shoe and examined it. "He could've hidden a small piece of paper between the lining and leather. The lining's hand-stitched on both vamps."

Forgotten, the sheet fell to her waist, baring her breasts. "Oh, my God," she said in a hushed tone, her eyes shining with excitement. "It's this shoe! Right here . . . see? The black thread is more brownish, and the stitches are a little larger than the others."

Matt retrieved the pocket knife he'd bought at Wal-Mart, intending to rip the thin fabric away, but Lili took it from him.

"Let me do that. Please." She sighed and carefully loosened several stitches. Once she'd done so, she pulled out the others. Slowly, she peeled back the fabric to reveal a scrap of yellowed, brittle paper, its edges uneven, as if it had been hastily torn from a larger piece. "Thank you, Joey."

"Careful," Matt warned as she eased it out and handed it to him.

Gingerly, he took the small piece of paper, straining to read the faded ink and scrawled words crushed together.

"What does it say?" Lili asked after several seconds had passed.

He read: " 'I left you a bit of money under them mums. If you can't get it, don't worry. I take care of my own. My last joke's ON YOU. Hold that dance for me, baby. Good-bye. I love you.' "

Slowly, Matt looked up, and met Lili's wide eyes. She wore an expression of confusion, and tears glimmered in her eyes. God, she was such a soft touch.

Good-bye. I love you . . .

Still, a sense of sorrow touched him as well. Maybe even killers like Mancuso had a saving grace, and his had been his love for a woman.

It was something Matt could understand, after all.

"My last joke's on you," he repeated at length. "He emphasized 'on you.'"

"Does he mean the actual *shoes*?" Lili asked, her gaze sharpening.

The rhinestones, sparkling in the low light, caught and held his attention. For a split second, Matt struggled against the obvious, then he said quietly, "Mancuso, you sonofabitch."

"What?" Lili snapped in frustration. "Dammit, Matt—"

"Diamonds," he said, tapping the broochlike decorations on each shoe. "I noticed a while back that a few of the rhinestones were loose in the fittings. I figured it was just due to wear, but I bet you Mancuso replaced some of the rhinestones with diamonds."

Eyes wide, Lili asked, "You mean I've been walking around wearing a small fortune in *diamonds*?"

He turned the shoe, smiling grimly. "Conroy never knew about the note, but he knew Rose's shoes had the diamonds."

"Did *she* know?" Lili asked, and Matt glanced at her. Damn; she looked sexy like this, naked and intense with concentration, her skin flushed with emotion.

Forcing his thoughts back to the immediate problem, he said, "Not everything, or else Mancuso wouldn't have left her instructions. Not that the 'under them mums' part does *us* much good."

"Why wouldn't he tell her? What were the chances she'd figure it out?"

"He didn't tell her for her own protection. She couldn't tell the cops what she didn't know, no matter what they did to her." As Lili's face paled, he added,

"Back then, the law was fuzzy on civil liberties. Getting their man—or woman—was all that mattered to the lawmen of the day."

"My God," Lili whispered.

"They'd have let her go eventually." Matt looked away. "Joey figured his partner might turn on him, and he planned on using those diamonds as a financial cushion. If he lived. I don't think Conroy ever said anything about the shoes to the cops, seeing as no hint of the truth ever went public, but Riley and Graziano must've known."

"So Joey stole jewelry, not money?"

Matt's gaze strayed toward her bare breasts again. "He made off with money, but he also took a wedding ring and, obviously, diamond jewelry. Maybe more, I don't know. Conroy might. I'm guessing the jewelry had some personal value to Mike Riley."

"Or Lou Graziano. There has to be a reason for his son to want the shoes."

Matt tiredly rubbed at his eyes. "Me and Willis Conroy are going to have a talk tomorrow. That old man's telling me the truth."

Lili looked at him, suddenly wary. "You won't hurt him? He's old and—"

"A killer," Matt interrupted harshly. "He doesn't deserve your sympathy."

It angered him that she even asked—but disappointment cut even deeper. "No, I won't hurt him." He hesitated, then asked quietly, "Do you really think I'd do something like that?"

"I think you'd do whatever you felt was necessary to keep me safe, whether you should or not," she said after a moment. "It's what we're paying you for—as you've told me so many times before."

Except he wasn't in this for the money anymore. After

he sent Lili home, he wouldn't take a dime of the fee. To hell with his plans for his agency. Everything would go to Dal and Manny. Christ, it was the least he could do.

"You said you made the monsters disappear," she said suddenly, not taking her gaze from him.

Unsure how to respond to this abrupt change in subject, or where she was going with this, Matt only nodded.

"By becoming just like them? Is that how it's supposed to work?"

Her words hit hard, physical as a blow. Heat rushed over him, blood roaring in his ears. Stunned, he stared at her.

"Jesus, Lili," he managed to get out. "How can you say that to me?"

Sudden tears welled in her eyes. "The truth, you mean? I told you I hate your job, but more than anything else, Matt, I hate what it's doing to you. Maybe your other clients never cared what you had to do, or what you had to be, in order to keep them safe. But I care. And I won't have it."

"You won't *have it*?" he repeated, and moved toward her on the bed.

She leaned away, something very like fear flashing across her face, and he froze.

"I'm not apologizing for doing my job or keeping you safe," he said after several seconds had passed, somehow keeping his voice calm and even. "And I'm not doing this for the money, Lili, but because I love you."

Her eyes went wide in shock, and as she opened her mouth, he slid off the bed. He grabbed his shirt and boxers, and stalked into the bathroom.

"Matt, wait!"

Despite her protest, he slammed the door. So it wasn't mature or cool or sensitive. Fuck it. He didn't want to hear what she had to say. Excuses, explanations, apologies. He pulled on the boxers, and as he straightened, glimpsed his face in the mirror.

Suddenly he was sixteen again—back in Pittsburgh, in that stinking hole of an apartment, listening to his father outside the bathroom door shouting at his mother, his sisters bawling—and hating what he saw in the mirror.

Take away his expensive house, car, and clothes, and he was still that angry kid who'd learned, too early, to use violence to survive. Lili saw it in him, despite everything he'd done to rub out the stain. It didn't matter to her that he was one of the good guys—he frightened her.

Closing his eyes tightly, Matt lowered his forehead against the cool glass of the mirror.

He loved her.

How could he have let himself be so stupid? Bad enough he'd done the unthinkable by falling for his own client, but then he'd gone and *told* her so.

And she'd looked stunned.

What had he hoped for? One of those Hollywood moments, when she said *I love you, too* and everything was magically all right?

No matter. He still had a job to do, and he'd finish it and get them both the hell out of here, alive and unharmed. The sooner she was back in her world and he was back in his, the better.

Opening his eyes again, Matt pushed back from the mirror.

Conroy had hit a nerve earlier, too. Matt didn't want to admit that maybe, without even realizing it, he'd come here expecting to meet up with the men who'd shot Dal and Manny. The thought of emptying a clip into the bastards for what they'd done to Lili, to his friends, filled him with a dark, cold satisfaction—and scared him. God, it had been so long since he'd known a fear like this.

A light rap cut across his thoughts, and he turned toward the door. His earlier anger had vanished, leaving nothing behind but a heavy weariness.

"Matt? Open the door, please."

Fighting with Lili was the last thing he wanted, but it wasn't like he could just walk away . . . he was her damn bodyguard, after all. Taking in a long breath, he said, "It's not locked."

He watched the knob turn, the door ease open. Lili had put on a shirt, and her face was pale and full of regret.

Oh, Jesus. He didn't need any pity party, either.

"I'm sorry," she said softly, her gaze unwavering. "I didn't mean it as criticism, Matt. I know you're defensive about your work, but I only said what I did because I care about what happens to you."

"Do you mean that?" Matt asked bluntly, tension tightening his muscles. "I'm not some little experiment in excitement? A new flavor of fun?"

She didn't look surprised by the question. "At the beginning, yes, but not anymore."

Not sure what to say to her honesty, he looked away. At length, he asked, "Why me, Lili? What in hell can I offer you?"

Now she looked surprised, and hot embarrassment filled him. He should've let the subject die quietly. Easier for them both to walk away in the end.

"There's a thousand little things, Matt, all part of who you are. I love your dedication, how you think, and the way you put pieces together into something that makes sense. I admire how you take chances, never letting fear hold you back. You're so physically powerful, but you're never arrogant or careless about it. You're so in control, so self-confident . . . I can't help but be attracted to that." She paused. "I love how you take care of me, but not in a way that makes me feel like arm candy. You ask for my opinions. You listen to me."

She colored slightly. "And making love with you . . . you're rough and gentle, serious and playful, you treat me like an equal, and still make me feel like a woman. You thrill me, alarm me, worry me, and I want to take care of you and protect you—"

"Protect *me*?" he interrupted. "I don't need protecting, Lili."

Anger sparked in her eyes, then she said quietly, "Somebody must've hurt you very badly in the past."

He looked away from her too-knowing gaze, amazed and humbled that, with all his skill at masking feelings, she could so easily see through to the heart of him.

"You can't let the past hold you down," he said finally, looking up again. "I look forward, never back."

"A good idea," she said. "In theory, anyway. But what's behind us, the good as well as the bad, makes us who we are now. Even if I could, I wouldn't go back to change a single mistake I've made in my life. Would you?"

It was a question he never expected. Always surprising him, his Lili. Making him think, making him work harder than was comfortable.

"I don't know," he said bluntly. "Some mistakes are just bad, and I've made my share of those. Lili, I'm not the man you think I am—"

"Of course you are," she interrupted, moving closer and brushing against him. "You just won't let yourself believe it."

She was all warmth and softness, perfume and woman. He couldn't think straight when she was against him like this; all he could do was pull her close and slide his hands under her shirt to bare skin, a purely primal satisfaction shooting through him at her low sound of pleasure.

Matt guided her back to the bed, still locked in an embrace, and eased her onto her back. Sighing, she twined her arms around his neck and whispered, "I have a question, too."

Matt looked down, meeting her gaze.

"What is it you see in *me*?"

The expectation and hope in her eyes was almost more than he could bear.

Without even having to think about it, he said, "You believe in me."

20

Early the next morning, Matt and Lili—with her backpack holding Rose's shoes—got into the car, and headed to Big Moccasin Lake Lodge to play "tourist." They were given the full tour, complete with bullet holes, blood stains, and the bedroom where Joey and Rose spent their last night. An entire wall of the first floor's common room was devoted to framed portraits of gangsters, vintage *Wanted* posters, and photos of lawmen standing outside old-fashioned cars, rifles in hand. Several pictures taken shortly after the shootings showed Joey's stolen sedan, thoroughly ransacked, and another showed two of Graziano's men lying on a dirt road like lifeless heaps of rags. The owner—not shy about playing up his lodge's single claim to fame and very knowledgeable in gangster lore—relished telling the gorier parts of the tale.

All the while Matt asked questions—focusing on the timing of the lawmen's arrival, the locations of blood trails and spent shells, closely examining the 1930s photos of the lodge—Lili kept watching him, almost as if she were seeing him for the first time.

Like he couldn't figure out why. He'd spent all morning acting like nothing had happened last night, as if he hadn't said what he had to her—but he knew better than to expect her to let it lie for much longer.

As they walked in silence back to the car, Lili said abruptly, "Did you mean what you said to me last night?"

No doubt about it, he knew this woman, inside and out.

Matt sighed as he fished the keys from the pocket of his jeans. "You know I did."

"I guess I needed to hear you say it again."

He knew what she wanted, but he didn't respond. Once, a mistake. Twice, a fool . . . and the once was bad enough.

As he drove back toward the resort, Lili's gaze remained speculative. When she took a breath to speak, he braced himself for a confrontation.

Instead, she asked, "What's the deal with those old pictures you kept looking at?"

Relief rushed through him at the reprieve. "I was checking out flower gardens. Mums in particular."

Lili briefly closed her eyes. "Of course. Damn, Hawkins, you're good."

He gave her small smile. "Except there were flowers planted all around the lodge. That doesn't exactly narrow down the search area."

"And the cops? Does it matter what time they arrived?"

"It might not; I'm just coming at the problem from different angles." Then he added, "The story the guy told us puts only fifteen or twenty minutes between the shooting at the lodge and the shoot-out on the road. That wouldn't be enough time for Graziano to dump any bodies."

"So what are you saying? That Joey and Rose just walked away?"

The thought had occurred to him, but if Joey or Rose had survived, somebody would've found out eventually. Habitual career criminals like Joey didn't just go straight. Besides, none of the facts supported the idea.

Matt shook his head. "The blood loss indicates at least debilitating wounds, if not fatal ones. A body was definitely dragged down the front steps. That's plain from the crime scene description. Graziano's men could've split up, a couple of them taking the bodies into the lake and then, when they heard the gunfire on the road, escaped into the woods. It's either that, or someone besides Graziano's thugs dumped the bodies."

"We have enough of a problem with Willis Conroy and Tony Graziano," Lili said flatly. "We *don't* need to add a mysterious third party to the mix."

"I know," he said. "But it's an angle, Lili. I look at all the angles."

Matt parked outside the cabin. With his hand on the small of Lili's back, he walked with her toward the porch—and suddenly slowed, grabbing her arm, as his instincts screamed in warning.

The front door was ajar.

"I shut and locked it," Lili whispered.

He'd already pulled the gun, and pushed her behind him. "Stay close."

"It could be the *maid*, Matt," she whispered, her fingers clutching him.

He nodded, holding the gun low. With a quick look around, to see if anyone was coming up behind him, he pushed open the door.

From inside, he could hear labored breathing, the sound of rustling papers. With Lili pressed against his back, he carefully looked around the doorjam—right at Willis Conroy's stooped back.

"Hello, Willis," he said, walking inside. "Is there

something we can help you find? A pair of old shoes maybe?"

With a grunt, the old man turned, eyes widening. Instead of alarm or embarrassment, his expression showed only irritation. Chin jutting, he snapped, "The hearing ain't what it used to be, or you wouldn't have caught me."

Matt glanced at Lili, who looked both surprised and hurt. He regretted her disillusion, but he'd warned her that men like Conroy didn't change, no matter how many years passed or time served in prison.

"Hands up, Conroy," he said, motioning with the Glock.

"I don't got a piece," Conroy muttered, even as he raised his arms, his hands shaking. "Not like I can hold one steady anymore."

"At close range you could still hit something," Matt retorted, and quickly searched the old man. When he was satisfied Conroy wasn't armed, he slipped the Glock back into the holster and pulled his shirt over it.

"Nice rig," Conroy said. When Matt said nothing, he added, "We didn't wear nothing that small back in my day. Shoulder holsters were big and heavy. Made your back ache like a bitch."

"What are you doing here?" Matt asked bluntly.

Conroy was wearing jeans and a plain undershirt with red suspenders. He'd had on a cardigan sweater, but had tossed it on the love seat—and Matt noted the two faded but unmistakable bullet wound scars on his upper arm.

Seeing the direction of Matt's stare, Conroy reached for his sweater and pulled it on. "Getting shot was a hazard of the job," he said wryly. "Something I reckon you know plenty about."

"Answer the question, Conroy."

"I guess you won't believe me if I said I was delivering fresh towels."

"I don't suppose we would," Lili cut in, her voice cold.

Conroy glanced at her, and shrugged. "I wanted Rosie's shoes."

Matt studied their geriatric burglar, trying to gauge from his expression how much Conroy really did know. "Why?"

"You haven't figured it out yet? Maybe you *are* as dumb as you look."

Lili gasped, but Matt held up his hand to calm her. "He's just trying to make me lose my temper." He stared at Conroy, but the old man didn't look away. "Yes, we figured it out."

Let Conroy stew over what, exactly, that meant.

"Where are her shoes?" Conroy asked at length.

"In a safe place," Matt answered.

Conroy's gaze shifted to the papers and photos scattered across the table. He turned, lifting one of the photos of Joey and Rose, and there was no mistaking the grief on his face—or the sudden spark of rage in his eyes.

"These were personal," he said, his voice cracking, and he picked up a copy of one of the letters as well. "He wrote the letters to her. It's not right, that anybody can see them."

"Joey forfeited his right to privacy when he started killing people," Matt said.

"Easy for you to be judge and jury." Conroy's mouth worked in an effort to control himself. His gaze flicked to Lili. "We wasn't so bad; we just got caught up in hard times, but then we got to where we couldn't go back no more. And you don't know what it was like in them prisons, being a kid and doing time with killers . . . what they did to us boys, what they taught us. You can't understand what it was like," Conroy repeated, turning back to Matt.

"When you don't got nothing and see all the other people who do, and you're just a kid, you think it's okay to take what you want. You tell yourself *you* deserve it, too, only life dealt you a bad hand. So you keep playing the game, hoping for the hand that'll take you outta the game for good. Joey wasn't so bad." Conroy's voice thickened with emotion. "He just didn't have no choices, see."

Matt closed on Conroy, his anger blooming dark and hot. "I know *exactly* what it's like to be born into nothing. My old man was a drunk and an ex-con loser who knocked his wife and kids around—until I got big enough to hit back. In the slums where I grew up, kids survived by learning to be mean, and to always carry knives and guns."

Matt heard Lili's sharp intake of breath.

But it was too late now to close that door to the part of him he didn't want anybody to see.

"I was seventeen when I was shot while trying to steal a car. When I was lying in that hospital bed, fighting not to die, I had a hell of a lot of time to think. I didn't want to be just another statistic, and after I left the hospital my probation officer helped me find a job. I passed my GED, and joined the army a few years later. When I got out, I took everything I'd learned—even the ugly shit—and made something worthwhile out of it."

He glanced at Lili, holding her shocked gaze for a moment, then looked back at Conroy, biting back a sharp resentment.

"I started with nothing," he said tightly. "And nobody expected more of me than to get shot to death or end up in prison. But I knew I had a choice, and I made damn sure I took it. Nobody else was in charge of my life, and nobody was to blame for my mistakes but me. I rose above what I was, Conroy, so don't give me any excuses."

"Rose above what?" Conroy's smile didn't reach his black eyes. "Look at yourself, with your gun, breaking the law, hiding out, gunning for the men who shot your pals . . . and you telling yourself those rich big shots you muscle for ain't as much a crook as some guy in prison with no nickel to his name." He leaned closer over his cane. "If somebody were to hurt that gal of yours, would you kill them? If you can look at me and tell me no, then I guess you're a better man than I ever was, all right, but you got that itch to kill. I can see it. You didn't rise above nothing."

Matt stared at him, the heat of anger replaced by a sliver of cold. "I'm not like you, Conroy, no matter how you twist facts. Try telling the families of those men you and Joey killed that you weren't so bad, and see what they'd say to you."

All at once, Conroy's defiance crumbled. His body seemed to fold inward, and his head drooped. "Yeah," he said, his voice low. "You're right. Joey wasn't nothin' but a no-good bum."

The quiet words were full of grief—but something about his response didn't feel right. Before Matt had a chance to examine it more closely, though, Lili grabbed his arm.

"I want to talk to you," she said, with a firmness he'd not heard before.

He didn't need to be Mr. Sensitive to tell she was upset. "You stay put," he ordered Conroy. "I'm not done with you yet."

He followed Lili to the bedroom, and the minute she'd shut the door behind them, she rounded on him.

"What the hell is the matter with you?" she demanded, shrugging off the backpack and dropping it to the floor. "You treated him like—"

"Don't fall for his act, Lili," Matt interrupted. "He's a manipulator and a liar, and he always will be."

"And how can you be so sure of that?"

"Because people like him can't change."

She gave him a long, measuring look. "For your sake, I hope that's not true."

Body tensed, he asked quietly, "What the fuck is that supposed to mean?"

"You know exactly what I mean."

He stared at her, speechless with anger—and that chilly fear he didn't want to look at head-on.

"Oh, come on, Matt. Don't deny it: The real reason you're angry with him is because you're afraid you're more like him than you want to admit."

"Nothing about that old man scares me," he shot back, and before he could stop himself, he added darkly, "So much for your belief in me."

"Don't." She took in a sharp, short breath. "After what we've been through and shared, I don't deserve to be shoved away." Her blue eyes were bright with anger. "You're ashamed of your past."

"Hell, yes!"

"Why? What you've done with your life is all the more remarkable for what you had to overcome. But you won't believe that, will you? No, it's much easier to believe I'm just a Pollyanna trying to make you feel better." She stepped closer, her face inches from his. "Let me tell you something else, Matt Hawkins: I'd much rather risk loving you, and maybe failing, than walk away from you without even trying."

"That's because you're not afraid of anything," Matt said after a moment. "I keep telling you that you have more guts than you give yourself credit for."

She stared at him for a long moment, the silence ticking by to the thud of his heartbeat. "We have something special between us. I don't want it to end."

Neither did he, but end it would.

"We live different lives," he said quietly. "Too different, and I can guarantee your family and friends won't jump for joy if you bring home a man like me."

"It's not their life. It's mine," she replied, and rubbed at her brows, as if she'd suddenly developed a headache. "What did he mean, that you're breaking the law?"

Matt didn't answer.

"Are you?" she persisted.

"I'm carrying a concealed weapon without a permit. That's illegal, but if I'm caught, I'll just get a slap on the wrist and a fine. It's why your father is paying me an extra bonus under the table, and why my boss brought me in. He knew I'd take the risk if I felt it necessary." He hesitated, then added, "The men after you aren't exactly obeying the laws, either."

"So what you're telling me is that your definition of 'illegal' depends upon the circumstances of the moment," she said quietly.

"That's right." He didn't look away from her troubled gaze. "And the chances of somebody shooting at me."

"Maybe we should call in the police now."

"I'll call Monica."

"I meant the local police."

"I'll call Monica," he repeated.

Her eyes narrowed. "If you won't listen to me, maybe you should listen to what Willis Conroy is telling you. Walk away from this, Matt. Come back with me to New York."

He'd seen this coming, but expecting it didn't make it any easier to deal with. Part of him wanted to believe he could turn his back on everything and go with her. For the first time in a long time, an inner need called out to him, challenging him to do more than just skate through the motions.

Instead of answering, he said, "You stay here. I have to talk to Conroy a minute. Alone."

Before she could respond, he'd walked out the door and back into the main room. A split second later, he heard her footsteps following. No surprise; he hadn't really expected her to stay in the bedroom.

Conroy was still in the room, his back to them, holding a picture of Rose McIntyre. Matt came up quietly behind him, and watched the gnarled finger, with its prominent blue veins, tremble as it touched the woman's smiling face.

The tenderness of the gesture struck him, and that earlier, indistinct feeling of something being all wrong suddenly fused with sharp, shocking clarity.

A wild, absurd thought, and yet . . .

Taking a deep breath, his heart pounding, Matt said quietly, "Hey. Joey."

The old man turned without hesitation.

Across the short distance, their gazes met and locked, and Matt whispered, "Jesus."

The old man straightened, as much as the weight of his years would allow, and slipped the photo of Rose into his pocket. His glare defying Matt to stop him, he walked past, feet shuffling, cane tapping on the wooden floor.

Matt watched him pass, stunned. He hadn't really expected that crazy hunch to be right, and when he swiveled around to look at Lili, he saw his own shock mirrored in her wide eyes.

As the old man reached the door, Matt turned and said, "Hold on. You owe me a few answers."

"I don't owe you nothing." The voice was low, steeped in weariness.

"Yeah, I think you do," Matt said. "For Lili. For my

two men who were shot because of what you know. What you did."

A dozen questions crowded his mind, not the least of which was what had happened to the real Willis Conroy—as if he couldn't guess. The old man turned, and their gazes again locked.

"Are you really Joey Mancuso?" Matt asked.

"Joey Mancuso died on a hot August night back in '33."

"And Willis Conroy? When did he die?"

"About 1978, as near as I can remember."

"And how did that happen?"

Mancuso smiled. "You think I killed him."

"Did you?"

The thin shoulders lifted in a shrug. "He was dying anyway, with a cancer eating away at him." Mancuso glanced at Lili, then back to Matt. "He didn't fight it none. He knew he deserved it. And we made a deal. I let him go on his terms, quiet-like."

"Did he know you were going to steal his life?"

"Neither of us had much of a life to steal," Mancuso muttered. Several seconds passed before he let out a long sigh and squinted at Matt. "You're a smart boy; I give you that. How'd you figure it out?"

"There were no bodies," Matt said. "Everybody assumed they were dumped in the lake, but there wasn't enough time between the two gunfights for that. The motor boat was found drifting, and when I saw how close the two lakes are, I knew somebody had escaped by boat. Somebody who'd been bleeding. It wasn't until you kept defending Mancuso, and I saw you touching that picture, that it all clicked. Willis Conroy never would've defended a man he'd betrayed."

"You got that right," Mancuso said darkly. "The lying sonofabitch."

"Why did you do it?" Lili asked, and Matt glanced at her. She still looked dazed.

A strange sense of regret touched him, that her romanticized image of Joey Mancuso had ended like this. In the space of a few minutes, two men had turned out not to be who she'd thought they were.

"Why? So I could come back here and spend my last days with Rosie. I buried her on the island," he said, motioning toward the lake. "Because I'm family, see, Susie and Frank agreed to scatter my ashes over there when I'm gone. They'd never do that for a stranger. It was the only way to be with her again . . . and Tony Graziano has no cause to bother Willis, but he'd never leave Joey Mancuso alone. I'm an old man; I don't want no more trouble. All I want is to die in peace and be with my girl."

Lili walked to the love seat and sat down heavily. "So nobody knows who you really are? Not even Susie?"

"Nobody knows the truth." Mancuso shifted his weight stiffly, both gnarled hands gripping his cane. "Willis wasn't close to his family and they never kept in contact with him while he was in the pen. It helped that we looked a little alike, but after over forty years of hard living in prison, nobody would know the difference, and it's not like anybody cares enough about old ex-cons to check too carefully. Not even when they bury them, and Willis went into the ground as Joey Mann . . . that was the name I went by after Rose died."

A long silence followed, tense with questions still unanswered.

"We found the note to Rose," Matt said finally. "And the diamonds."

The diamonds part was still mostly a guess, but he knew he'd hit it dead-on right when the old man didn't even react to his statement.

"A good joke, eh? All them diamonds, for my million-dollar baby."

"Yes," Lili murmured. "A good joke, Joey."

Mancuso looked at Lili, sudden tears filming his eyes. "I sure didn't want to see another girl killed by a Graziano. I was gonna steal the shoes and call Tony. It don't matter if his boys kill me. It's not like I got anybody left. My people, my girl, they're all gone." His gaze grew distant, bleak. "Funny, what'll keep a man alive . . . a fear of not knowing what's on the other side, a need for revenge that eats at you for years and years."

"You wanted revenge against Graziano and Conroy," Matt said, his gaze meeting Mancuso's in an uncomfortable understanding.

"You got it, boy. But by the time I healed up, ol' Lou had got himself rubbed out and Willis was in the pen. I didn't know what to do, but Joey Mancuso was dead, and I'd promised Rose I'd try to go straight, see . . . so I kept my promise to her." He paused, then added, "In my own way, I did. I headed up to Canada and found work in the lumber mills. I met a gal who'd lost her husband. She had two girls, and was in a bad way for money and a man to help her out."

"You married her," Lili said.

Mancuso glanced at her, and nodded. "She had red hair . . . I always had a weakness for redheaded gals. And she was good to me. We didn't have no kids of our own, but I got on well enough with her two girls. Then she died, and the girls married and moved on, and I got to thinking about Willis again. I found out when he was getting out, and I was waiting for him when he did." Mancuso suddenly grinned. "You shoulda seen the look on his face when he saw his old pal Joey."

Matt and Lili exchanged glances, and Lili shook her head in disgust and sadness.

"What's in the bag, Joey?" Matt asked.

"I told you. A wedding ring." Mancuso looked down. "A bit of jewelry, and a lot of money. It was a lot of money back then, anyway. These days, it wouldn't amount to much."

"Did the ring belong to Lou Graziano's wife?" Lili asked.

Surprised, Matt looked at her. That thought hadn't crossed his mind, but when he turned back to Mancuso, he saw the old man nodding.

"Maria Graziano was Mike Riley's mistress. One of 'em, anyway."

"Did Lou Graziano know?"

"Yeah, but he didn't want anybody else to know. Never figured that one out. He didn't care if his wife slept with another man, so long as nobody knew about it. He wasn't playing with a full deck, ol' Louie."

In Matt's opinion, assassins rarely were. Rubbing at the back of his neck, he fixed the old man with a thoughtful stare. "Mike Riley wanted his money back, and Lou Graziano wanted his wife's wedding ring."

"Yup. And Lou also wanted back the diamond necklace and earrings he gave Maria for their first anniversary. They was big as rocks, those diamonds. Who they got stolen from I don't know, but they were worth a fortune back then."

So far, everything Mancuso said made sense, and Matt asked, "Why'd you steal from Riley to begin with? You had to know he wouldn't let you get away with it."

"I was mad, and not thinking too good. It all had to do with Maria. I tell you, she was a crazy bitch. Pretty thing, but no better than an alley cat in heat," Mancuso said, his voice hardening with a decades-old anger. "She and Rose got into an argument one night—Rose called her a shameless slut—and Maria pulled a knife. Cut Rosie's arm real bad. I went to Mike about it. He laughed it off, like he always did. Truth is, he liked Maria because she was nuts. Then Mike started bad-mouthing my girl, and I lost my temper."

"You wanted to teach him a lesson?" Matt asked in amazement. "One of the meanest gangsters in Chicago?"

"No, I wanted to make a fool of him." Mancuso cut a sideways look at Matt. "I hit Mike where it'd hurt most, in his money and his woman. I pinched the dough from right under his sleeping nose. The jewelry was a last-minute . . . inspiration, you could say. There'd been a big party that night, and Maria had worn all her fancy jewelry. Before sleeping with Riley, she threw it all on the nightstand by the bed—even her wedding ring. Ain't that the craziest thing you ever heard?" He grew quiet, and when he looked up again, an intensity burned in his dark eyes. "I loved Rose, and I knew the way of a man and woman together is a gift, not cheap. People don't do what Lou and Maria did to each other and call it love. I wanted to make 'em all look like the animals they was. A joke, see. Everything with me was always a joke."

"Until Willis turned on you and Rose ended up dead," Matt said.

"No, that weren't so funny." Mancuso looked down, and angrily wiped at his cheeks. "I sure wasn't doing no laughing."

Silence fell over the cabin, and Matt heard Lili sigh beside him. He looked at her, and she simply shook her head, as if still struggling to believe what was happening.

"Seems to me this ring is more trouble than it's worth," she said.

This coming from the woman with the mile-wide romantic streak. Matt glanced at her, frowning, but he understood. He'd expected the answer to this old mystery to involve intricate plots and complications, but it wasn't that at all. It was personal—and simple. It was about pride. About honor, even among thieves and killers, and about family.

"Tony's as crazy as his old lady. He's got this idea that if he can get her ring and jewelry back, it'll rub off the tarnish of what his ma and pa did. Their shame has been hanging over him his whole life, making him feel like he had to make up for it." Again, Mancuso shifted, looking as if he wanted to sit down on one of the chairs.

Matt considered asking him to do so, but decided against it. He didn't want any of them to feel comfortable or cozy. It didn't seem right, somehow.

"Riley killed Lou so he could have Maria for himself," Lili said. "Not because Lou botched the hit and didn't bring back the stolen money."

"That's right, and because despite what the cops said about me and Rosie being in the lake, Lou knew better, and so did Mike. And Lou didn't exactly botch the hit," Mancuso said, his voice heavy with bitterness. "They shot Rose to pieces . . . I can't stand to think of it, not even after all these years. She never done nothing wrong."

Again, that heavy silence. Matt couldn't block out the images, and by the stricken look on Lili's face, he knew she couldn't, either.

"I got hit six times, but not bad enough to kill me. I passed out for a few minutes," Mancuso said at length, his expression distant, back in time. "I knew she was dead, and I couldn't leave her there. Cops pawin' at her body, her ending up on the slab, strangers gawking at her, and them damn newshounds taking pictures for the paper. I didn't want nobody touching her but me. I don't much remember that night, but I got to the boat. I was hurting bad, fighting to keep from passing out. I made it as far as the island, and that's where I buried her. It weren't much of a grave . . . she deserved a pretty stone, and roses."

"And what happened to you?"

Mancuso sighed. "The boat got loose and drifted away, so I was stuck on that little island. There was this trapper living nearby. Queer old bird . . . looked like a mountain man and lived like some damn Indian in the woods. He took me in and doctored me up. He weren't friendly, he weren't unfriendly . . . it was like he did it because I was there, like I was just some shot-up animal to him. When I was feeling up to it, I went after Lou and Willis but, like I said, I was too late."

Lili was staring down at her feet, a frown creasing her brow. Then she looked up and asked, "Does Tony Graziano know that Matt and I are here?"

"He suspected right off you might come to me. I got a call from him a few days ago. About now, he'll be sending his boys on up to check things out. He's crazy, but he ain't stupid."

Matt blew out a breath. "Then we better not waste any more time. Do you remember where the bag is?"

"I remember. Don't much care to ever see it again. It was all for Rosie . . . if she couldn't have it, I didn't want nothing to do with the money." Mancuso shifted again, the cane supporting his weight. "Why do you want it so bad?"

"I'm turning it over to the cops, along with the shoes. It's the only way Lili will be safe."

Mancuso nodded absently. "With the laws involved, Tony'll back off."

"I'll wait until it's dark before I go after the bag," Matt said. "And I want you to come with me."

The old man nodded again, then narrowed his eyes. "Get her out of here today. Whatever you plan on doing with Tony's boys, I don't give a damn, but don't you put that little gal in the middle of it no more."

"Excuse me, don't call me that and don't—" Lili began.

"I have no intention of gunning for Tony Graziano's goons," Matt interrupted.

But even as he said it, he knew it wasn't strictly true. He couldn't bring himself to look at Lili, fearing she'd see the truth in his eyes.

Mancuso stared at him for a long moment. "Just remember what I said to you. Hate my guts all you want, boy, but I still got sixty hard years on you. How many more bullets you gotta catch before you see that?"

21

A half hour later, Lili still didn't know which had rattled her worst: the shock of discovering Willis Conroy was really Joey Mancuso, the revelation that Matt had survived a horrendous childhood and wouldn't have said a word about it if he hadn't lost his temper, or the emotional bomb Matt had dropped on her in the bathroom last night.

He loves me . . .

Hearing him say it left her deliriously happy and absolutely terrified—and more determined than ever to make Matt see they were perfect together, if he would only open his eyes and look outside his box. For the first time, she'd truly felt she and Matt stood a chance to make it work.

And now this, bringing all the doubts rushing back.

"You should've told me," Lili said into the tense silence.

Matt was seated on the floor cleaning his gun, and her gaze darted from his face to the gun, and back again.

"What good would it have done?" he asked, not looking up. "Like I said, I believe in moving on, not looking back."

It chilled her, his inability—conscious or otherwise—to see how closely he walked the line between right and wrong. How long had it been since he'd been able to clearly see the difference? Or maybe he saw it all too clearly, being in the middle, knowing there were too many gray areas to make for nice, tidy limits. She might not be sorry he was breaking the law to keep them both alive, but it troubled her all the same. Perhaps there had been other alternatives, but he'd chosen the one he knew best: the right of might.

"Probably it would have done no good," Lili said at length. "But that's not the point. I think . . . it would've made me better understand you."

At that he looked up, his expression questioning.

"In particular, why a man who's so intelligent, capable, loyal, and full of compassion would still see himself as—"

"A street punk," he interrupted.

"Yes." She met his shuttered gaze. "Something like, 'you can take the boy out of the 'hood, but you can't take the 'hood out of the boy.' "

"And what if that's right?"

Her headache throbbed dully, and she massaged her brows. "And what if it doesn't make any difference to me?"

He looked back down at the gun, wiping at nonexistent spots. "You really think a shoe designer from New York with a wealthy family, and a bodyguard from Chicago with a juvenile rap sheet stand a chance together?"

"I think Matt Hawkins and Lili Kavanaugh have a chance, yes."

He paused, noting her pointed rephrasing. "That's because you're a romantic, Lili."

"And you're a damn pessimist," she shot back, angry. This man was a fighter, every inch of him—yet he was stubbornly determined to walk away from her without a fight. And she knew why, knew *exactly* what was going through his mind, and she hated it.

"No." He glanced up. "I'm a realist."

Despair rolled over her, overwhelming the anger. "So what you're saying is that when this is over, I'll never see you again."

She didn't miss the faint tightening of his mouth, or how his gaze slid from hers. He shrugged, as if that would be answer enough—but she knew better. He'd find excuses to stay away, "things" would come up. There might be a few phone calls, but they'd grow fewer and further apart until they stopped altogether.

She wanted to kick him for his stubbornness and complacency. Everything he said and did told her he wanted to be with her; how was she going to break through to him? If he didn't want to take that leap of faith, she couldn't force him. It took two to make a relationship work.

Maybe now was the time to start preparing for the hurt coming her way. But no matter what, she wouldn't cry or mope—she had her pride, dammit.

She pushed herself up off the love seat. "Are you going to call Monica again before we go find Joey's bag and that damn ring?"

Matt had called Monica earlier, but got no answer—probably working on a case, he'd said. Now, with a shake of his head, he began assembling his gun. "No. I've left a couple messages. She'll get them."

Lili nodded, and as she walked past him in silence, her

dignity intact despite the gathering hurt, he reached out and grabbed her hand.

"Hey," he said quietly as she stopped.

Looking down at him, she thought she saw an equal turmoil of pain and regret in his gaze. "Hey, what?"

"It'll be okay."

Lili only nodded, pulling free, and continued to the bedroom. Once there, she flopped back on the bed and stared up at the ceiling, wondering what he meant by "okay"—that she'd be fine without him, or that maybe they'd take a stab at a relationship.

Or maybe he only meant he'd be sure to keep her from getting shot until she was safely home.

After all, that was what he was being paid to do.

A shake on her shoulder woke Lili. She opened her eyes to a darkness broken only by a weak light from the bathroom, and saw Matt's face looming over her.

"Time to go," he said.

She pushed herself to her elbows, glancing at the nightstand clock: almost three in the morning. Since she was already dressed, all she had to do was roll out of the bed. "Where's Will . . . Joey? Is he still here?"

Not long after Joey had departed, Matt had decided he didn't trust him and had gone after him. Susie, who'd been sitting with the old man, had looked surprised, but Matt smiled and explained they had a checkers match planned, and promised to walk the old man back afterward. Susie had still looked doubtful, but Joey Mancuso had supported the lie with one of his own—and, Lili had noticed, a grateful expression that Matt had kept his secret.

Lili didn't know how she felt about that—it seemed wrong to deceive such nice people, especially since Joey had a hand in the real Willis Conroy's death—yet she had kept silent.

Nothing was simple and clear anymore.

"He's waiting in the other room," Matt answered. He was dressed in dark clothing from head to toe, as she was. When he'd picked out their clothing days ago, she'd never even noticed that he'd included clothes that would blend in with the night and shadows.

A little unnerving, sometimes, that control and mental chess playing. Not to mention completely alien to her own way of going about life. Could a man like this simply settle down for a nine-to-five job without going crazy from boredom? She'd think not, except he'd already told her he wanted "out of the front line," that he felt a need to move on.

Not much for a girl to pin her hopes on, but it was better than nothing.

"Let me brush my teeth, then we can go," she said with a sigh.

A faint smile tipped his mouth. "We're sneaking around in the dead of night, not going to a party."

She gave him a dark look on her way to the bathroom. Inside it, Lili made a face in the mirror. Like having fresh breath and a pearly white smile would matter to the cop reading her the Miranda.

With a long sigh, she finished up, then grabbed the backpack with Rose's shoes and followed Matt into the living room. Joey was sitting down, wearing an old black leather jacket over his jeans. His gaze flicked to Lili and his mouth thinned.

"Leave her here," he said.

"Can't," Matt answered flatly. "She's safer with me than alone."

The two men locked gazes, and finally Joey looked away. He raised a shaking hand and smoothed it across his shock of gray hair. Then he heaved himself up with the help of his cane and snapped, "What are you waiting for? Let's get this over and done with."

In silence, they filed out the cabin door and down the path leading to the dock. A car would make too much noise, so Matt had readied the old rowboat. Once they'd climbed in, Matt pushed off and rowed toward Big Moccasin Lake Lodge while Lili, clutching the backpack, sat with Joey.

Carefully, so no one would notice, she felt in the pocket of her black fleece jacket, to reassure herself the pocket knife she'd taken—without telling Matt—was really there. Just in case. She didn't want to be like those helpless women in the movies, who stood there screeching while people died around them.

Not that she was feeling very brave. At night, the lake looked eerie—thickly dark, blending into the sky, and the wind in the trees sounded like a low moan. The night was cloudy, the moon a pale smear behind dark clouds. She glanced at Joey and saw him staring out ahead at nothing, his gaze vacant, as if he were a million miles away.

More likely, seventy *years* away.

Matt pulled with powerful strokes against the oars. Before long he brought them to the lodge's pier, and once he'd tied up the boat he helped Lili out, then she and Matt helped Joey.

The old man felt frail and insubstantial in her grip, and while she hated what he'd been—and couldn't get past this ridiculous sense of disappointment that he hadn't died with Rose—she still couldn't help feeling pity for him. He'd outlived everyone he'd known, and for all the laws he'd broken and all the men he'd killed, he had nothing to show for it but a heavy regret that hung about him like a cloud.

"Can I see her shoes?"

Startled by Joey's question, Lili looked at Matt. He nodded once, his face oddly expressionless. She opened the backpack and pulled out Rose's shoes. The rhinestones— and as yet unknown number of diamonds—gleamed in the pale light. She handed one to Joey.

"She could dance the night away," Joey mumbled, running a finger over the shoe, tracing the ornament that Matt suspected held the diamonds. "Nothing made Rosie happier than to show off a pretty new dress. She lit up a room, and the boys never could keep their eyes off her. But she only had eyes for one fella . . . and she'd have been better off if she'd never met him."

This last was so quiet that Lili barely heard him over the splash of the waves against the shoreline. Lili swallowed back a sudden lump in her throat. She glanced at Matt, but he was focused on the dark bulk of the old lodge.

This late, the quiet lay like a blanket over everything, and no lights shone from the lodge's windows. While she understood Matt's wish to do this in secrecy—fewer complications, and quicker than negotiating with the lodge owner—she didn't like it.

Joey handed the shoe back to Lili, and she returned it to her pack with relief. She'd half feared the old man would turn and pitch it into the lake.

Matt stripped off his coat, leaving his gun and shoulder rig exposed, and grabbed the shovel from the boat. "Stay together and keep quiet," he whispered.

Not that there was much to say at moments like this. She and Joey followed him and when the old man stumbled, she took his arm to guide him.

"I'm sorry, Lili girl," he whispered.

Taken by surprise, she glanced at Joey and wondered what he was apologizing for—for being old, for being alive, for being what he was. Matt scowled at them over his shoulder, and she held back her question.

As they closed on the lodge, Matt asked quietly, "Where?"

Joey pointed toward the back. "I didn't bury it far, or too deep. Don't know why nobody ever found it. Maybe somebody did, and kept the money and the rest of Maria's jewelry, and said nothing about it. Then what'll you do?"

"I'll worry about that if we don't find it," Matt said, and began digging where Joey had pointed. The area was in back by the kitchen and storage area, well away from the sleeping rooms. If anyone heard the digging, they'd assume it was a raccoon or a stray dog.

Lili glanced at Joey, who again seemed lost in distant thought. They were standing not all that far from where he'd been shot, and she couldn't help saying softly, "It must be hard for you to be here."

"Ain't been near the place since that night, but I remember it, clear as can be," the old man replied softly. "I was loading up the car, so we could get away before the laws or Riley's boys could catch up. But Rosie . . . well, we didn't get going right away. I should've moved faster, but I was feelin' awful blue, and when I heard the cars on the road, I knew it was trouble. I grabbed my gun and ran." He paused. "She thought it was me, bringing the car around, and turned on the lights downstairs. Riley's boys opened fire. I came running, shooting like a crazy man, screaming, until they gunned me down, right there by the porch."

It was suddenly quiet, and Lili realized Matt had stopped digging. He was looking at Joey, his expression unreadable. After a moment he said, "No talking."

He resumed digging. The sandy, damp ground was soft, and a short while later, the shovel made a soft sound of contact. The smell of wet earth and rot filled Lili's senses as she moved closer.

"Is that the bag?" she whispered, and glanced around,

half expecting lights to flash on and angry shouts to cut across the quiet.

Matt's penlight illuminated the remains of a metal clasp. "Looks that way."

He sent a questioning glance at Joey Mancuso, who nodded. "Yeah, that's it . . . and in better shape than I figured. We both aged pretty well." When Lili and Matt stared at him, he added, "That was a joke. I was always makin' jokes when I was scared spitless. Better to crack a joke than piss my britches, I figured."

Incredibly, Lili found herself smothering a laugh beneath her hand. Even Matt smiled—a little.

"Now what?" she asked.

Relief rushed through her that this nightmare was over, and her life would soon be back to normal. But regret followed hard on relief, hitting her all the more intensely and painfully.

She looked at Matt through a sudden film of tears, at his broad back, and thought: *This is where the good-bye starts . . .*

"Now we call the cops," Matt said, not noticing her hastily wipe at her eyes. "Christ, I hope Monica got my message."

"Nobody's calling the cops."

The unfamiliar voice broke across the stillness. Before Matt could pull his gun, three men emerged from the darkness at the other side of the lodge where, obviously, they'd been waiting.

"Don't do it, Hawkins," the man said. "Arms up."

Fear gripped Lili. She knew that voice . . . Oh, God, she'd never forget that harsh voice in her ear at the Art Institute, telling her to shut up or he'd kill her.

Only this time she could see her attacker's face. Dark, ordinary. Medium build. Light eyes, but as cold and soulless as a shark's. The other two men—one built like a sumo wrestler, the other very blond and gaunt—had their guns aimed at Matt. The guns were dull black, and almost hidden in the darkness.

Lili went still, darting a glance toward Matt—and saw him looking at Joey with dark, silent rage. The violence of his expression terrified her.

Joey didn't look at either her or Matt, but stared straight ahead. Sickened and stunned by his betrayal, she whispered, "How could you?"

"Shut up," said the head thug tonelessly. "Do as I say, and I won't kill your bodyguard."

A lie. They had no intention of letting her or Matt live, or else they'd never have allowed a clear enough look at their faces to identify them.

"Where's the shoes, Conroy?"

Conroy? They didn't know the truth, either, then.

"Ain't my fault. I told you to leave her behind." Joey turned to Matt, gaze unwavering, then added, "The gal has the shoes in her backpack."

"Bones, get me the bag," the leader ordered.

Lili tensed, waiting for Matt to make his move, ready to run or dive toward the ground at an instant's notice.

The gaunt blond walked forward, eyes unblinking, gun ready. He brushed against Lili, and she shuddered at the touch. She could feel him behind her, smell the sweat, cigarette smoke, and the night's dampness rising from his clothes, feel his breath stirring her hair. Matt stiffened beside her, and while he looked calm, his hands in the air, she could feel the tense vibration of his body as he forced himself not to react. Lili took in quick, shallow breaths, trying not to think of the man behind her, and how easily he could put a bullet through the back of her head.

Sweat dripped down her spine, her scalp tingling.

Bones yanked off the backpack, and she stoically looked down at her feet as her body jerked back at his roughness. Fear beat at her like dark wings, but fury had its claws in her, just as it had that very first day.

Her life would *not* end like this, shot down like a rabid dog in some godforsaken woods out in the middle of nowhere. Not without a fight.

At that moment, moonlight caught on a silvery glint of metal. She froze. Beside her, Matt jerked in surprise.

Joey Mancuso had hauled out a gun from his jacket. His hands shook as he aimed, but the leader's back was just inches away.

The blond gunman yelled a warning, and Lili had just enough time to think: *Oh, God, not again . . .*

Matt yanked her behind him with one hand, pulling his gun with the other, as the first shot exploded with ear-splitting violence.

A split second of silence, then shouts and curses, and the answering roar of guns. She felt the recoil in Matt's body, crouched over her, with each shot he fired.

Caught between Matt and the lodge, Lili couldn't see what was happening. She knew a body lay in front of her, though, and as she felt Matt stumble and heard his low hiss of pain, she grabbed for her pocket knife.

Piddly or not, it was a weapon.

Matt suddenly slammed back, knocking the breath out of her in a painful rush. It took a moment for her to realize he was locked in a struggle with the huge gunman, who was intent on knocking the gun out of Matt's hand.

Matt was strong and quick, but this man had sheer bulk and brute strength behind him.

Quickly, Lili scrambled out from behind his protection and into the open.

"Lili, run!"

In a split second, her surroundings registered: the lights blazing in the lodge, panicked shouting erupting inside, and over that, the distant wail of sirens—somebody in the lodge must've already called the cops.

Three shapes lay on the ground, unmoving.

"Goddammit, Lili!" Matt's voice was strained, desperate. "Run for cover!"

She pulled out the knife and pried it open—and knew at once the small blade would have no impact on that hulk ramming Matt against the building, again and again and again.

Oh, God, he couldn't take much more of that.

Frantically, she searched for a weapon. Her gaze touched on the guns that had fallen on the ground, and skittered over them. She'd probably end up shooting herself or Matt.

Scattered across the lawn were rocks, sticks, and branches. She seized one of the largest branches just as Matt made a tight, low sound of pain, and his gun flew out of his hand.

No time for fear.

With a shout of rage, Lili ran forward and swung the branch down across the back of Matt's attacker with all her strength. It impacted on flesh and bone with a force that numbed her fingers, and sent tingling shocks down her arms.

With a grunt, the man turned and knocked her back with his huge fist. The blow took her on the side of the face, pain exploding outward, and she stumbled back, falling on the hard ground with a gasp.

"Dumb bitch," he snarled, as he pulled another gun and aimed it at her head.

Her first thought was to close her eyes, so she wouldn't see it coming—but instead she stared back, letting him see her contempt and anger.

Then half of the gunman vanished behind a dark, solid blur.

Matt rolled between her and the gunman, firing

rapidly, his face a tight mask of concentration.

Graziano's hulking gunman staggered back, shook himself, and took another step toward Matt.

Swearing, Matt fired twice more.

Over Matt's crouched body, the gunman's eyes met Lili's. A look of surprise crossed his face, then his expression went eerily blank. His gun fell from his hand. He opened his mouth, and a thin line of blood ran down his chin.

Lili squeezed her eyes shut, turning away, fighting back a wave of nausea, and struggling to control the dark terror pushing upward from within her. She heard the man fall, a boneless drop to the ground, heavy and dense and final.

But it took him several seconds to die, the gasping sounds he made terrible to hear. Finally, there was silence, and only then did she hear the sounds of her own weeping.

She opened her eyes to see Matt hunkered before her. Their eyes locked as she took a long, sobbing breath, shaking her head, as if denying it would make all the ugliness go away.

"Lili," Matt said.

He reached for her, and she saw the red smear on his hands.

She recoiled.

22

Matt stared at Lili, reading the fear and revulsion on her face. Stunned, he couldn't move, hurt beyond words, more than the white-hot pain in his arm where he'd caught a slug.

He dropped his hand.

Fighting back the pain and a hollow despair, he turned, holstering the Glock. For the first time, his focus widened, and he took in the scope of the carnage. Two of Graziano's men were dead; the blond was groaning and moving feebly. Joey Mancuso lay curled on the ground. Sirens sounded very close now . . . and he heard voices in the lodge, raised in anger and fear. The air smelled of cordite and blood.

More than anything, he wanted to sit down, but he had to take control of the situation before somebody lost their head and started shooting.

"It's all over, don't anybody panic," he yelled. His gaze touched on Lili's pale face, guilt and remorse hammering at him, before he looked at Mancuso's body and the wounded gunman. "And call an ambulance . . . now!"

Quickly, Matt retrieved the fallen weapons, and threw them into the bushes. Then, still facing the nearly unconscious gunman to keep an eye on him, he dropped to his knees beside Mancuso. He turned him onto his back, and whispered, "Oh, Jesus."

An old Colt .45 lay close by, and Mancuso's chest, rising and falling in erratic, rapid breaths, was dark with blood.

"Hold on," he muttered. Lili scooted toward him as the lodge's front door burst open. He met her gaze, and knew she'd see in his eyes that Mancuso wouldn't make it. "Help's on the way, just hold on."

The old man's eyes fluttered opened. "Lili . . . safe?"

Matt swallowed. "Yeah. She's safe."

"Good." With an effort, Mancuso dragged in air, and wheezed out. His hand suddenly flailed upward and Matt caught it in his own without hesitation.

"Hold on," Matt repeated, not understanding this stab of grief for a man he could never like, and who'd very likely betrayed him and Lili.

"Good God," said a voice from behind him. "What happened?"

"Aw, hell!" A new voice—the owner—full of shock and anger. "My place . . . you shot up my place!"

"Stand back," Matt barked, without turning or taking his gaze from Mancuso. "Watch that man over there. I don't think he's armed, but don't count on it. Somebody get me a towel!"

The sirens were close, and he could see the glow of red and blue lights. He was aware of the babble of voices around him, a warm hand on his arm, fingers painfully tight. Somebody shoved a shirt at him instead of a towel, and he took it, trying to staunch the bleeding.

"No good," Mancuso whispered. He took a long breath, and his lips twitched in what might've been a smile, or maybe just a grimace of pain. "Here I am bleeding all over . . . this same goddamn place again. Pretty good . . . joke . . ."

Mancuso shuddered as if seized with a sudden coldness, and then he gave a loud sigh, and went still.

Tightening his grip on the old man's hand, Matt leaned close and whispered, "Joey?"

But there was no response. Carefully Matt eased his hand free, and laid Mancuso's hand down against his chest.

He turned, and met Lili's gaze. A single tear tracked down the dirt on her face. Her lip was bleeding a little where Graziano's goon had hit her. Her hand was on his shoulder, and it had been her fingers digging into his skin.

Looking beyond her to the knot of a half-dozen men behind her, some wearing only underwear, he read confusion and shock on their faces.

"That's . . . Jesus, that's old Willis Conroy! Doug, you better call Frank and Susie," ordered the lodge's owner, toting a shotgun in a stance that said he knew how to use it. He looked at Matt, and recognition sharpened his gaze. "You! I remember you were here yesterday, asking questions . . . What the hell are you doing? What's this—"

The rest of his question was lost in the wail of sirens. Three squad cars careened onto the gravel drive, lightbars whirling red and blue, sirens blaring at ear-splitting decibels. Local deputies, followed by what looked like a park ranger's Explorer.

Matt stood. He turned from Mancuso's body, and raised his hands. "Get your hands up where they can see them, Lili. Now."

Her eyes glinting with sudden unease, she did as he ordered.

And none too soon, as cops poured out of the squads, guns drawn, and yelling. The general gist was: *Face down on the ground, hands behind your head! Everybody!*

"Do it," Matt said tersely. "Small-town cops can get a little nervous."

He eased himself to the ground, the rocks, sticks, and pine needles jabbing him, hands behind his head, his face in the grit. Lili followed, and then the men from the lodge, all of them silent and round-eyed, except the cursing owner, who was protesting loudly over the shouting deputies.

After his Glock was taken away, Matt found himself roughly hauled up and slammed against the lodge. The deputy yanked his hands behind him and cuffed him. The movement pulled at the torn flesh in his arm, shooting pain through him, and he grimaced, but said nothing.

Turning his head, he saw another deputy push Lili against the building as well. He met her eyes as the other deputy quickly searched her, seeing her fear and humiliation at such treatment.

He hoped she could see in his eyes how sorry he was for getting her into this mess.

A female voice he recognized shouted, "Hey! Take it easy—they're not the dirtbags, dammit. Are you blind or just stupid? He's bleeding!"

Monica Espinosa, way out of her jurisdiction and not letting that stop her from throwing out orders.

At least now he knew why she hadn't returned his earlier calls. He had no idea what she was doing here, but at the moment he didn't care. If ever he needed a cop on his side, it was now.

"Well, excuse me, Detective," a man snapped back. "But it appears I have a bunch of dead bodies and a helluva lot of firepower here. My job is to secure the scene first and make nice later."

"Sheriff Fitch, these are the people I was talking to you about: Professor Lili Kavanaugh and her bodyguard, Matt Hawkins," Monica said, parking herself between him and Lili. "Uncuff them, and let him sit down before he passes out."

With his face still pressed against the building, he could barely see Monica squaring off against a big man with a brush cut. Finally Fitch swore under his breath, then said, "Take the cuffs off this man and get him some bandages. Let the woman go. The ambulance is on the way, but it'll be at least fifteen minutes." He turned. "And let these other men up. Why the hell couldn't you people stay inside instead of sticking your nose where it doesn't belong? Is that one dead?"

The park ranger, hand on his gun, leaned over the blond hitman and said, "He's shot up pretty bad, but he's breathing."

"I recognize him," Monica said. "John 'Bones' Gallagher. The short one is Michael Fiore. I don't know the ox. Gallagher and Fiore are Graziano's men. Fiore is rumored to be his main hitman."

"Not anymore, he ain't." Sheriff Fitch rubbed his hands over his face. "Aw, please . . . tell me that ain't old man Conroy. He's a popular character around these parts, always had a joke, a good story to tell. What the hell are people gonna think about this? Christ, he was ninety-something!"

Matt briefly caught Lili's eye and leaned back against the wall. "They'll shake their heads, and talk about how Willis Conroy died a few feet from where the partner he ratted out seventy years ago was gunned down. Just one more chapter in the legend of Joey and Rose."

Lili didn't challenge the lie of Mancuso's identity. Maybe she, too, realized it wouldn't serve any purpose.

If it had been possible, he would've pulled her close to

comfort her and shield her from this rough handling and the brutal ugliness.

"What are you doing here?" he asked Monica as she came up beside him.

"Playing cavalry," she retorted. Anger burned in her eyes, but beneath it was concern. "I dropped by to talk to Crazy Tony and found out he'd left town. I had a real bad feeling about that, and when you didn't call, I decided I'd better haul ass up here and alert the locals to what was going on." Monica's gaze shifted to Lili. "You okay?"

"A little shook up." Touching a finger to her lip, she said, "But I'm okay." Lili moved to Matt, concern filling her gaze. "You're bleeding. What happened?"

"Caught one," he said tersely. "It's not bad."

"That's what you said the last time." Monica sighed and muttered, "I'm not sure I want to know what your definition of 'bad' is. I told you not to shoot anybody."

"It's not like I had a choice."

"Yeah, I know." Monica looked over the bodies of Graziano's men. "You tangled with some very bad people. We bagged Tony himself, by the way. The cocky old bastard was sitting in a little bar in town, waiting for his goons to show up, his limo parked outside. Two state troopers just walked in and took him into custody on the spot. We were on our way to Conroy Cove Resort when the 911 came in from the lodge here." She moved closer. "Who opened fire first?"

Matt glanced at Joey Mancuso. "The old man."

"Why?" asked Sheriff Fitch.

"I don't know. I didn't get a chance to ask." Matt dropped his head back against the lodge, struggling against a sudden wave of nausea and pain. A square-jawed deputy handed him a wad of gauze, and he pressed it against his arm, wincing. "Maybe he was trying to even an old score. He shot Graziano's main hitman in the back, and then all hell broke loose. The blond guy shot Conroy. I pulled my gun and took him down, just as the big bastard came at me. I was getting hammered, until Lili hit him with a branch. He knocked her aside, and was going to kill her, Monica. I didn't have a choice. I had to shoot."

"Nobody's going to mourn these bastards," Fitch said, "and it doesn't much matter to me who shot them. Self-defense, is how I see it."

Matt met the sheriff's dark eyes, then shifted his focus to Monica. Reading the warning in her gaze, he kept his mouth shut, and nodded.

"But what I'd really like to know is what the hell were you doing out here to begin with," Fitch said.

"That's a long story," Matt said.

"I reckon we have plenty of time," the man said dryly.

In a few minutes, Matt explained the whole tangled tale as best he could. One of the rangers poked at the old leather bag in the dirt and said, "I'll be damned. This is gotta be the craziest thing I've ever heard . . . all this trouble, over a wedding ring and a pair of old shoes."

"Shoes carrying a small fortune in diamonds," Lili said. She retrieved the backpack, and pulled out one of the shoes. All the men stared at it for a moment, and the ranger shook his head again.

"Crazy," he repeated.

Sheriff Fitch glared at Matt. "Maybe none of this would've happened if you'd had the good sense to contact me."

"Would you have believed me?" Matt asked. "A story like that?"

God, he was tired. And he'd begun to shake . . . whether from loss of blood, or from the realization that he'd killed a man, he didn't know. He wanted to slide down the wall and sit on the ground, and above all else, he wanted to kick himself for underestimating Joey Mancuso.

Damn, how could he have been so stupid?

Fitch grunted a noncommittal response to Matt's question—answer enough—and turned as another two cars arrived, both state patrol cars. "Well, well . . . here comes the big man. I wonder what Mr. Graziano will have to say about this sudden reduction in his labor force."

"I want to see him," Lili said quietly.

As everyone turned to stare at her, Fitch said, "I don't think that'd be a good idea. You're a little emotional—"

"Let her," Matt cut in, his gaze meeting Lili's. "We all need to face the monsters sometime."

Understanding flashed between them before she looked away again.

The sheriff sighed, then walked to the last car and opened its back door to reveal a handcuffed, elegant older man in a black overcoat, his silver hair carefully styled, his nose classically Roman. He stared straight ahead, his head at a regal angle, even as Lili walked forward.

"Is this what you were looking for, Mr. Graziano?" she asked, dangling one of Rose's shoes from her finger.

Anthony Graziano didn't respond. A man like him knew the game too well to show any emotion—yet Matt could've sworn the man twitched, as if he wanted to look.

"The diamonds from your mother's necklace. That's what Joey Mancuso stole, wasn't it?" Lili asked, moving closer.

Fitch followed, looking uneasy. "Don't get too close, ma'am."

Instinctively, Matt tensed . . . though he didn't think he'd be much use in a crisis right now.

"Did it ever occur to you, Mr. Graziano, to just give

me a call," she said, her voice tight with anger. "And make me an offer I couldn't refuse? That's what people like you do, right?"

At last, Graziano turned to Lili, his face expressionless—but his gaze shifted to the shoe only inches from him. Mere inches.

"You bastard," she spat, and hurled the shoe at him before the sheriff could stop her. The heel hit Graziano on the cheek, drawing blood.

"Whoa, hold on," Fitch snapped, and dragged Lili away.

For an instant nobody stood between Matt and Graziano, and their eyes clashed and locked across the short distance. Then Tony Graziano looked forward again, chin raised, ignoring the blood trickling down his cheek, and one of the troopers shut the door.

Nausea hit again, and the ground heaved.

"I'd like to sit down on the porch steps," Matt said abruptly.

Fitch looked at him sharply, then nodded.

Matt turned away from Monica, from the gathered lawmen and lodge guests, away from the disturbing scene behind him. Again, he caught Lili's gaze, and considered veering toward her and taking her in his arms—until he remembered how she'd recoiled from him, with that look of revulsion on her face.

He made his way to the steps and sat carefully. The gauze beneath his hand felt wet and warm.

Exhaustion rolled over him, a dark, suffocating wave. He lowered his head to his knees, eyes closed, struggling to block out the images flashing across his mind: Lili's horror, the big gunman's final gasp for air, and Joey Mancuso, dying in almost the exact spot where he'd been gunned down seventy years before.

Oh, God, he'd killed a man. He hadn't had time to

even think about it; he'd just rolled and started firing, as he'd been trained to do—but targets didn't have eyes that lost light as life faded away, or fight for every last breath.

Joey Mancuso's angry words echoed in his mind: *You rose above what? Look at yourself, with your gun, breaking the law, hiding out . . .*

Add killing to that.

No wonder Lili had turned away from him. He couldn't blame her, and maybe it was for the best. He'd known it would be like this in the end; that she'd see he wasn't the kind of man she should love. He'd tried to tell her, but she hadn't listened to his words.

This she couldn't reason away.

In the distance, he heard the airy wail of another siren. The ambulance, he hoped. He didn't look up, but he was aware of the exact moment Lili sat beside him on the step. Her scent, the vital feel of her charging the air around him . . . his body knew, without having to see.

"Matt, are you all right?" She sat close enough that he could feel the heat of her body—but she didn't touch him.

"Yes," he said automatically. Then, squeezing his eyes tighter against the pain, he whispered, "No . . . no, I'm not."

23

Sometimes silence could be louder than a city teeming with people—and what lay between her and Matt, as she followed him up the steps of his Lincoln Park townhouse, was one of those heavy, troubled silences that drowned out everything else but inner thoughts.

Spending the night at his townhouse, rather than going to a hotel, had seemed like a good idea at the time. Her flight out of O'Hare tomorrow was early, and she'd agreed to his suggestion because she didn't want to face crowds of people with her split lip and bruised cheek, and this new, embarrassing tendency to go weepy without warning.

Though she understood that her hyper-emotional state was a normal reaction to trauma, it didn't ease her embarrassment when she suddenly found tears streaming down her face in a restaurant, at a gas station, or in a supermarket.

Lili stared at Matt's broad back as he opened his door.

Facing a room of students right now might've been less stressful than spending her last night with this man.

"Come on in," he said quietly as he turned on the light and stood aside.

Wordlessly she walked past him, careful of his wounded arm in its sling, and into the foyer. He followed, and punched in the security code that deactivated the alarm.

The house had high ceilings, wood floors polished to a high gloss, lots of airy white wall space, vintage detailing in the plaster cornices, and carved window frames and doorjambs.

"It's lovely," she murmured.

"I hired someone to decorate it for me. It's not something I'm real interested in, but I wanted the place to look good."

"Well, I'd say you got your money's worth."

It looked "good," but where were the messes? The dirty socks and discarded clothing lying about, the piles of newspapers or junk mail catalogs, or any of the usual clutter of life? The place looked like something out of a decorating magazine, a showplace, but strangely . . . sterile.

"Monica said your luggage from the Drake is coming over later by taxi." He stood as if he didn't know quite what to do, as if having a guest in his home was something new and unusual for him.

Maybe it was. Bodyguards likely didn't have a lot of spare time to throw barbecues or Monday night football parties.

"It was nice of her to take care of that for me," she said, because she had to say something.

How incredibly awkward. Considering the physical and emotional intimacies they had shared in the past few weeks, and what they'd been through, the simple act of communicating shouldn't be so difficult.

Had they nothing to say to each other anymore? She could almost hear the walls coming down with a solid finality.

Matt cleared his throat. "Come on. I'll show you to the bedrooms. You can pick which one you want."

Bedrooms—plural. For the one man who lived here maybe a couple of weeks a month, when business was slow.

Pushing away her pervasive sense of sadness, Lili forced herself to smile and said, "Lead on."

He showed her two bedrooms, both of them perfectly decorated, but it was the one he didn't show her—his own—that intrigued her most. She left him in mid-speech about an attached bathroom and wandered down the hall to his room.

After a moment, he came after her. As she'd expected.

This room, at least, had a personality. Still light and airy, it felt lived in; and carried his scent. Books and magazines lay stacked on the end table, a pair of shoes sat on the floor by the bed, a jelly jar full of pocket change was on the dresser along with a bottle of cologne, and a leather bomber jacket was draped over a side chair.

He had framed Art Deco prints on his walls, one of a sleek bullet-nosed train above the bed—she tried not to look at the bed. She saw a framed photo of a sailboat with a smiling man on deck: Matt, in swim trunks and sunglasses, his dark hair wind-ruffled.

"Is this your boat?" she asked, walking to the picture. He looked so happy and carefree—much as he had in those precious few days they'd had together at the honeymoon cabin.

Since the shooting at Big Moccasin Lake Lodge, though, the shadows had returned to his eyes.

"Yes," he said, coming up behind her. So close . . . she could feel the heat of his body and she fought the need to lean back, to be enveloped once more in his warm, comfortable strength.

Lili nodded and turned, briefly catching his gaze—dark, shuttered, the lids half-lowered. A number of other framed photos were arranged on his dresser, and she walked past him to examine them, still very aware of Matt watching her.

She recognized Manny, and a couple of photos showed Matt with Monica Espinosa in obviously more cozy days. Amazingly, the jealousy stirred, and she didn't know if that made her happy or sad.

She headed again for the bed—plain Mission-style slatted foot- and headboards, covered with a masculine-looking navy duvet with burgundy corded edges. He must've reined in the designer a bit here. No frills, just simplicity in tones of blue, with an understated male elegance.

Sitting on the bed, she said, "I like this room. It's comfortable. Very you."

Matt rubbed the back of his neck. "You can stay in here if you want. I can sleep in one of the guestrooms."

"Matt. Look at me." When he did with obvious reluctance, she added, "Why can't we both stay here? I don't want to be alone tonight."

He let out his breath, and leaned back against the wall. He wore jeans and a red T-shirt, and looked vivid and vital against the white paint. "It'd be a bad idea."

"Why?" she asked bluntly. "Because I'm leaving tomorrow, and sleeping with me one last time would compromise your morals?"

"Assuming I have any morals left to compromise." Something in his voice raised the hair on her arms.

"Joey had his own agenda, and a skewed outlook on what was right and wrong," Lili said softly. "You're not like him."

He dropped his head back against the wall, and closed his eyes. "All I ever wanted was to be one of the good guys, Lili," he said in a low voice. "And to keep people safe from the kind of shit I grew up with."

For a long moment she didn't answer, not trusting herself to do so without betraying the tears just below the surface of her calm. She wanted to go to him, and hold him—just hold him—but she didn't move from the bed.

A sudden tightness came over his face, and he opened his eyes, meeting hers with piercing intensity. "In some ways, Mancuso was right. Maybe my clients don't kill cops or rob banks, but a lot of them didn't get to the top of a major corporation by being nice guys. I know what they do sometimes skirts the fine edge of the law."

"What are you trying to say, Matt?"

"I don't know," he admitted. "All I know is that I'm feeling like I shouldn't be around anybody right now. Not even you."

A chill stole over her. "It's a lot easier to feel sorry for yourself that way, isn't it? Being alone and pushing people away?"

A muscle in his jaw flexed. "I fucked up, Lili."

"So excuse you for being human. Even a master gets checkmated from time to time. How could you know he'd set us up?" When he didn't answer, she said, "He did set us up, right?"

"Maybe he did; maybe he took a gun because he had a bad feeling. Unless Tony Graziano talks, we'll never know for sure." He paused. "But Mancuso died trying to protect you. While I just stood there, not doing a damn thing to save our asses."

"He shot that man in the back." She looked away, trying to hold back the memory. "I still don't know how I feel about what he did."

Matt said nothing, but there wasn't much to say. Not a

born sociopath, molded by a series of poor choices and a hardscrabble existence, Joey Mancuso defied comfortable, tidy labels.

"Why didn't you want to tell anybody who he really was?" Surrounded by other people until just a few hours ago, she hadn't had a chance to ask before now.

"What good would it do? It wouldn't change anything, only hurt some people who don't deserve more hurting. Conroy's family doesn't need to know they were conned, and Mancuso's stepdaughters don't need grief like this coming out of the blue."

"I suppose that's true. And part of me is glad Joey and Rose will be together again." Lili looked up and saw the blank look on his face. "I know . . . me and my romantic streak."

"I wasn't—" He cut himself off with a sigh. "I'm glad you didn't lose that part of you, is all. Even after what I put you through."

Lili pushed herself up from the bed, and as she walked toward him, a look of unease crossed his face.

"I don't have any regrets, Matt." She looked him in the eye. "Except one, and it's nothing I can change, it seems."

Again, a muscle in his jaw clenched. "Don't stand so close to me, Lili."

"Why?" she asked softly, aware of a sudden, burning anger. "Am I turning you on, and you don't like it? Or do you think you're not good enough for me, tainted or dirty, and trying to be all noble about it?"

Irritation, mixed with indecision, sparked in his eyes, and she noted it with a dark satisfaction.

"You know, I thought we already went down that road, about you saving me from myself." She moved even closer, brushing against him—and close enough to feel his arousal.

"Lili, stop. This isn't going to do either of us any good."

He started to move away, but she grabbed his shirt in her fists and pushed him back against the wall, making his eyes widen in surprise before narrowing.

"Maybe," she murmured. "But I'm not getting on that plane tomorrow without first making damn sure you know what you're walking away from."

"A good fuck?"

If she hadn't expected something like this from him—and understood why—she might've been shocked, angered, or hurt. Instead, she smiled.

"Yeah, I am a pretty good fuck," she said, watching his mouth thin and his nostrils flare slightly. "Nice try, Matt, but you're forgetting I've been inside your skin, your head . . . I know what you're trying to do, and it won't work."

She released one hand from his shirt and slid it leisurely down his chest, feeling his belly clench, then down to his groin. His erection was hard beneath her stroking fingers.

"Mmmm," she purred. "I think the laddie doth protest too much."

He stood stone still, staring down at her from below lowered lids, his dark, thick lashes curled against flushed cheeks that were a dead giveaway.

She released his shirt with her other hand and yanked it from the waistband of his jeans.

"Dammit, Lili," he muttered, his voice thick.

Their gazes clashed—and Lili leaned into his tensed body and kissed him. Hard, aggressive; her anger and grief and love for him in every stroke of her tongue along his, as if she could will him to feel it. He made a sound at the back of his throat, raising the hand of his uninjured arm. Out of the corner of her eye she saw his hand hover for a split second, and then he cupped her head, his fingers tangling in her hair.

He kissed her back, his breathing rough, releasing his pent-up emotions in that kiss, in his press of his hips against hers. Moving his hand downward to the small of her back, he pulled her hard against him.

It was all she needed. With one hand up his T-shirt, stroking his chest, she worked at his belt buckle, his zipper.

Matt suddenly pushed her away, his chest heaving, jaw set. With a low curse, he ripped off his sling, then grabbed her by the front of her shirt and yanked her back against him, roughly fumbling with the buttons until he had the shirt off and his hands inside her bra, squeezing her breasts.

"Yes," she whispered, and their eyes met for a moment before Matt pulled her leggings and underwear down.

A moment later he had her against the wall, his jeans down, her legs around his waist, and he thrust hard into her, holding her between the smooth wall and his heated body. She could feel the tremors in his muscles under her clutching hands, from the force of his holding back—and need tore through her, making her gasp.

The feel of his hands on her, his breath on her neck, the eroticism of being against a wall with Matt deep inside her, moving with a merciless intensity, overwhelmed her in a haze of pleasure and she came almost at once. The aching impact of release stretched and elongated, swelling outward, and then dissolved on a shiver as she cried out sharply, curling against him.

Matt followed within seconds, head back, tendons straining, a low groan squeezed from his throat, his fingers digging into her bottom. Spent, he slumped against her, the heated dampness of his perspiration-sheened skin filling her senses.

Slowly, Lili dragged in a breath, and only then realized that in her anger and muddled feelings, she'd given him no time to put on a condom. She felt a moment of panic until she remembered she was due to start her period in a couple days. She was in the clear, but that had still been an incredibly stupid, risky thing to forget.

Had he even noticed?

At that moment, Matt raised his head. His eyes were scant inches away; his face so close she could see the striations of color in his pupils—the sudden regret and remorse that filled them.

Yet he didn't pull out of her.

"Stay with me, Matt," she murmured. "No one will ever love you like I do. That wasn't just fucking, and you know it."

She saw the answer in his eyes, but she tried one last time.

"Find another job. If you won't take the chance, then you're not the man I thought you were."

"That's the trouble, Lili," he said, his voice raw. "I never was that man to begin with. I tried to tell you all along, but you wouldn't listen."

All the hope inside her died, and Lili looked away from him, pushing him back and out of her. "I tried," she said wearily. "At least I can say that."

24

"*United Airlines Flight 896 with service to New York's LaGuardia Airport is in the final boarding process through Gate B-8. All ticketed passengers should now be on board . . .*"

Matt sat beside Lili, hunched forward, elbows on his knees. She leaned in the opposite direction, briefcase in her lap, arms crossed over it.

Not exactly the body language of young lovers unwilling to part.

Glancing at her, he said, "It's time for you to go, Lili."

"I know."

She was pale and quiet, her eyes hidden by dark sunglasses. The ache in his arm was nothing compared to the ache inside. Even certain as he was that saying good-bye to her was for the best, it still hurt.

And it would hurt for a good long while yet.

"This is it, I guess," Lili said, standing and pulling the strap of her briefcase over her shoulder.

Matt came to his feet as well, still stiff with the banging he'd received, his arm in the sling. "Good-bye, Lili. Stay safe."

She nodded. "Same to you. If you're ever in New York, stop by to say hi."

"I'll do that," he said, but it didn't sound convincing even to his own ears.

Polite untruths, acting like nothing was wrong.

"You're a good man," she said quietly. "Remember what you told Joey Mancuso, Matt. There are always choices."

He had nothing to say to that. Swallowing, he shifted his gaze to the few remaining passengers heading through the boarding gate.

"That's all I wanted to say. I have to go now." She leaned forward and pressed a kiss to his cheek. "Thank you for all you've done. Be happy."

Be happy.

Grief and anger burned at the back of his eyes. Abruptly, he took her by the shoulders and pulled her close, kissing her with hard desperation. No chaste kiss of friendship, no sweetly romantic farewell. He kissed her like a lover, deeply and thoroughly, until he felt her body tremble.

Finally she pushed away, and a single tear fell from beneath her sunglasses, tracking down her cheek, over the bruised and split lip. Her chin trembled, then she tightened her mouth, turned, and walked away from him.

The woman collecting the tickets noticed the tears— and probably the lip—and likely jumped to conclusions. She gently touched Lili on her arm. Lili, her face averted, shook her head and walked into the jetway, not once looking back at him, her shoulders square, head held high.

A good thing, Matt told himself. He didn't want her to

break down. No more than he wanted to sink down onto a chair, surrounded by hundreds of strangers, and cry like a damn baby.

Intending to put as much distance as possible between him and Lili's plane, he stalked away. Before long, though, he slowed, then stopped amid the constantly moving stream of people. Slowly, he turned and walked to a window, from which he could just glimpse her plane.

Matt rested his forehead against the glass, watching her plane back away from the gate, then taxi toward the runway. It took off, nose sharply angling upward, and he watched until it was only a speck against the clouds.

When he could no longer see it, he turned from the window and headed for his car. As he drove in the heavy traffic, all he could think about was that single tear falling from beneath her dark glasses.

Taking a deep breath, Matt tried to shake free of the memory. He had a dozen things to do—Dan Armistead wanted to talk with him, and he was supposed to go to the police station again. First, however, he needed to see Manny and Dal.

At the hospital, he steeled himself for the difficult visit as he walked down the bustling halls smelling of sickness and disinfectant. He sought out Manny first, and found him in a wheelchair, his leg encased in a bulky cast and propped up. His bandaged hand lay on his lap, and he held a TV remote in his other hand, rapidly cruising through channels. When he saw Matt in the doorway, the bored glaze of his eyes vanished and a grin split his stubbled face.

"Matt!" He motioned him in. "Hey, my man, good to see you."

In the brief instance their gazes met, a wealth of understanding passed between them.

"Good to see you, too, Manny." Matt squeezed his shoulder, and smiled. "How's it going? You look like shit."

"Thanks, you asshole." Manny grinned. "I'm trying to persuade the nurse that I can't shave myself left-handed and need her to do it. You should see her. She's hot, man. Real nice on the eyes." His grin faded, and his gaze took in the sling, the cuts and bruises. "You know, you don't look so good yourself."

"Been better," Matt agreed.

"Monica told me what happened. You're lucky to be alive." He shook his head. "I still can't believe this whole thing about shoes and gangsters and shit."

"I hear you," Matt said, sitting on the narrow hospital bed. He lifted his sling. "But I got the bullet hole to prove it happened."

"And a broken heart, yes?"

Matt glanced away. "It's for the best."

Manny was quiet for a moment. "What are you gonna do now?"

"I don't know." He looked up again. "Meet with Dan and hand in my letter of resignation. Go down to the police station for my slap on the wrist, and see if they'll give me back my gun. Take my boat out for a few days."

"Sounds like a plan." Manny nodded, meeting Matt's gaze briefly again. "Hey," he said. "You wanna sign my cast?"

"Sure."

Matt took the offered pen, and leaned forward. He signed: *To the luckiest bad-ass I know—get better. Matt.*

"So what's going on with this leg of yours?" Matt asked, too raw to handle any further questions about himself.

For the next hour, he and Manny talked about everything that didn't touch on anything too personal or painful, until Manny's easy-on-the-eyes nurse arrived with lunch, medicine, and a razor.

Manny winked, and Matt left with a grin. He headed to Dal's room, his smile fading, and spotted Jodie standing outside, talking seriously with a man in OR scrubs. He'd met Jodie several times before; she was a dark-haired, energetic woman, pretty and young—but today lines of strain marked her face, and her eyes held none of the sparkle he remembered.

Her eyes widened when she saw him. She finished her conversation with the doctor, and once he'd walked away she held out her arms to Matt, face tightening as she tried not to cry.

Matt took her in a hard embrace, squeezing his eyes shut, and felt her slight body shudder in his arms.

"Oh, my God, Matt," Jodie said with a sniff, pulling back. She gave him a wobbly smile, and tucked her hair behind her ear. "We were all worried sick about you. How are you?"

"Forget about me. How's Dal?"

"He's still drifting in and out of consciousness, but he's doing okay," Jodie answered, her voice tired. "He seems to be able to move without trouble, but he complains of pain a lot, and he has some trouble talking. The doctor thinks that's probably just because of the pain medication. But he's doing okay," she repeated, this time smiling a little. "It'll be a long, hard road to recovery, but it doesn't matter. He's alive, and that's all that counts."

"How are you doing?" he asked, searching her face.

"Tired, but I'm better now that he's awake. We'll beat this thing, me and Dal. I love him too much to let him give up." She smiled again. "He's going to be such a big baby, and I know this sounds weird, but I can't wait for the bad moods and short temper that'll mean he'll be fine."

Matt smiled back, knowing she meant every word. The road ahead would be tough for a few years, but she understood that and was prepared. "Dal's a lucky guy to have you, Jodie."

She blushed, and for some reason, the sight of her pink cheeks hit with a sharp, inner pain. He took a long, silent breath, trying to block out memories of Lili—laughing, yelling at him, loving him, attacking that hulking gunman. Without her, it felt like somebody had hacked a gaping, black hole in his life. Whenever he turned around, he kept expecting to see her.

"Can I visit with him?" he asked after a moment.

"Sure. I don't know if he's still awake, though. Come on."

Matt followed her inside. Unlike Manny's room, with its open drapes and blaring television, this room was darker, quieter. Dal lay on the narrow bed, covered by a blanket, hooked up to IVs and catheters. Bandages swathed his head, and his face was so swollen that he hardly looked like the same kid. Tears stung Matt's eyes, and he blinked them away.

He sat next to the bed, aware of Jodie behind him, her hand on his shoulder. He took Dal's cool hand, careful of the IV lines. "Hey, Dal. How's it hanging, kid?"

At the sound of his voice, Dal's eyes fluttered open and he smiled faintly. "Hey." His voice was low, difficult to hear. "I messed up, huh?"

"Nah," Matt answered, tightening his hand over Dal's. "Don't you even think that. It was my screw-up, not yours."

"You take them down?"

"Yeah." The brutal memory flashed to mind again, in all its chilling detail. He swallowed. "I did."

Dal's eyes drifted closed, then opened again. "I don't feel too good," he said, his tone apologetic.

"Considering what happened, I guess you wouldn't," Matt agreed. "I have to get going anyway. You take it easy, hear me?"

"Getting shot in the head's not so bad. Everybody knows us guys have a spare brain below the belt anyway." He managed another weak grin. "It won't keep me down."

"Better not." Matt grinned back. "Don't make me have to come in here and kick your ass out of bed."

Jodie laughed, and Dal made a huffing sound that might've been a laugh, too.

Not wanting to tire out Dal, or intrude on Jodie's time with her husband while he was awake and responsive, Matt gave Dal's hand a last squeeze, then left. Jodie followed him.

After making sure the door was shut, she fixed him with a steady look. "Tony Graziano's men—were they the bastards who shot my husband?"

Matt nodded. The wounded gunman had admitted as much, according to Monica. Matt, of course, hadn't been allowed anywhere near the man. Through clenched teeth, Monica had said: *You lie low and keep your mouth shut. We'll handle it.*

Jodie took a long, deep breath. "The men who died, did you kill them?"

He went still, not wanting to go back to that night, to the look in the big gunman's eyes before he toppled over, dying.

All he could answer was: "Yes."

Jodie stared at him for a long moment, then her eyes hardened. "Good," she whispered. "I'm glad. Thank you."

With a last quick hug and a dry brush of her lips against his cheek, Jodie returned to Dal's room, leaving Matt behind, stunned and cold with a deep, black fear.

Slowly, he turned away and headed back to his car, not even aware of the rush of activity around him. In the parking ramp, his footsteps echoed on concrete, and the wind moaned beneath the low ceilings. He opened the door of his BMW, ducked inside, and slid the key into the ignition.

Jodie's words haunted him; he couldn't get them out of his head. Instead of starting the car, he slumped forward, rested his forehead on the steering wheel, and squeezed his eyes shut.

25

Lili stared out her office window, her breath fogging the glass and hazing the view. Not that she was missing much. New York in November was bleak, without green leaves, grass, or multihued flowers in window boxes to alleviate the colorless tones of roads and buildings that blocked out the sky and pale warmth of the winter sun.

Considering her mood, not even sunny Cancun could cheer her up. She didn't want to pretend everything was fine. After spending two weeks at her parents' house, coddled and pampered, she'd returned home to escape her good little trouper act. She couldn't take more of their worry, how they handled her as if she were glass, always whispering around her, as if a normal tone of voice would shatter her.

What she'd needed was to be alone, to find her own way to deal with her grief and anger. She'd known leaving Matt would hurt, but she hadn't realized how much—and between the ever-present sadness and the nightmares that kept her from sleeping, she'd lost weight and had trouble concentrating. Even her students had noticed, and watched her with an irritating mix of awe and speculative curiosity.

Nothing like the notoriety of surviving a gun battle with professional assassins to improve class attendance.

Of course, everybody assumed her glassy-eyed stares and forgetfulness were because of her ordeal. Nobody—except her parents and Jared—knew that her biggest problem was a broken heart.

What a quaint phrase for this pervasive moodiness, the squeezing ache inside her, and restless emptiness. Broken implied a simple fix; a dab of glue here, and—voilà! Good as new.

If only it were that easy to mend her hurt and anger, and stitch up the tatters of her dignity. She swung constantly between tears and fury that he'd walked out of her life without so much as a backward glance.

She had really thought he would come with her, and her disappointment that he had failed her hopes cut as deeply as her grief.

With a sigh, she idly drew an unhappy face on the fogged window, then a heart. Realizing what she'd done, she frowned and rubbed the doodles away with the back of her hand.

Looking up again, she focused on the sidewalks full of people huddled in their coats, hurrying hither and yon, dashing between trucks and yellow taxicabs, rushing the *Do Not Walk* signal. Movement, movement . . . nothing ever stood still. Life hurtled onward, no matter what.

Which was exactly what she needed to do; just move on. She had a backlog of work to catch up on, and needed

to finish three new designs for next spring's bridal line—
and then there were all those boxes of files and computer
diskettes and whatnot that Jared had sent.

True to her word, she'd taken her first steps in becoming more active in her own business. She hadn't exactly
fired Jared, but had told him she didn't need him to baby
her along anymore and she wanted to learn the ropes.

After his initial surprise—and resentment; guys like
Jared didn't cotton well to being told they weren't
needed—he'd agreed to teach her. He'd been patient,
spending hours going over detailed reports and files until
she thought her brain would pop from information over-
load.

He'd argued with her about her decision not to expand
her line to nonbridal footwear, but she'd dug in and finally he'd admitted defeat.

For the first few days she'd panicked a little, uncertain
if she could really do this on her own. Investments,
schedules, profit and loss statements, payrolling, produc-
tion timelines, catalog mock-ups . . . it was a bit more
than she'd bargained for. She'd always been involved on
some level in all of it, but mostly superficially.

Trying to absorb these new tasks more fully had kept
her too busy to mope—at least during the daylight hours.

The phone rang, and she turned, considering letting
the answering machine take the call. But knowing she
couldn't hide away from life like this, she walked to her
desk and picked up the phone—and hated how her heart
pounded, still hoping to hear *him* on the other end.

"Lili Kavanaugh."

"Hey, Lil," said Jared, cheerfully.

Lil . . .

Another, deeper voice, rang in her memory: Matt's, so
clear it seemed as if he were standing beside her, and she

briefly closed her eyes. The first time he'd called her Lil was the night he'd kissed her for the first time.

"Lili?" Jared asked when she didn't answer.

Shaking herself free of the memories, she smiled and said, "Yeah, it's me. What's up?"

"Nothing much. Just checking up on you, like the obsessive-compulsive chump I am. How's it going?"

"I'm a mess, but I'm getting better."

Silence, then, "Have you talked to Hawkins?"

"No. And I'm not going to." Sensing the tension underlying his voice, she turned toward the window and abruptly changed the subject. "You sound upset. Did you and Olivia have another fight?"

Over the line, she heard his sigh. "I called and told her I wanted to drop by for a visit, she said it wasn't a good time, and the next thing I knew I was shouting, and she was hanging up on me."

Biting her lip, Lili said, "Do you want a bit of advice about Olivia?"

"I dunno. Depends."

"You've been too patient. Get more aggressive, Jared; let her know you mean business. Give her an ultimatum, and if she says no to you again, don't go back. You deserve better than to have her yanking you around like this."

"Aggressive? With Olivia? Somehow I have a feeling she'd kick my ass if I tried. She's not into that caveman stuff."

"You might be surprised," Lili said.

"Huh," he said after a moment. "Maybe I ought to drive over there, and drag her into the bedroom by her hair."

Lili arched a brow. "That might be pushing it."

"So why aren't you following your own advice and

calling Hawkins?" Jared asked abruptly. "Give him an ultimatum."

"I did," Lili said. "Me or the job, and he chose the job. End of story."

"If you're really that crazy about the guy, maybe you could give it a try with him anyway."

"I couldn't handle it, Jared," Lili said quietly. "Never knowing where he is or what he's doing, always worrying if he might be hurt . . . or worse. I got a good look at those risks he runs. I saw men shot, and die."

She had to close her eyes to hold back the images, the flash of blood, the final gasps for breath, the utter ugliness of it all.

Taking a long, steadying breath, she added, "I can't forget, and I won't ever live through that kind of fear again. If I'd stayed with Matt, pretending nothing was wrong, we would've ended up hating each other, fighting constantly, and eventually all the love would die away. I can't do that to myself, or to him."

For a long moment, Jared said nothing. "You're right. You deserve to be wonderfully, blissfully happy, Lil. I'm sorry it didn't work out."

"Me, too, Jared . . . me, too."

After hanging up the phone, Lili sat at her desk, staring down at the design sketches scattered across her desk.

Then her gaze settled on the phone again. Maybe she *should* try calling Matt. She didn't have his number, but she could call his agency and leave a message. If he was still there. What if he'd already left? He'd said she was his last assignment.

Beneath the indecision and longing, a familiar resignation stirred. If Matt had wanted to find her, nothing would've stopped him. And if he hadn't contacted her by now, nearly a month since they'd parted, he never would.

She swiveled her chair around, blinking rapidly, and several minutes passed as she focused fiercely on the framed antique shoe prints on her walls.

"This weepy stuff has got to stop," she muttered.

"Do you talk to walls a lot?"

Lili froze, her fingers gripping the armrests. Slowly, hardly daring to believe her mind wasn't playing tricks on her, she turned her chair and faced the tall, dark-haired man in jeans and a black leather bomber jacket leaning against the closed door of her office.

"Hi, Lili." Matt didn't move from the door, and she could sense the uncertainty vibrating from him. His gaze didn't leave her face. "You busy? I can come back later if—"

"No, I'm not busy. I'm . . . I have absolutely no idea what to say," she admitted baldly. "I never expected to see you again."

"I know." He paused. "I was in the area, and you said if I was, I should drop in and say hello."

Her heart pounded, a steady *thump-thump-thump*. "Why are you in New York?"

"I'm looking for a job." After a moment, he glanced around at the pictures crowding the walls of her office. "Nice pictures."

"They're all taken from my collection."

Oh, this was good . . . the man of her dreams walked back into her life, filling her with a hundred questions, and she discussed decor. Lili stood, but didn't move away from her desk. "Are you looking for a job in security?"

If her situation could get any worse, this would be it. If he were halfway across the country she could pretend he was safe, but if he were right here, in New York . . . Anger spurted. How could he do this to her?

"No," Matt said, looking straight at her. "I'm not in security anymore."

Lili abruptly sat down, tingling with elation, yet half-afraid to hope. Then the meaning of his words sank in.

"I see," she finally managed.

"Do you want to have lunch?" he asked.

"Yes . . . yes, I'd like that." She stood again, feeling a bit like a jack-in-the-box, and headed for her coat.

God, she wanted nothing more than to throw herself in his arms and hug him as hard as she could. She'd missed the press of his body against her at night, his arms around her, his quiet strength and quick mind. As she passed him, the heat of his body, the scents of cologne and leather, hit her with a visceral jolt, making her knees weak and the rest of her go all shaky.

"You're looking good," she said with deliberate calmness, and reached for her coat.

Matt helped her into it, then turned up the collar around her chin and pulled her closer. "So are you," he murmured, his gaze searching hers as he brushed the sides of her jaw lightly with his fingers. "I missed you, Lili."

"I missed you, too," she whispered—but pulled away from him, gently yet firmly.

She had too much pride to fall for him all over again—not until she understood why he was really here.

"You changed your hair color."

She touched her hair, remembering. "I was in need of a change." She left it at that, knowing he'd never understand why a new hair color had made her feel that little bit better on a bad day when she'd needed it most.

"It's . . . red. Kind of." He cocked his head to one side, studying her. "Or more like—"

He stopped, and made a questioning movement with his hand.

"Maroon?" she supplied. God, he was such a . . . guy.

"Yeah, more like maroon. I like it."

She smiled, feeling her cheeks warm. "If you're going for fake, why hold back? There's an Italian place a few blocks away. It's not fancy, but the food's great."

"Works for me," he said, and as he opened her office door, he crooked his elbow toward her.

She hesitated. He noticed but said nothing, only waited in silence. Still, he wasn't as calm as he pretended—she could see the lines of tension around his mouth, the wariness in those gray eyes. Finally, she rested her hand on his arm, oddly touched by his old-fashioned manners, and he led her outside.

They didn't talk as they walked down the noisy, crowded street and into the restaurant. It was warm inside, pungent with the scents of tomatoes and garlic. The same family had run it for three generations, and eating there felt like eating at an old friend's house. Because it was mid-afternoon, the hostess was able to seat them right away at a table toward the back. The woman smiled, placed menus on the white tablecloth, then left them alone to watch each other over the single red rose in a glass vase in the middle of the table.

How awkward—and strange. She'd shared a bed with this man, told him secrets, and had made love with him time and time again. All she had to do was close her eyes, and she could see his body in graphic detail. Yet it felt as if they were meeting as strangers, struggling for what to say, how to act.

"How's your arm?" she asked, settling on a safe subject.

"Almost as good as new." He shifted his gaze away from her, then back. "Did you ever get your shoes back from the police?"

Lili shook her head. "Not yet. There's a collector in

Las Vegas who's offering me an obscene amount of money for them, to go with his gangster collection. I just might let him have them."

"It could be a long time before anybody sees them again, or that bag they dug out of the dirt. Technically, I guess the ring and jewelry belong to Tony Graziano, but I don't think he's in any position to demand anything."

She smiled a little, and took a sip of water. "And Manny and Dal . . . how are they doing?"

"Manny's fine. He's been out of the hospital for a while, but he's still in physical therapy. He said to tell you hi." When she smiled, he added, "It was touch and go there for a while with Dal, but he's doing great."

"That's good to hear."

With the safe subjects exhausted, another silence fell between them. Lili shifted in her chair, wondering what to do next, and caught Matt's expression. "What are you smiling about?"

"You," he said. "You're squirming."

She sighed. "I don't know what to say. I'm happy you're here, but I can't help wondering what this is all about."

"I told you I'm looking for a job—or trying to, anyway. I wasn't taking the easy way out when I told you there's not a lot of work out there for someone with a work history like mine. Especially if I'm not looking at any more security jobs."

To give her hands something to do, she began playing with her spoon. "I thought you were going to start your own agency."

"I changed my mind." He sat back in his chair, taking in a long breath. "After what happened, I can't go back to that kind of work."

Alarmed she asked, "Did you get into trouble? Did they take away your license or something?"

Amusement touched his eyes. "No, I didn't get kicked out of the bodyguard club." Then he glanced away. "I killed a man, Lili. He was a lowlife animal, it was self-defense, and he was the one who shot Dal—but no matter how often I remind myself of that, I can't forget. And Joey Mancuso . . . what he said shook me up pretty bad."

"Matt—"

He held up his hand. "Let me finish. What he said made me do a lot of thinking, and in the end I didn't like what I came up with."

Lili reached across the table and took his hand in hers, squeezing it sympathetically. That night still gave *her* nightmares—and she hadn't been the one who'd pulled the trigger.

"What I'm trying to say is that the truth sometimes takes getting used to, especially since I was so damn sure I was right. But I wasn't, and there's no way I can ever go back." He brushed his thumb against the inside of her hand. "I did tell Dan Armistead I'd teach seminars at his training institute. It's good money for a few weeks a year, and I know I'll find a job soon enough. Even if it means flipping burgers."

The waitress arrived to take their order, smiling warmly at them—probably because she and Matt looked like two sweethearts, all lovey-dovey in their little corner of the world.

After the woman left, Lili pulled back her hand, a small hope rising within her. Unable to hold back any longer, she asked, "Did you come to New York for me, Matt?"

Quietly, he said, "I came to New York for us."

At the words she'd wanted to hear for so long, her heart skipped its regular beat, and she took a quick breath to keep from bursting into tears and embarrassing herself.

"I kept telling myself it'd be a mistake and wouldn't

work. We were too different, and a guy like me wasn't what a woman like you really wanted. Except I *like* how you're different from me, and I'm not so sure anymore what kind of guy I am."

"Well, I know." At his raised brow, Lili smiled. "You're *my* kind of guy."

A wide, answering smile broke across his face, reminding her all over again why she'd fallen in love with this man. He had so much heart, touching her like no one else she'd ever known.

A sudden inspiration took hold of her. Maybe a crazy idea, but she fixed him with an intent stare as she leaned across the table. "Matt, I sort of fired Jared. My business manager."

He raised a brow. "Good for you. How'd he take it?"

"I think he was secretly relieved, though he'd never say so to my face. He's showing me the ins and outs of running a business. I'm sure I'll do fine, and it'll be good for me to learn about the nuts-and-bolts end of things, but I know I'll need to hire somebody to help me out," she added in a breathless rush, trying to get all the words out before he could interrupt. "Like you said, sometimes it's hard to face the truth, but the fact is, I just don't have a good head for business. You want the job of running things for me?"

He stared at her, and a good half minute passed as she waited in an agony of anticipation before he said, "Me? You want me to work for you?"

"Why not?" she demanded, stung by his tone of voice, as if it was the most inconceivable thing he could imagine.

"Lili, I don't know a damn thing about shoes."

"You don't have to. Jared didn't. All you have to do is manage details, and I know you'd be good at that." She tried to look as serious as possible in the face of his continued bemusement. "I've been studying up on market analysis, profitability assessment, flow charts, and balance sheets . . . all that stuff you talked about that afternoon. I can understand it, but I have to tell you, Matt, it's not my bliss. You know what I mean?"

He smiled, rubbing his hand across his beard-shadowed jaw. "Bliss, huh?"

"But you think and analyze like a strategist. You see all the pieces of the whole, all the possibilities and problems that might play out. I need someone with your brain, because mine tunnels on color and form, design and function . . . not dollar signs."

"At last," he said, his smile slowly widening to a grin, "a woman who wants me for my brains, not my brawn."

"The brawn's a perk," she said mischievously, her gaze lingering on his shoulders and chest. "Can't have a business deal without perks."

He focused on her face with that unnerving intensity of his. "You're serious?"

She sketched an "X" across the chest of her tight, black knit dress—and observed how his gaze followed her finger across her breasts. "Cross my heart and hope to die."

He looked up from her breasts, his gaze full of sensual intent. "Do I get perks, too?"

Lili arched a brow. "Depends on how you perform. On the job," she added hastily, going warm.

"What if I screw up on the job?"

"I suppose you'd have to go back to flipping burgers."

"And the perks? Would I get to keep those?"

"Buddy, you drive a hard bargain." She laughed softly, still warm. "But most definitely. It's part of the package deal."

"All right," he said after a moment. "I'll take the job of keeping you organized, Lili, but under one condition— you have to marry me."

Lili jerked in surprise, nearly tipping her water glass. "*Marry* you?"

"Not right away," he added quickly. "We need some time to get to know each other better first."

She swallowed, uncertain of his seriousness. "True," she agreed.

"But those couple weeks were pretty damn unforgettable."

Their eyes met, memories of those days and nights sizzling between them. Matt shifted on his chair and rubbed at the back of his neck, looking so unsure of himself that she wanted to rush to him, fling her arms around his neck, and kiss him until he could hardly breathe.

Instead, she stayed in her chair, her hands clasped in her lap, waiting.

"I can't imagine my life without you in it," he said quietly. "I just can't."

Tears pressed against the backs of her eyes, and happiness rushed over her. "Oh, Matt, that is the most romantic thing any man has ever said to me."

"It is?" he asked, plainly startled. When she nodded, laughing, a smug look crossed his face. Holding his hand out across the table, he flashed that knee-melting smile and said, "So whaddya say, dollface? Is it a deal?"

She stared, then said in a low, provocative voice, "You want to shake my *hand*?"

"That's the way you seal a business deal."

She tossed her napkin aside and stood. "Not in my business it isn't."

His gaze sharpened with alarm. "Lili—"

Lili lifted one knee onto the table, then the other, and crawled across the table toward him.

Matt's jaw dropped.

Pushing the dishes aside, Lili kept one hand on the

table for support, then slid the other into his hair and angled his face toward her.

She kissed him deeply, with a whole lot of enthusiasm
and a touch of tongue. Matt made a low, surprised sound,
then reached up, cupped her face in his hands, and hungrily kissed her back.

At the sound of cheers and scattered applause, Lili
broke away and glanced at the customers and employees
who watched, some in amazement, others with broad
smiles. Looking back at Matt, she grinned into his half-
lidded, sexy gaze and ignored a faint flush of embarrassment.

"Deal," she whispered. "Sealed with a kiss."

A smile curved his mouth. "You know what, Lil?"

"What?"

"You're always surprising me."

"Is this a good thing?"

He laughed, pulled her off the table and onto his lap,
and gave her another long, deep kiss. "Yeah. It's a very
good thing."

EPILOGUE

**"Sugar and Spice, Naughty and Nice:
Shoes for Girls Who Just Wanna Have Fun"**

by Armand Brownlee,
photographs by Lisa Loomis
Harper's Bazaar

After five years of blazing trails in the smaller, more intimate arena of bridal footwear, Lili Kavanaugh and her trademark style of romantic fantasy have invaded the big, bad world of haute couture. While continuing her bridal line, Kavanaugh introduces a new line of fashion shoes in her fall/winter collection and, as with her bridal wear, she plans on offering both ready-to-wear and special order designs.

"Working with bridal shoes allows me to do everything from really retro—and I'm talking medieval or even earlier—to futuristic, from simply sexy to purely playful," says Kavanaugh. "There are no limits, except that the shoes have to be completely, totally feminine.

I'm taking the same approach to my new line, with feminine and sexy my only limits."

Indeed, "totally feminine" defines the sketches and demos I see strewn about her Long Beach, New Jersey, home office, which has a spectacular view of the Atlantic Ocean from the second floor's wraparound balcony.

It's a world away from her trendy new Soho boutique, but it's hard not to feel inspired by romantic days of yore when looking at such a view. I think of dashing captains on the decks of clipper ships, graceful women in silks and crinolines pacing along widow's walks. Then a pretty woman in a thong bikini strolls along the beachfront, and I think sexy and wild, and have an urge to beat my chest like Tarzan.

Life here has softer edges, and Kavanaugh eschews the New York scene for family life on the beach, although her business manager husband, Matt Hawkins, splits his time between New York and home. The couple's sailboat is their home away from home several months of the year.

As I sit here with Kavanaugh, charmed by her passion and verve, it doesn't seem at all strange that her recent past includes an episode that reads like a film noir movie script with Bogey and Bacall. Among her colleagues, you still hear the gossip about how her husband was also her former bodyguard, and saved her from a kidnapping attempt. Knowing a good thing when he saw it, Hawkins was smart enough to fall in love with the lady and marry her. Hawkins is the brains behind the company, and his calculated yet aggressive management—and intuitive ability to capitalize on trends—has taken his flamboyant wife's designs to the top of the industry.

"He keeps me grounded, I keep him crazy. It's a match made in heaven," Kavanaugh laughs. The couple's daughter, three-year-old Meggie, zooms around her mother's office in a hot pink swimsuit salted with sand, her curly hair the same honey-brown color as her mother's. The girl brandishes a large conch like a trophy, and leaves tiny, wet footprints on the polished hardwood floor.

"I can't get that kid to wear shoes," Kavanaugh says with a mournful sigh. "Can you believe it? It must be a genetic fluke or something."

We sit in the sunlight of late afternoon, listening to the surf and talking shoes, shoes, shoes. Kavanaugh is a bundle of energy, always on the move, showing me sketches, talking about her collection of historical shoes—currently on loan to Canada's Bata Shoe Museum—sharing pipe dreams, and sometimes I hear a note of worry in her voice as she prepares to launch her newest venture.

Judging from what I'm seeing today, however, she needn't worry.

Her husband comes in to collect Meggie, carrying son Alec, born ten weeks ago. Hawkins exudes the powerful physical presence of his former profession, and the incisive intelligence in his eyes seems to see right through you. He has an edge to him not usually found in Fashion Land, an edge that leaves you thinking he's been to far darker places than most of us can imagine. Even in Armani, with a burp rag over his shoulder and toting a newborn, he's not a man you want to underestimate.

And you can feel the love and affection between these two people. It comes to me that perhaps this is one reason that Kavanaugh's designs are so charged with feminine power. So self-confident.

Hawkins leaves with his loudly protesting daughter, and a moment later, Kavanaugh dashes off to retrieve yet another sketch. I can hear the excitement in her voice as she shows it to me. It's vintage Kavanaugh—rhinestone ornamentation, diva-red leather, the vamp encrusted with beadwork. It has a low comma heel, set back, and it's fun and sexy and flashy. It makes me think of speakeasies and Prohibition, and women showing their knees for the first time in thousands of years.

"I call it 'Rose,' " she explains, with a smile that dazzles. "It's an homage, something a little personal. Isn't it beautiful?"

I agree. I think I'll suggest to my partner that she buy a pair and we sign up for jitterbug lessons.

Every woman should own a pair of Lili Kavanaugh shoes. Every woman needs a little elegance, fun, and romance in her life.

"So." Lili rolled over on the bed, against Matt's warm, bare body. "What do you think of it?"

Outside the wind whistled and the surf, under the onslaught of a September squall, pounded along the shore. She let the magazine fall to the hardwood floor with a thump.

"I think it's pretty damn good," Matt answered lazily, twirling a lock of her hair around his fingers.

Lili snuggled closer against him. "I wish it had been longer."

"It was long enough. The photos of the shoes are great."

"I'm a little jealous. He seemed more enamoured of you than me." She glanced at Matt, his face shadowed in the low light of the bedside lamp.

An edge, the journalist had said. He'd hit it right on, and maybe it was because Matt was still active in security, teaching seminars a few times a year, and consulting on local jobs from time to time. If he sometimes seemed out of place in fashion circles, he probably seemed even more out of place at security seminars—the ex-bodyguard who now ran a shoe business for his wife.

Lili hesitated, then said, "I don't think he needed to mention that dark places rubbish."

"The guy had a good eye," Matt said after a moment. "I don't know that I'd describe what happened as film noir, but to somebody who wasn't there, I guess it might sound like *The Maltese Falcon*."

She went quiet, studying his handsome face. He rarely talked about the night Joey Mancuso died, and they'd both mostly put it behind them. Lili had no doubts Matt was happy, satisfied with his life, and utterly crazy about his wife and kids—but sometimes, she sensed he still brooded about what had happened and the man he'd killed.

They'd never learned if Joey Mancuso had set them up that night. Tony Graziano, the only one who knew for certain, had died of a heart attack before ever going to trial. He'd never talked. Lili knew Matt was certain Joey had betrayed them, but she held on to the belief that he hadn't—once a die-hard romantic, always a die-hard romantic.

The surviving gunman, just a flunky, had gotten life with no parole. The sentence satisfied both Manny Mendoza, who'd since married and gone to work for his uncle's construction company, and Dal and Jodie Farrell. Dal and Jodie had a little boy, and while Dal had lingering difficulties with fine motor coordination, he hadn't let it slow him down. He'd gone back to school and now worked as a teacher for children with disabilities. Even after five years, they all kept in touch.

Smiling, determined to banish the suddenly somber tone, Lili poked his hard belly. "You looked simply ravishing, dahling, with the diaper over your shoulder and holding Alec. That was a really sexy picture."

Matt grinned down at her. "And the shot of you against the deck railing in the wind wasn't half-bad, either."

"I looked like the cat that swallowed the canary," she murmured, fluttering her lashes playfully against his skin.

He laughed. "You looked like a woman who'd just had fast, hot sex in the john because her horny husband lost his mind when he saw you in that get-up. Christ, how'd they get that dress to stay on you anyway? Glue?"

"Tape." She couldn't help smiling back, or going a little warm as she remembered how he'd cornered her in the bathroom, flipped the wispy fabric of her loaner Versace gown upward and, in less than ten minutes, left her breathless and sloe-eyed with satisfaction. She'd tidied up and put herself back together, but the photographer had grinned knowingly, anyway. "Nursing does wonders for the cleavage, doesn't it?"

"I liked that line about Tarzan." His fingers stroked lower on her bottom. "You make me want to beat my chest and howl."

"Not too loud," she said archly. "Meg and Alec are finally asleep. We probably have . . . oh, forty minutes before *he* starts howling."

Matt shifted, rolling her to her back. "Then I'll just howl real quietly, right here." He kissed her ear, and it made her shiver with a delicious anticipation as he'd known it would.

She tightened her arms around him as he lowered his head, her love for him sweeping through her, powerful and strong. Smiling, she whispered, "Gotcha again, G-man."

"Yeah." He grinned. "Be gentle with me."

Lili was still laughing when he kissed her.

AUTHOR'S NOTE

The inspiration for this story came from *Shoes: A Celebration of Pumps, Sandals, Slippers & More* by Linda O'Keeffe. If you love shoes, this is a must-buy for the gorgeous pictures and fascinating trivia on shoes through the ages.

One pair of 1920s shoes so intrigued me that I built this book around them. Throw in inspiration from Alfred Noyes's poem *The Highwayman*, Bonnie Parker and Clyde Barrow, Al Capone's vault and John Dillinger's lost millions, a few old Hollywood films . . . and I had a story that was a heck of a lot of fun to write!

Research took me to Chicago and the fabulous Drake Hotel, a lovely place full of the glamour of a bygone era. I want to thank the Drake's assistant manager, Peter Schmidt, for his willingness to show me around the suites, including the impressive presidential suite. If you're ever in Chicago, do stop by to see the Drake, and have a drink in the Palm Court to the accompaniment of piano music and the trickle of the water fountain.

The Redhead Piano Bar is a real place. It's on Ontario Street, along Chicago's Magnificent Mile. Just follow the sign of the winking redhead, settle inside, and have yourself a James Bond martini!

The Moccasin Lake chain and resorts don't exist, but there are many small lakes and sport lodges in northern Wisconsin like them. Big Moccasin Lake Lodge owes its inspiration to the infamous Little Bohemia Lodge where John Dillinger's "missing millions" are allegedly buried, and where he and his gang engaged in a shoot-out with local sheriffs' deputies and bureau agents. Dillinger and his men escaped, leaving their womenfolk behind.

The term "G-man" is hard to pin down. Some claim it was already in use by the early 1930s, others claim it didn't come into standard use until a little later. I've introduced "G-man" into the story action of 1933, and my apologies to any gangster aficionados who feel it's anachronistic.

Finally, I must thank my friends Adele Budnick and Gail Shamasna for reading this story and offering both advice and support. You guys are the best! A heartfelt thanks as well to my editor, Micki Nuding, and my agent, Pam Ahearn. And, as always, love and kisses to Jerott, who never gives up offering me story ideas involving jet fighters and swords, even though I keep writing these mushy books.

Michelle Jerott

Dear Reader,

Satisfy your desire for unforgettable, sensuous romance by seeking out these Avon Books—all coming next month!

If you love historical romance, don't miss THE SEDUCTION OF SARA by Karen Hawkins, where you'll meet pert, pretty Lady Sara Carrington. Her brothers want to marry her off to a stodgy old man, so she's determined to find a husband who won't mind her willfull ways. She picks Nicholas, the Earl of Bridgeton—he's England's most notorious rake. He's willing to teach Sara the art of seduction—but marry her . . . never! Until she applies those lessons to him . . .

Cait London is an incomparable teller of tales and her contemporary romances have wowed her many readers. They're dramatic, romantic and filled with twists and turns that will keep you turning the pages. In LEAVING LONELY TOWN she's created her most memorable love story yet—between Sable Barclay, a woman desperately searching for the truth about her past, and Culley Blackwolf, a strong, silent man who just might know the answers to her questions.

Fans of Scotland—and there are many of you!—shouldn't let Lois Greiman's THE MACGOWAN BETROTHAL pass them by. Isobel Fraser is determined not to let Gilmour of the MacGowans steal her heart—even if his roguish ways are so very tempting . . .

And in Linda O'Brien's passionate BELOVED PROTECTOR, a young lady in need of a bodyguard expects to have a boring old man watching over her . . . instead she gets broad-shouldered, lean-hipped Pinkerton detective Case Brogan. Suddenly, Eliza Lowe isn't so sure if she wants him to protect her—or seduce her.

Don't miss any of these spectacular Avon Romances!

Warmly,

Lucia Macro

Lucia Macro
Executive Editor

REL 1001

Discover Contemporary Romances
at Their Sizzling Hot Best
from Avon Books